K.J. Backer was born in Corbett, OR in 1986. She grew up on a Christmas Tree farm enjoying the fragrant scents of Blue Spruce and Douglas Fir, surrounded by friendly animals, before moving to the Big Sky State in 1996. She credits her close family bonds, wild imagination, and love for books to her humble, country upbringing. She worked as a U.S. Capitol Intern in 2004, graduated from Montana State University- Billings with a degree in History Education in 2009, and taught History at a local high school for five years whilst "secretly" writing her first novel, *Nav'Aria: The Marked Heir* (published in 2019).

K.J. Backer has a huge love and appreciation for other cultures, adoption, travel, history, fantasy, and the written word. She lives in Billings, MT with her amazing husband, wonderful daughter, two adorable Pomeranians, and handsome tortoise.

Nav'Aria: The Winged Cresent is the third and final book of the *Nav'Aria* series. Follow Backer on social media and at kjbacker.com to learn more!

Cover design by SelfPubBookCovers.com/Jensen-Cook
Maps by K.J. Backer (Inkarnate Pro)
Edited and Proofread by Heather Peers

K.J. Backer
Visit author website at **kjbacker.com**

Printed in the United States of America

First Edition: November 2020

ISBN-13: 978-1-7329206-5-1

NAV'ARIA: THE WINGED CRESCENT

K.J. Backer

For Hunter.

Dad, thanks for taking me to get my first library card and for giving me your copy of *Eye of the World*. You set me on a path for *nerdom*… isn't it great to see where it's taken us!?

Nav'Aria

The Camp

Mt. Alodon

The Woods of the Willow

The Stenlen

The Shazla Desert

Rav'Ar

Nav'Alodon Mountains

Land of the Trolls

The Kingdom

Lure River

Castle Dintarran

Lake Thread

PROLOGUE

A Dream of Battle

Rinzaltan shook awake breathing heavily. The dream, or whatever that had been, felt so real. Clearing the dark images away, he tried to reorient himself. He knew he was lying next to his beautiful bride, for he could smell her fragrant, newly washed coat. Oils burned in the braziers, and the remnants of soup and barley from the evening meal wafted through the room. That felt like a lifetime ago.

"Is everything alright?" Elsra murmured sleepily.

Rinzaltan felt on edge. Worried. And terribly sad. He couldn't let her know that, though. "Yes, my darling. Forgive me for waking you. Last night's meal is not settling with me. I think I will take a walk."

"Do you need me to come with you?" The tone in her voice made it apparent that that was the last thing she wished to do.

He smiled knowingly; she despised being awoken in the night. He nuzzled her with his soft, velvety nose and whispered, "No, darling. You sleep. I will be back shortly. I only need some air."

That seemed to pacify her. "Alright," she murmured, already returning to her slumber.

He paused for a moment, watching her in the sliver of moonlight which shone from their curtained window. How he loved her. A shiver ran down his body then as the dream returned to him, and a tear rolled down his cheek. If the dream was indeed what he thought it was, then his time with her had just about run out. He closed his eyes, not wanting to cry anymore tears. Not yet, at least. Not when he was so close to her. It would do no good to cause her worry just yet. He glanced once more upon his headstrong wife, his gaze lingering….

She will go on without me. She will have to, the doleful thought weighing him down as he tried slipping away unnoticed.

Out in the corridor the cool night air seemed to refresh him. His heightened senses kicked in, and he felt his mind becoming more alert. There was work to be done this night—and in the many upcoming nights. He must send word to the King, and to his son. He flinched thinking of his children and felt almost cowed with the heavy weight of sadness.

No, he paused thinking, *if this is a dream from the Creator telling of what is to come, then it is no use crying over it.* His resolve strengthened, but his heart felt heavy with the image of his talented, beautiful children. Adults, perhaps, but they would always be his children. *Poor Trinidad,* he thought, his mind lingering on the bloody scene from his dream. The battle was coming. The evil scourge would spread across the land, and the King would be slain whilst astride his bonded companion Trinidad. A sacrifice would need to be made to save the King. A blood sacrifice. Rinzaltan's blood would run that day... and then his life would be no more. At least not here, for he would join the Creator and his spirit would live on in the Tree.

He shivered again but stopped himself, standing up straighter. This was of the Creator... and for King Rustusse. He had to live for the prophecy to come to pass. His son—and his son's son—had to be born and raised before the time of darkness strew its death and disarray.

But what of the winged ones? He did not understand why the dream had shown him that part, or why he had to be so furtive. His brow crinkled in thought as he headed to the Library of Kaulter. He needed to speak with his clerk Joh. Together, in secrecy, they would see that this foretelling came to pass. It wasn't as if they had a choice. Rinzaltan was the strongest and wisest of the unicorns. With great age and his blood connection to the First Horn, he had the gift of prophecy and foretelling. He knew with every passing moment—as he gained more clarity and his sleepiness fell away—that what he had seen would come to pass. There was no use questioning it. Now, all he could do was prepare for his own death.

***

Screams drifted upwards to Rinzaltan's vantage point. He watched, terror seizing him as his son rushed into battle. Trinidad's sheer white coat blazed through the swathed

Rav'Arians as his King swung his Marked sword arm, slaying the enemy. Roaring and shrieking to his left caught Rinzaltan's attention. The Winged Ones, just as they'd appeared in his dreams, had appeared on the battlefield. The sight of them was glorious. Their scales shone bright in the sunshine, making his pulse rise as he watched their ferocity in action.

As the fight reached its climax, they soared in and laid waste to the enemy, quickly igniting the scurrying abominations as one would tinder in a campfire. The flames and smoke took over the battlefield, and soon Rinzaltan lost sight of his son. A heavy fog began to roll in as the final battle cries sounded. The battle was nearing its end. The help of the winged ones had saved them all. All except one. For Rinzaltan knew from the dream that Rustusse was near his end… and thus, Rinzaltan's part in this fight was drawing ever nearer.

A throat cleared near him, and Rinzaltan turned to meet the wise stare of Saka, the Reoul elder. She stood with him in solidarity. She knew the price he would pay, for he had already explained it to her… a few times. Reouls, whom the Creator had given the southern lands in order to create peace and harmony between the winged and horned ones, had taken many of the soldiers by surprise. All of them really. None in Nav'Aria, save for the Kaulter unicorns, remembered their allies in the south. So separate were the species… but then the abominations had begun appearing and everything began to change. After his dream, Rinzaltan had known what to do. Setting his scribes to work, he had dug up anything he could on

the winged ones and then called out with his mind to
them. There had been a push back from Saka, until he,
rather forcefully, commanded her to come to Nav'Aria's
aid on the Creator's behalf. He had breathed a sigh of
relief when he'd heard their wingbeats in the distance this
day.

By the time his lifeblood ran cold, the deep spread of
his magic would release one final time. Aided by the
Creator, his will would cause all to forget the winged ones.
Saka had pushed back on this as well but grew
contemplative as he'd explained it. If knowledge of them
were to fall into the wrong hands, as his dream had
eluded, destruction would reign in Nav'Aria and Rav'Ar.
The winged ones had to remain separate for now not
because they were a danger or unwanted, but for their
own good. They must stay safely hidden beyond the
border.

To be destroyed by the monsters? No aid will come for us I see,
Saka had remarked.

And Rinzaltan had sadly looked upon her through eyes
that had seen more than his mortal life's memories. The
dream heavy with revelation. *Evil has come to Nav'Aria,* he'd
replied. Wasn't it obvious how the monsters scurried
north toward Nav'Aria, not reaching further south or
west? Something dark pulsed in the Kingdom, and
whatever—or whoever—it was should never find the
winged ones, or else grave days lie in store for all those
living.

Saka had not been pleased with this news but believed
him after he pressed his horn to her azure wing and

revealed a portion of the dream he'd been given. Saka had gasped, her wings and head sagging from the dream's doom. Making up her mind quickly, she sagely named one of her fighters, a fierce mossy green dragon, or Reoul, as they preferred to be called, as her successor. Though Tiakai didn't know yet that she would be groomed to take over the clan for Saka, the elder insisted that Rinzaltan leave her with the mark of remembrance, as well. She would keep them safe after Saka was long returned to the earth. And it would be her duty to prepare one as her elder should she fall before the time of prophecy.

She called her over toward the end of the battle, and as the powerful wingbeats blew swirling dust around Rinzaltan upon the ridge, he caught sight of his son far beyond the frontlines. The King was exposed. He knew Rustusse would fall momentarily.

"Tiakai, I thank you—and your kind—for joining us today. May you, and only you, remember us," she blinked, clearly unsure of what he was saying, looking toward Saka, who nodded, and urged her to listen. Rinzaltan continued, "May you always remember us in Nav'Aria, but never speak of it, until you meet one of us baring the Mark. All others will forget. The boundary must be maintained as the Creator urges us, so that evil does not make its way to you. But if it does, do not fear... the prophecy will be fulfilled... in time. Until then, wait for the Mark," as he spoke, he pressed his horn to her interior wing, leaving her with a small diamond-shaped symbol. She gasped in turn as he revealed an even smaller portion of the dream to emphasize his point.

Saka cleared her throat, and Tiakai murmured a quick "thank you," clearly very confused.

Saka whispered to her before Tiakai bowed her head once more and took to the skies. As she did so, she called out in a loud, urging roar. The battlefield now encased in smoke and fog, quieting in cries, erupted one final time with roars and wingbeats as winged ones surged up from all around. Bright yellows, greens, reds, and violets, the warriors' scales gleamed once above the fog heading back toward the border and their home in Rav'Ar.

All but Saka left.

Rinzaltan nodded to her before his gaze returned to the battlefield. He heard his son. Trinidad's cries tugged at his heart, for he knew that, though Rustusse would live and Trinidad's sprits would be restored, his heart would be torn asunder on this day, with his father's sacrifice.

"We honor the Creator... and we... I," Saka corrected, "will remember your sacrifice. You have my respect, Horned One. I will do my part to protect our clan from any outside evil... I will remember this exchange," she motioned to her wing with a diamond symbol that matched Tiakai's, "and prepare Tiakai for the days to come." With that, she spread her brilliant blue wings further and dove from the ridge, joining her retreating companions as instructed.

"Stay safe," whispered Rinzaltan, watching her go, for he feared that, even though his magic would protect them, their presence—and power—would be discovered. Yet, his time had come. He had done what the Creator had requested of him... and so he began his trek down toward his slain King and grieving son. For though his heart broke for himself, he feared even more for all those he was forced to leave behind. For the prophecy to be fulfilled meant that the Kingdom would be submerged in darkness, though with the Creator's help and the secrecy of the winged ones, most would come out unscathed, and peace would be restored quickly, he believed.

As he walked on, dodging corpses, strewn weapons, and the occasional scattered limb, he prayed. He prayed for Elsra. *May she have wisdom to rule Kaulter in my stead.* For his children. *May they have peace knowing I am with the Creator.* For a moment, he hesitated picturing Trinity's serene gaze, and Triumph with his tough exterior. He feared Triumph would be affected the most from his loss. He wished he would have told him how proud he was of him. Of all of them. He should have told them more often, he thought as his eyes fixed on his son up ahead. He prayed for his King. *May he rule wisely and soak up every minute with his son.* Despite getting a second chance at life, Rinzaltan knew that Rustusse's days were still numbered. He didn't know all the events that would transpire, but he did know that Rustusse would be betrayed—by whom or what, he knew not. Still, he was certain he was leaving Nav'Aria to face its darkest days yet.

As he came upon his son crying and grieving over the slain King whose blood pooled from a fatal stab Rinzaltan issued the command, and his friend Shale obeyed.

To the Creator I go. For Nav'Aria.

CHAPTER 1

The Usurper

Mounted atop Silver Seeker, Narco licked his lips excitedly as he charged down the hillside. The beast's hooves thundered, jostling Narco. He clung to the saddle and reins but could only hear Lyrianna's voice. He remembered her moans of pain from captivity. He couldn't wait to relive it very soon. She would know true loss today—and regret for having shunned his advances.

Repeatedly, he kicked his heels in time with his wicked thoughts. This day would be monumental. Narco was invincible.

He was better than Vikaris. Morta had assured him, and now with the Reoul blood coursing through his veins, he knew it to be true. There would be a defeat today... but it would not be his. He would slay Vikaris in front of both armies, and he would claim his Kingdom rightfully. And with it his Bride... after he beheaded her husband and son, of course. It would never do to let Darion live. Darion must die, and a new age would usher in his own heir, born to the captivating, broken Queen. He laughed aloud, Silver Seeker snorting and growling in thirst, seeming to pick up on his mood.

"Yes," Narco shouted to the beast, "We shall slay them all. But Vikaris is mine!"

Silver Seeker tossed his head violently—the light catching on the few silver hairs streaking his otherwise ebony mane—but continued toward the shining pair running through his troops' shoddy formation.

Both forces amassed, encircling the pair, fighting had ceased as all eyes were upon Narco. *Oh, what a glorious sight I must make*, he thought, considering his billowing cloak and shining breast plate. All other thoughts and insecurities had vanished upon accepting his nephew's challenge and moved to act boldly like he should have all along. Guzzling the Reoul blood helped too. Having had it in his system for so many years, he had forgotten how invigorating the blood could be. He already possessed physical strength from it, but it was what it did to his mind that made him nearly euphoric. His body trembled and his mind felt clear... no more worries or insecurities, no more thoughts of Morta and feeling weak; he was godlike when the fresh blood coursed through him.

Fresh gore, ripped corpses, and the foul Rav'Arians' odors filled the air. He closed his eyes, momentarily sucking it in his nostrils and reveling in the toxicity of his power. His eyes had not beheld his nephew in many years, for he'd elected to remain in his Castle while his forces fought. Coming closer, he saw the resemblance to his younger brother Rustusse. *Oh, how I hated my brother—the*

Marked Heir. The one who stole Mother's affection and my rightful place as ruler. Well, he had killed him, and he would kill his son this day, he vowed, smiling inwardly.

"Whatever happens, Narco is mine," Vikaris growled as he bent low in the leather war saddle, expertly riding his bonded companion.

Trixon rumbled his agreement.

Charging into the enemy's lines and challenging his uncle had been foolhardy, Vikaris knew. Yet this was the only way.

After leading his force against the haphazard onslaught of treacherous humans, Rav'Arians, trolls, and the midnight black unicorns, Vikaris couldn't stand to see any more losses. What would it mean to have a victory if it cost him the Kaulter unicorns? Seeing unicorns slaying unicorns was the most abominable, haunting thing Vikaris had ever witnessed, and he had realized in that moment, as his sword arm slew one and then another enemy, that this was exactly what Narco wanted. Pure evil.

The realization hit him… Vikaris didn't have to pander to Narco. HE was the rightful King, and HE would prove that by slaying the bastard in front of everyone gathered here today. There was only one more death needed on this battlefield. Let it be known that Vikaris rightfully unseated the usurper and claimed his birthright—his own throne— as the Marked Royal.

"It will be so," Trixon growled. His ferocity strengthening Vikaris's will ever further.

As the pair blazed across the battlefield, wafts of blood, Rav'Arian filth, and guts permeated the air around them. Vikaris shuddered inwardly as he gazed upon the already piling corpses and the crushed grasses and wildflowers of the once pristine Nav'Arian Plains. The soldiers on both sides had momentarily ceased fighting, making way for them. Narco, ridiculous cloak and all, rushed down the hillside toward him. A tiny sliver of doubt tickled Vikaris's mind. He was honestly a bit surprised to see his uncle willingly accept this challenge. He had thought him a fat coward, pent up safe behind the Castle walls, and yet here he was riding into battle.

"Creator, watch over us. Let justice be served on this day," Vikaris prayed.

As the words left his mouth, and as they passed his final lines of troops and corpses, he crossed into the enemy's lines. All worries vanished when his eyes beheld a Rav'Arian pinning down a writhing human soldier while another Rav'Arian hacked his limbs off, handing a bloodied leg to a nearby troll preparing to make a meal of their still-living comrade. Bile choked him at the abhorrent sight. Vikaris felt white hot rage so supreme that his Ruby glowed even brighter, as did his Marked arm alit with the ancient symbols of his land. His heritage.

As he ran by atop Trixon, the vile Rav'Arian stood to gaze at him, cackling with its face hidden behind its hood. Vikaris glared but did not halt. The Rav'Arians would be dealt with, but first, their Master had to be finished off.

Vikaris blocked the man's screams from his mind, along with the overwhelming rush of sounds and smells accosting his senses. He could not save him, but he could save the rest with this final contest.

Narco's crazed unicorn practically flew down the hill, heading straight for them. Its eyes roiling with demonic glee. Narco, though older, heavier, and clearly not a swordsman, held his sword aloft and looked surprisingly... eager.

They are both mad, Trixon spoke into his mind. *They must not be trusted or spared... that one looks rabid,* indicating the unicorn.

Nearing the edge of Narco's forces, the man himself appeared, pulling on the reins of his enraged beast. Eyes wild, the unicorn reared, snorting and kicking out as if to hit Trixon. Narco laughed aloud, and the hairs on Vikaris's neck rose. It had been cycles since he had last seen his uncle, let alone heard his voice.

"Ah, I see you have grown, nephew," Narco said, grinning awkwardly with his scarred, slack face.

Trixon snorted, he and Vikaris knowing full well that it was Trinidad who had sliced Narco's face while in captivity. His uncle's eyes narrowed as he looked Trixon up and down and stroked the mane of his wild, rearing unicorn.

"Uncle," Vikaris said curtly in acknowledgment. He and Trixon standing still and proud as soldiers should.

The beast lunged at Trixon, its horn narrowly missing Trixon's face before Narco cursed, pulling on the reins. "No, Silver Seeker," he bellowed angrily.

Vikaris grimaced. The pair of them were such an utter picture of incongruence. The product of evil and dark elements used by Morta, no doubt, from beyond the border.

Vikaris needed to end this quickly. He patted Trixon's neck and, without hesitation, jumped down with sword in hand.

The field behind had quieted as the forces merged and encircled the pair to watch the two leaders duel. The time had finally come.

"Narco," Vikaris called loudly for the ears of those around. "I challenge you right now for the Throne of Nav'Aria. My rightful place," raising his glowing arm with emphasis before turning his burning green eyes back to Narco. "Let us finish this."

Narco seemed to be ignoring him, petting his unicorn and speaking softly in the creature's ear. It had ceased rearing and shrieking its shrill, frenzied sounds, and yet... there was something eerie about its stillness.

I do not trust him, Vikaris, Trixon warned.

"Nor do I," Vikaris murmured aloud. "Warn the unicorns to keep a watchful eye and to act immediately if I am slain. Find Darion," he whispered as he leaned closer to his bonded unicorn for one final embrace before moving apart from him... finally drawing Narco's attention.

Narco opened his mouth as if to speak, but Vikaris cut him off. "Today, I challenge you, Narco, the usurper who killed my parents, your brother, in their beds. Whose reign has been filled with nothing but terror, war, and degradation. For Nav'Aria and for my family, I challenge you to single combat. Let you and I finish this war."

Narco patted his unicorn again and jumped down much more spryly than a man of his age and appearance would belie. Without speaking, the man dramatically unpinned his cloak at the neck and draped it over his saddle.

The soldiers, men and beast alike, began to shuffle. *What would he do? Vikaris had challenged, but Narco was ignoring him. Should they fight?* Vikaris could feel the hesitation and tension in the air. One wrong move and this day could still go awry now that their forces were enclosing them.

That will not happen, Trixon growled in his mind. *I will see you out of this safely, my King*. Trixon pawed the ground and turned to glare at the encroaching onlookers.

One look from the angry unicorn caused soldiers—on both sides—to back up, making room for a proper dueling space.

Narco then drew his sword smoothly and lunged into an offensive stance, slashing ahead of the unicorn.

Trixon growled, but Vikaris shouldered him out of the way. "No, this is my fight," Vikaris commanded through clenched teeth as his blade intercepted the wild slash inches from his shoulder. Vikaris held it and couldn't help but feel shock as the weight of his Uncle's sword pressed upon his own. How could he wield it with such pressure? He was an old man who had never seen battle.

"Ah," Narco cooed contemptuously, jumping back and momentarily withdrawing his attack, sizing up his opponent. "I see you are surprised to see that I can fight. Your father, and these creatures," he spat eyeing Trixon, "filled your head with fantasies about me. Did they tell you I was weak? That I would be an easy kill?" His upper lip sneered as he spoke.

Before Vikaris could reply, Narco danced forward, once again striking out offensively with his sword. He cut swiftly, moving in toward Vikaris's middle. The King was forced to take a step back in order to get his sword up in time to parry the heavy blow.

Such strength, unlike any Vikaris had ever expected. He gritted his teeth, holding off the attack. Narco broke contact first but then spun in a pirouette, slashing low toward Vikaris's right leg. The blade missed him by a hair. Narco did step back then, grinning widely, albeit slacked.

Vikaris felt stunned. His heart hammered. This was not anything near what he had expected of his uncle.

"Yes, I can see it now. They did mislead you. You poor fool, and to think, all this time, you have rebelled against me, thinking you were better than me. Stronger than me. And yet, look at you," Narco snickered, eyeing Vikaris's heaving chest and blood and sweat-slicked arms. "The Marked King bested by an 'old man'." Narco tsked, spinning on his heel to smile at the onlookers. He stood proudly in his ornate chest plate, his hideously scarred and pocked face shining with sweat in the sun, his oiled black hair clinging to his head.

He was an ugly, foul man. But maybe what he spoke was true? This wasn't the man Vikaris had been told about.

He eyed Narco's sword arm and the hand clutching the richly embossed sword hilt. His father's sword, he noted, his ire rising.

Narco looked to his sword, "Ah yes, I suppose you also think this your birthright. The sword of the Nav'Arian rulers should be in your hands? I do not see how that is possible if you cannot even wield it."

Narco jumped forward nearly faster than Vikaris could imagine, though he'd been expecting it. He moved into a defensive stance once more, staving off the harried attack from his uncle, who seemed not the slightest bit winded. Vikaris used both hands to hold his blade steady against the onslaught.

Narco laughed, "You are pitiful. Just as your father was. I knew he had tricked everyone into believing he was the better of us. I corrected that when I killed him, you know that right? It was my hand that slew first your mother, Elentra. I let your father watch her life slowly slip away as I strangled her." Narco broke off his attack, dancing backwards again, allowing Vikaris respite, for it did not appear that Narco needed it. "I slit your father's throat after that... slowly, of course. I placed the crown upon my head and laughed as his life faded away. My face smiling down was the last thing he ever saw... and then I went looking for you."

Vikaris growled, looking for an opening to cut the man down and end his tirade. His chest heaved in anger and frustration. He knew this had to do with Rav'Ar and whatever his uncle had discovered there years ago, but could he best him? He had believed it all these years. That if only Narco showed his face, Vikaris would kill him swiftly and justly. But now?

"I am glad it took this long though," Narco replied as if idly looking around the expanse. Vikaris lunged in with a sweeping slash, that Narco parried without even seeming afraid, as if it were a feather and not a sword aimed at his heart. Vikaris grunted as his uncle's boot came up in a swift kick, knocking him off his feet. He tumbled to the ground, clutching his sword expertly even as he fell back. He expected the blow to come and quickly rolled before jumping up once more. He knew that, while Narco had a supernatural strength, what he lacked was training and discipline. He desperately looked for an opening to exploit.

The two men circled one another, blades drawn, testing each other's reflexes and looking for weaknesses. Vikaris feared he was the weaker opponent, the likes of which had never happened before.

"As I said," Narco spoke softer, "I am glad this took so long, for it allowed me time with your wife. A ripe bud for the taking. Had I slew you as a child, I may not have ever discovered Lyrianna in the Kingdom. You brought her right to me... to savor slowly," Narco whispered, licking his lips. "Her body," Narco gasped, "Ah... it is an experience that I will know once again very soon."

Vikaris felt molten rage at the man's words. A bellow, an adamant charge, and a wild sword swing followed. Narco chuckled wickedly, staving off Vikaris's blows before landing a cut upon Vikaris's left arm.

Vikaris jumped back, gasping as he felt the blade slice open his upper arm. It hurt and rendered his arm heavy, but he knew it was shallow enough that he could keep fighting.

He is baiting you, Vikaris, Trixon boomed. *Shall I kill him instead?* The unicorn pawed the ground nearby.

Blood streamed down, slicking his hand. Vikaris hastily wiped it on his pants and eyed Narco, who stood still watching him as if he were already the victor.

Focus, Vikaris. Kill him, Trixon pressed.

Anger coursed through every vein in Vikaris's body. This had to end. He knew Narco was baiting him. Growing careless and rising to his taunts was exactly what Narco wanted. Vikaris took a deep, centering breath, fully opening all his senses. He was struck by the torrent of stimuli all around him. Smells of blood, sweat, dirt, and flowers mulled together. The groans of the dying, the whispers of the soldiers, and the... the deep inhales from his opponent.

Vikaris narrowed his eyes, analyzing his uncle. Though the man's mouth was closed, his nostrils flared heavily. The chest plate hid much of the chest's movement. The King smirked, *He can feign immortality, but his body tires too. He is mortal, whether he wants to believe it or not.* Vikaris clung to that fact. Feeling more and more of the weight and fear roll off his shoulders. He realized his uncle was not all powerful. He was winded and trying to hide it. Vikaris could use that.

Vikaris prowled the edge of the circle, his sword directed at Narco as he moved testing the bounds, just as he'd been taught as a boy by his father... whom this man had just admitted to having killed.

Narco, noting the change in Vikaris's mood, dropped the grin. He fell into his own defensive stance and the two circled one another quietly, only their shuffling feet and breathing could be heard above the silent crowd.

Ever the lover of drama—or so Vikaris had been told—Narco unsurprisingly filled the air moments later. "When I kill you, I will take her for my own and have her watch as I kill your son. Yours and Darion's heads will adorn my ramparts this night."

Spittle flew at his words, and though Vikaris had expected something like that, he felt the rage boiling. Keeping it abated and remaining focused was difficult. He clamped his mouth tightly shut and initiated small jabs in and out of the circle, keeping Narco moving but his blade at bay. He needed to tire the man out. And it seemed to be working, for Narco's tirades trailed off as he began to visibly fight the urge to breathe from his mouth. A few more shuffles and Vikaris began to press.

Narco cursed as Vikaris moved in between his blade and slashed Narco's forearm. Narco roared and lunged, and just as Vikaris expected, opened himself up, not thinking Vikaris had any remaining speed of his own. What he underestimated was the power that comes from being the Marked Royal as well as a protective husband and father. Narco would never harm his family again.

Vikaris thrust his sword, just narrowly missing Narco's neck but leaving a gash on his unmarked cheek. Narco's eyes widened at the impact. He skirted back to tenderly pat the torn flesh on his already hideous face. He pulled bloodied fingers back, and his eyes seemed unable to make out what was there before them.

He snarled, crouching low and attacking with a frenzy of sword parries.

Vikaris grunted as his blade met that of his enemy's, and again, he felt shock at the impact. The might of the man. But still he held his ground. Gritting his teeth, Vikaris held his uncle's sword and slammed into his shoulder, breaking their locked swords. Vikaris spun quickly, leaning low, and lunging with all of his force directly into the dazed man's lower torso. Sword met flesh.

The chest plate was gaudy and impractical, and it also gave the one wearing it a false sense of security. It wasn't a full suit of armor, and where its protection stopped short of his pants, Vikaris's sword stabbed with all the force an enraged man could muster.

Narco gawked, his eyes widening in an expression of incredulity. His sword, still in his clambering grip. As Vikaris's right Marked hand drove the sword into Narco's mid-section, his bloodied left arm clutched the man's sword arm, keeping back his weapon. He hadn't needed to look. His keen senses allowed him to catch the hand in midair.

Narco gasped while stepping back and breathing heavily from his mouth.

With a twist, Vikaris withdrew his sword roughly before kicking Narco free.

The man cried out in pain and fell to the ground, clutching his middle, just where his chest plate ceased to protect him. He spluttered, grappling with his blade that he'd dropped upon impact. The onlookers around gasped in unison. And then silence. All seemed to hold their breath upon the Nav'Arian Plains as monarch slew monarch.

Vikaris swept up his father's sword with his free hand, his gaze never leaving Narco's. The man rolled on the ground like an upturned beetle clutching his stomach, but he kicked his legs, as if that would keep Vikaris away. The Marked King of Nav'Aria grimaced as he approached the traitor. Again, without a glance he gripped his sword hilt in his right hand drove it into Narco's thigh as he lay sprawled back. The man screamed at the blade's progress.

Narco rocked from side to side, still clutching his stomach and trying to roll over. Blood pooled around him, and the gash on his face lent him a ghoulish appearance. His gaping, bloody snarl howled in pain.

"You are wrong, Narco," Vikaris said coldly, coming to stand over his long-time enemy, the tyrant of Nav'Aria. "I am not better than you."

Narco's bleary eyes seemed to focus for a moment. His confused gaze met Vikaris's. In a hushed yet lethal voice, Vikaris growled, "But my son is, and he will rule long after you and I perish. You see, you did not win. The Marked Heir of Nav'Aria will live on and take his rightful place at my side. And one day, his Marked Heir will rule… the tradition of Marked succession that you tried so vehemently to bring to an end will continue. And your name, Narco," Vikaris bent lower to stare fully in the face of the man that had nearly cost him everything, and then whispered, "Your name will be forgotten… for your legacy ends today."

Narco's eyes widened further, and his gurgled retort ceased as Vikaris slammed his sword—the sword of the Nav'Arian Royals—down, fluidly decapitating Narco in one decisive motion. Vikaris stepped back, tiredly looking at the vile head detached of body, then he changed his mind. He knelt quickly and stood, sword arm raising high the bloodied blade of his ancestors, and his other hand lifting the head of the slain usurper.

With the embodiment of majesty and tyranny aloft at once, Vikaris roared a cry so primal and guttural that onlookers would speak of it years later.

It was a cry of pain. A cry of rage. A cry of victory.

Narco was dead.

CHAPTER 2

The Confusion

"Triumph, can I talk to you?"

Though they had traveled together for a few days now, Triumph trembled with evident joy at the realization that his daughter Zola was alive. She hadn't been slain in the Coup, as suspected all those years before. It was amazing. A miracle, definitely. Darion didn't want to seem jealous... but Triumph's attention was so all consuming over his daughter that it left Darion unsure of their relationship. *Does he even want to stay bonded to me now that he has his daughter back?*

The pair continued lost in conversation upon their march through the foothills of Nav'Aria, making their way toward the Nav'Arian Plains and beyond to the Woods of the Willow. If they didn't find the King and his forces at the Plains, as Triumph suspected, then they would head for the Portals and to Kaulter. Darion felt a multitude of emotions, and after traveling so closely for the past few months through Rav'Ar and back, he felt alone. Nala and

Ati had left them before they crossed the border, and now it seemed Triumph was leaving Darion behind too.

"Wallowing is for lesser beings, my Prince," Triumph replied, approaching Darion, and snapping him from his reverie.

Darion blinked. "Hey, I wasn't wallowing, I was thinking, that's all." His eyes narrowed, "And get out of my head."

Triumph snorted, though his eyes sparkled with amusement.

His friend had changed, Darion observed. As if seeing Zola had awakened part of him that had been lost before, or rather, dead. Darion smiled. He was glad to see Triumph this happy.

"You're way nicer now... that seems appropriate since you're a Grandpa," Darion smiled innocently.

Triumph snorted again but remained silent. They fell into step together, and the close familiarity warmed Darion's heart, ridding away the doubts from the past days.

After he couldn't take the silence anymore, he turned to Triumph and sighed, opening his mouth to ask the question.

"Darion," Triumph whispered to him. His eyes shining as he looked deeply into his. "I will never leave you. While, yes, my heart feels like it could burst with happiness at seeing my daughter," his voice quivered with emotion, "you, Darion, are my family too. Nothing ever change that, and you do not need to fear whether you belong anymore. Your place is in Nav'Aria… and my place is with you."

Darion didn't want to start crying again. He felt like he had done enough of that after losing his Mom, who had been killed by an assassin in Kaulter, and crossing the treacherous Rav'Ar. He sniffed gruffly, trying to appear manly, like a Marked Prince should.

Triumph snorted a third time. The sheer annoyance of such a gesture interrupted Darion's melancholy. He shot the unicorn a dirty look.

Triumph laughed aloud, leaning into Darion and thus gaining the attention of the rest of the party. Their number had grown since they left for Rav'Ar. When Darion departed, he was running away. He wanted to find what fueled Narco's maniacal reign—yes, but he had desperately wanted to get away from the despair in Rick's eyes, the pity in Lyrianna's and Vikaris's, and the prospect of a Kaulter without Carol. But that was months ago. Upon his return, he was battle-tested, missed his loved ones, and possessed what he hoped would be viewed as valuable information.

Darion smiled broadly at his friends as he realized that he did consider Nav'Aria his home. Oregon felt like another lifetime. Another world. This is where he was meant to be, just as Triumph said. He patted his companion's neck, then picked up the pace to join Edmond, Soren, Zola, and young Trigger.

The youngling didn't engage with them much. He was clearly terrified of something. It's probably an infant thing. They set an easy pace to cater to him, though Darion wanted to press ahead badly. When they'd crossed the border and discovered Zola with the Merfolk at Lake Thread, they'd all seen the flash. The battle had begun! Darion knew his father needed him now more than ever. So, they trudged, and Darion could only pray that they'd make it in time.

Striding up beside Edmond, who gave him a nod, he listened as Soren explained much of Kaulter and the past years' happenings while Zola had been in captivity. She was rapt for information and, all things considered, seemed to have a strong mind. Darion knew Triumph took credit for that. *It must run in the family*, he had told Darion.

Zola was shaking her head. Soren, noticing her countenance, stopped mid-sentence. "Is something wrong?" He asked instead.

Darion studied her. She was a beauty—with or without her horn. In his other life he assumed all unicorns looked the same. This was certainly not the case They each had their own identifiable traits, mannerisms, and subtle differences in appearance. Zola had a full healthy form, having been well-fed her whole life, and her newly washed coat from her time with the Merfolk sparkled in the light. Darion saw much of Elsra's grace and fortitude in her face.

Triumph rushed up to the group, taking in the changing mood. "Zola, what is it?"

Her pace had slowed, and her chest was heaving.

Edmond, now having spent months with unicorns, elbowed Darion to step back a bit. As they did, Darion watched Triumph studying his daughter. Awkward moments passed by, and then finally Darion realized she wasn't upset, as in sad. She was furious. She looked up, her eyes ablaze.

"How could you leave us all? You have been hiding for years in this… this… Kaulter place. While I was…" Her voice trailed off, but the stare remained. Triumph, Soren, and Trigger sagely stepped back from the angry female.

Triumph was shaking his head but did not speak. Soren cleared his throat, but no words came out of his silvery muzzle.

She glared, waiting. None spoke. No one could retract her words. "You are pathetic," she said slamming a front hoof down to punctuate her words.

Triumph gasped as if he had been punched. "Zola," his voice broke.

She lifted her nose at him with the haughtiest expression Darion had ever seen. And he was bonded to freaking Triumph… the most tiresome of them all. Some mannerisms really were hereditary!

Darion watched in horror as she turned to whisper to Trigger, making as if to leave. He caught the word liar as she spoke quickly to her son.

Darion balled his fists angrily. *That's it? She's just going to leave Triumph after all these years?*

"You need to shut up, Zola," Darion yelled.

He ignored Edmond's wince and gasp. He knew his large friend probably would have told him to be more careful around angry unicorns, but… maybe he just wasn't a fast learner. Or maybe it was because this unicorn—her father—was one of the bravest, greatest beings alive. No one who knew Triumph would ever accuse him of cowardice.

A deep rumble rose in her throat as she looked up from her son and toward Darion. Her foot began slamming the earth again, and she lowered her head just a hair. Darion knew she was preparing to charge.

"So that's it then, huh? You are finally free and find your family, and now you're what? You're going to charge me? Attack me, the Prince? Ditch your Dad? I know you've been locked up for a while, but what you just said is completely untrue... so quit acting like an idiot and listen."

Triumph took the lead as mediator upon seeing his daughter fuming with sudden rage. "Darion, it is alright. Just step back, please," Triumph said, worry filling his voice.

Darion paused. *Does Triumph really think Zola would attack? Should I be worried?*

Darion looked back at her, stepping forward despite his friend's pleas, and did the one thing Zola didn't expect. He closed his eyes. Breathing deeply, Darion reached with his senses all around him. He could feel the tickle of wind across his forehead and throughout his shaggy locks. He could smell dirt and sweat upon their bodies. He felt heat radiating from Zola in her fury as he took one step closer and then another, his eyes still closed. Without having to look, he knew his Ruby was shining bright and his arm's symbols were illuminated. He could hear her swallowing repeatedly. As if she were dehydrated or trying to get a bad taste out of her mouth. And then he knew what to do.

"Zola," he said in a kinder voice, opening his eyes. "You are safe. And you are home. Whatever you do to try and push us away is fine. But you need to know now it's not going to work. We're not going anywhere, and neither are you."

He watched her tilt her head in silence. *She probably thinks I'm crazy.*

Darion had realized as he'd stood there, that she was going through something that Darion, while never in captivity, could empathize with. "Listen, the only enemy here is Narco. Master," Darion said softly, eyeing her. "He's the bad guy, Zola. What the unicorns did, they did for the greater good." He lifted his hand to cut her off as she was beginning to open her mouth to most likely retort... or bite him. "I said 'Listen' and I'm your Prince, so just do it." Darion heard a choking sound, unsure of whether it came from Edmond or Soren. Edmond probably just swallowed his tongue. Darion was close to it too, for now Zola looked really mad. Even more than before.

"Darion," Triumph whispered at him, urging him to step back.

"Zola... I've been there. Why do you think I'm returning to Nav'Aria? I had literally only returned a few weeks before Triumph and I set out on this quest. But you know what, I was running, Zola. I didn't want to face everyone after my mom was murdered. I blamed them all. I've blamed people my whole life. Why did I have to grow up in Oregon without my birth parents? Why did I have to come here to only have my mom stolen from me? Why me? Why me?!"

Darion thought Zola looked less mad. Maybe like a hair's width less.

"What I realized, though, was that I had spent much of my past searching and blaming, when I should have been grateful for the sacrifice my birth parents made to protect me. I should have been grateful to Carol for being my mom," Darion felt his voice quiver slightly at her name.

Zola swallowed audibly now, and Darion stepped even closer to her. "Zola, they didn't know you were there. Trust me. I've heard Triumph talk about the night of the Coup. If he had thought for even a second that you were still alive, he would have beaten down every door in the Castle to save you."

Zola looked away at that, and Darion reached his Marked hand up to her cheek and lightly, but firmly, brought her face back into view of his. The anger had left her, replaced by confusion and fatigue. Darion stared into her eyes before he spoke softer, "I have seen Triumph in battle with my own eyes, Zola. He has saved my life more than once. He is the most loyal soul I have ever met. You have to let the blame go. Or at least, the blame you're misplacing. Like I said, Narco is the bad guy. His monsters tortured Lyrianna and killed my mom. He kept you in captivity. He did it. The unicorns from Kaulter have been fighting with the King, my father, this entire time. No one left you there... at least consciously. OK?"

Without preamble she leaned in and rubbed her muzzle across Darion's cheek, and near his ear, whispered, "I see why he speaks so highly of you. You are wise... wiser than me, it seems." She stood back and seemed to have returned to a calmer demeanor. She looked toward Triumph, and as he approached, Darion stepped back to give them space.

Watching them, Darion couldn't help thinking of Elsra and how much she is going to love meeting her granddaughter.

Zola dipped her head lowly before Triumph. "I am sorry. I do not know what came over me. I... I did not think how this must have been for you."

Triumph rubbed her cheek with his own, lifting her head with his, but it was Soren's voice that responded. "Zola, you have nothing to apologize for. We are all victims of Narco... none more so than you. The King fights against his forces, we must go to them."

Darion nodded his agreement, and they all seemed to understand that even this short stop had cost them time. They could not dally any longer. Striding ahead, Darion walked through the lush grasses filled with wildflowers, all the while watching out for the occasional buried stone or shrub root. He heard his companions fall into line behind him.

A few seconds later his friend's voice whispered in his ear, "Good job back there," Edmond said, sounding impressed. "I thought she was going to charge at you," he laughed, subconsciously reaching for the sword at his hip.

Darion smiled at him and whispered conspiratorially, "Honestly, I did too."

Edmond blinked startled, then grinned, his cheeks reddening at his words. A slight stubble formed along his jaw and chin. "You might be the most brilliant or the most insane person in Nav'Aria, you know that?"

Darion punched him, grinning back. "Yeah, maybe... but I still kinda think Tony is the craziest of them all," and as if in thought of him, he stroked his growing facial hair as he'd seen Tony do with his goatee over the years.

While the grownups and two-legged creatures had been talking, Trigger kept hearing a buzzing sound. His mother looked mad. She scared him when she was like this. He scooted back away from her and the others, in case she attacked, remembering the night in the barn when she'd come for him... and killed the man with the whip. He could still remember the smell of the fire and hear the mean guard's howls of pain. He shuddered.

Buzz. Buzzzzzzzzzzzz. Buzz.

He spun around, completely surprised by the sound but couldn't identify it. He looked back at his mother, the human with the glowing arm was approaching her. He looked away quickly. He didn't want to see another person killed. He had terrible nightmares from *that* night still.

Buzzzzzz. Buzz. Buzz. Buzzzzzzzzzzzzzzzz.

Trigger flinched at the sound again, feeling a tingle down the length of his spine. Cowering low, he looked around with ever growing anxiety. *What if Mother is killed... what if she kills that human? Will they attack her? Will they*

*attack me… is she safe? Or should I go back to the other Master…
the one-handed man?*

Before he could decide, he heard his mother's voice as
she approached, "Come, Son. We must continue on our
way." She didn't ask if he was alright or explain what had
happened, but just ordered him to move.

Trigger didn't know what having a mom was supposed
to feel like, but he couldn't help thinking she was as
foreign and scary as Master. He was alone.

CHAPTER 3

The Trolls

Antonis couldn't believe his luck. All he had wanted was to stay in Nav'Aria and protect the King, as was his right. He had been the Royal Commander for years before being personally sent on a mission to another realm, Oregon, to protect the Marked Heir. And he had succeeded in his mission. He had brought Darion safely back to his parents, along with the other Keepers. He had been planning to reprise his former role as Vikaris's Royal Commander; although, to his dismay, it was already filled by his friend Garis. He couldn't expect to ask for the centaur to be demoted, but this... this had been foolhardy. He had been ordered to chase after his stubborn friend Rick, who had fled in the night—*like his stubborn son!*—to only get set upon by Trolls. He hated trolls! Their stench was bad enough, but now these filthy and ugly buffoons were his captors!

"You have grown soft, old man," he mumbled to himself. He had taken to talking to himself after being shuttled across the mountain lake to the island with the monster. He had been blindfolded and thrown into a wooden box. He had seen briefly what looked to be cages with other captives before being smacked on the head again—he was really getting tired of that—and thrown into his version of hell. It was putrid smelling, cramped, and dark. Give him a sword and a fight any day, but this, being locked away, unnerved and enraged him. Then, picturing Aalil and Rick, new fears pricked at him. They had been standing below the ledge during his attack. They'd followed him into the Troll holdings, and though he'd given his most urgent glare, Aalil only glared right back. Oh, how he loved her... and wanted to kill her at the same time.

He knew they were out there... somewhere... watching. *Please, Rick, do not let yourselves get caught too.* That beast, whatever it was, could not have Aalil. Though he wouldn't put a rescue attempt past them. They couldn't attack. He had known that when led to the Lake. There was no getting out of this, save for a miracle. *Just leave me,* he thought miserably, picking at a splinter jabbed in his thumb while staring at nothing in the dark, cramped box.

***

"Alright, here is what we will do," Riccus drawled softly. Carefully smoothing his palm over the loosened soil where they'd slept the previous two evenings, he spoke as if they were conversing over Sunday breakfast.

Aalil couldn't believe how calm he was. She had chewed down all her fingernails and began working on her lips. She couldn't stand the anxiety. This inaction. Antonis is down there... with that thing!

She stared at him, and he glanced at her briefly before going back to hiding their tracks upon the dislodged soil. He didn't seem the least bit intimidated by her. Something about that infuriated her and yet also made her trust in him all the more. He wasn't a simple soldier like some she had tossed around in the sparring ring; he was Antonis's best friend. They had spent years together in this Oregon place. She had to trust him. *You will trust him*, she instructed herself for the thousandth time. They must work together in order to save Antonis. She went back to chewing her lip, taut arms crossed before her. She wore her thick coat, glad to have brought it along. They had been lucky and caught a rabbit the previous evening, but after some vacillating decided not to risk a campfire. The rations Riccus had brought along were almost depleted. Still, they couldn't risk it. The trolls were everywhere, as if gathering for something. And there on the island each day, the hulking beast that was larger than any other troll stood roaring and hollering and slamming a hammer down on a shield. It made Aalil's whole body tremble each time... not for fear of herself, but for Antonis. She had not seen him since he was taken across to the island. They were keeping him somewhere... for something. She had to believe he still lived. He had to live.

"Hello, Aalil," Riccus snapped, "Shit, woman, stop daydreaming." Riccus spat, his voice and mood growing more and more gruff as the days went on.

She narrowed her eyes and clenched her fist.

He sighed, standing and wiping his dusty palms upon his pants. "I said, 'I think we have to try today. I snuck closer earlier this morning while you slept. They are getting ready to leave. We might miss our chance if we wait any longer.'"

Aalil's eyebrows shot up, and her heart fluttered with panic. "They are leaving?" She looked over to see that he was right. Up until now they had been gathering, but now it looked as if they were... departing.

"Look!" She felt panic flooding her body. Near the outcrop of stones on the water's edge, they'd been able to sneak close enough to see more of the happenings without being right in the action of the gathering. And yet, as they'd been talking—quarreling—she saw that again, they'd messed up. A large clustering of boats was returning from the island, carrying the females and children. And leading the party was the beast... and Antonis. The boat tipped, severely weighted down from the monster's bulk.

"What now, Riccus?"

Their plan had been to sneak across the water at night to rescue Antonis, having scouted the area and happenings for a few days. They'd found a seemingly unattended boat nearby. Their plan had been to use it, but now it was full light and there were hundreds of trolls upon the water and shoreline. They could never go undetected, and furthermore, Antonis was coming closer.

Antonis was coming closer! He lives, her mind whirled with new possible escape plans. She knew Riccus's silence meant he was doing the same. If Antonis was on this side once more, surely they'd be able to free him? This was actually better... or at least she hoped so.

CHAPTER 4

The Victory

Silence reigned for but a moment as all eyes looked upon the bloodied, decapitated head of the former tyrant of Nav'Aria. And then pandemonium.

Having seen his leader slain, Silver Seeker leapt forward, shrieking and kicking wildly, slashing any in his way. His reins flew behind him like wild tentacles.

Trixon glared. Digging his foreleg into the ground and bending low, he readied himself to pounce as soon as the beast drew near. It was obvious what the maddened creature intended. He was after Vikaris, of course. The King. *The rightful, uncontested King*, Trixon thought proudly.

But he had no time for reverie, for just as Silver Seeker headed toward him, a lumbering troll crashed into Trixon from the side. The gathered forces were reacting... badly. In a flash, the area had gone from a dueling ground to men and beast alike fighting. The Rav'Arians, hybrid unicorns, and trolls seemed to be reacting belligerently to the death of their leader. And now all semblance of order was lost. With bodies pressing inward, Trixon panicked, losing sight of Vikaris. He kicked and slashed wildly, bellowing for anyone present to get the King to safety. Kicking, out of instinct, he felt his leg connect with the shin of a troll, and he heard the troll's roar as he fell. Trixon hoped his bones had shattered, and he believed they had with the force of his enraged kick.

They had not fought this hard and this long only to lose their King just moments after killing the tyrant usurper. That could not happen. Trixon reared around. Knowing he was one of the mightiest of the unicorns present meant that he was also the biggest target... besides the King. He was the King's steed after all. He caught a glimpse of black and red before the flashing eyes and piercing midnight black horn nearly collided with him.

Narco's pet had found him.

Trixon noted the blood dripping from Silver Seeker's horn. Froth appeared on his coat as if he had run a long distance. *He is rabid*, Trixon thought.

After seeing some of their own slaughtered, Rav'Arians and trolls began to clear away from the enraged unicorns. It seemed even the Rav'Arians gave a wide berth to an angry unicorn.

Silver Seeker stood frozen, except for his head which swung low and from side to side, as if to the rhythm of his own war beat.

Trixon wanted to look around, reach out for Vikaris, but he knew if he took his eyes off this wretch, it could mean his downfall. He grumbled low in his throat.

"You, pet," Trixon growled. "You fight on the wrong side."

Silver Seeker didn't speak, but instead leapt over the corpse of a fallen soldier and reared, kicking polished hooves at Trixon's head.

Trixon had been expecting the move, knowing the pet—crazed as he was—had never been battle tested, much like Narco. He jumped to the side. Silver Seeker's hooves collided with the ground below, but not before his piercing horn cut right through a soldier who had ran into the fray in the worst possible moment. He was slashed open from clavicle to mid-torso before his face even registered the pain, eyes rolling upwards in his head as his corpse collapsed.

Trixon didn't hesitate, but instead used the moment of distraction as an opportunity to kick the pet's back leg. The knee buckled and a shriek escaped the unicorn's maw as he disentangled himself from the soldier's bloodied corpse and turned around swiftly. Blood and gore clung ominously to Silver Seeker's horn. He then turned to reveal a limping back leg.

Though fighting was all around them, the area remained fairly clear of interference, besides the occasional misstep of a soldier. All knew the unicorns were fighting to the death. Trixon shouted to Vikaris telepathically.

Are you alright? Where are you?

Vikaris didn't respond.

Trixon knew he could not be separated from the King. The Rav'Arians and trolls were hammering the area where they'd stood near Narco's body. Trixon needed to get to Vikaris, but this rabid creature would never let him turn away. They continued to stab and kick at one another. Trixon thought he heard a familiar voice yelling, but before he could identify it, a burst of silvery white light rushed to the scene.

The unicorns!

They had been instructed to stay behind during the duel. Vikaris's main force had stayed back, and had it not been for Garis's disobedience in sending his left flank to defend their King, Trixon knew they'd have been already killed. For as soon as Vikaris and Trixon had cleared through Narco's forces and the Tyrant agreed to the challenge, the nearest enemy force had begun encircling the dueling pair. It certainly was not Vikaris's best plan, Trixon brooded. *And he calls me rash*, he thought, exhaling forcefully to blow his bangs from his brow and combat Silver Seeker's unrelenting strikes—a few narrowly missing him. Trixon's attention was torn, and he knew that he needed to focus if he was to live through this trial and find the King.

Just then a familiar voice bellowed. The base of Trixon's horn tingled. *Vikaris!*

Fearing the worst, Trixon roared and rushed Silver Seeker headlong. He was faster than the creature, and his horn made contact with the powerful chest of his opponent. It didn't strike home, however, for the beast reacted immediately, jumping back and shrieking wildly. Trixon reared and kicked him, but his blows didn't land. Silver Seeker had stepped out of the way. Trixon was glad to see that he had at least bloodied his opponent. He limped on his back leg, and now with the gushing wound to the chest, he was beginning to slow. Still, Trixon didn't have time for this. He needed to get to Vikaris. How had he allowed them to get separated? Trixon cursed himself and backed away. Perhaps he could push his way through the crowd and Silver Seeker wouldn't follow?

Before he could decide, a white hollering blur slammed into Silver Seeker, toppling him to the ground like a bore tossing a challenger in the air with his tusks. So too did the unicorn upheave the startled enemy.

Drigidor!

Go to the King, the powerful unicorn warrior commanded.

Trixon nodded and turned instantly to the area he had last seen his liege. He didn't fear an attack from behind any longer, for he knew that Drigidor, Elsra's Second Mate, would guard his retreat with his life. Silver Seeker was no longer a threat to Trixon... to anyone, he thought. Then, as he heard Silver Seeker's maddened shrieks cut off mid-cry, Trixon knew Drigidor had finished him.

Pushing through, stabbing and kicking as needed, Trixon willed his way through the frenzy and into the main congregation. Though it was only feet away, it seemed nearly impossible to reach. Unyielding, Trixon forced his bulk through the mass, kicking friends and foes alike. Vikaris's welfare mattered above all.

Shoving aside a tottering Rav'Arian, grasping at—and failing to remove—the knife at its throat, the vacated space provided an opening into the scene. It was a splendor of death.

A green glow illuminated the area where Vikaris stood gallantly fighting against the onslaught of trolls and Rav'Arians who had crept in around him, shutting him off from Trixon and Garis's forces who hacked at the surrounding enemies. Through it all, Trixon could see one lone headless corpse... Narco's head lay a few feet away.

Trixon growled angrily and slammed into the skirmish, kicking and biting and slashing at anyone he could— anyone trying to harm the True King. Narco was dead... clearly, as his sightless eyes stared upwards from a trunkless head. The fight should be over. These creatures should know they've been beaten and surrender.

Vikaris didn't break his gaze or stride as his sword connected with the shoulder of the towering troll before him, but Trixon could feel his appreciation. An overwhelming sense of relief enveloped his aura. Trixon wanted to apologize for being separated. To grovel.... There would be time for that later. For now, he wanted to kill every last one of these monsters and be done with it. So, that's what he set out to do.

In quick order, he and Vikaris combatted the enemies, leaving none to Garis, the russet centaur and Commander who rushed in, sword prepared to aid his King.

Trixon breathed deeply under the weight of fatigue. He mentally tried to force it aside, for he saw many enemies left on the field. Though this portion of the army was contained, it looked as if Kragar's right flank had sought out the collective body of the enemy force and battled still upon the plain.

Why are they fighting? Their leader is dead! Trixon puzzled over it, coming closer to Vikaris.

"Well done, my friend," Vikaris smiled tiredly, though his expression seemed wan… and confused.

Garis, assured that Vikaris was well, had sent the remaining contingent of his troops to assist Kragar in bringing down the final combatants. Thousands of them fought, even after their leader was dead and an amassing number of them had been slain.

Trixon knew the fighting wasn't finished. A surrender seemed unlikely at this point. The Kingdom unicorns were deranged. He watched their glossy black chests heaving in exertion as they ran laps around the outer ring of soldiers. They hadn't engaged in the fighting after a number of their own—including Silver Seeker—had fallen. Now they ran… shrieking wildly. Crazed. It made Trixon's ears perk up anxiously. Something was very wrong.

Vikaris, who had been leaning down to search Narco's robes, now surveyed the unicorns and fighting soldiers with a befuddled expression as well. He could feel it also, Trixon knew.

Something wasn't right here.

***

"We are close!" Soren called back, and Triumph nodded his head solemnly.

"Soren is right, I can sense them too."

Darion gulped. After weeks away, he was about to
meet his father again and find out just what kind of
shitstorm he had left in his wake.

"Are they fighting? Is the battle over? Did we win?"

"Whoa, Darion," Triumph said softly, "we will find
out soon enough. We are near the Nav'Arian Plains. Can
you sense anything?"

Darion berated himself again for not thinking to reach
out with his senses. He had been too preoccupied
watching Zola and Triumph and thinking of this change in
the relationship. *Selfish!*

But as he reached out, he did sense something. A lot of
somethings. A huge field of war. He could smell it, hear it,
taste it. How had he missed this just moments ago? Blood
was in the air. And that feral shrieking sound? Gooseflesh
broke out along his arms. They were very close.

Darion stopped immediately, "Hold on," he said, and
his companions paused. Edmond drew his sword, wary of
any lurking Rav'Arians.

"Okay, we need to make a plan before we just walk
right onto a battlefield," Darion counseled.

Triumph and Soren nodded, and Edmond gave one
curt nod, tucking his now shoulder-length locks behind
his ears but remaining alert. Searching the area. Guarding
their backs while they deliberated. He really was a good
friend, Darion considered briefly before jumping into
hushed plans and scenarios with his unicorn companions.
Zola, he noted, stood to the side with her son. He
looked... darker than usual. Or smaller? Something was
different about Trigger, but Darion didn't have time to

think of the tiny hybrid unicorn. There was a battle being fought for his land... and he was missing it!

They decided to sneak closer. Soren and Edmond would go first before signaling for Darion and Triumph once they located their troops. Zola and Trigger were to stay behind until it was safe. Zola was displeased with this, but after Triumph looked meaningfully at Trigger, it seemed she realized that she could not bring him into this fight. War was no place for a child.

More quietly than before, they headed for the next big hill in front of them. The trees were sparser and the grass taller in this area leading out into the Plains. Once they crested the hill, Soren believed the battle would be below them. The unicorn shrunk surreptitiously, and Edmond crouched to follow suit and peer over the edge.

Darion chewed his lip nervously while awaiting the signal. He ran his hands through his shaggy, dark hair, briefly wondering what Rick would have to say about it. He prayed he was alive and safe... not down there fighting. Darion closed his eyes momentarily, trying to focus his senses. The Rav'Arians were there... in number, that much he knew. Their cloying toxic odor permeated the air, overwhelming Darion's senses. He could smell the metallic scent of blood churning in the muddied ground and crushed grasses below. Distantly he could hear war cries and metal upon metal. Sword fighting. It was still going on! *Father needs me!*

Darion opened his eyes, about to ask aloud what was taking Soren and Edmond so long, when all of a sudden,

Triumph's face was before his, eyes looming with a look of panic.

And then Darion heard it. Laughter. Wild, unbridled, maniacal laughter.

***

Still staring at the two forces clashing, Vikaris whispered, "Trixon, do you hear that?"

Trixon did indeed. His blood felt cold and his heart began to hammer. He glanced at the body at Vikaris's feet to ensure it had not come back to life. It had not. Narco still lay dead, his blood pooling around his crimson and black-clothed body. His breastplate tarnished and speckled with blood and dirt. But if he was dead... then who was that?

"YOU FOOLS. YOU VILE, PETTY, WORTHLESS FOOLS. YOU SQUIBBEL AND SQUABBLE AND FIGHT AND FUSS... AND ALL ALONG YOU HAVE BEEN PAWNS IN MY GAME. HAHAHAHA."

As if in a trance, a collective hush fell over the battlefield. The clashing swords stopped, the unicorns' shrieks ceased, and the Rav'Arians cackles faded away. All that could be heard was the foreign voice which blared in everyone's minds.

"YOU HAVE DONE JUST AS I HOPED YOU WOULD. YOU HAVE DESTROYED NARCO... HE WAS PITIFUL UNTIL THE END. A TOY, YES. A VERY FUN TOY. BUT DISPOSABLE. AND NOW THE REAL GAME WILL BE REVEALED... THE TOY MASTER... THE PUPPETEER... THE REAL EMPEROR... MORTA. HAHAHAHAHAHAHA."

Trixon couldn't speak. No one could. His eyes bulged as he met Vikaris's.

Trixon's eyes shot toward the soldiers. Many of them had their hands over their ears. Some were lying on the ground, rocking back and forth or slamming palms upon their foreheads to stave off the impact of Morta's proclamation. But before Trixon could question it further, the voice continued.

"RAV'ARIANS, TROLLS, AND MY PETS… I COMMAND YOU TO RETURN TO ME IMMEDIATELY. LEAVE THESE TIRESOME FOOLS TO WALLOW IN THIS REVELATION. THEY WILL SOON LEARN WHAT IT MEANS TO BE ENEMIES OF MINE."

The words had an immediate impact on the crowded soldiers, and with no decorum or order, the soldiers ran with reckless abandon—Rav'Arian, troll, and unicorn. No humans bade the call, however. It seemed most of the enemy soldiers had been either killed or were suffering from the pronouncement. One man, tall and seasoned-looking more so than the rest—perhaps a military leader for the enemy—stood. The insignia on his fine tunic matched Narco's. Trixon blearily watched as the man walked up to Narco and spat on the headless corpse, blood streaming from his wounded side. He tore the crest from his shirt before taking a blade from his belt and slitting his throat. The body landed with a thud.

Trixon walked as if his legs were in quicksand, slowly and stiffly nearing his King. Vikaris gratefully put an arm upon his neck.

While the enemy soldiers ran rapidly in the direction of the Kingdom and Castle Dintarran, Vikaris's troops stood looking as dazed as Trixon felt.

And then the voice continued one last time, softer than before. "For you see, Vikaris, I have been watching you for a long time now. I have always been watching…. You thought you were so powerful when you were with me at your Camp. Cutting off my hand." The voice purred, pausing with a tsk. "Such a brave leader." Laugher thundered in their minds as he continued, "You may have thought the war ended when your sword decapitated Narco… I hope you will see that the war has only just begun. Realize, I am no plaything, like Narco. Come fight me, King Vikaris… if you dare. HAHAHAHA."

Trixon couldn't see Vikaris's eyes, but he felt the despair as his King grabbed his neck with both arms and wept.

***

Edmond and Soren rushed back as soon as the "voice" began. Triumph and Darion looked at each other in utter shock. At the mention of "watching," all four voices gasped… "The watchers… of Tarsin."

After everything they'd been through and discovered in the desert, the final piece to the puzzle clicked into place. It seemed so terrifyingly obvious now.

Morta was Tarsin.

Tarsin was Morta.

Narco had never been the enemy… well, he was an enemy, but not *the* enemy.

Morta had set them up. He had set this in motion long ago.

And all they could ask themselves was, *what now?*

CHAPTER 5

The Promise

Once the voice seemed to have ended its freakish tirade, Darion and his party raced down the hillside and onto the Plains. The land was vast, but Darion could see the army's whereabouts spread out at the foot of Mount Alodon.

Triumph instructed Darion to ride him. He'd only ridden Triumph a couple of times when they'd had to run for their lives. This felt no different. He needed to find the King immediately!

"Do not worry about us, we will catch up... all of us," Soren reassured Triumph and Darion as he looked knowingly at Zola and the teetering, slow-moving Trigger. Edmond nodded grimly.

Before speeding off, Triumph reared and whinnied in response to his loyal friend.

"You could've warned me before you were going to stand up like that? I almost fell off," Darion grumbled as they raced upon the Plains.

"Ha!" Triumph snarked, "if you are to ride a unicorn—as my guest—then you would be wise to hold on and not dictate my movements, thank you very much, Prince."

"Here we go," Darion replied sarcastically, rolling his eyes. Their banter, though familiar and comforting, still didn't remove the fear.

Triumph didn't deign a response.

He must be as worried as me, Darion thought. He held on firmly with his legs and hands gripping Triumph's silvery mane, the unicorn's hooves thundering upon the grassy plains. Though still some distance away, he knew that normal eyes would be able to see them now. His heightened senses detected shouts of alarm as the lone rider headed toward the force.

"I am calling out to them; Drigidor says 'to approach'," and then more to himself than to Darion, Triumph continued, "Why does it always have to be him?"

Knowing that Triumph and his stepfather's relationship was anything but pleasant, Darion rolled his eyes thinking back to the time he'd been dragged before Elsra in the middle of the night to stand in the midst of one of Triumph's and Drigidor's arguments.

"You know that is rude, Darion. We were not acting childish," Triumph's haughty tone interrupted Darion's musing.

Now that Darion knew Triumph better, that's exactly what it was. "What's your deal with him? I mean," Darion added, sensing Triumph's anger... the growl was a dead giveaway, "I know he's not your Dad and could never live up to him, but can't you see he's trying?" Darion remembered the sting in Drigidor's eyes every time Triumph cut him down.

Triumph ran in silence toward the force, which was very close by now. Those that weren't injured or scouring the field to find the injured amidst the corpses waved in greeting.

Darion sat up straight under their inspection. He knew, unfortunately, that he and Triumph weren't done with this conversation. *Great,* he thought ruefully. *Triumph will probably lecture me later on as punishment for butting in.*

"Peace, Darion," Triumph whispered as their eyes took in the scene of death.

Rav'Arian filth clung to the air, and as they passed groans of pain came from injured soldiers awaiting help. Darion swallowed. The carnage was severe. He could barely make out the last of the Rav'Arians and trolls scurrying off, pursued by his Father's troops. Many still appeared to get away.

Darion felt shock, but before he could say anything, he saw a face he recognized. A man standing with another large unicorn froze as if in disbelief.

Father!

Darion felt all the unease, worry, and anger that had possessed him for much of his journey slip away as new emotions possessed him. Joy! Relief. Hope.

The King lives!

"Father!" Darion yelled and jumped swiftly from Triumph's back, closing the distance in a matter of steps.

Before Vikaris seemed to understand what was happening, Darion wrapped his arms around him.

Trixon whinnied softly, rubbing his cheek in greeting with Triumph, his uncle.

"Darion," Vikaris murmured, his hands squeezing his son's shoulders in a tight embrace. Bewilderment fogged his brain, but he knew this wasn't a dream. He leaned back to look at his son.

Bright, brilliant green eyes burned into his. "You have grown," Vikaris remarked. The boy that had run off after Carolina's death seemed to have entered into manhood. Darion looked harder. Stronger. Wearing fitted black pants and a sleeveless jerkin, much like Vikaris's own, Darion's long locks spilled well past his shoulders. His bared, bronzed skin—now darker than Vikaris's—revealed toned arms used to swinging a sword. His image struck a great resemblance to a portrait Vikaris had seen of his grandfather Valron when he was young. His eyes wandered to Darion's Mark. It had spread considerably. And his eyes.... They weren't the eyes of an untested, fearful youth; these were the eyes of a man who had seen hard things… and had come out victorious on the other side. These were the eyes of a soldier… and Vikaris would need every soldier for the coming days.

***

Morta stood immobile, peering into the murky, swirling liquid of the Chalice. He closed his amber eyes to savor the pungencies of the moment. No longer did he have to pretend to be the weak, aged adviser. What an enjoyable game it had been, but now that his plaything, Narco, had been killed, the charade was up. For this he was glad. It meant the next phase of his plan could unfold.

After calling to the forces, ordering his troops to return from the field, he had reached out with the liquid to make a few more commands. The trolls were on their way… and his border friends who had faithfully watched out for him for so many years were now braving the sunlight to join him. Together, with the hordes of Rav'Arian younglings leaving the tar pits, he would amass a force unlike anything Nav'Aria had ever seen before. Narco's force was only the precursor of what was to come in this Final Battle. Destruction would be imminent… and immeasurably pleasurable.

"I must look the part," Morta laughed wickedly. Without glancing behind him he snapped his fingers— with his remaining hand—at Dabor. The faithful troll, looming and silent as always, stepped forward, producing the menacing vials.

"Now watch and see true power, Dabor," Morta croaked, eyes intent upon the vials set before him on the table. One after another, Dabor undid the stoppers and poured the contents within. Acidic, metallic odors filled the room, and an ashy cloud burst up from Chalice. Morta threw off his cloak and stood up tall. His form, despite having feigned weakness, was actually much taller and stronger than anyone had given him credit. Standing upright, he thrust his stump into the mixture. A pain so great—and tantalizing—captured his entire nervous system. He felt electric with burning pleasure. Gritting his teeth, feeling the sweat break out upon his pale forehead, he smiled devilishly into the liquid, laughing. Pain was something he could handle. More than that, it was something he desired. This was only the beginning of the pain he would unleash. Vikaris may have slew Narco, but he would watch his land fall into the darkness that had claimed Tarsin's soul so many years before. That darkness reigned in Morta, and now the Nav'Arians would tremble in its contagion.

The liquid pulsated, rising higher and higher with some unseen force, never spilling from the Chalice but smoking dangerously, as if it were aflame. Morta could hardly see the liquid anymore, for the cloud of smoke was so great. He heard Dabor shuffling backwards away from the cloud.

And then, as if a window had been opened, an invisible breeze carried the toxic cloud away. It dissipated instantly. Morta closed his eyes, savoring the tingling sensations. And then in one smooth motion, he lifted his arm from the liquid… only this time it didn't end in a scarred stump. His left forearm lent seamlessly into a black, metal hand. He made a fist, squeezing it and wiggling his fingers. They worked exactly as if made of flesh, only the appearance proved otherwise.

A vial shattered behind him. He spun to see Dabor's eyes widen in shock. Morta laughed at Dabor, cocking his head. "You did not believe me when I said Narco was my pawn? I know you will not underestimate me again, will you?"

Dabor didn't speak, only shook his head, eyes downcast.

Morta smiled, breathing in the rich scents of metal, power, and fear. *This*, this was the moment when all who had underestimated him would be wiped out.

"Come, Dabor, we must not keep our guests waiting," Morta commanded, striding to the door and flinging it open with his glossy black hand.

***

"I do not understand," Vikaris said bemused. "How did you find us? Are you alright? Where have you been?"

Darion smiled, feeling utter joy at his father's evident worry and affection for him. He hadn't known what Vikaris's reaction would be.

Stepping back, he gestured to Triumph. "We have a lot to tell you. Triumph and Soren were able to locate you from their connection to the unicorns."

Darion could see Soren, Zola, and Trigger coming along, trailed by Edmond, who appeared to be watching vigilantly for any remaining Rav'Arians. Darion grinned at his friends, waving.

As they made their way through the troops, more and more came closer to hear what their King and Prince were saying. Many called out praise and welcome to their newly returned Marked Heir. Darion tried to appear confident and calm. Many were bleeding, having just fought in his name. He needed to appear grateful and proud of their efforts. He saw from the corner of his eye how confident his father looked; blood stains and grime did little to diminish the power exuding from him. His eyes burned bright, his Ruby glowed, and his Marked Arm illuminated for all to see.

Eyes drifting, Darion looked toward the body near Vikaris's feet. The head had been cut off and lay near it.

Vikaris followed his gaze.

"So that's Narco, huh?" Darion said, walking closer to inspect his evil, very much dead relative.

Vikaris nodded.

Darion searched the body, his eyes lingering on the emblem sewn into the former Emperor's clothing. It looked like a crescent moon with wings.

Triumph and Trixon approached the morbid curiosity.

The winged crescent, Triumph said quietly in his mind. *His enigmatic sigil for these past years.*

"The winged ones with his pets," Darion gasped, knowing full well that the crescent was a symbol for the unicorns.

Vikaris turned to look at his son, peering at him. Before Darion could add more, a low rumble sounded as a great silvery body barged into their intimate circle.

Without a word, Drigidor walked up to the body of Narco and kicked him once with his foreleg before bending down to the decapitated head. Drigidor's lips parted, and his teeth bit into Narco's oily exposed locks of hair, lifting the head up as if to carry it.

A promise, Drigidor's voice rumbled in their minds. *The Queen is expecting this.* And with that, Drigidor turned and began walking proudly in the direction of the Woods of the Willow. Soldiers parted in his wake. Many nodded their heads at the great unicorn while simultaneously spitting at the ground at the thought of that vile man's head anywhere near the pure, majestic being.

"Lyrianna," Vikaris whispered. And then, as if snapping out of a trance, Vikaris yelled at once, "We leave immediately. Make for the Portals. Make for Kaulter."

Vikaris turned to Darion and patted his back. "It is time to return, Son."

Darion nodded grimly. He knew they had much to discuss, but after Morta's wicked pronouncement, safety for his people—and his mother!—came first. They needed to get off the Plains, regroup, and plan. For it appeared that the war was far from over.

Triumph and Trixon stood together, both their heads bent in a submissive—rare—display of obeisance to their bonded companions. "Let us ride," they spoke in unison.

Darion looked once more at his father, whose lips tugged in the beginnings of a smile, though it didn't reach his eyes. There was too much going on for anyone to smile.

Darion and Vikaris swung onto the backs of their bonded unicorns, beginning the long march back toward the Woods and on to Kaulter.

CHAPTER 6

The Marked Royals

Pacing, the red-headed centaur's hooves pounded and tread so harshly upon the otherwise luscious landscape that rivets began to form in the grasses from her repeated steps. Lyrianna didn't blame her. She felt like pacing, herself. For now, she'd have to pacify the anxiety by subtly picking at one of her cuticles. There were too many onlookers around for her to appear nervous. She needed to be calm. Collected. Queenly.

Word had arrived only moments ago, causing the entire Fortress to erupt with joy, fear, and confusion. The nymph scout had returned with a verbal message.

Many casualties. Narco dead. Morta true villain as you predicted. Darion back. On our way.

Lyrianna had been with Elsra and Trinidad (and Cela, of course, her ever vigilant self-appointed bodyguard). The four of them met over lunch to discuss Trinidad's progress—or lack thereof—at the Tree. They had searched every nook and cranny and come up short.

Trinidad believed there was a way to regrow his horn, but if there was, they certainly had not figured it out yet. Lyrianna tried to push the glumness aside. They would find the answer. She worried that if she gave into despair, Trinidad would be able to detect it given their unusual bond. She couldn't let that happen.

Standing at the Kaulter Portal entrance, they waited. Nervously, she reached her fingers up to the Mark which she now bore upon her forehead. *What will Vikaris think? And Darion... how will he react to seeing me?* She laced her hands together in front of her, squeezing her fingers tightly. Nervously.

I think he will surprise you, my Queen, Trinidad spoke telepathically. *I have a good feeling about him. Your connection to him while we were... you know... could not have taken place, in my opinion, had it not been with a willing heart. The fact that Darion was able to hear from you makes me confident that he longs for his mother, just as his mother longs for her son.*

Lyrianna glanced at him, her eyes filling with tears, nodding in thanks. Though she didn't speak, she knew he picked up on her gratitude. Breathing deeply and trying to calm her nerves, she began to sense something at the pool. The waters began swirling, giving off a green glow.

This is it, she thought.

"Step back from the Portal everyone," Elsra's commanding voice carried to the surrounding villagers, including soldiers' families and the guards.

Mothers began urging children back in place, holding them close. Lyrianna felt her stomach grip at the sight of them. Some of those children may have been made fatherless. She wanted to weep for them. *Get a hold of yourself*, she thought forcefully. She shook off the emotion again, feigning calmness. *Cool, collected, queenly*, she repeated. That is what they expect from her. What they need from her. That is what Vikaris had believed she was when he left her in charge, along with Elsra. Lifting her chin, she straightened her spine ever further and awaited what would come.

Fixing her eyes on the growing movement in the pool, she sensed Cela, who came to stand on her other side. While Lyrianna knew she was moving out of the way, Cela's hand on her blade did not go unnoticed. No enemies would get through the Portal and live long. Lyrianna didn't fear for enemies at the moment, though. Her husband had sent a message, and while yes, they had considered that the messenger could have been compromised and sent with a lie (since there was no handwritten note), she didn't think that the case. The mention of Darion had sealed it in her mind—and her heart. This had to be it.

Painstakingly slow, figures began to emerge from the pool. Many of them. She knew the full army would be spilling out of the Portal, and she made to back up, signaling to those around to continue making room on the hillside so the beleaguered soldiers could get out. Guards stood nearby in case the crowd of villagers turned moblike. Seegar could be seen directing groups this way or that.

A few grooms leading teams of horses passed through the Portal before a towering, familiar form emerged from the pool, heading directly toward Lyrianna and her party.

A cloth bag was belted upon his thickly muscled neck parting his silver mane as he approached. A young human soldier trailing behind him kept his eyes downcast. As the figure approached, Elsra leapt forward and nuzzled him affectionately. "Thank the Creator," she breathed. Drigidor was home.

Lyrianna kept one eye on the pool, but since it appeared to be all soldiers for the moment, she focused back to the Regent's Mate. The cloth bag caught her gaze, and she scrunched her face in an effort to distinguish what could possibly be important enough to mar the beautiful, pristine coat of a unicorn.

Drigidor jerked his head toward the soldier accompanying him and whispered something. The soldier nodded his head sheepishly and with fumbling fingers unsecured the belt from Drigidor's neck. Holding the sackcloth, the soldier looked again to Drigidor, who nodded to him, before approaching Lyrianna himself.

Her breath caught, and her stomach clenched as the young soldier reached into the bag.

It was Narco! Or at least, what was left of him. His face loomed before hers as the soldier clutched the evil man's oily hair and lifted the decapitated head before them as instructed by Drigidor.

Lyrianna felt sick.

Drigidor stepped forward, nudging the soldier aside. "A promise kept, my Queen," his low voice rumbled.

Lyrianna inhaled, nodding forcefully, keeping her eyes on Drigidor's dark orbs. "You have kept your word and done well, Drigidor."

Drigidor interjected quickly, "I did not slay him, my Queen. Your husband saw to that. I only ensured his head was brought to you as requested."

Vikaris killed Narco? Her head swarmed. A million questions flooded her brain at his words, but they would have to wait, for a hushed whisper had fallen upon the hillside, and the green glow grew to a brilliant light. *The pool!* She had become distracted and ceased glancing at the oncoming soldiers. But as her eyes searched the area, they fell upon a lovely sight. Her family!

Vikaris, Darion, Triumph, and Trixon emerged from the pool, standing proudly and filling her with such immense pride at their wondrous sight. The air seemed to crackle with energy. Magic. For the Marked Royals astride their bonded unicorn companions of the First Horn's lineage had returned to the Isle of Kaulter.

***

Darion sat atop Triumph, with his permission, of course, looking out upon the Kaulter hillside near the portal pool. He breathed in deeply, remembering the sweet, crisp air of Kaulter. It seemed like a lifetime ago when he had come here with Seegar, Edmond, and young Anton. He remembered seeing Merfolk waving from the sea, the beautiful waterfall and bridge that led into the village, and the spectacular wooden Fortress built into a gigantic tree.

"You know the last time I was here I didn't really like you," Darion murmured, patting Triumph's neck.

The unicorn snorted in response, "I think we can agree the feeling was mutual, my Prince," Triumph said, and though joking, he recaptured the snappish tone he had used previously very well.

Too well for Darion's taste.

Triumph laughed aloud at Darion's discomfort. "Ah, but it is good to be back," Triumph added happily, his horned head moving all around to take in the sights.

Looking beyond the brilliant light and beautiful surroundings, Darion's eyes found those gathered nearby. The whole village seemed to have come out for their return, and smack dab in the front stood a resplendent lady.

Mother, he thought. His heart soared with love. So much so that it surprised him. He glanced at his father and Trixon who nodded. All were headed toward the beautiful blonde-headed queen standing amidst the Unicorn Council... and next to a very imposing—and gorgeous—red-headed centaur. Darion loved it here.

He jumped down from Triumph and hurried over to his mother, as did Vikaris. Darion slowed his step to allow Vikaris to get there first. It seemed only right, for as he neared her, he felt a tremor of anxiety. Was she mad at him for leaving?

Though, drawing closer, it appeared he and Vikaris noticed her newest feature at the same time, both freezing mid-step. Vikaris, in his rush to hug her, paused and held her shoulders firmly at arms' length. Mouth agape, he inspected her magnificent, yet changed, brow.

She had tears in her eyes and a tremulous smile as she searched her husband's face. Darion stepped closer. His mother had a silvery diamond-shaped symbol cresting her forehead. He was sure that hadn't been there before, and he would know. He had been sketching her face, unaware that it was his mother, weeks before coming to Nav'Aria.

"What is that?" he blurted. His cheeks flushed immediately as his parents both looked at him.

Vikaris's mouth appearing permanently ajar.

Lyrianna laughed a melodic sound that made the back of Darion's neck tingle. He loved to hear her sound happy—and safe. He didn't think he'd ever heard anything so beautiful in his life.

"We have a lot to discuss," Lyrianna exclaimed in her sweet voice, giving him a slight wink. She glanced to Trinidad, who still lacked his horn but stood tall and proud. Warmth and kindness radiated from him.

Vikaris made a gargling sound as if trying to speak, but Trixon beat him to it.

"You two are bonded? Father, how is that possible?"

Bonded, Darion thought, feeling confused. *But she's.... she's not a Marked Royal. How is that possible?*

Now it was time for Trinidad to chuckle. He replied enigmatically, "As the Queen said, I think we have a lot to discuss." He stepped forward to nuzzle his son and murmured quietly, "It warms a father's heart to see his son home safe. I am glad of it, Trixon," before turning in greeting toward Triumph.

Trixon whinnied at his father's side, taking on the momentary image of a pleased youth.

Darion smiled at the reunited unicorns.

Vikaris laughed, "I do not know what you two have been up to in my absence, but you are surely a happy sight," and with that Vikaris leaned in and kissed his wife before embracing her in a firm hug. She hesitated, eyeing his bandaged left arm, before tenderly hugging him back. Keeping his uninjured arm around her shoulders, Vikaris turned toward Darion.

Their faces filled with love. Joy beckoned him closer. Lyrianna had tears spilling down her cheeks but laughed happily as she reached to embrace Darion. As he stepped forward smiling at them, his parents wrapped their arms around him in a warm family embrace.

"Welcome home, son," Lyrianna whispered, standing up on her toes to kiss his cheek. "Welcome home."

In that moment, having their loving arms around him, Darion knew true peace. He closed his eyes and allowed himself to just be—to breathe in the light citrus scent of Lyrianna's hair and perfume near his face and feel the strong grip of his father's hand upon his back. This... this is what he had always longed for... and yet, reality struck him.

Letting go of the embrace, he took a step back, his eyes searching the rest of the group gathered around. There were two faces he didn't see.

"Where's my Dad?" Darion asked. "And Tony?"

The look that swept across his birth parents' faces told him much. "Are they—" Fear gripped him. He couldn't even say the word.

Vikaris stepped forward, placing his hands on Darion's shoulders and looking intensely into his eyes. "After you and Triumph left," Vikaris shot a scowl at Triumph. The unicorn shifted uncomfortably on his feet.

Darion swallowed guiltily. *Yep… we're still in trouble for leaving.*

Vikaris continued, "Riccus took it upon himself to go in search of answers in the mountains. I sent Antonis after him," pausing to look at Lyrianna and Elsra, who shook their heads lightly, before Vikaris continued. "To my knowledge, we have not heard from them since."

"The mountains?" Darion spluttered. And then he remembered his lessons from Triumph and Seegar. There were inhabitants in the mountains. Mysterious, dangerous inhabitants.

"To the trolls?" Darion felt sick, like he'd been punched in the stomach. *DAD, WHAT WERE YOU THINKING?* And then he understood. Rick would never just sit by. After his Mom's funeral and leaving him, Rick was probably angered… and sad. He needed to move. To act. So, he went on his own quest.

Darion exhaled heavily and felt moisture tickling the corner of his eyes.

Vikaris looked solemn. "As Lyrianna said, we have much to discuss. We should go to our apartments where we can discuss privately."

As he said it, Darion looked around him at the hushed citizens gathering nearby. Many whispered softly, and looks of alarm creased their brows.

Darion felt stupid. He should know by now that everyone looked to the Royals for guidance, and here he was looking crestfallen and causing the mood around them to change. Mothers were burying their children's faces in their arms as if to protect them. Darion tried to lift his lips into a smile, or at least a more pleasant face than the look of horror he had only moments ago. He stepped aside, allowing the people to see his parents' faces. Vikaris stood proud and nodded regally to those around him.

During their discussion, the number of soldiers emerging from the pool had become sparse. Moments passed before another guard or two carrying the injured came through. Elsra and Drigidor stood closer to the portal, directing the last of the soldiers. And after a long lapse of no one coming through, many on the hillside began to turn away and begin walking back toward their homes. Many women and children embraced their men returned from battle, covering them in kisses and clutching to their shirtsleeves; other mothers cried softly, hugging their children close, knowing their fighters had paid the ultimate sacrifice.

Darion knew Vikaris had spread the word that upon their return all were to go home to get medical care, food and rest. He would send word to their officers once he spoke to the Unicorn Council and knew the plans for what was to come.

More severely injured soldiers were being led to the Fortress, and as the crowd began to thin out, one family of centaurs stood. The female's stoic face began to crumple as she gazed forlornly at the Pool.

And then as if something snapped inside her, she wailed, "Garis! Sire, where is my Garis?" The two shaggy haired younglings whimpered at her side.

Vikaris glanced back at the pool, but before he could comfort her, a rippling glow came at the pool one final time. And as Commander's form began to materialize, his wife's wail of joy erupted from the hillside. She and her younglings rushed closer toward the portal entrance.

Garis, Royal Commander of the Nav'Arian forces under Vikaris's leadership, of course, emerged from the pool, along with Edmond, Soren, Zola, and Trigger, bringing up the rear.

"What is that?" Lyrianna whispered.

Elsra and Trinidad both whinnied in alarm at the sight, for though the other unicorns had seen the infant, this was the first time the Kaulter unicorns had seen Trigger… and his mother.

Triumph rushed toward them, nuzzling Zola and looking at Trigger, who looked a little frightened but comfortable. He, it appeared, had not been able to keep pace with the marching soldiers, and so it was that a tiny black unicorn was draped upon a shaggy centaur's back. His hornless mother looking cautiously on one side, and Edmond standing on the other with a protective hand placed on Trigger's back. Soren stood nearby looking oddly affectionate.

No infant could have had a better group looking out for him.

Darion didn't speak. He couldn't. He could only watch, his eyes itching with moisture once more as he heard the words his friend had always longed to say.

"Mother, I would like to introduce you to someone very special. This is Zola... your granddaughter."

CHAPTER 7

The New Leader

Both pausing for one last moment of indecision, Rick and Aalil knew this was it. If they didn't do this right, they'd either die in the effort or be captured to die alongside Tony.

"Well…," Rick grumbled, moving to a crouched position behind the rocks. Aalil must have taken his grumble for the signal because she was up on her feet and already moving to her position farther down the trail.

Rick watched her, waiting until she gave the return nod.

A moment later she crouched behind another large rock, nodding curtly. Her ferocious stare could have cut glass. Rick knew she blamed him for not acting sooner. Hell, Rick blamed himself.

Spitting, he shook himself, knowing that more than ever he needed to focus. The boat carrying the beast and its captive, Antonis, from the island was near the shore. The trolls with their strange gaits bustled all around, bowing to the beast and packing their weapons. Though he hadn't spent much time around trolls, he felt certain they didn't used to limp. It seemed strange, but he stuffed the idea away for the moment. For just then, the boat struck the shallow edge of the crystal lake, and the beast jumped out. He seemed even larger this side of the water. Towering over the trolls, the water splashed around him as he jumped out and walked with long strides, dragging the boat Antonis still sat in. He looked child-size next to the creature.

Rick knew this was it. All they could do was kill the beast. That was their only option. Then, in the chaos of its death, Aalil would sneak down to cut Tony's bonds, and they'd get away before any of the lumbering idiots even realized they were gone. Aalil had gone back for her bow, and together they had planned to strike from multiple positions to create more confusion. Rick didn't have a bow, but he had a slingshot. It seemed silly in light of her actual weapon, but he was a tracker. He could make traps and tools from anything. That's all a weapon was, in his mind. A tool. He used bows, blades, slings, traps, whatever was at his disposal while hunting. This seemed no different. That big lurking monster down there still needed to be brought down. Who cared what did it as long as the job got done? Though he had felt his cheeks grow a little warmer when Aalil eyed his slingshot.

Squinting his left eye, he examined the beast barking rough, guttural commands. From his higher vantage, Rick bounced a stone in the palm of his hand, licking his cracked lips and watching for his moment. They had poured over the placement and positioning of their attack. He knew trolls had thick skin and sometimes wore leather jerkins or strange chest plates. They needed to do the most damage with their first volley, for it may be their only chance.

Rick glanced back to Aalil, who was still staring at him with her severe gaze. Rick exhaled, blowing his dusty bangs off his forehead. He loved his friend, but boy did he have strange taste in women. Aalil was… well, she wasn't Carol, Rick thought. Carol was nurturing and loving, Aalil… she was downright scary.

He looked back to the beach and saw that the beast was standing alone; all other observers had scattered away to do his bidding. Antonis was still in the boat. This was it. Their moment.

He looked back at Aalil and mouthed, *NOW!*

Without hesitation, she drew the bowstring and fluidly released one, two, three arrows before most soldiers would have had one knocked. He sucked in his breath at the sight. *Well, that was something to see*, he thought begrudgingly.

Tightening the leather sling in his hand and closing his left eye to zero in on his target, he speculated. He had never shot a stone this far but hoped that gravity would come to his aid. With a soft whistle, he released his own volley of stones, one after the other. He noted that just after the arrows hit—all striking home—his own stones toppled off the beast's head.

It roared as the arrowheads pierced the thick skin at the base of its skull and near its armpit. All made contact, but none seemed to do much harm.

"Shit," Rick grunted, filling his sling with more stones. They had expected that it would take a lot more than that, but any delay stole their element of surprise.

Crouching low, he crawled to his next position. They had mapped out two to three large rocks to hover behind, to make it appear like the attack was larger than a two-person volley.

Aalil reached her next spot and began loosing arrows. *One. Two. Three.*

Rick launched his next stones, smirking as one struck the beast directly in the eye. They moved so swiftly that the beast stood flinging its arms about amidst bellows. Trolls rushed toward the beast, looking toward Rick and Aalil's position. Rick knew they were down to moments. Seconds really, before their position was discovered.

Still the beast stood.

"Shit, shit, shit," Rick spat again... dropping to the ground and moving toward his third and final position, as was Aalil. This was her last volley. She had only had nine arrows. Two of hers had missed in the last volley due to the beast's erratic movements.

He looked to her. Her braid was loosed. Long strands of hair blew in the wind and stuck to her sweaty face. She nodded at him, determination in her eyes, then jumped up to unleash her final arrows.

Rick watched as they soared through the air. One after the other struck both the beast and the nearest unfortunate troll who had stepped into the line of fire. That troll, too, roared in pain and twisted himself trying to reach the arrows protruding from its back.

Rick launched a wave of stones and then, realizing that there was no other volley coming, drew the blade at his belt.

Aalil's bow clattered to the ground as he heard her approaching from the side. Her sweaty, terrified face revealed more than he'd hoped. *Had they failed?*

No, he thought sternly. *We can still fight.* The trolls moved slow compared to him. Only a few amassed on the beach, trying to pin the beast and troll down and pull out the arrows. A few were turning and looking, yelling commands and pointing at the rocks near the last position. Rick and Aalil didn't hesitate. Staying crouched, they both began moving in closer to attack. There would be no retreat today. They had to save Tony.

They made to hurry, but their footing wasn't secure here. The entire hillside was littered with giant boulders and loosened gravel. It was great for hiding behind, but terrible for stealth. One wrong foot and they'd go sliding down the hill, probably being knocked unconscious—or worse—in the process.

Rick turned to Aalil to whisper orders, but what he saw paralyzed him.

"How did you—"

Pain erupted on the side of his head, and the last thing he saw before collapsing was a troll's arm tight around Aalil's neck, squeezing the life out of her.

***

Morta stood atop the ramparts overlooking the Kingdom and the surrounding areas. Behind him were his tower and the barn (Chamber, as Narco had tried idiotically to dub it, which had mostly burned down due to that dreadful accident with Zola). It all belonged to him now, and he didn't have to remain hidden. The next phase of his plan was in motion. He gripped the stone wall with his newly embossed black metal hand and looked out upon the dammed Lure River. He could see movement beyond the water and knew his forces were returning. He could smell them. Hear them. He bade them to move faster and faster... and they obeyed.

Morta cackled as he watched the first Rav'Arians driving the remaining human soldiers and trolls onward, back to their true Master. The ebony unicorns ran wildly shrieking on the outskirts of the mass.

"It is as you said, Master. They return to you so quickly," a voice purred nearby.

Morta looked over to the speaker. He had known this individual for a very long time. A loyal pet, indeed.

"Did you doubt them? I thought you, out of anyone, would know that my creations live to obey me. It is best if you remember that, Tav'Opal."

The pale woman, with her proud face and greying strawberry blonde hair pulled into a severe bun, inhaled slightly, otherwise betraying no other emotions on her face. With a seemingly serene nod, she replied, "I could never doubt you, Master. We are the watchers of Tarsin. We live to serve and obey you, just as your... creations."

Morta grinned, turning fully toward her and motioning for them to walk, "I am glad to hear it, for I have a special task for you to carry out." He grinned wickedly, enjoying the sight of her widening eyes.

Her demeanor seemed impervious. Oh, he would enjoy cracking her tough façade very much... but not yet. He had never held affection for anyone, not since... well, since he went by a different name. Morta cared for no one but himself and the power and destruction he would wreak upon this land. Tarsin had cared, but Tarsin was dead. Reborn as Morta... and he would sew despair and darkness through every soul in Nav'Aria.

But Tav'Opal, he admitted to himself, had shown expertise in maintaining watch all these years. She would be rewarded... as a loyal pet should be. They were all pets to him: no one could stand equal to the swirling power within him. He had no need of advisors or military leaders. He would enjoy breaking each and every one of them. Breaking the entire world. Nav'Aria would fall... forever. The thought warmed him considerably.

Stroking his metal hand, he smiled widely, his yellowing teeth matching Tav'Opal's, "I have someone I would like you to meet."

CHAPTER 8

The Reveal

Darion felt clean—like *really* clean—for the first time in a long time. He paused with the bar of soap gripped in his hand as he sat in the steaming iron tub. Servants had hauled buckets and buckets of steaming water up flights of stairs before pouring a few scented oils into the water and handing him a bar of crisp-smelling soap.

Though perhaps not the same feeling of cleanliness as a scalding shower offered back in his other life, this was definitely an improvement from the recent past. He laughed to himself. He had not been properly bathed in quite a while. After scrubbing behind his ears as his mother had jokingly instructed, he finally lay back to soak… and think. The warm water and time alone helped him process what the hell was happening.

He closed his eyes, resting his head on the lip of the tub. He knew his father and soldiers were also seeking medical care, baths, food, and rest. They had been instructed to take care of themselves, and the Royal family and Unicorn Council were expected to dine together this evening.

Darion thought about what he would say. *Where do I start? At the beginning? Killing the first Rav'Arians? The Shazla Viper which almost killed Edmond? The…* his mind froze, fixating on one image. *The pool with the laughing, stark-naked sisters.* He smiled, eyes still closed, picturing his and Edmond's nervous first meeting with the females. He let his mind wander… *what is Nala doing? Is she safe?*

He prayed to the Creator—whom he believed had to be real after everything that had happened to him— "Please watch over Nala and Ati." After a pause, he remembered the child. *What was his name?*

Biting his lip, trying to remember the name of the child that had been placed in Nala's arms, Darion felt a slight sliver of jealousy rising up. *Valon,* he remembered. He was the reason she left Darion. He felt his anger rising, even though he knew it was irrational. *It's not the kid's fault his family and neighbors are a bunch of psychos.* He shuddered thinking of the Watchers. It was good that Nala got the kid out, he concluded. And, though it hurt him to admit it, she had to go back to the Reouls. Someone needed to tell Zalto and Tiakai of the Watchers and Rav'Arian breeding grounds nearby. They weren't safe.

Darion felt the pressure building within him. There was so much to tell, and now with Morta being Tarsin… Shaking his head, he tried to relax again. But try as he might, he kept picturing the terror in Tav'Raka's eyes as she thrust her child into Nala's arms. She had known

Tarsin's terror... it seemed only a precursor of what was to come with Morta.

"Please, Nala. Be careful," he whispered. And then his mind drifted to his Dad. And Tony. Squeezing his eyes tightly, he splashed water over his face multiple times, as if that could wash away his worries.

Out of nowhere a tap at the door made him jump. He splashed water over the very full tub at the sound of Triumph's voice in his head. *Darion.* Triumph spoke in a soft, inquiring voice. Not his eye-rolling lecture tone, but in a caring tone. Like a friend. Like family.

Darion, I am your family, Triumph chided, adding softer, *Are you alright?*

Though Darion knew his companion couldn't see him, he still tried to sit up and put on a brave face before responding. Without thought, his fingers traced the small flower Triumph's horn had etched above Darion's heart to seal Carol's image in his memory during their journey. He smiled. Triumph's company would calm him.

Speaking telepathically, once so foreign, came naturally to Darion. *Here, hold on. I'm coming.* He jumped out of the tub, grateful for the towels set nearby, for he had no idea what clothes to put on.

Strolling to the door with bare chest and simple towel around his waist, he prayed no female servants were out there. He threw it open to welcome his companion.

"Come on in," Darion said, opting for a cheery tone.

Triumph walked in, chest puffed out and head raised proudly... he really was majestic, Darion thought.

Triumph's hoof clattered, as if he had slipped, and his head turned back, now with a severe gaze. "I did not 'strut.'"

Darion could only shake his head and sigh, *here we go*, he thought. "Yeah, ok, whatever, man," Darion said, smacking Triumph's rear as he walked by, "You keep telling yourself that."

Triumph grumbled inaudibly and inhaled deeply. "You smell much better, I must say."

"So do you," Darion retorted, noting the shimmering coat and pristine mane of his friend. "You really needed a bath."

Triumph raised his head as if to argue, then shook out his mane and whinnied. "You are right. I feel much better—and more prepared to see Mother this way."

"What are you doing here anyways?" Darion asked. "I thought you'd be with Zola?"

Triumph cocked his head, "Mother is showing her around and had some female attendants in tow to see to her and Trigger. Lei was called for to check them over as well... Soren said he would watch over them while I freshened up and came to check on you."

Darion smiled perceptively. "Not wanting to uh... be alone with your Mom, huh!?"

Triumph snorted indignantly, "And what exactly do you mean by that?"

"You know what I mean, we both left without telling our parents... and now we have to face them." Darion looked over at Triumph, who was beginning to shift his bulk and fidget... "Are you nervous?"

"Me? Absolutely not. That is ridiculous to even suggest. I am a grown unicorn and responsible for my own destiny."

"You're totally nervous!" Darion laughed, turning to look toward the clothes that had been laid out upon the divan in the corner of the room. As he walked toward them, he felt a cool breeze, and then his bare ass was out on display.

"Really?" He glared over his shoulder at Triumph, who was trying to kick the towel he had just pulled from Darion a second ago. Darion glowered at him, "Grow up."

After quickly throwing on the clothes, a dark pair of pants with a gold-spun tunic and fitted green overcoat with fine boots, Darion walked toward the mirror to take in his appearance. It was more formal than anything he had ever worn. He rubbed the woven fabric almost reverently. His nerves started up again. *Why the fancy clothes? Is this a trial? Are we gonna be punished? Banished? Executed?*

Triumph snorted, "Darion, these are, in peace time, the ordinary clothes worn by the Royals. You have come at such an odd season, only seeing bloodied soldiers and swordbelts. These," he pointed his sparkling horn toward the shirt sleeve, "these are the clothes traditionally worn in Nav'Aria… at least, they used to be."

Before glancing back at the mirror, Darion regarded him to make sure he wasn't messing with him. His hair had grown well past his shoulders. Running his fingers through the wet tendrils, he found a bit of black lace set near the wash bowl. He tied his hair back with it and took in his appearance. With the beginnings of a beard, he looked... older. Stronger. Nav'Arian.

He was surprised by his reflection. For the first time in his life he didn't mind what he saw. Dark hair, tanned skin, bright green eyes, a strong chin, and a regal outfit. It all seemed... right. Even his slightly crooked nose no longer bothered him. It gave his appearance more edge. Along with his heavily Marked Arm and glowing red Ruby at his throat, he looked... cool, he thought.

He turned toward Triumph, who had dropped the banter, taking in Darion's confident body language. The unicorn raised his head proudly, "Shall we, my Prince?"

Darion smiled warmly, "We shall." He added, merrily, "Try not to strut too much though."

Triumph blew his bangs forcefully and appeared to roll his eyes. His good behavior was usually short lived, Darion thought wryly, throwing open the door as the pair headed toward the Council dinner.

The dinner was in Elsra's rooms, which Darion was glad to find. His parents' room didn't appeal to him any longer—not after Carol had been killed there. Darion shuddered at the dark memory.

Triumph leaned close to him, and Darion placed his hand upon Triumph's neck. Together, in this familiar posture, they walked toward what they both knew was going to be an uncomfortable occasion. Yes, it was a time of war, and, yes, it was months ago... but they still had left without anyone's permission. Darion had a feeling that Vikaris wasn't going to just let that go without a word. Oh no, he knew that he was about to receive the paternal lecture of his life. He could feel it… and at his thought, he felt a tremor pass through Triumph. His companion may act all cool and calm… yet it was clear he feared Elsra's reaction to their absence. Their trials. Findings. Zola and Trigger.

***

Lyrianna paced. Now that she was behind closed doors and no longer visible to all the hillside villager's eyes, she paced and paced, caring not if she wore out the carpet. Vikaris had just left to go check in with some of his commanders and would meet her at the Council dinner. And while she understood that he had his duty to perform, she still wanted to smack the man. *Leave again! He had only just returned! And what about Darion?*

She wished more than anything to run to him and hold him in her arms, having been denied her maternal role for so many years. She loved him yet hardly knew him. She felt a little shy thinking of entering the dinner without her husband for support.

"Lyrianna! Stop this," she growled. After everything that had happened—was happening—meeting her family at dinner had her pacing? Childish. This is the type of evening she had dreamed of and prayed for… for years! She stopped pacing and spun to look at the single flower she had in a small vase near her bedside. She had always loved Riccus's pet-name for his wife. *Springflower.* In memory of Carolina and her sacrifice, Lyrianna had taken it upon herself to keep one bloom near her bedside at all times. Looking at it, she felt her heart slow its racing. She breathed in and out, calming her nerves.

With eyes fixed on the blue petals, she spoke softly, "Carolina, I would like to get to know the boy you raised. Be with us now." She closed her eyes, smiling and feeling a rush of peace come over her. That beautiful woman had faithfully kept her son safe all these years, but more than that, she had given him a home… and a mother's love. And while Lyrianna now questioned, at times, how to navigate the future with Darion, she had nothing but respect and admiration for the woman who had given all for her family.

"My Queen," a rich, kindly voice sounded from the other side of her doors.

She ran, throwing it open without hesitation. "Oh Trinidad, I am so glad to see you." She rushed and threw her arms around her bonded unicorn companion.

She cracked an eye as she heard a muffled snort nearby. She looked over to see Cela standing there with a bemused expression. "Should I give you two a little time alone?"

The Queen's jaw dropped. *How dare she speak—*

But then she heard the loveliest sound she could ever recall hearing. Laughter. Trinidad was laughing, and of all things, he was laughing full-heartedly at Cela's crude joke. Trinidad's chuckles filled the hallway, and unable to hold it in, Lyrianna's melodious laughs reverberated off the hall, as well. Cela stood with her hands on her ivory hips looking pleased with herself.

Before they could speak further, hooves clattered upon the floor, and Cela spun ever alert.

Approaching them were Darion and Triumph. Lyrianna's chuckles faded away, but her smile did not. Her son. He was perfect in every way. She loved his long hair, bright eyes, and strong jaw. She loved his height, and his sun-kissed skin. And she loved seeing that he had been properly bonded to a unicorn as he should be... as the true Marked Heir.

His face broke out in a grin at the sight of them, and Lyrianna couldn't help but chuckle once more, as Darion's eyes widened upon seeing Cela... and his cheeks flushed slightly at the sight of her oozing bosom escaping the very small vest she wore atop. Cela grinned coquettishly, brushing a long red lock of hair off her shoulders. *The tramp*, Lyrianna thought, but did not mean it. She loved her fiery guard (and friend) dearly. But that was enough ogling for the moment.

"Darion," Lyrianna said clearly in greeting. "Will you escort me to dinner?" She smiled regally, raising her chin for effect... not for Darion, but for Cela, who without delay stepped back to resume her guard duties.

"Uh... sure," Darion replied. He rounded the unicorns whose heads were nestled together in greeting and hushed conversation.

"Those two brothers have much to catch up on I assume," Lyrianna smiled warmly at them as Darion joined her. She delicately held her pink satin and chiffon dress up at the side with one hand, while taking Darion's proffered arm as they strode toward the Regent's chambers.

Darion glanced at her. "I think we all have a lot to catch up on… Mother," Darion added, the word seeming foreign but warm on his tongue.

She nodded her head at him, searching his face, memorizing every detail as she once had of the babe she held in her arms. Now she studied the man. "We definitely do, my Son."

As they neared Elsra's door, Lyrianna felt Darion straighten his back ever further at the sight of Vikaris. He stood at the door dressed in what could only be described as resplendent attire. Unable to hold in even the slightest sigh at the sight of him, she smiled widely. She had not seen her husband this clean and polished in… well, quite sometime. Thinking of their earlier bathing experience, she warmed inwardly. She had only been too glad to help rid him of the grime and the neckbeard that emerged while away fighting, careful of his injured arm, of course.

Now, with oiled hair and a short but kept beard, he looked regal… especially in the deep black and gold attire which subtly matched Darion's. She had chosen them both herself, as well as her own gown that she had set seamstresses to work on immediately after Vikaris left to face Narco. The need for a gown had made it all seem normal. She would commission a gown for the return of her husband and son. She had known they would come back… and if it took having a dress made to give her a little extra hope and sense of normalcy, then so be it. She plucked her fingers lightly upon the pink rose fabric with the faint silver diamond pattern interwoven throughout the dress to shimmer upon the overlay.

Without releasing Darion's arm, she curtsied to her husband. Darion clumsily bent down in a bow at her instruction. Vikaris grinned widely at the two of them and bowed his head slightly in acknowledgement. *Ever the King,* she thought. Though, sadly, she had never seen him upon his rightful throne, she knew his bearing and leadership skills all came from his great family line. He would be magnificent upon the throne, and she would shine with pride at his side, along with Darion at his opposite. Glancing at Darion, she decided he would need a little work on his posture. She released his arm with a light squeeze before moving to Vikaris.

"Husband," she greeted. "Look at the fine Nav'Arian I encountered in the hall," she cooed gaily. Now standing with Vikaris and getting another look at Darion, she couldn't help but beam. He was perfect, whether he could bow or not. He was her son. Her heart swelled.

"A fine Nav'Arian, indeed," Vikaris echoed in a voice so joy-filled it took Lyrianna's breath away.

Darion smiled, his boyish pleasure at his father's praise dancing across his face before he could school his features.

"Come, son," Vikaris added, "there is much to discuss."

Lyrianna's feelings of joy wavered when she saw the smile disappear from Darion's face at the King's words. Without wanting to spoil the moment further, she smiled at them both, and putting on a voice of levity, gushed, "Mmmmm, the dinner smells incredible! Shall we go in? I am sure you are both famished from your journey."

Darion's stomach lurched with an audible growl that broke the solemnity, and even Vikaris chuckled, patting Darion on the back. "I think you are right, my dear. Let us dine together as a family."

The servant standing near the door bowed low as he held the door open for the Royals and members of the Unicorn Council. The aroma wafting from the room made even Lyrianna's stomach growl, and she realized she had missed her midday meal. Food would be good for everyone, she thought, glancing at the two men in her life. She only hoped that it would help stave off any intolerable mood swings from any gathered there. She had a feeling, though, even with the food and return of so many, that this was going to be a big, uncomfortable event. Looking over her shoulder, she smiled at Trinidad, who, while pleased to be standing with his brother and son who had just approached, also seemed to reflect the same sentiment. There were a lot of strong personalities about to be grouped in this confined space.

Led into the chambers by her husband and trailed by her son and unicorn friends, she could only hope for the best… and that they were able to at least eat before Vikaris laid into their son about his hasty, secret departure.

CHAPTER 9

The Stone

Dabor moaned, tossing and turning in his sleep, succumbing to the dark nightmare which haunted him most nights. Twisting his childlike memories and his fears of today together.

A black, ominous cloud swirled around his dream-self as he walked through the mountain path. He could see them there. He should be with them. His mother and sisters wailing from the opposite beach. And there stood H'kalff. Narco's beast sent to destroy everything the reclusive trolls had ever known.

Dabor hid behind a rock watching, trying to keep out of sight from the cloud. He could feel eyes on him… eyes everywhere. Watching. The cloud swirled into a funnel around the cages of females and children, their shrill cries for help tearing at him. For he knew what came next.

No, he moaned… wishing himself awake. But the dream seemed to have a hold him. He was paralyzed by fear.

There on the beach, as the swirling vortex began to dissipate, stood H'kalff. Huge. Menacing. God-like. A monster in the mountains. His eyes blazed red, and the evil that he manifested made Dabor want to flee. Run away from everything here. But he couldn't. He stood transfixed facing the cages. His eyes trained to the spot where he knew his family was held... where he had been held all those years ago.

Dabor tried to shake himself awake again but to no avail. He may be free of *that* cage, but his mind was a prison in which his memory would forever hold him.

His dream-self shifted closer to the opposite beach. No one looked at him, but he was there to witness it all... again.

H'kalff had arrived one day seemingly out of nowhere, though Dabor later learned he had been created by the pale hooded human, Morta, and sent to force the trolls to submit to the stranger's will. Narco wanted the strength of the trolls to bolster his forces.

When he arrived, it had been the warmer season. In the mountains there are really only two seasons, warm and freezing. There is no heat like what is felt on the Nav'Arian plains or closer to the border. In those warm months the trolls would migrate and hunt. They clung to the Lake area but moved in and out of the cave tunnels, hunting and sending messages to other troll clans. It was a time of feasting, mating, and celebrating their survival of another year. And one particular evening, when the moon hung low and full, a beast unlike any of them had ever seen strode up to the leaders' circle. Cookfires and circles of kin dotted the expanse, and so it was that Dabor found himself watching, like many of the others, as the beast slew their leader. He drew no weapon, only reached out with his great hand—long nails like talons—and ripped out their leader's throat. Not a word was spoken... only quiet shock. Then the screams came.

The pristine evening exploded into a night of terror as the beast, who towered over all the trolls, including the great warriors, roared the most terrifying sound Dabor had ever heard. And then, as if he had been calling them, a multitude of cloaked creatures emerged from the caves, clicking and cackling as they surrounded the trolls and their cookfires. Dabor now knew them as Rav'Arians, but as a child had thought them demons arising from some hidden abyss. He hated them... and how they still brought out his worst fears even a cycle later.

He watched, once more frozen in terror as the Rav'Arians surrounded each kin circle, slaying any who seemed to oppose... and then the beast spoke louder than Dabor ever thought possible.

"I AM LEADER NOW," H'kalff bellowed.

Dabor's memories and fears shifted again, transforming and affecting the nightmare. It returned to daylight on the beach where he stood outside of the cages.

He tried to cover his ears, tried to squeeze his eyes shut again, cowering like the small young troll he had been.

"The prisoners," H'kalff roared. The Rav'Arians outside the cages went to do his bidding. He had them built swiftly, slaying any troll who opposed him and declaring that he was sent from beyond the land to lead them. He was their god-king, and they must obey him or face his wrath.

Many of the males had died that moonlit night—Dabor's father included—the corpses dragged away by the skulking creatures whose unnatural odors seemed offensive in the otherwise pure, clean mountain air.

After some of the males were killed, the rest were gathered up and forced to sit and watch—some did not, but died nonetheless—as all the females and children were taken in small boats. The beasts had been planning this attack and were well prepared. Without a word, as the boats were carried down, the females and children were forced upon them and taken across the lake to a center island. The males roared and grunted. Some pleaded and wept, but H'kallf only laughed.

Now in this daylight portion of the dream, the beast stood on the beach once more, as the guards pulled the young males from the pens.

"No. Sick. He sick," Dabor's mother pleaded.

Trying to wake up, Dabor knew what was coming and fought it. He covered his ears as the tears rolled down his grey leather-like skin.

"Sick?" The Rav'Arian at the cage entrance croaked with a menacing laugh. Its talon-like fingers dug into the youngling's arm, causing him to squawk in protest as he was dragged before H'kalff.

Dabor, now back beside his mother in the pen, his memory fully immersed in the nightmare, watched in horror as H'kalff inspected his older—yet sickly—brother, Dezbos.

Dabor felt himself trembling. Crying. Just as he had that day. As H'kalff ceased his inspection of the scrawny troll, who wept openly and called for his mother, H'kalff took him, and in one giant bite, bit off Dezbos's head, throwing his body to the Rav'Arians to feast on.

The crunching, the wailing, the roars.... blood pounded in Dabor's ears as he tried to forget. Tried to block it out. But he never could.

"Any more sick?" H'kalff shouted, blood smearing his lips and fangs as he sneered at the pens.

No one spoke this time.

The beast's glare then moved to Dabor.

The youngling trembled but did not cry out as his brother had. He squeezed his mother's slack arm, looking at her tear-soaked face, not knowing that would be the last time he would see her and his little sisters.

As he was dragged out, the Rav'Arians quickly pinned him. The first one, he had no idea what was coming. He wanted to kick them off, scream or shout. But he didn't, either through fear or pride or a little of both. He would not be killed.

He felt his pantleg being rolled up, and a blinding pain shot through his leg as something struck above the back of his kneecap. At once, everything changed... shifted.

Awaking, though still upset about his brother's death, he felt only numb. All thoughts of fighting back and killing H'kalff vanished, and the nightmare that was Dabor's reality came true. Dabor was under H'kalff's control, and he couldn't do anything about it. For if he ever removed the small dark stone embedded behind his knee, H'kalff would know... and he would eat Dabor's sisters. Dabor was trapped... loyal to first Narco, and now his evil successor.

Dabor awoke trembling. His knee throbbing freshly as it had years ago. The pain was a small comfort to Dabor; it helped remind him, he was not the monster that they forced him to be. He hated who he was, but even more so he loathed what Morta and the Rav'Arians were doing. He had to find a way to the mountains. To remove the stone only once he knew his family was safe. But in order to do that, he would have to disobey Morta... and that was impossible so long as the stone remained in place. Even thinking about it made the small stone burn hot. Its dark, magical hold kept him obedient. It kept him—and all the male trolls—enslaved, limping and loyal.

Dabor felt his cheeks. He had cried in reality as he had wept in the dream. The mere recognition of this provoked profound sadness. If only he could feel that... the numbness of his waking existence was setting in.

***

Licking his fingers, Darion savored the last mouthfuls of herb-roasted hen. His father had toasted him only moments ago and nodded to the attendant, a pretty woman with dark brown hair and an honest face, to fill his glass with wine. Darion didn't love the taste of it, but he wasn't complaining. He knew this meant he was a man in his father's eyes... and where there was wine, there would surely be ale to come. Triumph had spoken of it often, and Darion looked forward to trying it. With Edmond. He seemed like a fun drinking buddy, and besides, Edmond needed to stop thinking of Ati. Maybe ale would help?

Ale never helps, Triumph said haughtily, interrupting Darion's pleasurable daydream.

Darion, while trying to appear calm and mature, scowled in Triumph's direction but didn't reply. It had been a while since they'd been in civilized company.

…And if you're trying to appear 'mature,' then stop eating like a child. Do you see any other adults licking their fingers?

Darion felt his neck grow hot and immediately set his hands in his lap, trying to wipe the flavorful grease with his napkin.

Better, Triumph murmured.

Darion wanted to kick him but knew that, too, was probably something a toddler would do. It was still fun to think about, though.

Before Triumph could intrude upon his thoughts again, Vikaris stood up at the head of the table and raised his glass. "And now that we are all finished eating, I would like to take this moment for a toast."

Vikaris looked every part the King in the candlelight, with his dark coat—the gold trim and design work shimmering in the light. He stood tall and proud, and though smiling, his eyes had the cast of someone in control… and with a deep fire burning within.

Darion swallowed nervously and sat up, knowing that soon he would be expected to share before those gathered. He looked around the gilded room, and though at one time he would have found it odd to see unicorns speaking and conversing with humans, and a voluptuous centaur guarding the door, it all felt familiar. The room had been set up to accommodate their diversity, with varying table heights and methods for eating and drinking.

The long table was decorated with boughs of ivy and willow branches strewn about, subtly accentuating the fine trim of the porcelain dinnerware. Braziers burned in every corner of the room, releasing exotic, earthy scents, which combined with the wine, made Darion's head swim.

He shook it subtly. He needed a clear head for what was coming. The unicorns gathered at the next table. This one stood much higher so the unicorns could stand and graze off the giant platter filled with fruits of all kind, grasses, wildflowers, hay, and varying types of greenery. A large trough of ale sat next to their table. But now that the King spoke, they came nearer the human table, surrounding it. Trixon loomed beside Vikaris, Trinidad near Lyrianna—now bonded... however that came to be—and Triumph's towering presence appeared beside Darion.

"A toast... to my son Darion, and the return of he and his companions," Vikaris stared boldly and directly at Darion, adding in a softer voice, "we have much to hear from their ventures."

Darion felt his stomach grip. *He's so pissed*, he thought, trying to keep a calm expression upon his face.

Nod at him, Triumph urged in his mind. *Nod at your King in respect, and to show that you are unafraid. He will not be 'pissed' once he hears of everything we have experienced, but rather, proud.*

Now nod as a Prince of Nav'Aria would in respect of his King's toast.

Darion raised his glass a smidge higher in the air and dipped his head at his father in acknowledgment of the toast.

Vikaris's stern gaze softened and he nodded subtly. Darion felt relief flood his body but remained sitting upright and looking hopefully, as a prince should.

"I also raise a toast to my Queen and Regent Elsra for safeguarding Kaulter in my stead."

Lyrianna, Darion noted, smiled and tilted her head in acknowledgment too. Elsra released a small snort, Kaulter was hers after all—along with the King's—but she, too, dipped her head in acquiescence.

Vikaris continued, "And to the great warriors that we lost in our recent battle, I..." Vikaris's voice faltered as he pressed his lips together, exhaling loudly through his flared nostrils. "Their deaths will not be in vain. We killed Narco and many of his beasts. Though the war continues, I say today we toast to our fallen Nav'Arians and to our purpose. We must plan, and we must continue the fight. Now more than ever we must remain together."

Trixon stamped his hoof as Vikaris concluded. The powerful unicorn emanated strength even at this social gathering. Darion neither missed the slight caution his father threw out glancing toward Darion and Triumph nor Trixon's severe gaze.

The attendees' moods seemed to change, and the lively dinner environment morphed into a solemn moment of silence. "To Nav'Aria," Vikaris spoke softly, then sipped from his gold trimmed glass.

"To Nav'Aria," they whispered and all drank, the humans from their glasses and the unicorns from their trough, one at a time. Elsra led, followed by Drigidor, Trinidad, Triumph, and Trixon.

Cela did not drink, being on guard duty, but kept her head down, as if in prayer, until all had drunk.

"Now, let us hear of the great escapades of our returning friends," Vikaris said with forced cheer. Elsra echoed his words and directed a stern look toward Triumph while both motioned for Cela to allow the attendees in to move the tables out of the way so they could gather in the center of the room for this monumental discussion. While chairs and tables were shifted or carried off to create a more intimate circle, Darion snatched his glass from the table before the attendants could take it. Forgetting his earlier thought of a clear head, he drank greedily, downing the contents in a few big gulps. He thought he'd find Triumph behind him with a rebuke, but when he turned around, he caught his companion guzzling mouthfuls from the ale trough.

Darion wanted to laugh… or cry. *The King is so pissed… and Trixon looks like he wants to kill someone.*

The King certainly is… displeased, Triumph agreed, *and so is my Mother. Don't go near her, she bites! And I think that is what has Trixon so upset. He would not challenge me… his uncle.* And then more to himself, he added, *at least I do not think he would.*

Darion's eyes widened, glancing at Triumph. *Well, that's comforting,* Darion chided, feeling his heartbeat increase.

CHAPTER 10

The Tested Heir

Recounting their voyages took many hours, the daylight soon turning to a violet and amber sunset. The room seemed smaller as the evening shadows emerged. Or perhaps it only felt smaller because everyone was staring at them.

Seriously, Trixon looks like he might kill someone by the time this is all over, Darion thought. He didn't remember such open hostility from the unicorn before... but he supposed he had been seen in a better light back then as the returning Marked Heir and not the skulking "coward" who fled in the night.

Darion started things off, but it had grown a little awkward when it came time to recount meeting Nala and Ati. With face flushed, he looked pleadingly at Triumph, who was only too happy to carry on the tale. As the unicorn spoke, Darion watched the listeners gape.... Triumph was a good storyteller, so Darion happily let him tell most of it, interjecting only when necessary or to clarify for the King, who every few moments made them pause for questions.

"And so it was that we left the Winged Ones... the Reouls, after learning their leader refused to aid Nav'Aria... even though they believe Darion to be the Chosen One. And... the fact that Tiakai, their leader, bares the mark of Rinzaltan from the beginning of this war. She knows the evil we face, and still they sit. They are no threat... but they will be no help either, Your Majesty," Triumph concluded somberly. "They prefer to waste away in the desert."

That caused quite a stir, but surprisingly not as much as Darion would have expected. Elsra and Trinidad both gasped at the mention of Rinzaltan, and Darion knew they would speak of it further, but beyond that, no one seemed as surprised about the Winged Ones.

What is wrong with these people? Dragons!? That's a pretty big revelation, at least he and Triumph had thought so. *Why isn't anyone surprised?*

His mother interrupted his thoughts, sharing that they had seen the transformation of the giant frieze in the Kaulter Fortress, so they had assumed the prophecy had been shared. It had included winged symbols, and they had already discovered Vondulus's journal with mention of *winged ones*, so they were able to make the connection quite easily.

Darion couldn't believe what he was hearing and had so many questions of his own, specifically regarding his Mother's Mark, Rick and Tony's mission, the prophecy, and changing of the frieze. That would have to wait, for

Triumph had captured everyone's attention with their "findings."

"Darion caught scent of them long before Soren or I did. And once we snuck up to the area, we discovered the Rav'Arian breeding ground."

All went still in the room, save for a few gasps.

Drigidor stepped forward involuntarily, as if he thought the enemy about to break into the room.

Trixon rumbled a low growl, eyeing the door; Cela raised her head proudly, placing her hand upon the blade at her waist.

No enemy was coming, Darion knew, but he also felt proud to know that none would make it into this room alive. He stood amongst some of the most formidable warriors of Nav'Aria.

Feeling inspired, Darion picked up the story, "They have their eggs floating in these giant tar pits... which absolutely reek. You know how they smell like death? It's because they're soaked in tar as eggs. We saw some cracking and the infants floated in the liquid. Some others that looked a little older were closer to the edge, and bigger ones walked out of the tar and the guards held them down and cut off their tails. They're born with tails! And they..." Darion paused, glancing at his mother, whose face had taken on a slightly sickly pallor and finished lamely, "they... well, yeah... you can guess the rest. It was nasty."

"Thank the Creator you were not seen," Lyrianna said in a hushed voice, her knuckles white from squeezing the chair leg where she sat.

"Well… about that," Darion grimaced, "We were. And this is where it gets even crazier."

Triumph nodded vigorously, "Indeed. The guards caught sight of us and raised the alarm. We heard booming roars, and I demanded Nala and Darion jump on my back. As we rushed away from the breeding grounds, we were set upon by a terrible beast. A monster unlike anything we have ever seen before. I pray that we never see the likes of it again."

Darion noticed that the skin around Vikaris's eyes seemed to tighten, but he otherwise did not reveal any outward emotion, besides glancing subtly at Trixon, who now stepped closer. Intently.

"What was this creature?" The King asked.

"It…" Triumph paused, as if trying to find the right word for it.

How do you describe that thing? Darion thought, then it struck him. He blurted, "It was a mutant! It looks wrong, as if it was part alligator and troll and Rav'Arian—and maybe even dragon—all rolled into one. It was deadly!"

"And Darion killed it," Triumph announced proudly. "He slew the horrid beast, saving not only my life but that of Nala as well."

Darion looked down in embarrassment. His gut clenched at the memory. Thinking that the beast had hurt Triumph, that it had killed Nala, he had gone into a rage. Yet, while it was true he had killed it, he had never liked being the center of attention. He kept his eyes down and tried to calm his breathing.

"How?" The King asked, his voice carrying a different sound… one Darion hadn't heard from him before.

"I… well, like I did with the viper and again with Gamlin when Narco possessed him, I… I don't really know how to describe it. I just reached out with my senses and told it to stop. And then I stabbed it."

Idiot, he thought to himself. *That sounded so lame!*

Darion still didn't look up. Instead he stared at the shadows dancing upon the floor. Triumph pressed his horn to the wall sconces, as he had done in the Great Hall while first getting to know Darion. Yet the scattered sconces did not light the entire room, and as the candles upon the tables began to melt away and splutter, the room became more and more intimate, hiding the attendees' expressions in the growing shadows.

When no one spoke for a few long moments, Darion looked up hesitantly, fully expecting a reprimand. Instead, what he found shocked him.

His father's face had such a strange expression… *what is his deal?*

Awe, Triumph whispered. *He is in awe of your abilities, my Prince. Not all Marked Heirs can call upon their senses to speak and control others as you do.*

"Triumph fought it, too, it really wasn't only me," Darion said in an attempt to brush it off. And then before the moment carried on any longer, he continued, "Then after that, we headed toward the border… and that's when it got really weird."

Triumph snorted, whispering, "Very eloquent. You have a true knack for this."

Darion scowled at him, pushing at Triumph's thick neck and motioning for him to continue.

"The Prince speaks true, though his casual manner still makes me laugh," Triumph continued, trying to lighten the mood.

Still no one spoke.

Tough crowd, Darion thought, eyeing Trixon who growled clearly becoming impatient with their pacing.

Triumph let out a small sigh but sagely carried on the tale. "One evening, Edmond went to bury our dinner scraps. There he discovered a buried skeleton. Two, actually."

Darion closed his eyes picturing it. He could still smell the fresh earth as they dug up the remains.

"One of a giant, winged creature... and the other, a human skull."

Lyianna reached for Vikaris's hand, both looking intensely at Darion and Triumph.

At Triumph's words, Darion took the yellow ribbon from his pocket, which he had only thought to bring along at the very last moment. Holding it up, he added, "This was tied around the skull, so we assume it was a female's skull. And once we discovered the gravesite in the woods, things really got strange," he said, looking at Triumph earnestly. "An old woman, super pale and creepy, appeared out of nowhere and made us follow her. She kept muttering something... 'we watch, we watch, we watch.'" Darion felt goosebumps forming along his arms with the memory.

Vikaris tilted his head as if trying to piece it all together.

Trixon looked as if he was about to ask a question, but Triumph interjected in his authoritative, lecturing tone.

"She led us to a secret human community... and they do not serve you, my King, but rather Tarsin."

"Who the hell is Tarsin?" Vikaris demanded.

"That's exactly what I said," Darion exclaimed, a small smile escaping as he looked at his father. "It took us forever to figure out... we barely made it out of that community alive," he grimaced after hearing his mother's gasp.

Darion became more serious but continued, "Father, they serve the Rav'Arians. They sent word to them to come and attack us. They were going to sacrifice us under the moon. They had a whole festival planned. This Tarsin," Darion looked at Triumph, "we think is Morta. The same man... somehow," Darion paused. He knew it sounded crazy because that skull and creepy community was so old, but it had to be linked. It was linked. He just knew it.

"Son, I want to believe you, but none of this makes sense. Who is Tarsin? And why would a hidden human settlement be serving Rav'Arians? I cannot fathom how they would survive, if the beast you spoke of moments ago had been roaming the land... why would humans stay there? Would they not want to take refuge in Nav'Aria? Under my protection?"

Darion knew he had muddled his explanation. He felt insecure sharing it all, but Triumph came to his rescue.

"Darion speaks truly. If it pleases you, my King, may I try to piece it together for you before any other doubts are voiced?"

Vikaris sat up straight, as if he had been reprimanded, for in a subtle yet clear way, Triumph had done just that.

Trixon's eyes blazed challengingly. The room was silent....

Shit, Darion thought. *Trixon is seriously going to kill us!*

And then a loud booming rumble filled the corner of the chamber.

All heads turned to see Drigidor... laughing. He had been silent most of the evening, besides a murmured response here or there at dinner.

Triumph stood up straighter, raising his head high, and Darion knew that these two were probably about to erupt in a shouting match. *Even better,* Darion mused, *let's have three unicorns fight right here.*

Surprisingly, though, Drigidor spoke. "Your Majesty, my stepson—though he loathes to be called so, speaks truly. Let us hear from him, and him only."

Darion didn't miss the look directed at him by the intimidating unicorn warrior.

"Triumph and Darion clearly have experienced much and learned more beyond anything our scouts have for years. Let us hear it... and see this discussion through."

Elsra, though she did not speak, ahemmed in agreement at his side, and Lyrianna and Trinidad both nodded their heads. Vikaris glanced around, then threw up his hands, "Bah! You are right. Please share the rest of your findings, Triumph. I will reserve my comments until the end."

Trixon gave a resigned growl and stepped back, much like a guard dog settling down after a near upset.

Triumph went to work... much more eloquently than Darion's interruptions had been. After explaining all that they had learned about the Winged Ones, Rav'Arians, the Watchers, and Tarsin... the pieces of the puzzle began to come together.

"Though I have no idea how it is possible, it is our belief," Triumph concluded, tilting his head at Darion, "that Tarsin was tainted many, many years ago, and over time he became known as Morta. With the use of some foreign dark magic, he created these hybrid monsters— including the Rav'Arians—and has been the true enemy all along. Narco was his pawn," Triumph hesitated before a steely edge came to his voice, "and now, the true fight for Nav'Aria—and the good of all—is upon us. This... this is the real fight. I do not know what has transpired in that wretch's heart, how he has been able to live so many cycles, or what his ultimate goal is, but I fear that the destruction of Nav'Aria is atop his list." Triumph ceased speaking, and Darion assumed he was finished.

Looking around the room, everyone seemed to be lost in their own thoughts. A wise, soft voice spoke into the stillness. "It is as you say, brother. I can sense it to be true. And if I may go one step further, I believe this prophecy you spoke of with the Winged Ones—and which we saw here on the Frieze—speaks of Darion." Trinidad's clear blue eyes looked up and seemed to envelop Darion whole.

"You, my Prince, you are the one that must defeat Morta... and rid our land of this evil darkness."

"But—" Vikaris and Lyrianna both began.

Elsra's serene yet commanding voice cut through the air. "It is foretold. Darion *is* our hope." Elsra stepped forward eyeing them. "I, Regent Elsra and leader of the Unicorn Council and Kaulter, declare Darion to be the true and tested Marked Heir of Nav'Aria. Let it be questioned no more if he, though raised in a foreign land, has the makings of a true Heir or not. He bears the Mark, he has faced battle, he has killed an enemy, he has kept his wits, and he has served Nav'Aria by obtaining this information valiantly," Elsra paused, shooting a glare at Triumph, "though, I wish his companion would have thought to send word to us of their discoveries... and whereabouts."

Darion could hardly breathe for the supreme power emanating from Elsra as she spoke, "Do all gathered here agree? The time of questioning and testing has come to an end. See before you now, the true Marked Heir of Nav'Aria... and the chosen one to lead us through this season of peril."

Darion swallowed nervously, expecting his father to explode. To cast doubt. He looked toward Vikaris, again surprised by the expression on his face. His father looked... intrigued. Pensive. But not upset.

"I agree and declare it so. Darion is my named and Marked Heir. Shall I fall in battle, he is to take my place as King." Vikaris looked at him proudly.

Lyrianna, standing up beside him, nodded in agreement.

"I agree with the Regent and His Majesty. If the King falls, we will serve you, Prince Darion." Trixon's deferential words after his earlier intensity shook Darion the most.

Darion's eyes bulged. *King? No way!* He was only just getting used to being called Prince. He prayed that his father would live to be an old man.

Before anyone else could say anything, another voice filled the room. "Excuse my interruption, but... how do the trolls fit into all of this?"

Everyone glanced at the door and gawked at the curious centaur—who technically wasn't supposed to speak while a Council/Royal meeting was in place—but no one stopped her. She had served Lyrianna well, Darion knew, and it was a valid question.

During the last hours of discussion and being in the hot seat, Darion had forgotten the trolls—and with that, his dad and Tony.

"And I want to hear more of Zola... and her son," Trinidad added.

Vikaris sighed, his weariness breaking across his stern façade. "Valid questions. All of them. We have much more to discuss. Please sit, and let us continue."

The attendees nodded their thoughts while their worries scampered intermittently across their faces. It wasn't until most of the candlesticks had melted away that the party dispersed to rest, with strict instructions to meet again first thing in the morning.

Darion's eyes felt heavy, and he could barely mumble a "goodnight" as he left the chambers for his own. He took comfort in Triumph's quiet, steady presence in the cold, dark hallway.

CHAPTER 11

The Unease

Zola felt nervous. Outside hers and Trigger's room, she could hear servants and guards beginning their morning duties. Sounds from the village began to make their way to her window as the Kaulter populace awoke to another day. Birds chirped from the tree branches interwoven, it would seem, from the impressive wooden fortress built into the largest tree Zola had ever seen.

She looked around her room. The air smelled crisp, clean, and sweet. The room was decorated lavishly. Two satin divans had been placed in there for sleeping in the utmost comfort. The room was beautiful. It was also a prison. Four walls and a door.

She loathed the feeling of it. She felt trapped... so many years she had spent behind four walls and a door. She needed to get out of here. Clear her head. *Did I do the right thing in bringing Trigger here? Did I have a choice?*

She looked at the tiny colt lying upon the crimson divan. His head shook slightly in his sleep, dreaming. She only hoped it was a good dream. A few sleepy squeaks uttered from his mouth.

She hardly knew what to say to him. Though she felt a profound need and compulsion to protect him, she knew next to nothing about being a mother. Nothing about being a unicorn. Nothing about being free. She needed to get out of here. Observe. Learn.

She thought of Triumph... her father, though it had taken her many days to fully believe his claim. She pictured Darion, the Prince. Her father fawned over the boy. She couldn't quite understand why. She distrusted humans... Darion's father looked dangerous. She didn't trust any of them. Not yet. She could not until she knew for certain she and her son were truly safe. She could not let her guard down.

Rising from her divan, she paced softly upon the carpeted floor so as not to wake her son. She was supposed to meet with the Unicorn Council and Royal family this morning.

She pictured Elsra. The first female unicorn she had ever met. She had felt supreme awe...and shame. Where Elsra oozed grace, power, and radiance with her dazzling lavender eyes and sparkling horn, Zola had stood fattened and weak from captivity... without a horn. And to add to her embarrassment, which shamed her most of all, was her involuntary feeling of disappointment as Elsra inspected her son... unlike any unicorn ever seen in Kaulter. She felt inadequate, and it burned a fire within her. She hated feeling weak and different. But she supposed she was different, and the only way forward was to embrace that. Even her father spoke nonstop of her gaining her horn once coming to Kaulter. As if once she had her horn, then—and only then—would she be worthy. She blew angrily from her nostrils, shaking her now clean mane.

And then she thought of one other individual. The only one who seemed to take her as she was.

She pictured his stoic face, remembering the scars from his battle-tested body. He seemed solid and safe. Where others made her promises or asked repeated questions of her captivity, Soren listened. He didn't press her. She felt her worries fade away whenever in his presence. The tender way he looked at Trigger filled her with an unknown tingly feeling. With him, she didn't feel different or judged. She felt heard. But, she fretted, could she really trust him? *Can I trust anyone?*

***

As the villagers awoke, the sounds of hooves clattered upon the square, roosters crowed, birds chirped, washing women chatted softly on their way to the well, and the aromas of baking bread and morning porridges filled the air. At the sparring grounds, however, the area stood empty... save for one.

Edmond had grown over the past weeks, even larger and more defined, if that was possible. Standing at the weapons rack, with his muscled back to Darion, who approached on soft feet alongside Triumph, Darion didn't feel threatened any longer, but still... just a little perturbed. His best friend had to be part-giant! Seriously, the dude was huge. Tony was going to fawn all over him whenever he got back.

A tremor of fear wracked his body remembering his friend's mission. *Can't think about that now,* Darion chided.

"Hey!" Darion called, getting Edmond's attention. He hadn't seen him since they had arrived, for Edmond had opted to accompany Soren and Zola until he found his little brother, Anton, who was being well cared for, Seegar had assured them.

The High Councilor had greeted them upon the hillside, having recovered from a wound he took when the Camp had been attacked. Darion was relieved to find that his aged friend was alright. Seegar had made sure everyone had proper accommodations, having been given the position of overseeing Kaulter's day-to-day affairs while Elsra met with the Royals and military leaders. There was much to be done in so little time. Seegar had looked slightly frazzled, not cool and collected as usual. Darion was surprised by that until he figured it out. Poor Seegar had to find a place for the entire Nav'Arian military to sleep… and make sure everyone was fed and that the infirmary was ready to care for the injured. Darion pitied the man but was glad he was the one with the job and not Darion. That sounded like an awful lot of work… and worry!

"Slept in, I see?" Edmond grinned.

Darion mock-glared at his friend, ducking under the wooden beams that created a fenced barrier surrounding the area, while Triumph went to unlatch the gate with his horn.

"Yeah right, I was up way later than you, and I'm still here... right on time."

"Are you—I mean, we—in trouble?" The youth glanced around, cheeks flushed, as if looking for a Nav'Arian guard to appear out of nowhere and take him away.

Darion decided to make his friend sweat a little. Drawing his brows together worriedly, biting his lower lip, and sighing, he quietly replied, "It's not good. Triumph and I, well, we got yelled at by our parents." Triumph grumbled, and Darion hoped that he wouldn't give him away just yet. "But... well, you and Soren...," Darion hesitated, looking away for effect.

Triumph spoke quickly, "I am sorry, Edmond. We really did everything we could for you. But you are to receive," as the unicorn spoke, Edmond's eyes goggled and his Adam's apple accentuated a fearful gulp, "a penance. A public display of humility meant to embarrass you and teach you—and others who may one day wish to do the same—a lesson."

"Wh—what lesson?" Edmond squeaked.

Darion glanced at Triumph.

Edmond's brow furrowed while his head swiveled back and forth between them.

"Oh, you two stop that," Soren snorted, appearing like an apparition, coming to Edmond's rescue.

"Are you kidding me?" Edmond exhaled forcefully and threw his hands in the air for emphasis. "I thought they were going to cut my hand off or something."

"My, my, Edmond. What a vivid imagination you have," Triumph said haughtily, with feigned disgust. "Who do you take us for?"

Edmond still glared while Darion laughed. "Soren, you ruined it! We were kidding, Edmond. You're all fine. No one is in trouble... well, except for Triumph. His mom is so pissed—"

A sudden impact made Darion tumble. When he looked up, Triumph's head was tilted upwards inspecting the sky.

"Dude, are you even allowed to do that to me? You're such a child."

"I'm the 'child'? You are the one playing a malicious trick upon our good friend Edmond here."

Darion rolled his eyes, but before he could say anything, Soren spoke.

"I had a feeling you would be here," he began, already knowing what Triumph's first question would be. "I wanted to hear how everything went last night—besides our supposed 'penance'," he gave Triumph a stern look of his own and then rubbed his cheek upon Edmond in familiar greeting. "And I wanted to let you know how Zola and Trigger are."

Triumph snapped alert at the mention of his daughter.

Darion jumped up, too, wiping his palms upon his pants.

"Zola is fine," Soren said, his voice taking on a warmer tone. "She and Trigger were taken to apartments not too far from your own. I stayed and dined with them," but at a glance from Triumph, he added hastily, "And Edmond and his brother joined too."

Darion grinned. He had a feeling something was going on there… and he liked where it was headed.

What? Where WHAT is headed? Triumph piped in.

Darion rolled his eyes once more. "Get out of my head!"

"Then guard your mind, Prince."

"Oh, here we go," Edmond grumbled, walking back to the weapons rack.

"Anyways," Soren pressed. "What happened last night? How *did* they take it?"

"We told them everything we could think of. My father was intense… as usual. But I think they believe us. We have to meet them again soon," Darion informed him.

"I think you should accompany us this morning, at least at the beginning, Soren," Triumph said, "And you, Edmond. In case they have any other questions for us."

"Well then, we better get busy," Edmond pronounced. "Do you still want to spar?" He gestured toward Darion.

Darion felt extremely tired… and now thanks to Triumph's little tantrum, his tailbone hurt.

I will not be blamed for that, Triumph countered.

"Ughhhh, yes! Anything to get me away from this guy for a minute," Darion jested, patting Triumph on the back and promptly jumping away before he could get knocked down again.

"Alright then," Edmond winked. "But I would not put your back to him just yet."

Darion froze and spun around, as if expecting an attack.

None came. Triumph had sauntered over to the edge of the area to speak in hushed whispers with Soren.

He turned back around to see Edmond looking pleased with himself.

"Yeah, I deserved that," Darion said, feeling more amused by the minute.

These moments with Edmond, Triumph, and Soren felt the most natural. They had become so close throughout their journey, and he was glad of their company. Grabbing a blade, he swung it around a few times, having grown more and more comfortable, each and every passing day, with the grip of a sword in his hand.

Edmond gulped and stood straight, instead of launching into an attack as expected.

Darion turned to see his father alongside Garis, Myrne, and Kragar, approaching. The towering centaurs looked impressive nearing the opposite fence where Triumph and Soren stood. Kragar, steely-eyed and intimidating as ever, stood arms crossed. Darion didn't know the man well, but always felt nervous around the quiet, yet deadly, Lieutenant Commander.

To be fair, he didn't really know any of them well, his father included.

Walking, he smiled upon seeing that Vikaris had given up his ceremonial dress for more practical clothes. Battle attire... same as what Darion and Edmond wore. While the fancy, gold-trimmed shirt and coat had been a nice change, it wasn't practical. Darion had gladly thrown on his dark, worn pants—cleaned and folded by the wash women—and a light tan, sleeveless shirt. His hair tied back in a ponytail. His father wore his leather jerkin, arms bare, as was his habit. His Marked Arm, covered in even more symbols than Darion could remember, was visible for all to see. His Ruby tight across his throat. Eyes penetrating, Darion swallowed nervously.

"Son," Vikaris said in greeting. "I was just telling Garis and the others here of our discussion last night. They will be joining us for the War Council meeting this morning, which will begin soon," raising an eyebrow in a very paternal manner, "but before that begins," he paused....

Darion straightened. He would not be admonished in front of everyone for sparring. *Isn't that what a Prince is supposed to do? You haven't done anything wrong,* Darion counseled himself. *Face him!*

Vikaris continued, "Garis brought up a good question that I wanted to ask you—and your companions," the King added, waving toward Triumph, Soren, and Edmond as they surrounded Darion.

Darion was grateful for his friends in that moment. "Alright. What question, Garis?"

The towering, bearded Commander dipped his head in acknowledgment of Darion before speaking. "My Prince. The King has regaled us with a summarized version of your exploits," he looked over at Darion's companions, as well. "The part I am struggling to understand is your time in this hidden community. *The Watchers*, is that what you called them? Well, if it is as you describe and they have sworn allegiance to Morta and the Rav'Arians, what is the connection with the giant skeleton that you dug up—if any? Did a winged one kill before? Are you truly sure they are peaceful as you say, or could they be secretly harboring the intent to join with Morta? Perhaps once more?"

CHAPTER 12

The Lair

Rick's head felt like it had been hit by a train... or a troll's club, he reckoned. A gasp of pain escaped his lips as he tried to take inventory of his condition.

"Shhh. Do not make a sound, Riccus."

Rick knew that voice. Familiar. Authoritative. But it sounded like it was in a vacuum. So distant. His ears felt muffled, and the blood pounded in his head with intensifying pain. But he kept quiet.

Cracking an eyelid, he saw darkness. *Where am I? And where is Tony?*

It had been his voice alright, Rick was sure. Unless he had imagined it. He blinked blurrily, trying to make out any shapes or forms. His right eyelid was swollen, he observed as he tried to open both eyes. Slowly, he focused on his arms and legs, noticing for the first time that he was bound. *Netted like a fool!* How had he let himself get captured?

Aalil! Where is Aalil?

Though his head thundered as if that train was really ramming into him, he tried to focus. Squinting with his one good eye, he realized he could make out a person in front of him. "Tony?" he whispered.

"I said, 'shhhh'," Tony growled softly. "They have her."

Rick tried to make sense of what he was hearing. Why would the trolls keep Aalil separately? Why wasn't she held captive with Rick and Tony?

"Where?" Rick uttered, barely audible to even his own ears.

"With the females," Tony whispered back.

Rick discerned fear, anguish, and anger in Tony's bitter reply. Rick swallowed painfully. He knew that if she died, his friend would never forgive him. And just hours ago, the situation had been the reverse, with Aalil threatening him over Antonis's captivity! It should be him here alone... as had been his plan. He didn't want anyone else getting hurt, and he certainly couldn't fathom anyone else dying. Trying to maintain his breathing, he didn't speak aloud again for some time. Instead, he tried to discern his surroundings. He listened for guards. His arms had been tied with a thick rope behind his back, and his feet were bound together tightly, so much so, that his feet felt near numbness. He needed to get out of these bonds and free Antonis quickly. Then, together, they'd go after Aalil.

They had seen more than enough to know that this hideous beast was one of Narco's evil creations. His hold on the trolls had been due to one of his monsters—much like the Rav'Arians—all along. That is the news they'd take to Vikaris. That, and that they were mobilizing, most likely preparing to join the fight.

It was time to go. *But how?*

Aalil pretended to sleep as she lay on her side with the foul-smelling females and children on the heavily guarded beach. They had been brought out from their cages, the females and males allowed to mix throughout the afternoon. Many obscenities had played out right before her eyes. She clenched her teeth, trying not to recall the open coupling that had taken place around the beach. The massive black beast with the red eyes strode up and down the shoreline, yelling and grunting jeers. They would leave at dawn to join the attack on Nav'Aria. Today was intended for making more trolls. All soldiers were ordered to fornicate with the females, whether they had a wife or not. Aalil knew from the desperate protesting grunts that this was not consensual. One female had pushed a male away. Aalil remembered how he'd motioned for the strangely limping guards to pin the unruly troll down before the beast took her himself. Aalil shuddered. The female was then sacrificed to the beast, and everyone ceased their activity to kneel and bow before their idol. The beast cut off her head before throwing it in the lake, wiping her spilling blood down the sides of his face. No other males were denied their exploits after that.

Aalil had sat, seemingly forgotten, tied in a boat just out of reach from the edge. She watched as the troll younglings clustered and held each other's hands in small groups, many of them covering their eyes or ears as the males set upon the females. After watching a pair of younglings sneak over to the corpse of the slain female and cry upon her headless body, Aalil wept. Though these were vile creatures—evil cohorts of Narco's—children were children. They should not be exposed to this. She may loathe the beast and the male warriors, but from what she had seen, the females and children were victims, and her heart broke for them. This very reason is what had led her to desire a life as a warrior rather than a wife. She had wanted to be strong... stronger than her mother had been. She did not wish to bring children into this cruel world, remembering Queen Lyrianna's tales of the female chattel rescued during her escape. No. She would not be a mother... at least not until Narco was dead.

As tears streamed down her face, she tried to shut it all out. Later, a male troll came and picked her up as easily as a child would a doll, throwing her down next to the many curled up forms of younglings and females asleep in clusters upon the beach.

She laid there listening. Trying and failing to fall asleep. She wondered what they intended to do with her. Her thoughts returned to Antonis and Riccus. She had not seen either of them after being dragged away by the captor who had left in an opposite direction of the one carrying Riccus. She prayed both men were alright.

What felt like days ago had only happened that morning, she reflected. When she had seen Riccus knocked down, she jumped immediately into action. Out of arrows, she had gripped her bow preparing to swing it at the troll who had clubbed her friend. Without a word, she had stepped closer. Initially the troll didn't seem to notice her. She whistled softly to get its attention and was glad to see its hideous eyes take on at least what she assumed was a surprised expression. She was about to tell it to step away from Riccus, when, out of nowhere, a large arm wrapped around her neck from behind and pressed a jagged blade against her throat. Cursing to herself, she froze, not wanting to drop her weapon yet aware the gag was up. She had been caught. They had been caught. The rescue attempt had failed. No one would be coming for any of them now.

Peering down at the blade pressed to her throat, she had considered elbowing the troll or slamming her bow toward its face. But before she did, a huge hand with grey-like skin reached over her and pulled her bow from her startled grip. It clattered against the rocks at their feet, and at once, she felt like a child next to the looming trolls.

"You quiet… or die," a guttural grunt muttered behind her.

Thinking of her botched reaction time again, she contemplated if she even deserved Atonis's love. *You are no warrior,* she thought bitterly. *You failed him.*

A howl broke through the night's stillness… and her heavy thoughts. An ear-splitting, soul-rendering cry. Somewhere in the mountains, another creature was hurting. Grieving. Possibly dying. The thought brought no comfort.

***

"Tav'Opal, I want you to learn everything you can from this creature. We will enter the Portals to Kaulter and slay all that stand in our way."

Morta gave her a look so fierce that it brokered no argument. He knew the stubborn creature probably wouldn't share anything else. But she needed a task. He wasn't sure how long he would let her live... or any of them. He would not tolerate being challenged for authority, and yet, she had been a good servant throughout the years. She had her uses... for now. And, she had a darkness within her, though she kept a stoic exterior. He could see it when he gazed into her eyes. The loathing. Yes, she would serve him well for now.

Morta glanced around the area. Since the burning of the great barn, the maddened unicorns which returned from battle had been corralled in a large open expanse near his tower. A rickety fence had been quickly thrown up, though Morta knew it would never hold the beasts if pressed. They could easily jump right over it... but they wouldn't. They served him now.

The corral was outdoors, but the guards had made a makeshift tent high enough that a unicorn could stand under it if expected to speak to Morta or a guard. Otherwise, they milled aimlessly—angrily—about. Without the return of Silver Seeker, their unofficial leader, they seemed at a loss. And within the middle of their meanderings was a wretched creature strapped to a giant stump, the tree having been felled before the unicorns were restricted to the area.

Smiling at the writhing being, Morta chuckled. *Yes, Tav'Opal will enjoy watching over this one.*

He glanced at her pursed lips as she studied him. "Well, I will leave you to it," he said, signaling to the Rav'Arians and one troll that gathered nearby. *My guards*, he laughed inwardly. They had learned early on he was not Narco… and certainly not weak. He would bring destruction upon the world and the only hope they had to survive it was to obey him and stay out of the way. The heads adorning the rampart walls included now a human Watcher's, a Rav'Arian's, and a troll's, all of whom had irritated him at one point or another. No one was safe… save for the unicorns and Tav'Opal. He would use them… yet their ultimate fate, he cared little about.

"I hope you enjoy your new friend, Bertin," Morta said, his tone oozing with venom as he smiled wickedly at the strung up male nymph that had been captured at the battle's end. With his wings torn and his face covered in cuts and bruises, he was almost unrecognizable, save for his chestnut eyes burning with hate.

Morta sneered. Nymphs were good for only thing. Information. They knew the Woods of the Willow better than anyone, he had come to learn. His helpers would extract every scrap of information they could from this creature. And then his head would join those upon the ramparts. He had not seen a nymph's head atop the ramparts for far too long.

"To the Tower," Morta instructed coldly. He had someone he needed to visit. He laughed evilly as he strode from the unicorns' pen toward his room, and in it, the

Chalice. Another creature awaited him… and this one had already succumbed to his power. *Victory is near!*

CHAPTER 13

The Surprise Entry

Rushing to get cleaned up, Darion threw on clean clothes. Still choosing casual battle attire versus the ensemble from the previous night. He knew he only had moments more before he'd be considered late for the Morning Council meeting. Upon his father's departure from the sparring round, Edmond and he had managed a few rounds, though their "fight" seemed lackluster. What Garis spoke had left them distracted. It couldn't be true, could it?

Darion thought back to their time with the Reouls. He recalled his connection with Gamlin as he chased off Narco from the young one's mind. Darion had been there... seen and felt it all. There was nothing malicious about Gamlin. *Zalto*, he hesitated in his thoughts, *was intimidating at first.* He laughed at such an understatement, recalling the forest aflame! And yet, Zalto had raised Nala and Ati, whom Darion had gotten to know very well. They were good. Kind. There was no way the Reouls were secretly evil and plotting, despite what Garis eluded to.

Whatever had happened all those years ago, causing that winged skeleton to end up there, had to do with Morta... Tarsin. Darion just knew it.

You need to be firm then as you explain that today, Triumph counseled, standing in Darion's doorway.

Hastily dressed and running his hands through his damp hair, he joined his friend to make their way down the hall and back to Elsra's compartments.

Edmond, Soren, Zola, and Trigger stood awaiting them outside Elsra's room. Darion knew Triumph was right. He had to make them see that, though the Winged Ones wouldn't be coming to help, they were not the threat either. The Watchers, on the other hand, could only be assumed as traitors and would most likely be joining Morta's numbers, as would the Rav'Arians from the breeding grounds.

Darion looked at his friends... squaring his shoulders, he nodded at them all. "Here we go."

He walked purposefully into the inner chambers where they had met late into the previous evening. He had informed his father that Soren and Edmond would be joining them today. Vikaris had looked as if he may argue, but Darion had stood firm. After Garis's questions— Darion didn't fault him, knowing the centaur Commander was only trying to play it safe and understand their enemy. Darion argued that it would probably be best to hear from Soren and Edmond then, since they had seen everything, as well. They may remember something that Darion or Triumph had forgotten to mention. His father had looked at them with that appraising scowl before nodding. "Very wise, Son. I agree. Do not be late."

***

The King marched on ahead with Trixon quick on his heels. He chewed on his inner cheek thinking of all that had just been said. So much to process. So much more to plan. *How could Morta have been behind all of this?*

Vikaris angrily picked up his pace as his heartrate climbed. He had had Morta in his clutches back in the Camp. *Why did I not kill him and be done with it?*

That was his greatest mistake, he admitted to himself. He had discounted his enemy based upon the man's weak stature. An aged adviser. A miscreant. A nuisance. But *the* true enemy? That had never crossed his mind.

"Fool," Vikaris spat.

His bonded companion stopped him, "My King, that is not fair. If you are a fool, then I am an even greater fool for not seeing through this ploy. I am the one who found the miserable man in the woods. I should have killed him then with Antonis and Riccus."

Vikaris glanced at his friend. They both knew—even as rash as Trixon was at times—that would have definitely crossed a line. The King had needed to see him… to have him interrogated.

"We both know that is not true."

Trixon rumbled but ceased at Vikaris's silencing raised hand. The pair strode aggressively, their intensity parting a path through now jumpy servants and passersby and across the beautiful thoroughfare beyond the Fortress where the Shovlan Tree had last been sighted.

The magical tree often shifted and could appear whenever a Marked Royal or Unicorn of the First Horn's line needed it... appearing with its gleaming silver branches and crystal needles. The spirits of old. Within the Shovlan Tree was the Cavern of Creation where so long ago Vondulus and Tribute had remained hidden until the time was right to reveal the first Marked King of Nav'Aria. Vondulus had been sent by the Creator to usher the realm into a time of great prosperity and peace.

And I will forever be remembered as the King that squandered that peace, Vikaris thought bitterly.

The morning discussion had not gone as well as he would have liked. Darion had taken it upon himself—*himself*—to invite not only Edmond and Soren, as he'd said, but also Zola and Trigger. Those two made him uncomfortable. *How could they be certain Morta did not have his clutches in her? Another spy? And why did her son look like that? What dark magic coursed through his hybrid veins?*

Trixon cleared his throat. Vikaris knew his companion had mixed feelings about his cousin and her child—if they were truly Triumph's kin. Such oddities this week was bringing. So many problems to fix... and an even larger, more enigmatic adversary still eluded Vikaris. He felt like a lost fawn surrounded by a pack of hungry wolves. He forced himself not to look around for hidden eyes. *But how to make sense of it all? And how would Darion defeat Morta? Should we really base our entire survival off a supposed prophecy and my son? And what about these winged ones? Dare I even hope for my friends' success in the mountains?*

Without realizing it, so lost in thought, Vikaris came right to the Tree. Stopping suddenly, he looked up, his breath catching at the sight of silvery white sparkling crystals spinning lightly above from the tiniest breeze. He exhaled and closed his eyes, trying to regain his inner calm. Opening them once more, he trained his mind to focus only on the Shovlan Tree. The splendor of the crystals, and within them, the spirits of the many unicorns that had gone before them.

Hurried footsteps behind him announced the arrival of his son and the other Unicorn Council members. Turning, feeling a slight sliver of shame for his sudden, angry outburst and departure from the meeting in Elsra's apartments, Vikaris was surprised to see Trinidad and Lyrianna still with the party.

Her crystal blue eyes pierced his heart like a blade, and he knew they would have words later. His wife had always been a treasure. Beautiful and wise. But her captivity had changed her, giving her more spirit and revealing even more strength than he'd have credited her with, to his great shame, he admitted to himself. But still... why had she come? Hopefully not to reprimand him before he and the Council disappeared into the Tree.

Without a word, Lyrianna stepped forward, Elsra, Drigidor, Triumph, Darion, and Trinidad remaining behind.

Vikaris smiled at her... and then gaped.

For his beautiful bride did not walk up to his side to give him a kiss a or quiet word, but rather, walked right up to the Tree and placed her forehead, where the diamond symbol now adorned her face, against the Tree. Vikaris marveled—and spluttered—as the Tree began to open at the access point designated for the unicorns. Vikaris and Darion—using their Marked Arms and Rubies—could access a different place on the Tree. But this? This was unheard of!

Vikaris felt Trixon start at his side.

Standing up to her full height, Lyrianna turned, nose slightly raised in the air, and said sweetly, "Would you care to join us, husband?" And with that, she spun on her heel, skirts swishing softly, and walked through the entryway, Trinidad hurrying behind her into the Shovlan Tree. The magical tree that, to anyone's knowledge, had only ever admitted Unicorns of the First Horn's line... a Marked King or Queen and a Marked Heir. Lyrianna was not of the Meridia line. She did not bare the Mark. She wore no Ruby. How could this be?

Standing agape, Vikaris watched Elsra and Drigidor and then Triumph and Darion enter the Tree in succession. Soon, only Trixon and Vikaris stood outside.

"We did not see it, Vikaris," Trixon spoke in his low voice. "She *is* Marked now."

Vikaris's jaw dropped at the realization. He knew a symbol had been etched onto her forehead, but the idea that she would now be considered "Marked," as an equal to him in more ways than one, gave him pause.

Trixon laughed, moving toward the entryway. "You underestimate your wife, Vikaris. Something I do not believe she is going to let you forget anytime soon."

Vikaris gulped. Trixon was right. "Fool," Vikaris murmured once more. *I am a fool in more ways than one it would appear.*

Once gathered, and everyone—namely Vikaris and Trixon—grew accustomed to having the newly admitted Queen within their secret gathering place, the party set to work. They needed to plan, strategize, and discover everything they could about Morta, this enigmatic Tarsin, and how they could defeat him.

"How Darion will defeat him…" Triumph boomed interrupting Vikaris's musings.

The King felt raw terror at the thought. How was his son supposed to defeat the enemy? He had never seen a full battle, and with the exception of his Rav'Ar trials, he was untested. The entire Rav'Arian horde, peppered with trolls and indoctrinated humans left in the Kingdom, would prove the ultimate test. There had to be something else. Wasn't there a scrap of paper containing this so-called prophecy? His aides had set to work tearing apart the entire Kaulter Library but had come up empty handed. It was as if they were all in a fog. Everyone seemed to agree that there was a prophecy, but how or what Darion was supposed to do seemed unclear. Just walking up to Morta and stabbing him in the heart seemed unlikely. Darion would die in the process, Vikaris feared.

The Frieze in the Kaulter Fortress, as well as the Reoul drawings that Darion and Triumph described, sounded the same. An image of a Marked Royal straddling the border between what could only be perceived as Rav'Ar, land of the Winged Ones—and Rav'Arians. Vikaris had not forgotten Garis's questions pointing to the two groups' possible connection. The figure in the frieze then straddled what appeared as Nav'Aria, the home of the unicorns and other Nav'Arian peoples.

"Yes, but how can we be sure that the image is of Darion and not of myself? Do I not also bare the Mark and wear the Ruby? Perhaps the prophecy speaks of me, and Darion can remain here in safety?"

Elsra snorted, annoyed. "Vikaris, we have gone over this many times. Trinidad and I both agree that Darion is the Chosen One. The signs all point to it… Triumph, Drigidor, and Trixon, do you agree with our summation of the prophecy?"

The unicorns' heads bobbed. Vikaris did not have to look at Trixon to know he, though standing behind him, was also nodding his head.

"Yes, but—" Vikaris paused, glancing at his son. "I mean no disrespect, Darion, but you are too young. This is too big of a fight."

Something in Darion seemed to snap, for as Vikaris spoke, he was surprised when his son stood up to his full height, matching that of his own. Darion stared Vikaris in the eye, and all suggestion of youth and inexperience faded away. Vikaris stepped back, bumping into Trixon from the intensity in his son's brilliant green eyes.

Darion's stance and gaze dared anyone to challenge him. *Who was this child?* Vikaris already felt like he was married to a stranger, with his wife's position now as a Marked Royal. Did he not know any of them?

"I'm going to talk now," Darion said coolly, eyeing Vikaris.

The King crossed his arms, glaring, but did not speak.

"I get it. You don't think I'm ready; you think you need to be the big hero and save the day. And I'd love for that to be the case, Father. But you need to know one thing. I am no 'boy.'"

With Darion's intense proclamation, his arm glowed, and his Ruby shined bright, fully illuminating the dark cavern. Vikaris felt goosebumps rise upon his forearms. His peripheral revealed Lyrianna sitting up alert, eyes aglow and transfixed. As Darion continued, he emanated even more light.

"Since coming to Nav'Aria, in only a few months, I have learned that I'm a Prince, I've met my birth parents, I've lost my Mom, and now I've faced more enemies and crazy situations than I could've ever imagined. What's more, I have bonded a unicorn, I have killed monsters, and I will face Morta. He must suffer for killing my Mom. So, my King." Vikaris couldn't help but flinch at the derisive tone in his son's voice.

Darion pressed on, "Do not ever again say I am just a 'boy' or 'too young'. I am Darion! I am your son, but I am also the son of Rick and Carol, and they didn't raise me to hide away while others fight—and die—for me. My Mom didn't die so that I could play it safe here like a little kid. My Dad didn't offer to go off and find the troll secrets just so I could sit this one out. I am going with you."

At Darion's last forceful words, a flashing green light eclipsed within the Cavern of Creation, knocking them back as if from a great gust of wind... all but Darion. He stood—with eyes far older than his years—and waited silently.

Elsra and Drigidor put their heads together and murmured. Trinidad whispered into Lyrianna's ear. The rest, Triumph, Vikaris, and Trixon, stood looking stunned.

Softer than before, Darion added, "I am going with you, and," Darion smiled, softening his features, for which Vikaris was glad to see, "I will defeat Morta—with your help... Father."

And then, as if coming out of a trance, the force left his voice, and he plopped back into his chair.

Vikaris felt a rush of mixed emotions. *What just happened? Is he trying to usurp my authority? How could that much power have issued forth from him?*

As if in answer to his questions, Trixon spoke aloud, his booming voice filling the quiet Cavern. "And so, we have our answer. Prince Darion is indeed the Chosen One, as the Creator has revealed in full to us here... a promise has been made. Darion is our only hope for defeating Morta. I propose that, instead of questioning *if* he is the one to kill the wretch, we set to finding out *how* Darion is to succeed... and how we must partner with him."

Vikaris felt slight embarrassment, and yet, why should he? *He was indeed the King and this boy's—no*, he stopped himself—*this man's father.* He had had to be sure. *And now*, he admitted, *I am sure.* He looked around to see the dazed expressions upon many of the other faces. *We all are.*

Trinidad's wise voice, softer than his male counterparts, broke the stillness. "My son has spoken wisely," Trinidad said, warmth and peace radiating from him even without his horn. Trixon whinnied softly under his father's praise. "As has yours, my King," Trinidad continued. "I have been thinking on much of this, and I am embarrassed to admit, but I believe my never-ending desire to regrow my horn..." speaking faster, as if he feared he'd be interrupted, Trinidad continued, "it is my belief that this is all connected. There are so many unique and strange events taking place, that I believe they must be. Darion's return. Carolina's tragic death. The discovery of Winged Ones. The loss of my horn... and that of Zola's," Vikaris heard Triumph's slight intake of breath at the mention of his newly found daughter. "These hybrid unicorns. Narco's death. Lyrianna's Mark. The 'Watchers.' All these events are unique and coming about so quickly, I can only deduce that the end is near. We must puzzle out what this means... and how exactly Darion is to defeat Morta. Furthermore," Trinidad paused. If it had been anyone else, Vikaris would have thought it for effect, but he knew this not to be the case with his humble friend.

Trinidad exhaled softly, eyes closed for a moment before continuing. "It is my belief that the signs—and the Creator's presence even here today—are pointing toward Nav'Aria."

Vikaris frowned, about to interject. *Of course, things were pointing to Nav'Aria. That is what we are fighting for, is it not?*

Be still, Vikaris, Trixon spoke into his mind, quietly. Commandingly. *Please hear him.*

Trinidad stood, and though he was without his horn, he seemed to grow larger, more impressive, and majestic as he spoke his concluding thoughts. "It is time to march on Castle Dintarran."

Vikaris felt his heart sink. Trixon rubbed his cheek with his own in reassurance.

"We have come to the end, my King. The darkness is growing in Nav'Aria, and I fear that now we are not only fighting for the liberation of Nav'Aria, but for life itself. This new enemy—one that has lain in wait for years like a coiled snake, hidden in the shadows and ready to strike— does not wish to dominate. He wishes to destroy. I can feel it… and I know when you search your hearts, you will feel it too. We have come to the end." Trinidad continued, raising his voice to show finality, "What we do will decide the fate of all. We need to attack before Morta has more time to prepare."

Vikaris sat, feeling all the heat from Darion's explosion fade away. Taking a moment, Vikaris placed his head in his hands. What Trinidad spoke was not much different from what Garis, Myrne, and Kragar had said to him earlier. And yet… to press into the enemy's territory? To his rightful home? To see destruction within his palace? Could he do it?

A hand lightly settled upon his shoulder and he looked up to see Lyrianna's beautiful, calm face smiling upon him. With a reassuring squeeze she nodded her head slightly before stepping back.

Vikaris looked around the table to his friends. His family.

"Elsra, do you as Regent of Kaulter agree with Trinidad? Is this final battle to be fought in the Kingdom?"

Elsra's lavender eyes swept over the table and returned to Vikaris. The shimmer of tears not taking away from the resolve in her voice as she spoke. "It is time, my King. Kaulter will always be a safe refuge for you, but it cannot withstand this populace for long. It is time to reclaim your throne."

Vikaris stood, feeling his regal responsibility now more than ever. They would lose many in this fight. He would carry their deaths and the weight of this decision for his remaining days. He swallowed, feeling his resolve strengthen as he looked at the stoic faces of the Unicorn Council and Marked Royals.

"Then it is time. I will inform Garis. We will assemble all of our fighters and march upon Castle Dintarran. Darion," Vikaris paused looking at him. "Before we are to leave, we need to have a plan for how you are to defeat Morta. Search this cavern. For if we do not find answers, we are walking blindly into battle."

"I will help search," Trinidad said quickly.

"Me too," replied Lyrianna.

"As will I," Triumph echoed.

"I will join you, my King, and help gather the troops," Drigidor boomed.

Vikaris nodded, expecting this as well as Trixon, who rumbled his agreement.

"And I will prepare to leave," Elsra added.

Vikaris looked at her in surprise. What? Elsra was the Regent. Her place was protecting Kaulter.

"I have sat out of the fight long enough, Vikaris," Elsra's warm, yet authoritative voice rang out. "This vile man has imprisoned my family, tortured them, and stolen what is most precious to a unicorn," she said this, eyes falling upon Trinidad, whose head dipped at her words. Her tone turning to steel, "I will not let others go in my stead, as Prince Darion spoke earlier. This fight will take all of us together. We must defeat Morta, or else Kaulter will fall too."

Silence reigned for a long moment at the meaning of Elsra's words. Vikaris couldn't believe that they'd come to this point. He had thought killing Narco was the end, and now, the weight of all that hung in the balance threatened to overtake him. But he could not give into fear or weakness. For Elsra's power and tenacity was infectious. She was the Mate of the great Rinzaltan. Her kin was of the First Horn's. She was the wisest and most powerful unicorn in all the land. Perhaps with her presence they would have a fighting chance.

"So be it," Vikaris said, softly. "Prepare for war."

CHAPTER 14

The Blessing

A small tug on Aalil's elbow caused her to wake with a start. *What time is it? Where am I?* All at once the chaos of the previous day and evening flooded her memory as she looked around a beach filled with waking trolls. The females and children with whom she was kept were beginning to rise. Heavily guarded, they were unable to do much beyond sitting up and waiting. The beast was prowling, shouting guttural commands, and the male trolls hastened to do his bidding. Their departure was underway.

"Food?" A small, timid voice whispered to her.

Distracted with inspecting the beach she had not even acknowledged who had woken her. Glancing to her side, she saw a female adolescent with a couple smaller younglings clustered around her. The female glanced back at the beast, and then at Aalil. Subtly she looked down at her hand which held in it a small portion of bread. It had been torn off. "You sleep," she added, as if in explanation.

"I…," Aalil paused. Was that true? Had they distributed food whilst she slept? Not knowing this seemed unlikely since she was a warrior. She slept lightly… always alert. She felt an even greater shame. One mess up after another. She had let herself, her friend, and her lover get captured, and then had managed to sleep comfortably through the night? She wished she could punish herself further, beyond biting the inside of her cheek. Push herself on a long run or through multiple training exercises. She forced herself to admit that most anyone would have succumbed to the exhaustion of her capture and the horrific evening events. *Still…*.

Sweeping her eyes around, she observed that none were watching the females closely. She reached for the bread and took it, keeping it in her lap and out of view as she tore tiny pieces off to suck on. If this was all the food they were going to get, then she needed to savor it.

From her peripheral, she examined the female who sat calmly… nobly even. Her chin raised just slightly. Though Aalil had not spent much time with trolls, she could see that this one was pretty… for a troll. Her grey-like skin did not appear bulbous like many of the men's. She had a petite look to her, even though she was huge compared to Aalil. Beyond this, Aalil noticed other features: dark unwashed hair framing her face and her large coal black eyes looking around her from sweeping lashes. Her mouth was set in a firm, resigned position… not a frown and, yet, not a smile. Simply calm.

How does she do it, Aalil wondered as she chewed the bread hungrily, forgetting her earlier thought to savor it. A bundle of anger and nerves.

"Thank you," she said around a mouthful, then quickly added, "What is your name?"

The large dark eyes swept back to Aalil, and the foreign face did smile. "I am D'Ania."

Aalil felt her own lips upturn with a smile. Though trolls terrified Aalil deeply, she did not feel any hidden agenda or malice from this one, nor from any of the females or children, for that matter. She did note how differently the females and males behaved. Was it simply a gender thing… or was there something more to it? Remembering the barbarism stabbed at her gut.

"Thank you, D'Ania. I am Aalil," she replied. "Are these your children?" Though she doubted it, she wanted to keep the conversation going, realizing that this could be her way to obtain information on the trolls… and Antonis's whereabouts.

D'Ania's face returned to the serene gaze as her eyes drifted around. "Quiet talk," she murmured but quickly added, "No. I help."

Aalil gave a nod in response. Though D'Ania's speech was fragmented, Aalil was able to understand her. "That is kind of you," Aalil offered, looking at the three younglings, one looking only just a few years old. The children stared hollowly with sleepy, scared eyes. Dressed in tattered rags, they leaned on one another, dozing in and out of sleep as D'Ania talked.

"You from..." D'Ania lifted one large finger toward an opening in the mountain which led to the Cave tunnels... and beyond.

Before nodding, Aalil looked to make sure they had not been spotted talking.

"Want go," D'Ania whispered, pointing at her chest and then nodding at the children.

Escape? Aalil wondered. She would be happy to flee and even perhaps take D'Ania along—she might be useful—but not children.

"Know a way" D'Ania whispered, her voice sounding more urgent.

"I..." Aalil began, but before she could respond, heavy footsteps kicked up loose gravel nearby. She dropped her eyes and wrapped the edge of her coat around the bread just in case. With her eyes lowered she could still make out large feet and lower legs belonging to a large creature. A male.

"We march," the low voice growled. The females and children—Aalil included—stood up. No one wanted to be seen disobeying the males, particularly after what they had done the evening before. Aalil ground her teeth at the memory. If she could get free and to her friends, she was going to make sure these males learned a few things... starting with that hideous beast.

It prowled the beach, but as if on cue, as she looked at it, its predatorial gaze shot over, like it could sense her. She didn't know why they kept her alive, but no one had come for her, so she assumed it best to remain hidden with the females. Hidden and forgotten... until she could strike.

Antonis woke first. He and Rick had slept fitfully on the cold stone floor. Rick still lay there, his brow furrowed even while asleep. Saying they were stressed was putting it mildly. They were prisoners... and had not seen or heard anything about Aalil. Antonis felt such anger... mixed with terror—the likes of which he had never known. This was why he had vowed never to commit to a woman. Best to remain loyal to his King and country alone. And then that woman had shown back up, with her leather vest, taut stomach, strong uppercut, and changed everything. "Damn her," he muttered, looking around cautiously. He was surprised to find they were alone.

Seizing the opportunity, he kicked Rick hastily and started scooting backwards. Rick groused sleepily, taking his sweet time to wake up. *He really is an old man! Unbelievable*, Antonis thought. He'd have enjoyed nothing more than kicking his friend again, but wasting time and alerting the enemy simply wasn't worth it.

Without a blade, it would be nearly impossible to cut their bonds. But he had to try. Antonis backed up and began rubbing his bindings frantically upon the wall... hoping to either ease them off or rub the rope away. He knew it was a hopeless plan, but they had felt all around them for sharp rocks and come up with nothing. His feet were bound, as were Rick's, and together they were tied to a post in the middle of the area. If they could first free their hands, then Antonis could free their feet, and then....

"Stop," a youth's voice said, trying—and failing—to sound menacing like the adults.

Antonis froze, glancing around to meet the eyes of the youth who now stepped from the shadows. He sighed in resignation. Though much smaller than the adults, this one could still raise the alarm—*or club me*, Antonis admitted, eyeing the youth's weapon—before he ever got rid of these cursed bonds.

As the adolescent stepped closer, Antonis thought he recognized him. He had been a messenger to Antonis's earlier guards. Could he get him talking? Would he have news of Aalil?

"Sorry," Antonis mumbled, eyes down, "My arm itches."

In the pale early morning light, Antonis could just make out his features. A yawn sounded nearby as Rick, finally deeming it time to awake—*blast him!*—sat up.

The troll stopped, staying out of range of them. "Lie," he snorted.

No fool then, Antonis considered. He had hoped the troll would come close enough that he could trip him and get the club away from him. It had been unlikely, but still.... Looking at the youth some more, Antonis decided to be blunt.

"Why are you keeping us?"

The troll looked at him, and then away from Antonis's gaze, as if not wanting to be heard. "You fight."

Antonis opened his mouth in protest. He had defended himself after they set upon him!

The troll stepped closer, dropping his voice. "Master wants."

Antonis swallowed. *So, Narco knew of his presence here?* That seemed unlikely, but at least he knew that they would not be killed until they were presented at the Castle.

"Do we leave for the Castle soon then?"

The youth nodded. "Now." And then, without another word, the troll spun on his heel to march toward the cave opening. Antonis watched his rigid back, trying so hard to emulate the other guards. Antonis had seen it time and time again. Younglings peacocking as if they too belonged with the soldiers, even though their sword arms were untested and their blades not yet bloodied.

The youth paused before looking back at Antonis. His eyes red in the shadowed cave. "Food," the troll called, throwing a bundle as an afterthought.

Antonis clenched his jaw. He would not crawl for this youngling's amusement, though his stomach protested. Once the troll took a few steps further, Rick scooted on his belly toward the bundle, muttering curses before he was forced to drag it over to Antonis with his teeth. What ensued can only be described as humiliating, for they both tried to tear into the two pieces of bread with only their teeth.

"Have I told you that I hate trolls?" Rick drawled.

It was the first time Rick had spoken more than a curse this morning.

Antonis chuckled, his stomach rumbling along with him. "Good thing you set out on this quest then," Antonis sarcastically countered.

Rick groaned but kicked at Antonis's foot anyway.

"I hate them too, buddy. We need to get out of here... and fast."

Rick's face became stone again, and his eyes glittered angrily. "We certainly do."

***

"Well, why don't you show us what you've found and we can start there?" Darion suggested. They were back in the Tree today—this time without the King. Vikaris planned to march by the end of the week, and so their need for information and answers was eminent. Otherwise, they would be, as he had said, "marching in blind."

Trinidad and Lyrianna seemed set upon discounting each and every one of Darion and Triumph's ideas. *Did they want to figure out the prophecy or not? Wasn't finding a way to grow Trinidad's horn the most important thing to him?*

Lyrianna and Trinidad both stood next to the largest heap of documents—scrolls, notebooks, journals—that they had compiled from the various Cavern archives. They claimed they had scoured the documents for hours upon hours to no avail.

Triumph had nudged them aside with his horn, illuminating the corner with the small beam of light streaming from the tip of his horn as he nosed through the documents. He had claimed that the unicorns had all the Kaulter histories memorized long ago, but these did not appear to be documents he was familiar with.

"Hasn't anyone ever gone through this stuff before?"

Triumph and Trinidad looked at one another sheepishly. "If someone did, it was most likely our father, Rinzaltan," Trinidad admitted. "We have been... distracted with other matters."

Triumph snorted in agreement. "Yes... war takes precedence."

"Yeah, but even I can tell there is important stuff in this room. Someone should have had this duty." Darion eyed them both as he spoke.

"Oh Darion, please. Do not lay all the blame at their feet. Yes, someone should have... so let us do so now," Lyrianna spoke, ever the diplomat.

Darion sighed looking at his mother. Lyrianna's radiant face and melodic voice entranced him. He could look at it all day and know warmth and joy. He wanted to memorize her face as it was now, happy, not in pain or under Narco's control, as she'd looked in his dreams. He wanted to sketch it next to his last image of her as if to redeem all that had been taken. But not yet. She was right. Their duty now was to search for answers within the Shovlan Tree.

Darion paused. He closed his eyes and let his senses search outwards. He remembered the first time he'd come to the Tree, and how it had pulsed teasingly at him, edging him closer and closer toward the Marked Royal entrance.

As he closed his eyes, he felt a deep sadness emanating from ahead of him. A heaviness that he had not sensed before in the Tree. A confusion. A despair. A... loss.

Darion opened his eyes and met the aquamarine pools of Trinidad's. He gave the unicorn a weak smile. He had a feeling Trinidad knew what he had been doing while Triumph was busily scattering pages around—to no avail. Ever the haughty instructor, Triumph wasn't exactly patient. Darion feared he'd tear the pages with his frenzied movements and swift leafing of pages with his illuminated horn.

Darion considered Trinidad. Lyrianna stood at his side, one arm upon his neck as she held a scroll aloft, reading it silently.

Darion closed his eyes again, narrowing in on the pair. What he found surprised him ever further. The connection, it seemed from their touch, allowed Darion to sense their mixed emotions, as if one. Where Trinidad discharged a mixture of despair, loss, and a dim hope, Lyrianna's life force dazzled Darion. So much light and vibrancy radiated from her aura. She was light. Hope. Love. Darion could sense it. And all thoughts that he'd ever had about her, comparing her to Carol, fell away. She was as authentic and pure a person as one could ever encounter.

Darion focused on it... that light. Concentrating his senses, he could hear a soft vibration. As if jubilant soundwaves spread out from his mother. And as she touched Trinidad's neck, his heaviness seemed to lift... just slightly, but lift the aura did. It was as if there was a break in the clouds that had not been there before. Darion focused on that. Breathing deeply, without even realizing what he was doing, he reached out his hands, ignoring his mother's startled gasp, as he placed one palm upon her Marked forehead and another upon Trinidad's stump.

Connected as they were, through Lyrianna's touch upon Trinidad's neck, and now Darion's touch upon their foreheads, Darion felt a wave of power rush through him. It felt as it had the few times before, but so much happier. He couldn't describe it, but there wasn't the element of fear that had been there when driving Narco out of Gamlin or scaring off the viper and the hybrid beast in Rav'Ar. He felt pure power. He felt light.

He gasped as it shined brighter and brighter, and the songs radiating from his mother's aura grew in volume. The pulsing beat of the Tree again caused his arm to tingle and glow while it made his Ruby shine. He kept his eyes firmly closed. This was it. This was the key to Trinidad, he knew it.

Focusing on the song and light, Darion imagined what Trinidad would look like restored. Gleaming. Majestic. Magnificent. And then he remembered how Trinidad— and Lyrianna—had looked in captivity. Broken. Dirty. Vulnerable.

It made him angry, and he seized even more onto the light and the image of majesty. This was what a unicorn was meant to be. A protector of the Realm. A pure spirit guided by the Creator. That had been taken from Trinidad, and yet, even within his nearly broken spirit, Darion could feel the thrum of hope. It was there. It had always been there. The connection between the three made Darion even more sure that the hope of regrowing Trinidad's horn was not in vain. It was not for Trinidad to regrow his horn, or even for Vikaris to win this battle; instead, the deep, buried hope in both of these bonded hearts was for Darion. The love that was written upon Lyrianna's heart and etched in Trinidad's mind would save Nav'Aria. It was unwavering. The selfless love and belief in Darion's capability.

While it nearly broke his heart, it also renewed him. He seized on that impression of selfless love and loyalty to Nav'Aria and the Marked Heir. Trinidad did not long solely for his horn; Lyrianna did not long solely to be a mother. These two, joined as one, believed unequivocally that Darion would return to save them all.

Darion grasped onto this thrumming belief and pulled on it. His senses brimming with music, light, and tingling beyond anything he'd ever experienced. And into the light he spoke, "Creator... Spirits of Shovlan... reward this being for his humble loyalty to you and to Nav'Aria." And without so much as a doubt, Darion pushed his mind toward that image that now grew brighter and brighter. The images of their captivity fading away as if the pages from his sketchbook were being ripped out and thrown into a fire. Instead, he focused on the light gleaming off of the pristine, shining coat of the majestic Trinidad, whose horn sparkled like diamonds in sunlight, standing next to the resplendent Queen of Nav'Aria, whose scars had been washed away as she was given the shimmering gift of a Marked diamond shape upon her forehead. A kiss from the spirits of old.

Darion focused, eyes firmly closed, and as he had drawn the evil away from Soren's wounds, Darion began to draw his palm away from Trinidad's forehead, slowly... His focus absolute. His hand still upon Lyrianna's brow, he retained the connection to their bonded senses and pulled on the selfless love and purity that wafted in huge waves from the pair. As he drew his hand away, his senses noted the movement upon Trinidad's brow. A horn slowly began to knit together, as if from thin air, but Darion knew better. He was connected to it all. To the pair. To Shovlan. To the Spirits of ancient unicorns. To the First Horn. To the Cavern of Creation... and the Creator himself. He was connected to it, and he knew that all were working together to gift this creature, so deserving and wholly pure, with the gift of a new beginning. Darion did not create the horn. He was the vessel for its return. When he finally opened his eyes, what he saw caused him to break out in a giant grin.

There before him stood a mesmerized Lyrianna, looking somewhat dazed as she pressed her palm upon her own forehead, Mark shimmering brightly. Abundantly clear was her adoration for the majestic unicorn standing at her side.

Trinidad was nearly unrecognizable. Though Darion had known he was a unicorn rightfully, he had not looked like this before.

The transformation was awe-inspiring. Trinidad's pure coat was nearly blinding, and as he stood lifting his head high for what seemed the first time in months, his horn illuminated the area far beyond any other had done in the Cavern. He was light... he was restored. This was who Trinidad had always been on the inside... and now was apparent for all to see on the outside.

"Brother," Triumph spoke reverently, stepping toward Trinidad. "You look just like Father. You are like Rinzaltan."

Trinidad beamed and laughed merrily, rushing to rub his cheek upon first his brother's, and then Darion's.

Rich laughter broke out from each of them.

Lyrianna's melodic chuckles and glossy eyes only made her lovelier. "Oh Darion, you did it!" She gushed hugging her son in a tight embrace.

Darion smiled but pulled back, looking from her to Trinidad. "No, you two did it. The Creator can see your pure hearts and has given you this gift. I didn't do anything... I only focused on what was already there."

Lyrianna's face broke into a tearful smile as she looked at Trinidad and nodded, wrapping her arms around him. "You are whole my friend. You have always been whole to me."

Trinidad's cheeks glistened with happy tears, and Darion leaned upon Triumph, watching them joyfully celebrate this monumental moment.

Thank you, Darion, Triumph said softly.

I—Darion was about to argue.

No, you did a lot here today. The Creator has blessed us all... with you. I will not forget what you have done for my brother. Not ever, and with that, Triumph rubbed his own wet cheek upon Darion's.

Darion smiled, then deciding that was about as much mush as he could handle, added aloud, "So... about that prophecy?"

Lyrianna and Trinidad broke their embrace, and soon the four of them laughed as they returned to sifting through the documents on the table, aided now by Trinidad's bright light.

CHAPTER 15

The Buzz

Mother! Zola! You must come quick! Triumph called out telepathically as he drew near to the Fortress.

Triumph had hardly been able to contain his excitement after Darion—*his bonded companion*—had worked the miraculous. *He healed Trinidad! Well, according to Darion, he only did what the Tree Spirits and Creator led him to. Either way,* Triumph regarded, *our Prince is all powerful. If he can do it once, he can do it again. Zola will have her horn!*

After spending a few hours searching, they had agreed that Vikaris and Eslra needed to know about Trinidad. The news would be good for morale around Kaulter. Triumph had offered to go find Elsra, while the rest headed to Vikaris.

Triumph, as he ran through the Fortress in search of the females who held his heart, smiled. He felt elation thinking of the brilliance of his brother. No jealousy or envy could ever arise when he thought of his eldest sibling. His only sibling, since Trinity had been slain many years before. Trinidad had been Rustusse's companion. He was wise, humble, pure, courageous, and powerful. He had survived Narco's captivity and escaped… helping save the Queen of Nav'Aria, along with many female prisoners. And now…what was always inside his heart was once again visible in his shining coat, horn, and build. He had been rewarded by the Spirits of old, and this was something to celebrate! This was a day filled with hope!

As he rounded a corner, he slid to a stop as Elsra and Zola, followed by a tottering Trigger and patient Soren, approached.

"Oh good, you are all together," Triumph breathed out relieved, feeling slightly winded from his exuberant canter.

"Son, what is it? Is Kaulter compromised? I have heard nothing from my guards," Elsra questioned immediately.

Triumph laughed, "No, no, it is nothing like that Mother, I assure you. I bring you good news… Hope!"

Elsra cocked her head, as did the rest of them.

Triumph felt giddy. Elated. Jubilant. And he didn't care for a moment if he looked a fool bouncing with joy before their eyes! "You must come. We are to meet Vikaris and others at the War Tent, where he is meeting with Garis and Kragar."

Elsra sighed. "Son, I have only just come from there. I was relaying to Zola and Soren what was discussed in the Tree. We must prepare. I do not have time for this—"

"Oh, you will want to make time for this, Mother," Triumph said so forcefully, all the while smiling like a fool, that his Mother paused to study him.

"What is it? Why are you guarding your mind? I could have read it and moved on by now, Triumph. I have much to do."

"It is too good to see in my mind, Mother. You must come... All of you, must come. Especially you, Zola," Triumph concluded beaming at his daughter.

"I—" Zola began as if to say no, looking back at Trigger.

Triumph nudged her with his nose in greeting and finality. "We all go to meet Vikaris. That is the message. Now please come along. Quickly!"

"Message from whom, Son? Vikaris is ordering us there? Why? What has changed? I was with him only moments ago."

Snorting, Triumph emphasized, "Mother, listen to me."

"Triumph," Elsra said, an icy tone creeping into her voice, "this better be worth it," then raised her head proudly and began in the direction of the War Tent.

"Impossible!" Vikaris whispered, as Trixon simultaneously rumbled, "Father?" as if in disbelief.

Trinidad astounded all when he entered the Tent. Garis and Kragar both took steps backwards as if a gust of wind had blown through. The light radiating off Trinidad was nearly blinding... Darion hoped that would lessen a little or else they were going to need to invent sunglasses here real soon.

Trixon rushed around the table in the now crowded tent to get to his father. They pressed their cheeks together in a happy display of affection and greeting.

Trixon looked like an excited child, his entire body seeming electric with energy. "How did this happen?"

"Yes, how?" Vikaris spluttered.

Lyrianna beamed at Trinidad's side, her hand on his neck, and answered simply, "Darion."

The King flopped into his chair, eyes bulging.

Darion smiled. He enjoyed seeing his Father a little flustered... it made him seem more human. Vikaris moved his mouth, but sheer awe stole his words. At the tent flap's opening, Trixon, Trinidad, Lyrianna, and Cela moved further inwards to make way for the newly arrived Elsra, Triumph, Soren, Zola, and Trigger. Now it was time for the Prince to explain.

Like Vikaris, Elsra couldn't contain her gasp. Bulged eyes and mouth agape, she had many questions. Darion grinned, knowing Triumph was also enjoying the sight of his parent flustered.

"My son, but how?" Elsra whispered, approaching Trinidad as if he were a celestial being. Her reverence and awe warmed Darion as he watched Trinidad bow his head in greeting to his Mother, while Trixon stepped out of the way, respectfully making way for his Father and Grandmother. The two unicorns' horns touched, and a dazzling light mixed of silver and lavender showered around the tent with a spark. Elsra gasped.

"Prince Darion healed me, Mother." Trinidad's voice caused goosebumps to rise along Darion's arms. He sounded so full of life. So beyond any earthly being. He was utterly magnificent.

Large tears pooled in Elsra's lavender eyes as she looked at Darion, who had stepped up to the table strewn with maps where his father still sat in shock, and Garis and Kragar stood rigid, mouths still agape. "Is this true, Darion?"

Lyrianna's head bobbed as she cried freely with a giant smile and came to lean upon the seated Vikaris. "Come in, come in everyone," she ushered them. "Darion, please share what you did."

Darion swallowed, suddenly feeling a little unsure of what to say. He didn't really do anything; after all, *it just sorta happened.*

Don't be dim, Darion. You, with the aid of the Creator, just worked a miracle! Now tell them what you did, Triumph spoke into his mind. His tone as happy as it was upon finding Zola.

As Darion shared, the room grew hushed, and he watched his Father's face turn from shock to awe as the news was delivered. Trinidad and Trixon came to stand near Lyrianna and Vikaris. Darion tried to look at Vikaris and Elsra equally as he shared the events. Elsra's reaction was even more amazed. Just as he finished, the tent flap moved again, and a towering figure, Drigidor, stuck his head in, abandoning all formalities.

"I just heard—" his low booming voice filled the Tent. "Well, I cannot believe it—" He barged in, dark eyes wide as he saw Trinidad shining like a diamond. Elsra pressed her body upon her Mate's in greeting, though her eyes remained transfixed upon Trinidad's.

Before anyone else could speak, Triumph's excited voice filled the crowded tent. "Yes, and now he will heal Zola too. Right, Darion?" He looked from Darion to Zola, whom he nudged, as if encouraging her to step forward. "Now, Darion. You must. Heal her too. You can do it."

Darion froze. *Zola?* "I—" He hesitated. *Can I do it again?* He didn't really understand what he had done before.

"Darion," Triumph chastised aloud. "Quit with the humility. You have already done it. Now do it again."

Darion swallowed. It sounded more like a demand than a request.

"It is a demand," Triumph said aloud.

Darion looked up startled. For Triumph to betray his inner thoughts before this audience was rare. Triumph was very intent on this outcome. Darion bit his lip nervously.

"Triumph, please calm yourself," Elsra's motherly, yet authoritative, voice murmured. "You do not command the Prince."

"Right," Vikaris echoed firmly.

"Forgive me," Triumph interjected, "But in this instance, I will. Darion, heal my daughter."

Darion recoiled… he wanted to punch his friend. *My so-called friend.* This was a lot of pressure… couldn't they have talked about it before being put on the spot like this? Darion's eyes wandered to Zola's. She hadn't spoken, but Darion could sense that she was on high alert. Could he do it again?

Before anyone else spoke or he lost his will, he acquiesced, "Alright, I will try, Triumph. I can't promise it'll work again. I don't even know exactly what happened the first time, like I said."

Vikaris, Triumph, and Elsra all started speaking at once. And a strange buzzing sound tugged at Darion's ears.

He raised his hand to silence them. "I said, 'I will try,'" Darion replied in a stronger voice... silencing the voices but not the buzzing, whatever that was.

"You heard the man," Triumph said. "Make room for the Prince."

Darion wanted to roll his eyes. It was just like Triumph to call him Prince now and ooze with proper respect, as if this was Darion's idea. *Such bullshit*, Darion thought.

"Fine. I'll try... if you want me to, Zola?" Darion asked.

Looking from him, to Trinidad, to Triumph, and over her shoulder toward Trigger, Zola's determination seemed to strengthen. She stepped forward, replying, "Yes."

Darion exhaled, feeling his nerves ratchet ever higher. "Great," he said, though he didn't feel confident. "Everyone who doesn't need to be in here, please leave."

Vikaris nodded and as Garis and Kragar filed out, followed by Drigidor, a grumbling Cela, and after murmuring in Zola's ear, Soren led Trigger outside. That still left a pretty full tent with Trixon, Vikaris, Trinidad, Lyrianna, Elsra, Zola, Triumph, and Darion.

Hurry up with this, Darion. We have a war to prepare for, Triumph said haughtily.

This time Darion did roll his eyes... and thought of a few choice words for his "friend" in retort.

The interior of the War Tent felt cramped. Illuminated only by a few candles, and a blindingly white light coming from Trinidad, it was distracting. This space wasn't meant for this many bodies.

Vikaris had had it set up temporarily while his full force of troops were scattered all over the Kaulter countryside in rows of tents. Their War Camp had come to Kaulter, and there were people—and creatures—everywhere! They had to get them back to the mainland or else there would be no food left. Darion could hear bustling outside the tent flaps. Soldiers, fletchers, cook women, laundresses, blacksmiths, all the hustle and bustle of a camp. This wasn't the quiet, inspired atmosphere that the Shovlan Tree had been. And Darion hardly knew Zola. Granted, he hadn't spent a terrible amount of time with Lyrianna or Trinidad, but still! Everyone was just standing there looking at him. The intensity in his Father's eyes made him nervous. *So much pressure*, Darion thought, running his hands through his thick curls. The braziers had long since burned up the herbs, giving off an ashy smell. Combined with the Camp odors and close quarters filled with human and unicorn sweat, it didn't create a pleasant work environment.

Unicorns do not sweat, Darion. Now get on with it, Triumph pressed.

Triumph, Darion pleaded. *It doesn't feel the same this time. I can't force it. What if I need to be in the Tree?* He didn't want to voice his concerns aloud but needed to try one last time with Triumph.

Without replying, Triumph urged Zola toward Darion. "Alright Zola, just do whatever Darion says," though he sounded calm, he shot a look of authority at Darion.

Darion knew he had to at least try or else he'd never hear the end of it. "OK fine... Zola stand here, please. I'll put my hand on your forehead and then... well, we'll see what happens."

Zola looked skittish. Her nostrils flared and head reared. Though Darion was fairly tall, unicorns were much taller.

"I'll need to be able to reach your head," he mumbled awkwardly.

She exhaled heavily, and at Triumph's nearby soothing words, she settled, bringing her head down where Darion could comfortably reach it. He stood on the opposite side of the tent from his parents and their respective unicorn companions. Their eyes burned into him. He could feel the hairs rising on the back of his neck at being the gathering's sole focus. Zola was no better. She eyed him suspiciously, and Triumph, off to the side, still murmured soothing words to her while continuing to dog Darion with his commands.

Darion placed his sweaty palm on Zola's stump. He felt her start at the contact, but she did not move. "OK, here goes nothing," Darion whispered, and then closed his eyes.

As soon as he placed his hand upon Zola's forehead, his senses jerked alive. It was as if a force was pulling him under water. He gulped, letting go abruptly and stepping back.

Though it had only been a split-second, Darion felt like he had been held under water for nearly a full minute. His heart pounded, and blood pulsed in his ears. Considering it, he didn't feel fear, just curiosity. He glanced at his Father. "Can you sense her?" he asked him directly.

The King furrowed his brow and closed his eyes momentarily. "No, Darion, nothing beyond the fact that there is a unicorn standing nearby. I... fear I do not 'sense' things as deeply as you do. What did you find?"

"A—"

Zola cut in, "Problem?" She shied away from his raised palm while he tried to calm her.

"No, no, Zola... well, I'm not sure what it is. Can I try again?" Darion asked.

He was still annoyed that Triumph had pushed him into this, but his Father's revelation suggested that perhaps Darion was the only one who could sense what was hidden within beings. Yes, if Darion closed his eyes, like Vikaris, he'd be able to point in the direction of every unicorn in the room and single them out. One could sense—through smell and sound, plus a tingling sensation—whenever in the presence of such majesty. Both Marked Royals could do that, but to sense what was buried within, at one's core—the swirling vortex of hidden emotions—*that apparently only I can do,* Darion considered. *But what is that in Zola?*

As Darion studied her, waiting for her to respond, a softer voice piped in.

"I can sense... something... I think. Like a building storm," Lyrianna said, her face inquisitive as she looked at Zola.

You fool! Darion thought, abashed. His Mother was now Marked too. But in a different way... not with the Marked Arm of a human ruler, but with the mark of a unicorn. *She's the connection*, Darion thought excitedly.

"Mother! Yes! That's it. Will you come help me, please?"

Zola snorted, stepping back and eyeing them in growing suspicion.

Triumph stepped up to join her. "Darion," he said quietly, "what is it?"

"We were wrong. It wasn't just me that helped Trinidad. It was only through the connection with my Mother. I..." he paused, smiling at her as she stepped up to him, "*we* did it. Somehow, she is a link to the unicorn power. That's what her Mark is; it's different from ours," Darion said, gesturing to Vikaris, who was also now standing.

Vikaris looked skeptical, but to his credit, he didn't speak. Darion knew the King was intrigued or else he would have already left to go about his work. Elsra stood immobile... watching intently, as did Trixon and Trinidad, but they did not interfere.

"Mother, do what you did with Trinidad, and if it's okay I'll touch both of your foreheads at the same time, as I did in the Tree. Alright?"

Lyrianna's presence seemed to have a calming effect on Zola. The Queen murmured something in her sweet voice before placing her hand gently upon Zola's neck, lightly running her fingers down Zola's mane.

Darion exhaled, excitement building. This was something. He just knew it. Once Lyrianna and Zola were connected, Darion took a deep breath and placed one palm on Zola's stump and the other on Lyrianna's Marked forehead, his eyes closing to focus.

What he found nearly swept him away. A tempest of power and swirling light threatening to pull him under. Clenching his jaw, he stood firm. He knew there was something to all of this, and he had to identify it. This was nothing like his previous experiences. This was a fountain of power. *But who is controlling it? Zola? Lyrianna? A hidden force?* Then Darion's mind shot straight to Morta.

Standing against the torrent was difficult, but Darion began to think of himself as firm. As if he were invulnerable to this force. The winds that seemed to be coming against him lessened, and he began to notice new things within the force. A deep sadness welled up in him as he navigated through what he was beginning to identify as Zola's emotions—powerful feelings that were near the brink of eruption. What he found as he sifted through this storm was a confused spirit. Strong and terrified. Powerful yet so weak. Proud but insecure. Maternal yet childlike herself. Zola was conflicted. And deeper down, as he looked through the pure swirling vortex of light and immense power, there was a tiny, wriggling, black essence. It looked like a worm lying at the bottom of an ocean of light.

As Darion identified the worm, a reeking scent of tar filled his nostrils. He gagged internally, surprised by its bitterness. When he looked upon it, it seemed to enlarge, growing and filling more and more of the land beneath the serene sea. The light waves began to crash around him, threatening Darion's position once more. He combatted the waves of fear, anger, rejection, humiliation, and outrage, focusing solely on the receding, peaceful waves. He imagined those growing and casting the others out. Waves of peace, joy, radiance, and love. The seas calmed and a quiet stillness broke out.

The worm decreased in size but remained below the surface. Darion felt fearful that he was at an impasse. If he focused on examining the worm again, the darker emotions would take over, but if he left it there, he knew—without really needing to know why—that she would never become whole. Zola would never rise to her position in society as a leader amongst others, being kin of the First Horn. She was tarnished. Captive. Imprisoned by this wriggling darkness infesting her core. Like with any vermin, it needed to be eradicated.

Darion let his mind wander to Lyrianna's spirit. Unsurprisingly, she was a beacon of light. Where Zola was a turbulent vortex, Lyrianna's spirit shined like the clearest night sky dangling a hanging crescent moon glowing and framed by a multitude of bright stars. Music seemed to fill the air, and a warmth flooded through Darion's body as if renewing his energy. He rubbed his thumb reassuringly upon his Mother's forehead but did not break concentration or open his eyes.

I have to kill the worm, he thought, not totally understanding what it was or meant. As he thought it, a frenzied buzzing sound came from somewhere nearby. He seemed to remember hearing a buzzing earlier, but he couldn't place it. *No time for that now*, he admonished. Breathing deeply, he focused all his energy upon the worm while holding back the rise of waves crashing angrily against him.

Go away. You do not belong here. This one is claimed.

Upon hearing this, Darion felt strangely unafraid. He actually laughed. This... *this* worm was going to try to claim a unicorn? *Not gonna happen*, Darion thought.

It cannot imprison her spirit. Darion sensed this coming from his Mother.

Imprisoned. If anyone knew what that was like, Lyrianna did. This emboldened Darion further.

No! He yelled in his mind at the darkness. *This one is light! This is a unicorn of the First Horn. The mightiest, most beautiful creatures of the land.*

The darkness seemed to grow and squirm.

Darion began drawing it out, as if grabbing ahold of it with his own hands. The worm needed to be pulled out of the core and thrown away, much like Soren's infection.

The darkness grew even larger, more encompassing, and the waves began to crash down hard upon Darion, making his head pound with the torrential force. A wicked laugh erupted from the maelstrom. Darion began to lose his grip on the worm while waves pounded even harder. The laughter grew louder as the being sensed a victory over this intruder.

You are weak, it teased. *Weaker than this one.*

A thought trickled into Darion's mind at the mention of weak. *Zola… weak?* Images flashed in Darion's mind.

Zola birthing another foal only to have it taken from her.

Master petting Zola.

Master abusing Zola with his lies and instruments.

The effects of Zola's drugs wearing off.

Seeing Trigger for the first time.

Master taking Trigger.

Killing his fat helper.

Destroying the Barn and the guard who hurt Trigger.

Finding safety with Triumph.

Triumph! Darion's heart soared. Zola wasn't weak! She had been a victim. She was the child of Triumph, the most incredible and powerful and loyal of friends. New images flashed in Darion's mind. The waves then started to recede, and the laughter morphed into howls.

Triumph crying over the loss of his family.

Triumph slaying more than twenty Rav'Arians singlehandedly at the sight of his injured friends.

Triumph standing up to the beast outside the Tar Pits to protect Darion.

Triumph facing down Zalto, a fire-breathing dragon!

And the sight of Triumph running toward his daughter when he sensed her at the Lake. Triumph had nearly burst with joy over the sight of his child. Triumph did not see her as weak. She was his beloved daughter!

Zola was not going to fall to any darkness nor be subjected to Master's evil taint any more. She was of Triumph, which meant she was Darion's family now.

Finding a strength unknown even to himself, Darion stood straight-backed, imagining himself greater and stronger and in complete control during the storm. He renewed his pull upon the worm that had now shrunk to a miniscule wriggling entity. It was trying to bury itself and hide from the building green light washing the surface as Darion's spirit and force came after it. Darion viewed it as a maggot in his food, or worse, on his body. One does not leave it there to fester. The maggot must be removed.

"She is mine," Darion growled at it and imaging himself yanking the maggot-like worm, grinding it up in his fingertips, and throwing it away from himself. It loosed one last ear-splitting scream before bursting and disappearing instantly. As it did, the waves that Darion had long since stopped paying attention to, settled. It was like the calm that comes after a hurricane, when the waters still and the onlookers release their breath. There is a peace that comes... not an inexperienced one, like that of before the storm, but a deeper peace that comes from having survived it. Zola would know that peace, Darion could feel it. The life waters of her soul seemed to feel it too. Light, as if a sunrise, began to bloom all around, swirling yellows, golds, and violets.

Darion took a deep breath. He could feel with his right hand that the horn had not grown. He focused on it for a time, but nothing else came.

Opening his eyes, his head felt heavy, and he was hit with extreme fatigue... surprised to find that Lyrianna's face looked worn too. He looked into Zola's eyes, which he thought—knowing full well it could be simply his imagination—seemed more alive. He felt an energy from her that he had not felt before.

"Zola, I'm sorry I couldn't—"

Before he could finish, she rubbed her cheek upon his, and in a singsong voice, gushed, "No... You have done everything! I feel free!"

Darion felt surprise... and a deep joy at hearing it. She had never sounded like that before.

Triumph walked up and rubbed his cheek upon Zola's, and then Darion's.

"You have done a wondrous thing today, Darion. Two wondrous things," Elsra's regal voice declared, nodding to both Zola and Trinidad.

"But I couldn't get your horn to grow back, Zola. I'm sorry, I don't know why. There was a... barrier. But it's gone now. Hopefully your horn will come back some day... maybe I can try again."

Zola was nodding. "I could feel it—all of it. Under Master I felt nothing, but since then, I have felt too much. You have given me control, Darion. I can be in my own head now without feeling shame."

Darion smiled, unsure of what else there was to say. Looking at Triumph, he worried that he had let him down.

Don't be an idiot, Triumph sighed. Then added warmly, *You make me proud everyday, Darion.*

"That was..."

Darion turned to look at the last speaker. His Father.

"Darion, that was incredible. Though I could not sense all that just took place, any of us could see that you have supreme power. The Creator has gifted you greatly." Vikaris strode up to Darion—and Lyrianna, who still stood there looking tired yet pleased. Grabbing Darion by the shoulders, Vikaris's green intense stare looked into Darion's.

He was surprised to see tears in his Father's eyes.

"Son, please forgive me for my ignorance. You have grown greatly. I see that now. You are our hope. Like the image on the frieze, you will be the one to destroy Morta. I will help you—and I may question you now and then, as is my right as King and your Father," he hesitated, smiling now, "but I will never again deny the truth of what you are. A man." Vikaris squeezed Darion's shoulders with emphasis.

Darion smiled, but before he could answer, a dazed looking Soren burst into the Tent.

"Is Trigger with you?"

CHAPTER 16

The Spy

Deep below the cool water's surface, Shannic searched. He knew it was fruitless, but how else would he fill his time? They were trapped without a way to return to the waters surrounding the continent and the farther Isle of Kaulter. None of the landwalkers seemed to know that the waters connected. *How else did they suppose the Merfolk had inhabited both areas since creation?*

He thought of the ignorant humans and beasts he had observed over his many years, his last encounter swimming up in his mind: the hornless unicorn who had escaped with her unique son. While Shannic had little contact with the unicorns, he knew that it was not common to see one missing a horn and the other dark as the deepest waters. Unicorns usually wore a shimmering silver coat, like the glow of the moon upon the sea. *How had that child come to be,* he wondered for the millionth time as he swam aimlessly. He knew the futility of scouring the lakebed once again. He liked to swim, though—alone. It helped him clear his mind of the pressures of caring for the imprisoned Merfolk. The weight of responsibility fell upon his shoulders all too often. His kind were trapped. Hungry. Scared. Hopeless. No one was coming for them... they had long since let go of that dream.

No Rav'Arians had come for many days, for which Shannic was glad. But it left them with foreboding. Narco had always sent his minions for food... and to bring about despair wherever they could by harming them into submission. *What was happening on the outside? What did it mean if the landwalkers stopped coming to their holding?*

Shannic searched on. He knew that treading and listlessly waiting for another torturer to come was ridiculous. This may be the opportunity he had always prayed for. He knew that long ago, when this war began, he had heard of a key which could unlock the dam. He had always looked for it, but now he renewed his focused energy on one purpose. Saving his remaining kind. If the Rav'Arians were not coming, then he needed to use this time to his greatest advantage. He needed to bring down the dam and get out of here... to reunite with the Kaulter survivors and never again allow themselves to be netted into the humans' games.

***

"We must hurry," the hushed voice commanded to Trigger, as he tottered behind.

Trigger trembled slightly at the sound of the voice. His mother had saved him from this man before. She had said he would never hurt him again... but he was here. He had found Trigger. He had been in his dreams ever since the barn, though Trigger was too young to understand it and alert anyone. No one paid him much attention anyway.

His mother's intensity scared him. The Kaulter unicorns' scornful looks made him feel ashamed, though he couldn't say why. He had never seen his image, after all, and knew nothing of his differences... only that they looked down their noses at him. Morta, the hooded man with the creepy laugh and pale skin, told him time and time again of his distinction from the Kaulter unicorns. He was nothing. He was worthless. He was too different. Undesirable. He would never belong. But, Master, as Morta now referred to himself, would care for him. Trigger wasn't so sure, but he had no one else. He believed no one and in nothing. His mother was self-consumed, busy reuniting with her father, and had too little time for her son.

Trigger stumbled. A stinging sensation captured his attention as Morta smacked him hard with the flat part of his blade. Trigger sucked in his breath as he caught sight of Morta's hood falling to reveal a stern expression. His eyes were not friendly eyes. They were... scary. Trigger worried that he had done the wrong thing not telling his mother. But Morta, wicked as he was, had been the only constant in his life that he could remember. Trigger felt resignation well up inside of him. Whatever happened to him was probably what he deserved, since he was nothing to no one. No help would come, he assumed sadly. Morta was his home now, and he would do best to remember that.

As they ran up the hill toward the Portal, a large unicorn, one from the Kingdom, stepped out from the surrounding brush, followed by some of the palest humans Trigger had ever seen... distinctly different from the bronzed Darion and his father. These humans looked as if the sun was hurting their eyes, scrunching them up and keeping their hoods drawn so that only ghostly white faces stared out. They looked sickly—and terrifying. Trigger looked from them to Morta. *They look alike,* Trigger realized.

And then to his horror, one of them dragged out a prisoner. Trigger had seen some of the nymphs flitting by as he walked with his Mother and heard her conversation with Soren about the different species. Nymphs guarded the Portals and worked as messengers surrounding the Woods of the Willow and beyond. They came in all sizes and colors, and the females wore little clothing. And they had wings and hovered above the ground. Trigger remembered thinking that he wished he had wings because he found it hard to keep pace with the grownups.

This one didn't look like the rest, though. This one's face was bloodied and bruised. To Trigger's horror, as the nymph was thrown to the ground, he saw that bloodied ridges remained on its back. His wings had been torn off! Trigger felt his pulse skyrocket, and he began shaking everywhere as he watched Morta draw his blade. Unconsciously, Trigger started backing up, thinking of nothing now but escape.

A low rumbling came from the unicorn near him, cutting off his retreat. The large beast wreaked even more terror in Trigger. He froze, unable to take his eyes off the nymph who was trying, despite his many injuries, to stand. The male jutted his jaw out and spat, "You will never be King. You are an imposter."

Morta laughed, throwing back his hood.

The sound made Trigger's skin crawl.

Morta threw off his cloak to reveal a more upright, powerful looking man than what Trigger remembered. And his hand... it was back! Trigger specifically remembered that he had only had one, and now that he looked at the man with the pale, mottled skin and balding head, he saw that in proper clothing, and with his metal skin and blade drawn, he looked powerful.

In one smooth motion with his metal hand, Morta grabbed the nymph, raising him in the air so that they came face to face.

The nymph's eyes widened.

In his cackling voice, Morta whispered, "You are correct, Bertin. I have been an imposter long enough. I no longer hide in the shadows, for now," as he spoke he slammed his knife into Bertin's chest. The nymph groaned and his body spasmed as Morta continued, "now, I will destroy you all."

And in that instant Trigger knew he had chosen wrong. He watched as Morta threw the body to the side of the Portal entrance where the guards' bodies were already littered. Morta waved his hand in a smooth gesture, and before Trigger knew it, he was being pushed toward the Portal by the large, towering unicorn and pale-skinned strangers.

Morta smiled a serpentine grin. "Come, my pet. You will be my greatest prize. You will grow to become my steed."

Trigger felt his heart plummet as his hooves hit the water. He had chosen wrong… now he was on the wrong side.

Mother, he thought panicked.

Another blow came, this time with Morta's fist colliding with Trigger's head. "Enough of that," he growled. "You are mine. No one will be coming for you." And then, as if to himself, he laughed wildly, nodding at the large unicorn to use his horn—however he did it, Trigger did not know—but as the water began to glow and their exit drew near, Morta whispered softly, "I have made sure of it."

***

The tent erupted as worried family members darted out, following on Zola's heels as she interrogated Soren. Darion and Triumph shared a look of concern. Triumph was his grandfather, after all.

"He was just here!" Soren was saying, panic edging his voice. "I told him I sensed something… it felt wrong, and the next minute I was surrounded by villagers all coming to see if I had word of the war. They surrounded me, obscuring my view, and when I told them that this was not the time and that the King would share soon, they departed. And when they did, Trigger was gone! I followed them quickly, but I could see for myself he was not with them. I circled our tent and then came here to you. It has only been moments. I am sure he is alright," though the panic in Soren's voice said otherwise.

"A wrongness," Elsra murmured, "You are right, Soren. I can sense an evil that was not here before. It feels as if it is washing over us."

The worm, Darion thought, feeling more terror than he had in a long time. Now that the moment had passed with Zola, he could still sense that wriggling darkness. That terror. That hold upon them all. Morta was here!

"Darion believes it is Morta," Triumph blurted. And though under normal circumstances Darion would have been annoyed at his friend for reading his thoughts and revealing them so quickly, this was not the time for pettiness.

Zola whinnied, her eyes rolling and her head swiveling to study the area. "No," she whispered. All sense of peace and calm that had washed over her moments ago seemed to be fading as her maternal instinct to protect her child rose. Darion could see the wall coming up again within her. They needed to find Trigger... and fast!

"We split up... search everywhere," Vikaris commanded, his hand going instinctively to the sword at his belt.

Trixon's booming voice added, "We will ride to Garis and Kragar to alert the guards and search the area," as the King jumped upon his back. "Have faith, Zola. We will find him."

Darion looked at the party, momentarily frozen, watching the King ride off on Trixon. "Well, let's split up!" Darion snapped. "Everyone spread out... and be careful. He could be anywhere," Darion warned.

Triumph was whispering in Zola's ear. She shook her mane, and whinnied angrily, "I will not allow others to look for my son. I am going now!" Zola snapped forcefully and began walking toward the back of the tent and beyond. Triumph looked at Darion, but before they could speak, Soren cut in.

"I will go after her," he added, nodding to them.

"If you see any of those villagers, you should have someone interrogate them... and find Edmond too," Darion called as he was walking away. Darion knew his friend had been with his brother again while the Royals and leaders met. He was trying to spend as much time with the boy before they set off to lay siege, no doubt, to Darion's rightful home.

But Darion couldn't think about that at the moment.

Get on my back, Triumph ordered, breathing heavily. Angrily!

Darion didn't argue. He swung up with ease upon his companion's back and was surprised to see Lyrianna already sitting upon Trinidad in his silver brilliance.

Elsra had already departed, rushing toward the Fortress to secure it and warn the guards there.

"We will head toward the Portal and surrounding hills," Triumph said hastily, already beginning to walk.

Trinidad nodded, calling, "We will search the interior of the camp and village."

Darion turned to wave as he heard his mother's sweet voice call out, "Be careful."

"Darion," Triumph said softly as he galloped through the village, surprising many a passerby. He was moving fast. "I have a very bad feeling about this. Whatever it is that was in Zola, I can still sense it. It is everywhere. Spawning. Evil has come to Kaulter, Darion. And I fear what we will find."

Darion knew exactly what he was talking about. He could sense it too. He closed his eyes and focused his senses in time to discern a residue to the air. "Shit," he blurted. For it was as if an arrow pointed directly from his position toward the evil taint. The Portal. And in that moment, he knew. They were too late.

"Hurry, Triumph! He's taken him to the Portal."

Triumph cursed while speeding over the ground faster than Darion ever thought possible. Skidding to a halt at the side of the pool, where the Kaulter Portal was accessed, they found a terrible sight.

"NO," Triumph roared as he neared them. Discarded corpses at the edge of the Pool. Darion recognized one of the corpses, a guard from the sparring ground. As he looked closer, he saw, too, a nymph's headless corpse.

UNICORNS… to me! He has taken him through the Portal! Triumph's panging cry was so loud and feral that Darion flinched at the sound.

Hours later, Elsra, Zola, and Soren returned to the Fortress, along with Cela and Edmond for protection. Though no one had asked Edmond to guard them, he felt sickened and truly guilty about having enjoyed a game of cards with Anton while the foal was being abducted.

After the shocking discovery, the smoldering anger in King Vikaris, the intensity in Zola, and the rage overtaking Triumph—having to be held back from going after Trigger immediately—and the shrieking wails of Bertin's sisters, Darion fretted, exhaustion tugging at him. He had, after all, healed Trinidad and Zola (well, not fully, but that worm was gone, at least), and after Trigger's abduction, Darion longed for his feathered bed. He was nodding off in the War Tent, his head falling back and then waking with the movement. Breathing deeply, he tried to shake himself alert. The air was stuffy, and Darion's lids felt heavy. He sat in the tent with Garis, Kragar, Vikaris, Lyrianna, Drigidor, Triumph, Trixon, and Trinidad.

"My King, we have waited long enough. As we saw today," Garis pressed, nodding slightly in Triumph's direction, "Kaulter is no longer safe. The enemy is emboldened. We must move. The food stores here are not enough to sustain our force. If Morta resides in the Castle, then it is there we must strike."

"Yes, but…" Vikaris circled his fingertips on his temples, "the Castle and Village around it are heavily fortified. What are you suggesting, Garis? Lay siege to my rightful home? Invade the Castle?"

Darion wanted to roll his eyes. Sometimes his father could be so obstinate. Though not yet a seasoned warrior, even Darion knew that this was the only way forward. They had tried to fight Narco's forces… for years on open ground. And though they'd won and held the enemy off from invading the Camp or Kaulter, Morta was a different enemy. He was cunning, and he was gathering forces. They needed to attack him immediately before he came to them. Again.

"With all due respect, Your Majesty," Kragar croaked in his steely voice while crossing his muscled arms, "it would not be the first time the Castle has been invaded."

Vikaris's glare could have cut glass! "Yes, I am aware of that, Lieutenant. That is the night that my parents were slain in their beds."

Kragar shifted slightly on his feet but did not break his stare. "Then we know it is possible to infiltrate," Kragar said in a softer tone, though softer for Kragar still could have made the toughest of men nervous. He was a hard man.

Darion stifled another yawn, fearing the wrath of the warriors. He wondered if he could sneak out. Looking at the ferocity in his father's face, he was not about to ask him.

"Say we do 'attack' the Castle," Trixon cut in. "What do you suggest? Throw our full force at it, or do you have something else in mind?"

The candlelight danced at his words, and an audible catch sounded from Trinidad's throat. "You mean to sneak someone inside the Castle?" The wise unicorn sounded horror stricken.

"Now just hold on," Garis raised his impressive arms in a gesture to stave off argument.

Vikaris looked as if he had swallowed rocks. "Another soul to be thrown mercilessly into the enemy's clutches?"

Garis scowled at the comment. "My King," he began in a kind, but authoritative tone, "what happened to

Gruegor is not your fault." Hurrying on, before Vikaris could retort, he pressed, "And furthermore, we need someone on the inside. To scout… and to open the gates. It would be so much easier that way."

"And our troops would be where?" Vikaris looked angry but refrained from an argumentative tone. For the sake of planning, he was at least trying to understand his Commander's idea, for which Darion was glad. He was tired of arguing. The abduction earlier had frayed everyone's nerves.

Darion thought on that, looking at Triumph from his peripheral. His friend had not spoken during this entire exchange—*he's uncharacteristically quiet,* Darion thought. Triumph looked to be in a daze. The events of the day hadn't just worn him down… no, he was feeling great shame for letting Zola down. Darion patted his companion's neck, causing Triumph to shudder at his touch. Darion paused, looking at him.

"Are you okay?" He whispered to his friend. Triumph's eyes looked hollow.

He shook his head once but did not reply to Darion's question. Darion swallowed uneasily. Triumph did not usually admit to his feelings… especially in front of others. Darion feared Triumph's worry would have a ripple effect and its weight would reverberate throughout the Council. Darion could not let that happen.

"We will get him back, Triumph."

Triumph's one visible eye bore into Darion, but still he did not speak.

"I will go," a thunderous voice announced into the silence.

"Drigidor, I appreciate your willingness, but we need you to lead the Unicorn warriors, as is your role." Vikaris said quickly, waving away his offer.

"And I," a warmer, but no less resolved voice, chimed in.

Darion gaped. *Trinidad!*

"What? No, my friend, that is madness…" Vikaris stood, looking alarmed, shielding off his friends' words with his Marked hand, while at the same time, Trixon boomed, "No, Father. You cannot risk yourself."

"As will I," a musical voice added as Lyrianna appeared at the tent flaps.

Vikaris's face spoke volumes. "There is no way I am letting you go back there," he snarled. Darion knew it wasn't anger at his Mother, but rather, fear for her well-being.

She can't go!

Lyrianna strolled up to the table, passing by Trinidad with a brush of fingertips through his now shining mane as she walked toward Vikaris. But as she did so, she stopped in front of Darion.

It was at that moment that Darion noticed a note in her hand.

Foreboding filled him, though he couldn't say why. The look in her eyes. The way the paper appeared to have been crumpled and then smoothed back out. Whatever it was, it wasn't good. Darion had spent more time with his

Mother in the last few days and was beginning to see the depth within her.

Her lips lifted, attempting a smile that did not reach her eyes.

"Word has just arrived from our furthest scouts. It came to the Fortress, and I brought it here as soon as I received it."

"My dear," Vikaris said quietly, "You did not need to bring it at this hour. A messenger could have carried it," Vikaris said, reaching for the note but still not quite seeing what Darion sensed.

"I... could not," she replied. "It... it has to do with," here she paused looking at Darion, "Riccus and Antonis."

Darion felt his heart begin to hammer in his chest.

"They have been captured by the trolls. The nymphs who roam the passageways upon and around the mountains have sent word. Two men appear to be with them... alive," she added, looking at Darion's expression.

Lyrianna's announcement was met with a volley of questions from the men, unicorns, and centaur.

What? How many Trolls? What about Aalil? Where was this report from? When were they sighted?

"Here," she said, thrusting the paper into her husband's outstretched hand.

Darion barely resisted the urge to rip the paper out of Vikaris's hand.

Triumph, now coming out of his daze, leaned upon Darion in reassurance.

After scanning the document, Vikaris looked up and met Darion's eyes. Darion bit his lip, fending off his own questions... or tears.

"Son," Vikaris nodded at him, "it is true. They have been sighted. Their appearances described here... it is them. No mention of Aalil though."

Darion recalled his excitement for Tony when he'd heard about their romance. Oregon Tony would have never taken the plunge. Darion felt his stomach plummet. *What had they done to her? Antonis must be heartbroken.* Darion felt sick at the loss of another life. This Tony will be heartbroken.

"There is a large force coming down from their mountain holds. They will head to the Castle, under Morta's direction, no doubt. Garis is correct, we must hasten toward them, for if the trolls are already arriving, we can only assume the Rav'Arians and these... Watchers... from Rav'Ar are as well. We must attack the Castle." Lyrianna's voice was firm.

"I'll go," Darion blurted. Looking at Triumph and then his parents. "They have my Dad. I'm going. If you need someone to get inside the Castle, it should be me."

Vikaris was shaking his head before Darion had even finished, which made him angry. "You said it yourself," Darion glared, pointing at Garis, "we need someone on the inside. It should be me."

"Darion, that is impossible," Vikaris countered. "The Prophecy speaks of you defeating Morta... we cannot risk you being killed or captured before the time is right. I am sorry, Son. I do not want to sound heartless, and I too wish to free my friends, but it cannot be you."

The room suddenly shifted. The air felt tense and dark, but a brilliance was growing to Darion's right. He could sense something happening. Glancing over, he saw Trinidad stepping forward, and with him, Lyrianna. She moved steadily toward her bonded unicorn companion. As she placed her hand upon his neck, the Mark upon her forehead gave off a glow.

"We will go," Lyrianna spoke serenely.

Vikaris slammed his fist down angrily. "Absolutely not. You are my wife. You are the Queen. You have only just been freed from them!"

Darion felt the hairs on the back of his neck begin to rise at the intensity of his father's vehemence. Strangely, Lyrianna did not seemed cowed by it, though even Kragar had taken a slight step backwards at the anger fanning from his King.

"We know the Castle and the enemy better than any of you do presently, Vikaris," Trinidad replied softly. "Because we were there most recently, we know their weaknesses. We will get in, locate the captives, and open the gates."

Vikaris folded his toned arms, his Marked Arm beginning to glow on its own, and shook his head stubbornly.

Darion felt he was betraying his father because he was beginning to see the merit in Trinidad's words. They did know the Castle layout and dungeons better than anyone... certainly better than Darion would.

"Mighty Trinidad, how do you expect to remain hidden? I mean, you are glowing," Garis said waving his hand toward Trinidad.

It was a good point, Darion capitulated. Trinidad definitely does stand out.

"There are ways," Lyrianna cut in. "And... we are going. We are the only ones who can. Vikaris, please see reason. I know it is difficult, but..." at this, she sighed before looking at Darion. "Darion, I will not watch you lose Riccus too."

The strength of her gaze, shoulders squared and chin held high, could've rivaled any warrior's, Vikaris's included.

"Dear, you are the one who must see reason," Vikaris pleaded, panic edging his voice. "Do not do this. Should Darion lose you in exchange for Riccus? The cost is too great. I am sorry, Darion, but it is. I will not have my wife risk her life out of guilt for Carolina's death. It was tragic and terrible, yes, but my darling," Vikaris's voice softened as he walked around the table to join Lyrianna. "You are not at fault for her death. You have to stop blaming yourself."

Darion felt like he had been slapped. *Blaming herself?*

Her chin rose an inch higher, yet she reached out to grasp her husband's hand. "Whether that is true or not, I have made my decision, Vikaris, and..." at this she placed a hand upon the King's cheek. "We are expendable, where none of the rest of you are."

Vikaris reared back at her words.

Darion coughed in startlement.

"You do not say that ever again…" Tears formed in Vikaris's face, fully illuminated by the glow of Lyrianna's Mark.

She stepped back, looking to Trinidad, who stood upright and nodded. "We have discussed it, Vikaris. You must lead the troops," she paused to gesture at Darion, "and you, your place is with your Father, and, of course, Triumph, Trixon… and Drigidor," she looked over at the towering warrior, and motioned to Garis and Kragar. "You all have a place. You all can fight. I cannot…. Elsra has Kaulter, and even she is choosing to fight, and I…" she stood straighter. "I am expendable," she lifted her hands to ward off arguments. "I speak the truth. I will not go down in our historical records as the Queen who was foolishly captured and then sat out the remainder of the war, idly picking flowers… at the expense of everyone she loved. No," her voice grew in cadence and authority. "I will not sit this fight out, Vikaris. We all must play our part, and I know the Castle. I know the enemy. And," she paused in resignation, "I know that I will never be able to look myself in the mirror if Riccus is killed while I do nothing."

Surprisingly, Darion actually agreed with her… not with the expendable part, but with her having a role. Who else could they send to the Castle? She had been there most recently, and she knew the passageways in and out of the surrounding area. He felt terrible guilt and shame at the thought, though.

"It is sound reasoning," Triumph spoke for the first time all evening.

Vikaris, working his jaw but not uttering any intelligible words, glared at him.

Trixon rumbled with ferocity surpassing that of his King. It was his father, after all, that Lyrianna was thinking of placing back in danger. Trixon was shaking his head resolutely, "No, there is nothing sound about this. I disagree," Trixon rumbled, turning toward his father, "You are a unicorn, not a spy. Your place is here in Kaulter, Father. Please."

"They will not be alone, Your Majesty," and though uninvited, Cela pushed her way through yet again. Her ivory coat, pale skin, and flame red hair suddenly appearing as if an apparition, she stepped up to Lyrianna's opposite side.

Trinidad rumbled, raising his head ever higher. His horn sharper than any blade. His eyes remained fixed on Trixon and Vikaris. "We have decided."

Trixon dipped his head, though the angry and fearful aura did not fade from him.

Vikaris walked back to his seat without a word. "So be it," he said icily. "You three will go ahead and enter the Castle, and the rest of us will begin to march the main force toward the Castle... and Creator help us, we can only pray that we will all meet once this is finished."

CHAPTER 17

The Getaway

The jagged rocks and loose gravel made walking difficult. Aalil stumbled along blinded by the bright sunlight as they left the cave tunnel to march a path marked out by the guards. The female and children captives, as Aalil came to think of them, for they certainly weren't free like the male trolls, were dispatched after breakfast. They were told nothing except to remain silent and to move quickly. Aalil was grateful for D'Ania's presence and the small gift of bread earlier. That had long since worn off, but Aalil knew that any food intake meant energy and she needed fuel in order to get out of here and find Antonis and Riccus. She had neither seen nor heard anything of their whereabouts since being captured. She had overheard some mulling guards on the beach speak of "the war" and "must hurry," but beyond that, she knew nothing. She assumed her group was moving to the heart of Nav'Aria, but being this high up in the mountains, it would take some time to get there. She shivered recalling her earlier climbs. The dark cave interiors lined with scraping, swooping bats! If the females and children were being marched, then that meant the males must not be far. They had to all be going in the same direction, right? Or—she tripped on a loose stone, bumping into D'Ania. She grimaced an unspoken apology, quickly righting herself.

What if they were taking the males to Nav'Aria and the females deeper into the mountains? They hadn't seen a large force of males since the beach, come to think of it. She had been so consumed with her worry for Antonis and her feelings of shame for being captured and then fretting over hunger pains, that she had completely missed the many obvious signs before her!

Idiot! Antonis might be moving in a different direction.

Swinging her head around, she surveyed their surroundings. She realized that she needed to get away from this captive line soon and find the force of male trolls headed toward Nav'Aria. *Narco is mobilizing... he might remember Antonis and Riccus. That is one reunion that cannot happen!*

She observed there were far fewer male trolls accompanying her party than there had been earlier. She had assumed they were moving at a faster pace to keep up with the males ahead. But what if the males were headed to the "war," and they had left guards to take the females to another hidden location separate from the battlefield? The more she thought on it, the more likely it seemed. They wouldn't bring the females and children to the fight, not if they were being treated like this. From what she could tell, they didn't have blades or battle experience.

The females and children would only be in the way. Yet as she looked at them, she felt an inkling of hope. She realized these trolls, though large and fearsome, were not fully grown males. These looked to be adolescents.

It made sense, she reasoned. They left the younger, inexperienced trolls in charge. *And yet this*, she thought smugly to herself, *is something I am used to after years of putting up with crap from my male counterparts.* It gave her an edge, she thought, looking at them. They may have sent off their warriors, but they didn't realize they had left one in the thick of it. She smiled to herself, turning her attention to the guards' behaviors. They had left a snake in a children's nursery, and they didn't realize it. *Good,* she thought, looking around. Time to use her hunger pains, shame, and worry to feed her rage and propel her forward.

I need to kill them, get away, and save Antonis and Riccus. Not so hard, she thought, knowing that it would be near impossible. And yet, whenever she felt moments of doubt, she thought of all the battles she'd faced previously in her life. She was a tested warrior, and this was just another challenge for her to prove that she was indeed capable and did not need a rescuer. Smiling inwardly, she thought how much she would enjoy holding this over Antonis's head for years to come. The one time she saved him from the trolls. It would be a good story, and they would tell their children and laugh about it… but it hadn't happened yet. That was the future she desired. Now, she needed to act to make it happen.

As the sun reached its zenith, Aalil and the other captives were led to an alcove in a tunnel that let some sunlight stream in. The light and temperature changed as they went from cave to path and back to cave bothered Aalil, but she chose not to focus on it. One younger guard approached her and the others near her. Though their hands were bound, their legs had been left free for marching. The guard handed out a piece of dried meat to each troll, but passed over her awaiting hands. She knew he was staring at her, hoping to goad her into arguing. She chose to play the submissive, fearful role. He looked as if he were trying to decide whether he should tease her or not. Lifting his ugly face into the air just a hair, he turned and swaggered back to the other guards to enjoy a good chuckle.

D'Ania, Aalil noted, seemed to pick up on the social cues easily. She feigned an uninterested expression, but as soon as the guards moved back to speak, backs toward their captives, she handed her piece to Aalil.

"Share," D'Ania murmured, giving Aalil the food.

Aalil paused before taking a bite, eyeing her. "How do you know I will not just eat it all?"

D'Ania's face, with troll features and strange greyish skin, seemed more expressive than the others Aalil had seen... or perhaps, she just hadn't studied the species long enough. D'Ania's eyebrow raised slightly, and then she looked away calmly. "We share."

Aalil snorted softly. Though she knew she couldn't trust anyone here, she was beginning to like D'Ania. Could she use her?

She tore off a chunk of the meat with her teeth while keeping her eyes on the guards. It was tough, whatever it was. She regurgitated a bit at the thought. *What is this?*

D'Ania must have guessed her thoughts, for she took the meat and tore off a chunk with her larger, sharp teeth. "Ram. Not troll."

Aalil smiled. "I… knew that."

D'Ania chortled, eyebrow raised, but all the while her eyes bespoke friendship and mischief.

Eyeing the guards, Aalil continued to chew, savoring it as she formulated her plan.

"D'Ania, we need to free our hands if we are to get out of here."

"Yes," was all the troll said, and then turned to whisper into the older youngling's ears. The little ones huddled together, sharing their meat as well, for it seemed the guard had not deemed them worth an adult portion—if that's what they called this. Aalil's stomach growled loudly.

But before she could worry about her bodily discomforts, her eyes widened. The child withdrew a thin blade from the interior of its tattered clothing.

Aalil's eyes darted back to the guards. Their backs were to them. There were only three presently. The other two had gone on to scout. She could not be sure how long they would stay away, but she believed this was the opportunity she had been waiting for. She had to act.

Before a word was spoken, D'Ania snatched the blade, even though all hands remained bound at the wrists. She was fluid with her movements, transferring the blade to Aalil smoothly.

The female troll's features remained aloof as she pretended to survey the other captives looking in the opposite direction of Aalil. The guards roared with laughter, and one slapped the other on the back in jest. They possessed huge hindquarters of meat that they munched on while drinking greedily from horned waterskins.

Aalil set to work sawing away at her bindings. The thick corded rope abraded her skin. Darting glances at the guards, she forced herself to remain calm. She wanted to hoot with glee as the bindings fell away. She reached for D'Ania's hands, keeping them low, and began to saw away at her new friend's holds. That took a deal of time longer since her larger wrists had required more rope, but Aalil was methodical. She just kept sawing. Finally, D'Ania's bindings also fell away, and she grabbed the knife to begin removing her foster children's bindings too.

One child's rope remained. Other females became aware of what was happening. They began shifting and looking toward D'Ania.

Panicked, Aalil realized they were going to give them away before the blade was back in her hands. Eyes glancing at the guards, she noted one was beginning to stand.

"Look away," D'Ania's quiet, but forceful whisper urged.

Aalil worried it wouldn't work. She kept her eyes down, not wanting to get the guard's attention just yet.

Footsteps approached. She quickly grabbed the rope and laid it across her coupled wrists. D'Ania keenly feigned the same bound position. The group fell silent.

An approaching guard came closer to examine them. Crunching gravel, its booted feet appeared and stopped in front of Aalil. She froze, her breathing coming more rapidly.

"You," the youth's voice growled. "Tonight."

Aalil squinted. *What?* Then risking a glance, she realized he hadn't stopped in front of her, but D'Ania. He was eyeing her lustily.

"Yes?" He asked, though he knew her acquiescence was moot. "Feel good," he laughed, kicking dirt in the faces of the group before once again sauntering back to his companions. The guards roared ever louder with laughter. The younglings were crying softly, and Aalil could feel the tension emanating from D'Ania.

Aalil kept her eyes on the guards, who were all looking their way. As soon as they drifted back into conversation, she spoke, "We need to kill them."

"Yes," D'Ania replied, and Aalil was surprised by the vehemence in her voice.

She had feared the troll would have qualms about killing her own kind. D'Ania assured her otherwise as she returned to carefully sawing away at the child's bindings. More of the female trolls—this time quietly but more intently—leaned closer. Their looks of apathy and despondency were beginning to break, and now an energy began to pulse from their corner of the cave. Aalil wondered if she could trust them. With all the captives fighting back, these three males could be dealt with swiftly.

She leaned into D'Ania to whisper, "Can we trust these others?"

Dania glanced at the side, as if pondering it, then jerked one quick affirmative nod.

Aalil whispered hurried instructions into D'Ania's ear. Keeping her eyes on the guards, she listened as muffled voices began to relay her message. The knife was to be passed around as fast as possible and the captives were to free their hands. Then, they would attack at once. If the guards approached, the knife was to be handed back—quickly—to the human for the fight.

Before the knife was returned, the guards began standing. One walked toward the cave entrance and urinated in full view of the captives. The other two rolled their shoulders, cracked their necks, belched, and packed their belongings. They strapped their horned waterskins to their belts, tossed aside bones from their midday meal, and turned toward the captives.

It was now or never, Aalil thought. "Knife," she yelled.

The guards, slow and untested, looked at each other, not quite understanding what their human captive had said. They seemed surprised to hear her speak.

Urgently, she looked at the group of females as the males neared them.

"Up," the males roared at their captives, waving their arms with emphasis and glaring at them wickedly. One of the males kicked the nearest female in the stomach. She choked in pain and startlement.

"Fast!" The guard roared, standing over her and yanking her up by her hair. The meat still clenched in his jagged teeth and the gleam in his red greedy eyes completed his image as the monster Aalil knew him to be.

The female cried out in pain and tried to get up, but the troll kicked her again to disable her leg.

Aalil watched, her rage boiling.

The other troll, the one who had spoken to D'Ania, approached, this time with eyes fixed on Aalil.

She knew the charade was up and honestly didn't care. She wasn't any good at playing the submissive weakling. She was a warrior, and she'd rather die with her head held high, blade in hand, than scrape before this bastard troll.

Just as the boots skidded to a halt in front of her, cool metal touched the skin of her palm behind her back. As the troll snarled, she smiled.

Its expression changed as understanding came just a moment too late. Aalil swiftly brought the blade forward and slammed it into the troll's throat. Blood poured out immediately from the gash, and the guard fell clutching his neck. Aalil ripped the thin blade out forcefully, kicking the tottering troll backwards and out of the way. The other guards, one hastily pulling up his trousers while the other ceased harassing the female at the end of the line, both bellowed angrily. Pulling clubs from the fastenings on their backs, they charged.

Pandemonium erupted. For though they knew the human had slain their comrade, they had not expected half of the females to have freed hands... and deadly intent. A group of four females jumped from the line and onto a guard, screaming, biting, punching, and slashing with their long nails. Yes, they were females, who had been held captive, but they were large and enraged… and four against one. The guard fell, gnashing his teeth and roaring as he tried to fend them off, his club never quite making contact with his assailants.

The savagery of the moment froze Aalil. She watched in horror as the females pinned down his arms and legs, and another from the line jumped in to draw the blade from his belt. She stabbed him again and again and again, until his limbs had ceased quivering and the life had left him. Only then did the females pull their dagger-wielding friend off of him.

The last guard watched in horror, his jaw working soundlessly as he backed up, snarling at the group but maintaining eye contact. Aalil knew he'd either fight or bolt. And they couldn't let one get away to warn the others.

"Get him," she cried out, rushing the thick, towering guard.

Just as she reached him, and he swung his club to connect with a female's head, dropping her instantly, a voice screamed, "NO!"

Aalil stood in a defensive stance, covered in the blood from the other troll, and tossed the blade in between her hands. As she and the troll began their dance of death, a figure pushed through the other females. She was old, much older than the majority of the trolls Aalil had seen in the group, and by the looks of her, had known harsh treatment. One of her eyes was missing, and her hair had mostly fallen out. Her skin had an ashy look to it, and her tattered garments barely hung upon her skeletal frame.

The guard paused just for a moment, his eyes flicking toward the female speaker. That gave Aalil just the time she needed to jump at him. She stabbed his arm and simultaneously landed a front kick to the club in his hands, causing it to drop away from him. He growled but stepped back surprisingly, making no attempt to retrieve his club. He looked at the skeletal female again.

"Who is he?" Aalil demanded, looking at the old troll and signaling for D'Ania to scoop up his weapon.

"My son," the woman crowed.

Aalil spat. "Your son is a monster. It would be better to kill him and get away from here. He cannot live to tell the other males."

"Son," the old troll said again, pushing the final trolls in the front out of her way to emerge just before the much larger, towering adolescent troll. "My last son," the old troll sobbed.

The male snarled, "Master's. No son."

Aalil looked around. They had to end this… but then she saw the younglings at the back of the group cowering.

"Damnit," she grumbled. "Fine. Pin him down, but do not kill him. We will get information from him." She was an experienced military leader and knew how to make people jump at her commands. Her cutting, authoritative voice broke up the confusion, and immediately the female trolls leapt to do her bidding. Before the male could react, D'Ania jumped forward and punched him hard in the face, his nose crunching and blood spurting out at the impact.

The old woman shrieked in objection, but it was over in a matter of moments. The felled troll clutched at his wounded face. The females quickly disarmed him of his other weapons. Aalil then found some remaining rope near one of the corpses and bound the troll's hands.

Standing, Aalil glanced at the old troll. "What do you hope to happen now? He is evil like the rest of the males. Why spare him?"

The troll woman scowled at her, and then without speaking, walked up to the male. She motioned her hands as if telling the females guarding him to roll him over. As they did, she pulled at one of his pantlegs pushing it up to reveal, just above his boot and below his knee, a stone embedded into his veiny grey calf.

"What is that?" Aalil asked, curiosity winning out. The black stone looked as if it had burned away the skin. Red tendrils spread out from its position in the leg.

"Evil," the troll mother spat, glaring at the stone. "Why evil," she pressed, staring at Aalil and back to the stone.

"The stone makes him evil?" Aalil guessed, and then the truth dawned before her. Why were the males evil, while the females and children seemed normal? Why had the trolls all of a sudden turned against Nav'Aria so many years ago, after living in peace for many cycles?

"What is it?" she asked stepping closer.

"Gift," the old female croaked derisively.

"What would happen if I cut it out?"

At this, the guard began to wriggle in his bonds. Females from all over the cave came to lend their weight and sat on his limbs, pressing his bloodied face into the dirt while the rest stood with Aalil to inspect it.

"I do," D'Ania announced. She motioned for Aalil to hand her the knife.

Aalil couldn't think of a reason to say no, so she gave her the blade and barked for females to guard both entrances to the cave.

Aalil grabbed a scrap of rope from one of the females cut bindings and shoved it into the troll's mouth for him to bite down on. He was trying to speak, but his words were garbled from the rope.

D'Ania hovered over him, looking to Aalil. "Do it," she ordered her.

What ensued next can only be described as nightmarish. The stone seemed to have grown into his leg, and it wasn't as simple as digging in and popping it out. Rather, it needed to be torn out, spiked tendrils and all. The troll reared and fought with all his might, his agonized cries filling the cavern. The old female troll had to be held back and kept from interfering. But finally it was done. D'Ania stood up looking dazed. Her hands covered in a dark, oozing blood. The stone, with its jagged spiked tendrils was tossed aside. None wanted to touch it. Aalil ordered for his leg to be wrapped. By this time the troll had passed out from the pain.

The females broke into small groups—all except the ones pinning the troll down—to discuss the day's events.

And then a soft, timid voice snapped them back to attention. "What happen?"

Aalil turned, breaking off mid-sentence with D'Ania to look at the male troll. He looked... nicer. She couldn't explain it, but it was as if his entire appearance had changed. His face was still was covered in blood from his broken nose, and his grey bulbous skin gave him a ghoulish appearance, and yet....

"Eyes," D'Ania murmured.

That is it!

His eyes weren't the frightening red color they'd been earlier. Now they had returned to a deep brown, and his mouth was set in a worried, yet kind, smile.

The old woman sobbed, pushing forward and kneeling down at his head. "Son," she cooed.

"Mother?" The troll's voice sounded softer, less threatening and aggressive, truer to one his age.

Aalil signaled for the females holding him to move, and she watched as the troll guard, so threatening and evil from earlier, embraced the weak female carefully. Lovingly.

And just like that, Aalil had freed herself and the female captives. But that's not what made her heart pound excitedly. She had done it! She had come to the mountains to find Riccus, but also to figure out the enigmatic hold Narco had on them. And now she knew. Vikaris needed this information. The trolls were being controlled by the Beast... and these possessive stones. If they could all be removed, Narco would lose an entire section of his army. Hope was in sight!

She glanced at the stone that had moments ago been festering into the youth's legs… and mind. *What power does it hold?* She eyed it, and D'Ania, who was at her side, began inspecting it also.

"We should destroy it," Aalil announced.

D'Ania murmured in agreement, "How?"

Aalil looked at it, not wanting to even touch it. As she considered it, the old troll female approached. Looking her over, Aalil realized that it was not age that had her so withered, but maltreatment. She looked younger close up, her skeletal frame bespoke starvation. *What had they done to her?* Aalil realized there were no old trolls in the group. Only abused survivors, so near death from their captivity and hunger. Aalil felt a fire beginning to burn in her belly. She would see those stones destroyed and that beast beheaded… or die trying. These females—and all that had been suffered silently here in the mountains—would be brought to light. *They will have vengeance*, Aalil vowed.

"I… break," the troll mother replied, dragging her son's club with her. She walked to the stone that had possessed her son, causing him to commit all kinds of atrocities. The club hovered over the stone and with a guttural cry—and more strength than Aalil expected—she slammed the club down to shatter the stone. The shards dissolved into dust, and a swirling black cloud swept over them before escaping out the cave tunnel. The evil that had been housed in that stone was no more. The mother slumped, using the club as a crutch, as she tottered back toward her silently weeping son.

We have to move, Aalil realized. For the first time in days, Aalil's thoughts drifted back to her duties. She was a warrior for King Vikaris. She could no longer sit crying about Antonis, even though it broke her heart to admit it. She had information... very vital information that the King needed. A whole force of trolls led by a terrifying beast was headed his way, and the only way to stop them would be either mass slaughter or removing those stones. She had to get to Nav'Aria and send word. And then she would come back for Antonis and Riccus, wherever they were. She could only pray for their welfare. For now, the fate of the Nav'Aria was at hand.

CHAPTER 18

The Castle

Little Trigger wept.

After emerging from the Portal, he had been roughly tied up and strapped onto one of the other towering unicorns he recognized from the Barn. He thought this one was Number Ten or Eleven, but he hadn't had time to memorize them all before they'd been led to battle many days ago. His memories were fuzzy. Everything was a blur.

His head lolled to the side as he hung from the unicorn's back. Once they'd come from the portal, Morta had backhanded and berated Trigger. He had been crying, and Morta had snarled, "You thought you could leave me, did you? Who do you cry over now? They are nothing. They are all going to die and if you keep this sniveling up, I will make you watch!"

Though it wasn't the first time this man—or the mean guard back at the Barn—had hurt him, Trigger felt shock and confusion.

A woman's voice had interrupted Morta. She placed a pale hand upon his shoulder. "We must go, Master. They will be coming for us."

Morta had spun on her with a verbal berating for touching him, before glaring back at Trigger. "We will leave... but you will tell me everything you have learned about the enemy as soon as we stop."

And so, Trigger had arrived at this side of the Portal to find a group of dark unicorns and pale humans waiting to lead them back to the Castle... to Trigger's prison.

That had been over a day ago. And still he cried— silently now. He tried not to sniffle. The unicorn he was strapped to growled anytime he heard a noise from Trigger and certainly let him know he didn't appreciate having to carry the runaway.

Trigger felt bewildered. He had heard Morta's voice in his mind for days. Calling to him. It had at first sounded like a buzzing sound. Then the words came. Morta had sounded kind then. Almost cooing. Zola had been so distracted in Kaulter, and Trigger had begun looking forward to the voice's kind words and reassurance each day.

He now knew it was all a lie. Morta had been teasing him. He had successfully lured Trigger away from his family. From safety. And Trigger feared more than anything that no one would come for him. Why would they? He looked different than his mother. He didn't feel safe and so he hardly spoke. He had seen the looks his supposed grandmother had cast upon him. Though... his thoughts paused on Triumph and Soren. Those two hadn't seemed ashamed of him, or his appearance. Soren, if anyone, had seemed almost... happy to be in his company.

But that could not be, Trigger thought. He was no one special. Soren had probably already forgotten about him. Zola was so worried about her horn, she probably didn't even remember she had a son. She was happy to be in Kaulter. She wouldn't leave there. Trigger cried harder. He had already had one beating today when he didn't answer Morta's questions fast enough.

"Quit crying," the unicorn growled once more.

Trigger tried to stem his tears, but the anger in the unicorn's voice only made him cry harder.

"You are weak. You have let the enemy's weakness rub off on you," the unicorn snarled.

Trigger didn't reply but thought about it. He didn't think that the Kaulter unicorns were the enemy, but he knew he shouldn't have those thoughts. If Morta "entered" his mind, he might find out that Trigger liked them and then hurt him even further.

They kept a fast pace, and the awkward positioning of being strapped to an adult unicorn made him feel sick. His tiny head throbbed and his stomach ached. He needed his mother.

A stinging slap made him start.

Morta, astride a large unicorn with a saddle, came inches from Trigger's face. "I have decided I will make you watch her die. Your weakness must be broken. It will be beaten out of you once we return to the Castle. We will be there soon. Rest now, young one, for you and I are going to have a long discussion this evening."

Trigger trembled all over as he watched Morta ride ahead. Once the man was out of sight, his stomach heaved. Gagging and choking on his sobs and fear, he was met with scathing disdain from the unicorn he was strapped to. Misery was Trigger's companion.

***

After coming through the Portal, Darion watched as Garis, Kragar, and the pale sisters of the slain Bertin secured their position before allowing Vikaris and Darion to walk out.

Trixon and Triumph followed them, along with Trinidad and Lyrianna. Edmond, Soren, and Cela were behind them, as was Drigidor.

Elsra had elected to stay behind and ensure all was left in good hands at Kaulter, with the promise to catch up to them soon. She had ordered Zola to remain with her. Though the young mother was enraged, she had seen reason as Elsra explained it. Zola was without a horn and not conditioned to fighting. She could help Elsra in other ways while the warriors pressed forward first to search for Trigger. She had seemed angry, but Darion was relieved that the darkness he had detected from her earlier had not returned. She had been healed of that... at least. But her worries had not lessened. She was still without her horn, and more importantly, her son. Triumph had been conflicted, Darion knew, but had not wavered in his march through the Portal. His place was with Darion, and they both knew it. Darion would need him in these final days—and the strength of the military.

Warriors of all shapes and ages flooded into the Woods of the Willow. Centaurs, nymphs, humans, and unicorns kept coming. Thousands of warriors, armed and alert, poured from Kaulter back into mainland Nav'Aria. This time they knew it really was the last battle. The hope of the world clung to their success. Morta was not Narco. He would not hideout behind his fortifications forever. He had just infiltrated Kaulter undetected... twice, actually, if you counted his manipulation of Alice. He was a new enemy... and Vikaris had made it clear to all that he, if left alive, would destroy everything. This was no longer a fight for the King or Nav'Aria, but for life itself.

"I do not like this," Trixon grumbled again. He had wanted scouts to go ahead before exposing the Royals. "Perhaps I should go ahead and look around?"

Vikaris rolled his eyes upward. "Trixon, for the millionth time, NO." Though he kept his voice quiet so only the Royals and Unicorn Council nearby could hear him, Trixon shifted uneasily as if embarrassed... or contemplating disobeying.

"It is safe... for now. Morta will have raced ahead and back to his forces... to *my* Castle," Vikaris growled. While he wasn't angry at Trixon, Darion knew, his father's sharp veracity still gave them pause.

Darion had overheard his parents arguing late last night. Though he couldn't make out the words from his room, his heightened senses had allowed him to hear their raised voices from afar. He knew his father was petrified by the idea of Lyrianna going back to the Castle. And though it sickened Darion, he still agreed with her.

Lyrianna stopped and wrapped her arms around Vikaris's waist, belted blades and all.

Feeling his cheeks flush, Darion looked away quickly as Lyrianna planted a huge kiss on Vikaris, who didn't take long to reciprocate. The two passionately locked lips right there in the middle of the gathering.

Darion's heightened senses picked up his father's voice as he whispered in her ear, "Please, there must be another way."

Darion, though still not looking, felt nothing but compassion for his father in this moment. To let her go was breaking his heart. Darion questioned why he, himself, was alright with it? Was it rationale? Insensitivity? Fear?

You trust her, Darion... and my brother. That is why you are not questioning it, nor am I. We have faith in them and must believe in their success. There is no other option, Triumph spoke quietly into Darion's mind.

Darion considered it, turning to look at his friend who walked near him. *I think you're right,* he concluded. *They can do it.*

Thank you, Trixon's booming voice cut in.

Darion glanced at him, startled.

Triumph whinnied softly in annoyance. It wasn't polite for non-bonded unicorns to listen into telepathic conversations.

Trixon snorted and moved away from the still-interlocked couple. As he did, Trinidad approached, as well, nuzzling his son with the velvet of his nose. Darion, though surprised by Trixon's interjection, wasn't bothered by them. These were Triumph's family members who were bonded to his parents. They were then, by extension, his family. He wanted to get to know them better.

"Uncle, you know I cannot help it. You are speaking of my father... your belief in him," Trixon paused to glance at Trinidad, who emanated serene calm, "gives me hope. You two are right in your thinking. We must have faith."

Trinidad nodded, the light shimmering upon his magnificent horn. "We will be successful. No harm will come to the Queen, I promise," he said with such force that Darion was reminded that he was still a warrior, the former bonded companion to the late King Rustusse, kind and wise as he seemed.

"See that no harm comes to you too," Drigidor's authoritative voice added as he approached. And then, as if an aside, he added, "Elsra said I had to give you a parental warning," he chuckled.

Triumph snorted.

Trinidad bowed his head slightly at hearing his mother's command and his stepfather's words. "She is not one to disobey," Trinidad said, his voice warm and melodious, smooth as silk. Trinidad did not sound afraid. If anything, he sounded eager. He was healed and ready.

Darion didn't spend much time thinking on it, though, for soon the light began to radiate around him as he stood in the center amid the most powerful unicorns in the land. He felt himself gaping a little.

"Guys, can I have a little space? I'm starting to feel a little claustrophobic," he blurted.

Trixon chuckled.

Gales of laughter erupted from Triumph but were drowned out by the booming guffaw of Drigidor. And just like that, the crowding unicorns stepped back. Darion was grateful for a little air. The massive creatures, while met with awe, could be most oppressive. He was also glad his words had broken the tense atmosphere. He couldn't handle much more of it, anxious as he was. At the laughter, his parents walked hand in hand over to them, the unicorns parting to make way for the monarchs, and together the group planned for the march ahead.

Darion felt Edmond and Soren sneak up behind him. The comfort of his friends' familiar presence was most welcome.

By this time, most of the armed forces—and a multitude of horses—had come through the portal and were making their way toward the base of Mt. Alodon, where Garis and Kragar had commanded them to gather. They would sleep there before pressing south toward the Stenlen... or what was left of it. Rumors were that Narco's forces had decimated the village. Vikaris had explained he felt obligated to check there in case there were any remaining supporters alive. *What good was a King if he left his people to suffer? I have allowed this to go on far too long,* he had said sadly.

Hours passed by, and the troops were all bound for their meeting place. Lyrianna, Trinidad, Cela, and the lilac-

haired nymphs parted ways with the Nav'Arian army...
and Vikaris.

Lyrianna had cried, as had Vikaris.

Darion had stood somber but not fully dismayed. He
clung to his faith in his mother.

Tell her that, Darion, Triumph urged.

As Lyrianna hugged her son goodbye, Darion
whispered, "I believe in you, Mother. I know we will win.
I will see you when this is over."

She had looked up, cupped his face, and then kissed
his forehead. "And I believe in you, Darion. You are the
greatest thing to have ever happened to me and your
father. Stay safe. And trust in your abilities. You are
stronger than you know." She rubbed his cheek with her
thumb before turning and embracing Vikaris one final
time. After another drawn out, passionate kiss, Darion's
father helped Lyrianna up to Trinidad's back. He watched
Vikaris lean in to talk to Trinidad. The radiance of
Trinidad and Lyrianna illuminated the area surrounding
them. Trinidad whinnied in response to the King before
tilting his head toward him reverently. Darion smiled
watching his father pat Trinidad's cheek. He was glad to
see his father part ways amicably, even though Darion
knew how worried he truly was.

Cela, ever the warrior, had a bow in hand and looked
ready to fight any enemy that came near her Queen.
Darion trusted her fully. And he felt pride as he looked at
them. Trinidad and Cela were wholly sworn to Lyrianna.
They clearly loved her, and Darion felt peace knowing his
mother was in good hands. She would infiltrate the Castle,

find Rick and Tony, and make entry easier for the main Nav'Arian force.

The nymphs flitted ahead of Lyrianna, leading her to the ancient pathways that had helped her escape the Castle and Narco's control only months before.

That had been hours ago. Darion now marched alongside his father with their bonded unicorns. Edmond and Soren strode just behind. He could hear their whispered conversation, identifying plants and animals, seemingly picking up right where they'd left off in the Shazla Desert. A small comfort.

Yet as they marched, Darion began to stew. Something was tugging at his mind, though he couldn't make out what it was. All he knew was that something bad was imminent.

When the unicorn questioned his rising anxiety, he shared with Triumph, *Call it whatever you want, but something is coming. And we're not gonna like it.*

CHAPTER 19

The Mistake

"STOP," the disgusting beast bellowed for the hundredth time. Antonis rolled his eyes. Though bound, gagged, and draped over a massive troll's shoulder, he still felt annoyance. The leadership here was completely ridiculous. There was no order. This beast roared and barked at intermittent times, and the trolls who were meandering down the mountain trails would stop randomly. No salutes. No crisp lines. No "yes, sirs." *Bah! Despicable,* Antonis thought once again. *How did I let them catch me?* he wondered, feeling his ears warm with the humiliation.

He was Antonis Legario, Royal Commander... well, former Commander and High Keeper of Prince Darion. And now he dangled off a troll's stinking shoulder like a hunting prize. He looked around cautiously. He could make out Rick's slightly smaller frame hung off a nearby troll. He knew they'd be hastily dropped in a matter of—

Thud.

And once again the stupid troll dropped him without any warning. His tailbone ached, and he swallowed a growl at the impact. He didn't want to give them the pleasure of knowing it had hurt, and he didn't want to draw any more attention to himself. They had been moving steadily, though these sporadic stops for whatever reason did disrupt the journey. Antonis noticed they took no food, drink, or trips to make water, so why stop?

A moment later, another thud sounded, and Rick was dropped next to him. Though gagged, Antonis made out his friend's garbled words, "son-of-a-bitch" and something or other. Antonis glared at him. *Leave it to Rick to cuss them out,* he thought sardonically. *This is not the time,* he hoped his look imparted.

Rick scowled at him but quieted.

Antonis searched the perimeter. Thick conifers crept skyward, enclosing portions of the mountain trails, reminding Antonis of Oregon. *Gorgeous terrain, if you were not strapped to the back of a stinking troll.*

Rick scooted closer, their guards leaving them for a moment to join the others a small distance away. Rick mumbled something.

Antonis scowled at him again and shook his head once. He didn't have the patience for his friend's complaints right now. They couldn't draw the trolls' attention. His eyes searched for the beast. It had called for the stop, so where was it?

Rick mumbled something even louder, his gag garbling his words.

And then Antonis understood. His eyes flashed back to Rick. *They are lost!* Antonis wanted to smack himself. *Of course.* The beast was searching for their direction and left all the trolls milling about confused. *They really are idiots!*

Rick nodded once with a wink. Antonis knew that look. Rick was a tracker, the best of the land, certainly… and he looked as if he had a plan formulating.

Antonis scooted closer, leaning his head slightly.

Rick didn't speak, but something cold touched Antonis's wrist.

He didn't look, fearing to draw the troll's attention, though he knew his eyes widened.

A blade! Where the hell had that come from?

Sawing expertly and efficiently, Rick soon had Antonis's hands free. Looking around, Antonis knew the trolls were still preoccupied. They were growing restless. They were distracted.

Rick soon was sawing at his own foot bindings. His hands had already been freed, so it seemed, though he'd kept up the charade. Antonis was impressed!

Quickly, Rick handed Antonis the blade. Antonis pulled the gag from his mouth, as did Rick. Both men searching the area for detection.

"Do you have a plan?"

Rick nodded nonchalantly at the thick trees eastward. The forest there was dense, and though the land sloped, the descent didn't look deadly. The trolls had been avoiding much of the thick forest, choosing instead a roundabout way down the mountains. Their bulk hindered their mobility through the overgrown forest.

We could do it, Antonis thought, looking around and nodding once.

The final fibers of the course rope were sawed away, and he felt, with jubilation, that he was free! He wanted to rub his ankles and crack his neck but did neither. For just then an earth-shaking roar sounded from somewhere behind. The beast must have picked up the trail again… and did not sound pleased. This seemed like an excellent moment to get the hell out of here.

"Now," Antonis whispered. Leaving their bindings and gag behind and armed only with one knife, which Rick must have picked off a troll, they crept away from the gathering.

They made their way toward the trees seemingly undetected… until they heard yells of alarm. Their troll guards finally realized they'd escaped. With all pretense of stealth dropped, Antonis and Rick sprinted toward the trees. As they entered the heavily wooded area and began dodging tree limbs and thick underbrush, a roar louder than any either of them had heard before erupted at the edge of the forest. And then… crashing, thunderous sounds came from behind.

Shit! Antonis thought. "Run, Rick!"

The beast was coming for them… and by the sound of it, he was gaining on them—dense forest or not.

***

Elsra paced the hallways for the final time. As soon as she was finished here, she would head to join the others on the mainland. But there was much to be done before she could do that.

After bidding the warriors goodbye, her hours had been filled with overseeing administrative duties... something Vikaris forgot about all too often. He had no Castle and had been on the run for his entire reign. Furthermore, the ever faithful Seegar had taken on far more than his station required, overseeing many of Vikaris's affairs so the King could go off to battle.

She snorted at the idea of Vikaris sitting at a desk sifting through grain reports and livestock counts. Managing a kingdom—not that Kaulter was exactly a kingdom, rather an extension of Nav'Arian rule—was difficult work all the same. She had citizens that needed caring for. Petty squabbles to be adjudicated. Alimonies to be paid for families of the slain soldiers. Grain counts. Livestock counts. Orders and reports from hobblers, fletchers, blacksmiths, ... reports of unforeseen issues. A roof fire. A death. A sickness. A theft. Reports from every clan elder... check ins with the nymphs, merfolk, centaurs, unicorns, humans, ... the duties went on and on. Life on the Isle thrived, she knew, because of her efforts. It wasn't vanity or hubris that drove her, but an ever-longing desire to honor Rinzaltan... the True Regent. He, the wisest leader of unicorns, had been the most magnificent unicorn of her time—maybe of any time, beyond Tribute himself.

She wandered aimlessly as she recollected her years spent with her First Mate. The wonder he filled her with at each glance. The joy that had sparkled in his eyes as he'd looked upon the birth of all three of their children.

The ferocity that burned in his eyes when he spoke of the darkness which he felt beyond the border.

She walked through the rich wooden halls, her hooves clinking softly as she peeked in rooms watching maids going about their duties. She wandered toward the Kitchen and Medical Lab to give her final instructions to the staff. Seegar, she knew, would care for Kaulter sagely. He had been a welcome presence on and off throughout the years. He cared greatly for Nav'Aria and for the children above all. Though he had been initially worried when Elsra had asked him to stay in her place, Vikaris had assured him that that was his wish as well. Seegar, seeming gratified, had humbly as ever vowed to watch over the land until Elsra's return.

She knew he was capable. Yet still, a great leader did all that they could to prepare… and so she personally visited with the staff, giving parting advice, words of encouragement, and tender farewells.

As she walked, she became filled with sadness at her final memory of Rinzaltan, when the news had come to her that her husband had sacrificed himself for King Rustusse, her son Trinidad's bonded companion. Her eyes welled with tears at the memory. Even after all these years, she could still feel the same rip upon her soul as when her beloved husband had left this world. She remembered the long hours she had spent with Trinidad, crying and requiring him to tell her again and again what had happened. She tried to reason it out. Was there anything else that could have been done? But though it broke her heart, she had known that Rinzaltan, who'd always had the gift of foresight, had made the right choice. Vikaris was far too young at the time. The nation needed a leader, and Rustusse had been a great one.

What a world they lived in now without those two formidable male leaders. *Creator, watch over the males that I have left,* she thought, picturing each of her loved ones in turn. *And my female too,* she prayed silently, her thoughts landing on Zola. What was she to do with her granddaughter?

The girl had been raised in captivity. She was confused, vulnerable, and, at times, aggravating. Elsra also feared for Trigger. There was a darkness upon him and Zola. She had felt it since they first arrived. It made her spine tingle to be in their presence for long. Not that she believed they were evil, but rather, Morta's taint was great. She had fallen into his games before, having allowed Alice—*his illegimate daughter!*—to slay her granddaughter Xenia and nearly kill Drigidor. It shamed her to think on it, for she had always been a wise ruler. Capable of reading hearts. How had she missed the evil in Alice, and even further, allowed Morta to infiltrate Kaulter again and steal Trigger? She felt such shame. She had let them down... all of them. Had she lost her abilities? Was she growing careless? Reckless? Was her mind becoming feeble with old age?

Considering it, Elsra acknowledged that she felt sympathy for Zola, but not trust. She couldn't fully let her guard down. Darkness still permeated Kaulter. She could feel it.

After visiting with the final Fortress staff members, she descended the steps that led into the village to meet with the caretakers of the newly orphaned children whose parents had died in the fight or of sickness. She cared deeply for her citizens. Families would be found to provide for these children… she would make sure.

"Tell the Regent, thank you," ordered Lina the kind, children's home matron.

Tiny centaur and three human children mumbled their gratitude.

Elsra nodded her head at them, knowing that they must yearn terribly for their parents.

As she left the children's home, she decided on a whim to visit one more place. She had a feeling she would find someone there. Someone that she needed to smooth things over with.

As she crested the hillside, she peered down toward the waters. There, near the pristine beach and clear cerulean water stood a beautiful creature kneeling down in deep conversation with the merfolk. *They had come!*

She stood watching for some time.

Elsra recalled her conversation the previous evening with Zola. Elsra had once again asked her about her time in captivity and her escape. She had heard mention of a merman in the telling before but, so overcome with emotion of the tale, hadn't commented on it. This time, however, she had wondered aloud if someone should check with the merfolk to see if they knew this Shannic.

Zola's eyes had widened as she realized that Elsra could only mean that merfolk were here.

"There are more?" she had questioned.

Elsra was glad to see that Zola had taken it upon herself to come here. As she watched the afternoon sun glaring off of the water she felt joy. Zola looked... well... happy. Even without a horn, she seemed animated and more comfortable speaking with the merfolk than she had while speaking with her own grandmother.

A pang of guilt struck Elsra. Had she been too distant with Zola? Perhaps if she'd welcomed her with love rather than mistrust, Zola would have spoken to her with that much enthusiasm.

Troubled, Elsra turned away. It wasn't that Zola didn't have a horn, contrary to what Triumph had said in his departure. She knew Zola was her kin. Trinidad had not been diminished in her eyes because of his lack of a horn. But there was the strange foreignness about her... and her son. Zola did not know what it meant to be a unicorn... she didn't know anything beyond the controlled world she'd experienced under Narco. That darkness had left her spirit scarred. It had taken her innocence. Her right to a family. Darion himself had had to battle the evil, insidious hold upon her soul. Her darkness was all around. Now that Elsra thought of it, as the evening shadows began to emerge upon the empty hillside, she shivered. She could feel the evil everywhere. Her eyes widened as realization struck her. *This evil isn't Zola, this is—*

A piercing stab caused Elsra to rear and shriek with pain. She jumped, all four limbs rising off the ground, growing alert and spinning around. As if out of thin air, four hooded creatures—humans, by the looks of their size—came at her with blades drawn. She snarled angrily. She had allowed her mistrust and distracted exhaustion get the better of her. It wasn't Zola! It was Morta's "Watchers." They were just as Triumph had described. Pale. Creepy. Evil. And she had fallen right into their trap, on the hillside without any protection or guards.

She shrieked in anger and pain as another slice cut into her rear. She spun, slashing out wildly with her horn. The area around her just barely lit by her gleaming horn. She focused on it, making the light around her grow. The humans—creatures, more like—balked at the light, lifting their arms to shield their eyes. She growled knowing that these vermin had lived most of their existence underground, in wait for Morta's command. Well, they would not have her. They would not have Kaulter!

She dove forward, her horn piercing through the shoulder of the male in front of her. He fell back with a cry and clutched at the gushing wound. While she had him pinned, the others had seemed to recover from their shock and pressed in.

Elsra exhaled noisily. She was winded already. Age and lack of fighting had left her vulnerable. With another wild slash, she cut the arm of one of the humans, but he only flinched. Surface wound. The male laughed and lunged at her with his dripping blade. He must be the one that had stabbed her. The wounds upon her side and rear stung, but she couldn't think of it now. She tried to dodge the man but felt panic. The other two dug their blades simultaneously into both her sides as they ran by.

An ear-splitting scream erupted! She could feel the blood pouring from her wounds. All three males jumped back and stood in front of her, blades bloodied.

Her head began to feel light, and her limbs felt slow. She had lived many cycles. This was not how she was meant to die. There was a war. Her family was waiting for her to join them. She hadn't said all that needed to be said!

Tentatively, she tried to back up, but her feet fell upon the wounded man who yelled and thrashed under her. This momentary distraction was all the other three needed. They came at her, blades moving quickly. Elsra stood her ground. Her final thoughts were of Zola. They would come for her next, and there was no one to stop them. She stood just below this hill, alone and vulnerable, save for the merfolk. But Elsra knew they couldn't help her. She had left Kaulter weak. No warriors to protect them. She had let down Zola. She had failed Rinzaltan.

With one final scream, picturing Rinzaltan's majestic and powerful form, she let loose all her aggression and anger. A flashing light burst from her, knocking all three fighters to the ground. Unfortunately, that final energy release sapped most of her strength. She could feel it waning. And though she tried to remain standing, her wobbling legs betrayed her. She fell to her front knees before her back limbs crumbled and she collapsed on her side.

The injured man, having been trampled, now lay dead beneath her. She tried lifting her head, but the fight and blood loss had left her weakened. One by one, the men stood, and as her light began to dim and the evening shadows crept ever farther, they smiled yellowed, rotting teeth wickedly and approached her for the killing stroke.

"What was that?" Zola looked around, all laughter and conversation with the merfolk forgotten as a shriek unlike anything she'd ever heard sounded from above. She had taken a narrow, winding trail down to the beach where she'd stood for hours visiting with the kindly merfolk.

They had been thrilled to hear from her, and though evidently worried for their kind imprisoned behind the dam, they seemed hopeful. Many remembered Shannic and knew that if he was alive, there must be others. She confirmed this, explaining how the others had helped carry her and Trigger across.

The sun was beginning to fade, a brilliant colorful sunset broke out across the land and danced upon the water's surface as twilight came. She swept her eyes all around in search of whatever had made that sound.

"It sounds like someone is hurt," Marzan, the friendliest of the merfolk, replied.

Zola's stomach seized in fear. "I have to go," Zola said, already turning back toward the path.

"Wait, no! You do not know what is up there!" Marzan called, his brilliant, iridescent blue scales shimmering just beneath the water. His dark eyes, framed by curling brown locks, looked worried. They were lying flat on their bellies in the shallow water nearest the beach, tails splashing behind.

"I have to find out. What if someone needs me?" Zola called back, already finding the path. She peered upwards but could see only the rocky cliff above. She needed to get higher up.

"But you said, yourself, that Elsra had you stay behind because you are not a trained fighter? Stay here with us! Hide!"

Zola turned back, lifting her head proudly. "Thank you, Marzan. But no. I will never hide again. Elsra needs me."

And with that, she hurried up the steep trail, noting how much harder it was going up than down. She didn't look back but could hear the murmuring voices of the merfolk as they withdrew into deeper waters, their fins splashing and slapping the waves.

As she rounded a bend in the trail, she was able to see up ahead. Atop the hillside, though shadows were growing in the coming evening, a glowing unicorn fought off attackers.

Elsra!

Forgetting her earlier trepidation, Zola ran up the trail, her chest heaving not with fatigue, but anger!

She was still so far off, but with her enhanced eyesight—Soren explained that unicorns have some of the best senses in the world, besides the Marked Royals—she could see them surround Elsra and strike. She watched in horror as the villains stabbed her grandmother who, though fighting and giving her best effort, was visibly tiring. In one final surge, light burst from Elsra, knocking the men over.

Being a good distance away, it did not slow Zola, but she did feel its warm breeze blow through her mane. She pushed harder as terror gripped her. Elsra fell and the men began to encircle her.

"You cannot have her," Zola screamed as she headbutted one of the men from behind, barely reaching them in time to stop their fatal cuts. The man that she had struck flew over Elsra's body, landing with a heavy thud. The other two men spun. One of them, she watched, licked his lips in lusty anticipation. He reminded her of the guard that had hurt Trigger. And she realized, staring at these abnormally pale men, that these were the Watchers who had abducted him. There could be no doubt. They had stolen her son and were now turning their malice on her grandmother.

Without a word, she let her rage fuel her and guide her movements. She went for the bearded one first, and in one breath, downed him with a front kick before slamming her sharp hoof through his chest cavity, just as Triumph had described doing in his forest battle. *Effective*, she thought. So swift had her attack come, the man hadn't even uttered a sound. The other man seemed to be contemplating escape. He was stepping backwards and beginning to look around.

"You cannot hide from me," she growled.

He set his jaw, lifting his blade.

Zola watched it with satisfaction. A nearly imperceptible quiver gave him away. He was afraid. *Good*, she thought, baring her perfectly white, straight teeth.

The man's eyes widened. "You…"

Whatever he was about to say, Zola would never know, for she came at him and reared up on her back legs—the movement foreign to her untested legs as if a primal fighting instinct had come to her. Zola's hooves slammed heavily down on the man, crushing his collarbone and skull with a disgusting crunch.

She turned to look at her grandmother, but just as she began walking toward her, the man she had thrown with her head—and forgotten about momentarily—jumped up. Slashing wildly, his blade glanced off her shoulder. A scratch really, but it infuriated her all the same. She whinnied, and as he made to slash again, she did the first thing that came to her mind. Catching the man's wrist in her mouth, she bit down as hard as she could, tasting the metallic blood spurting from the man's nearly detached wrist. His agonized screams broke the stillness, and as his blade fell to the ground, she released him. He stumbled back, nearly tripping on Elsra, clutching his dangling and bloody hand. He turned as if to run.

Zola wouldn't give him the opportunity. She kicked low, colliding with his kneecap, the man's leg buckled beneath her heavy blow. He whimpered as he fell, rolling on his back. Before he could move again, she slammed her hoof down upon his right leg. His femur bone snapped and tore through his flesh and pantlegs. The man screamed, rearing from the pain and trying to reach his leg. With her head, she knocked him back, and with another heavy step, she broke his other wrist. His screams turned to moans as he lay there broken. Satisfied that he wouldn't go anywhere, Zola turned and came around to Elsra's head.

Zola knelt down, pressing her ear toward Elsra's mouth. She could hear shallow breathing. "Grandmother," Zola asked softly.

Elsra's eyes fluttered open. "Z-Z-Zola," she spluttered, eyes widening and searching the darkness. "H-how?"

"I killed them, Grandmother. I am sorry I was not here sooner." Zola dipped her head low, feeling her rage turn to shame. She should have been here.

Elsra's wide eyes regarded Zola's face. Then took on their familiar serene gaze, and though her body was failing her, her mind remained active. "You are a warrior, Zola. I should have seen it."

Her grandmother's body shuddered, and Zola gasped, panicked. "I can get help," Zola blurted, thinking of Seegar. He was probably in the Fortress. She could get him. He could help.

"No," Elsra whispered. "Stay." She took another shallow breath, then looked at Zola. "I am sorry to leave you after just finding you... Granddaughter. And I am sorry if I was hard on you, I... you," Elsra's voice cut out, and Zola felt tears spring to her eyes.

"You are... have always been... loved, Zola."

Zola felt her heart breaking. The words she'd so longed to hear ever since her strange, drugged state had worn off, came now as her grandmother bled out in front of her.

"I am sorry, Grandmother. I should have been here. I am sorry. I..."

"Zola," Elsra whispered, her voice growing nearly inaudible. "My Zola, I recognize you as kin of the First Horn… and… welcome you to the Unicorn Council."

Another flashing light burst from Elsra. This one larger than when fending off the attackers, bringing another warm gust of wind. Zola felt caught up in it, as if trapped in a funnel, remembering the feeling of Darion inside her mind earlier, drawing out the evil and calming the waves of her life source. And as if in a dream, she felt herself becoming whole. The blinding white and silver funnel moved faster and faster and then… evaporated. As the winds ceased, Zola was surprised to find the entire area upon the hillside lit… and coming from her! The light was coming from within her. And from her horn!

Elsra's eyes opened one final time to gaze at Zola's splendor. "There she is, my warrior," Elsra's gentle voice spoke, before her eyes fell closed with a sigh.

As Elsra's last breath drifted upward and away, a thin trail of silver light blew toward the water below. Zola watched it, and just before it dipped beyond view, a shimmering, giant white tree with crystal branches appeared. She gasped in wonder as her grandmother's spirit blew around the tree, seeming to land upon a branch. There Zola squinted and could just make out where a new bud—a crystal—appeared. And as quickly as it had come, it was gone.

Zola questioned its reality. And she felt the world dim as the Tree, and with it, her grandmother's spirit, disappeared. Bowing over Elsra's body, she wept. Suddenly she remembered that unicorn's horns have powers. Standing, she awkwardly pressed her horn toward the sources of blood pooling around Elsra. Again and again she tried, but it was in vain. No movement returned to Elsra's body. Nothing changed.

"It will not work," a gentle, aged voice spoke, interrupting Zola's racing thoughts.

She looked up sharply, feeling ready to attack and protect her grandmother's body—no matter what. But no threat came; it was Seegar.

He stood, surrounded by ten guards—human and centaur—who had been selected to remain at the Fortress and protect Kaulter. But they had neglected their charge, Zola thought, bitterly looking at her grandmother's body. They had allowed her to go around unprotected, and now she lay before them dead.

Zola felt her drying tears tighten her cheeks as she looked at Seegar.

He approached her, and as if able to read her thoughts, shared, "This is a heavy weight we will carry unto our graves. We have let Kaulter down. I saw the flashing light and came as swiftly as my old bones would carry me. I am sorry, Zola. The Regent was," his voice quivered with emotion, "she was magnificent in compassion and splendor. I have loved serving her—and the King—all these years."

Zola felt chastened as she watched a tear roll down the man's wrinkled cheek. Who was she to cast blame? Seegar had known her grandmother far longer than Zola. They all knew how headstrong she had been. If she said she was going to do something, who could stop her?

Seegar approached Zola and placed his hand upon her neck in comfort. He looked at her then, and added, "I heard her words to you, and saw your transformation. Elsra," he paused looking down upon her body, "she gave her final powers to see your rightful place restored. A true unicorn of the council." He smiled at Zola, tears filling his eyes, "and now, we must win this war... in her memory. And of so many others."

Zola nodded, her tongue suddenly feeling heavy. She had no words. *My warrior*, Elsra had called her. Zola questioned it, though as she surveyed the area, she wondered. The bodies that littered the area were a mangled, bloody mess. Seegar's guards had begun inspecting them. As they dragged the bodies over, the severely injured man moaned.

Narrowing her eyes, Zola called, "He will tell us where my son is."

Seegar nodded. "Yes, we will find out everything he knows."

After more guards were called to fetch a wagon and Elsra's body was loaded onto it, the moon made its grand entrance into the starry night sky. A heavenly procession welcomed Elsra, First Mate of Rinzaltan, Regent and Leader of the Unicorn Council, and Protector of Kaulter.

"Goodbye, Elsra," Zola whispered softly, watching her horn shimmer in the moonlight above her eyes.

***

Elsra felt life returning to her limbs. Looking around her, she found herself lying in a field of flowers and soft grasses. She felt confused, but oddly, not afraid. She sensed something... familiar. She couldn't quite place it. The darkness that had claimed Nav'Aria, and now Kaulter, was gone. Rather, the air smelled sweet and the land seemed clean. Pure. She peered down the length of her body, surprised to find that her wounds were gone. Her coat, having always been pristine, was glowing softly. She shook her head and smelled flowers. A circlet of gold was woven with wildflowers and placed atop her head. She gave it no thought, though, for at that moment, she caught sight of something she'd longed for for so many years.

Rinzaltan approached with soft footfalls.

"Is this a dream?" she murmured, rising gracefully to face him, the love that had been taken from her all too soon.

"No, my darling," Rinzaltan's rich, musical voice danced in her eardrums, soaring around her as if in a caress.

Her whole body tingled, and her heart soared! "I am really with you? You are real?"

Instead of replying right away, he stepped forward and nuzzled her softly upon her cheek.

She inhaled deeply, remembering the spearmint fragrance that had often accompanied him. He smelled clean... and safe. "How is this possible?"

"You have joined me in the life beyond," Rinzaltan replied. "The Creator has returned you to my side, my love."

Silver tears of joy fell with abandon, and Elsra laughed. A full, joyous laugh, letting go of all the shame, terror, anger, and sadness she had carried on and off over the years. This was no dream. And he had not come back to life, but rather, she had died and found new life. Whatever this was, and wherever she was now, she wasn't going to question it. Being with Rinzaltan again made her feel whole; it was right.

And yet, she remembered all of those she'd left behind, Drigidor coming to mind. "But what of the others? What of Nav'Aria?"

Rinzaltan smiled. He did not seem worried at all. She could sense his calm spirit. "This is how it was meant to be. The darkness that has come into the world shall not win, so long as the prophecy is fulfilled."

"And if it is not?" she questioned.

"Have faith, Elsra," and then he added softly, "for if the prophecy fails, then there will be no Nav'Aria. We must lend our faith and strength to the Tree, to help those we have left behind to fight... including your Drigidor."

"You are not mad?" She asked softly.

As if on cue, the Shovlan Tree appeared. Rinzaltan looked from it to her, "I could never be mad at you, my love. You chose a strong mate to partner with you and help lead Kaulter. You honored me in memory... but, most of all, you continued to live."

Tears streamed freely from her cheeks. Rinzaltan nuzzled her, before glancing back toward the Tree. It did not seem firm, but rather a blurring image. They walked toward it, and Elsra felt a wash of cold air as she walked right through its silhouette.

She knew then for certain, that her time in the world of the living had come to an end. She pictured Drigidor's handsome face again. She felt a pang of sadness for him. And for her sons. And granddaughter. For now, all she could do for them was believe and pray that the Creator keep them safe, until they join her on this side.

"All will be well, my love," Rinzaltan murmured, and then as they walked toward a stunning valley filled with flowers and enchanting, sweeping trees... the sky broke over the valley with rich, vivid, swirling colors of sepia and violet and azure. She could hardly breathe for the sight of it. It looked like the Nav'Aria she remembered... before it had become tainted. It was as if she were in Nav'Aria again—not as it was, or even perhaps as it had been, but as it should be. How the Creator had imagined it to be. She walked, breathing in the smells of juniper, lavender, lilac, and rose, and watching fat bumblebees and elegant butterflies fluttering around marigolds, daisies, nasturtiums, and hibiscus flowers. The diverse abundance of life astounded her.

She stopped midstride to gaze at the splendor.

"This is only a fraction of what I have to show you, Elsra. But first, there are some unicorns waiting to see you."

Elsra's heart leapt as she looked toward the horizon and saw with complete and utter astonishment that it was her beloved daughter Trinity... and with her, her daughter Xenia, both having been savagely slain. But now... now they were whole and happy and radiant. Elsra didn't hesitate. She ran to them.

And as the sun set upon her, she danced and reared and laughed in reunion with her husband, daughter, and granddaughter under the glorious sky. Life had not stopped for her, but rather, it had been returned.

CHAPTER 20

The Widower

Triumph walked in deep conversation with Trixon. He had always enjoyed his nephew's company, despite his rashness. The quiet camp, save for the War Tent at the center, allowed them time to share their thoughts.

The unicorns had left the King and Prince, along with Garis and Kragar. Trixon had seemed restless, and Triumph had suggested they take a walk. It had been a long time since they'd been alone to catch up, and with Trinidad now going off with Lyrianna once more, Triumph knew Trixon was worried. He felt it his duty to comfort him.

"Tell me, Trixon. What do you make of the prophecy? Do you see a way that Darion can beat Morta?"

Trixon looked levelly at him.

"I want the truth, I promise. I will not react."

Trixon snorted, speaking lowly, "How gracious of you, Uncle."

They both knew Triumph had a tendency to become riled and, on occasion, go on a self-righteous tangent. But Triumph was working on it. Darion made fun of him so much, that he had come to see how difficult he had been to get along with.

"Just spit it out," Triumph growled.

"And there is the uncle I know," Trixon boomed, chuckling. He pulled up short at the edge of the camp, searching the darkness before speaking more seriously, "I believe in Darion, and Vikaris trusts him... though neither of us really understands how he is supposed to do it. The image of him straddling the land... I guess I thought," he stopped, shaking his head, his jaw working silently.

Triumph studied him, waiting. "Well... what?"

Trixon glanced at him, "I assumed it meant that these so-called winged ones would join us in the fight. Without them, I fear for him."

Triumph felt a pit in his stomach, for it echoed his greatest unspoken fear. *It is because of Tiakai and her stubborn decision to stay in Rav'Ar and let her kind die*, he thought angrily. Having been an instructor for years and familiar with the old texts, he had also believed that the meaning behind this prophecy was figurative rather than literal. Darion was meant to "destroy" Morta by unifying the creatures of the land, and yet... that is not what had happened. So now what? Is Darion supposed to challenge Morta to a duel? Plunge a blade into his chest? As much as he wished that to be true, Triumph felt it seemed too easy.

Trixon murmured something.

"What was that?" Triumph asked, distracted with his thoughts.

"I said, 'I sense something' headed right toward us."

Triumph blinked, growing alert. As if a beacon went off in his mind, he looked directly in the direction of the one approaching. He would know that individual anywhere.

"Why in Creator's name is she here—alone?"

Trixon and Triumph hustled toward the growing light. A dazzling radiance began to spill upon the land around them, casting away the shadows.

"Zola?" Trixon asked, sounding confused. Though they could clearly sense and see her plain as day, she looked different. "You got your horn?" And then, perceptive as always, his tone grew solemn, "It came at great cost, I see."

Triumph looked at him and back to Zola. Goosebumps broke out along his spine.

Guards began to mill about, catching sight of the approaching visitor, and a runner was sent to the King's tent. Triumph ran to her. "What are you doing here?" Looking around, Triumph felt confusion and fear grip him. *Where is Mother?*

One look at Zola, her eyes glossy and head held aloft, confirmed it. Elsra wasn't coming... she never would.

Before he could ask, though, a booming voice sounded as heavy hooves pounded from the center of camp. "Where is Elsra? Where is my wife?"

Triumph couldn't breathe. He felt sick. Drigidor's intensity seemed to have sucked the wonder out of everyone and everything.

As Darion and Vikaris ran up, Garis's hooves thudding heavily at their side, Zola spoke. "She is dead." Zola's clear voice cut into the night. "Killed by the pale humans of Morta."

Triumph couldn't breathe. He felt like he was hyperventilating. Catching Darion's eyes, he realized they knew of whom she spoke. *The Watchers.* They had stolen Trigger, but not all had left Kaulter. Triumph felt intense remorse. They had taken all the warriors with them, leaving Elsra and Zola vulnerable. They had failed them. *We failed Mother.*

"NOOOOOOOO," Drigidor's voice thundered as he reared and landed heavily, his eyes maddened with grief and rage. He landed and prowled in front of her, "You lie. I would know if she were gone," and though he looked menacing, Triumph saw his stepfather's love for his mother... seemingly for the first time. He *had* really loved her. Drigidor, the powerful—most often annoying— Second Mate of the Regent was weeping. His wife had been slain, and Triumph's heart broke anew for him.

Taking in the tragic news, Vikaris rubbed his hands over his face. "Is Seegar..." the King's question trailed off.

Zola quickly assured him of Seegar's help and capable charge of Kaulter. "We believe the remaining Watchers were killed, but Seegar will be surrounded by guards day and night."

The King nodded, murmuring, "good" but did not cease from rubbing his eyes and temples. Darion simply stood frozen. What greater grief could befall the land?

Garis shook his head sadly as he studied the ground. Triumph knew his wife and children were in Kaulter still. He sent up a silent prayer for Garis's children and all remaining in Kaulter. There was nothing that could be done now.

Succumbing to his grief, Drigidor was snorting and sniffling, being ushered aside with Kragar, whose head leaned in close to comfort his long-time friend.

Zola stood, shining bright, her horn illuminating the area.

And though his heart was crushed, Triumph—ever the intellectual—still had to know, "yes, but how did you get your horn back?"

Zola looked toward him, and her voice seemed to soften, "I killed her attackers, and she called me her 'warrior,' naming me to the Unicorn Council. With her last breath she used her powers to call to the Creator to return my horn, and she smiled at me... before closing her eyes for the final time. I saw her breath leave and her spirit join the Shovlan Tree."

Trixon and Triumph both gasped at this, as did Vikaris.

"The spirits have rewarded your bravery and loyalty to the Regent. And she, in turn, gave her last power surge to you," Trixon's voice rumbled reverently. "You have done well, my cousin." And then, remembering tradition, Trixon stepped forward, bowing his head before her in acknowledgment of her equal status as a Council member, before nuzzling her and stepping aside. Triumph followed him, tears falling freely for the death of his mother and the healing of his daughter. Drigidor did not come to pay her respects, but Triumph understood. His stepfather was overwrought with emotion. Triumph knew firsthand the pain of losing a spouse, and again, felt only compassion for his stepfather.

Darion stepped forward to Zola, making as if to bow his head too. "No need, my Prince," Triumph's voice croaked, the emotion thick in his throat. "You and your father do not need to bow to anyone."

Zola shifted uncomfortably, the light around her dimming slightly.

Darion smiled sadly at Triumph, "I don't totally agree," he responded. Then turning, he directed his words to Zola. "Zola, I know what it's like to be a foreigner here. To be different. And I know how creepy those Watchers are. What you did today was very brave. I am proud to also welcome you to the Unicorn Council," and instead of a mere nod, Darion bowed low at the waist.

The shimmering glow that gushed from Zola was palpable. She stepped back and bowed her head in turn, her dazzling horn mere inches from Darion. "Thank you, Prince Darion. My horn is yours in this fight."

Vikaris strode up to Darion and placed an arm around his shoulder, tears streaking his face.

Triumph watched Vikaris, the King, also bow to his daughter in welcome. Triumph knew this to be a monumental moment. *Elsra would have loved to have seen*

Vikaris bowing to anyone! "That man's pride will swallow us all," she used to grumble behind closed doors. The thought made Triumph smile, though his heart felt heavy. Truthfully, he had not parted ways with his mother as well as he would have liked. Another mistake to add to his ever-growing guilt....

Knowing full well Triumph's self-loathing, Darion embraced him. "I am sorry for your loss, Triumph. But please," and this time Darion looked him in the eye, grabbing his horn for effect, "do not for one-minute think that I'm going to let you blame yourself for this. She knew how much you loved her, and she was so proud of you... of us. Elsra died knowing that her family was strong, and that we would win this war."

Triumph sighed, and then shook his head to free his horn from Darion's death grip. "You are right.... Now let go of my horn before I decide to use it on you," Triumph growled.

Darion smiled at him, releasing only the grip on his horn.

Triumph closed his eyes, begrudgingly grateful for Darion's words and presence. He knew Darion was right. But it wasn't his nature to let things go. Elsra would be avenged. He would mourn later. His thoughts turned to Drigidor. Perhaps he couldn't say goodbye to his mother, but he could make things right with him.

Vikaris ushered them back to the War Tent. A growing audience had filed in silently behind them as soldiers of all shapes and sizes had been drawn from their tents. As the party moved inward through the rows of tents and remnants of cookfires, a fluttering sound made them all turn. A nymph flitted by and collapsed before Vikaris. Trixon's horn illuminated the area around them. Gasps could be heard, and Triumph pushed closer to see.

The nymph was bleeding from a thick shaft which protruded from its stomach. "They are coming," the nymph whispered.

"Who?" Vikaris asked.

Garis signaled for more guards to set up watch.

Blood began to spill from the nymph's mouth as it lay convulsing on the ground.

"Who did this to you?" The King yelled.

The nymph raised a shaky, copper-toned finger in the direction he had come. "Trolls," he whispered, his breath leaving him and his hand falling with a light thud as he died before their eyes.

As if on cue, a thundering sound began. *Footsteps*, Triumph realized. Hundreds of them. Heavy footsteps coming straight for them. And then the horns and war chants began.

"We are under attack," Vikaris roared, calling his soldiers to arms.

Garis blew his own horn, and in moments the camp was ablaze as lanterns were lit and soldiers hastily tied on their belts and blades, rushing toward the horses at the edge of camp.

The battle had come to them.

***

"Rick, keep going," Antonis called, looking for any large rock or tree branch that could be used in defense.

Clutching the thin blade, he knew for a fact it wouldn't be enough to fend off the beast. But.... What else was there to do? The beast was coming for them. Its roaring crash through the forest was hard to miss... and from the sounds of it, it was gaining on them.

"Fuck that," Rick growled, slowing his pace. "I am not leaving you. Either we both run or we both fight."

Antonis felt near explosion with anger. "Damn you, Rick, RUN!"

Rick stopped, turned around, and spat.

The beast was nearing them; another breath or two and he'd be in sight.

Antonis ran forward, his arms and legs scraped by thick branches and tree needles. "We have to move," he said, pushing Rick forward.

Rick, though smaller than Antonis, became an immovable stone.

As trees began to fall, Antonis felt his heart skyrocketing. The beast had found them.

"Shit," Antonis snarled, looking around for any defense. Bracing himself in a fighter's stance, he raised the blade and prepared for what he knew to be his final fight.

The air around them felt darker and fouler.

Rick sucked in a breath, cursing and squaring his shoulders, fists balled. His right eye still swollen shut.

Antonis felt near hysteria. It was so like Rick to think he could box his way out of this. "Damnit, Rick. You need to run," but as Antonis glanced at his friend, he saw his attention was elsewhere.

Antonis peered ahead to see the beast climbing over broken tree branches and felled trees—of its own making. Its red, maddened eyes glowing, and huge snout oozing snot. A deep purple tongue flicked out and licked its lips. The beast towered over them. Its broad, muscled chest and thick limbs could crush them both with one swipe of its arm.

Antonis snorted and spat, cracking his neck as he did so. "Well, come on then," he challenged.

The beast's eyes narrowed on Antonis. His savage bellow blasted both men.

But before it leapt straight for Antonis, Rick barreled into his side. Antonis went crashing down. He looked in horror at the leaping beast headed straight for his pig-headed, stubborn, brave-as-hell best friend. Knowing Rick was about to be killed before his eyes, he hurriedly clambered to get back up. "No," he cried, seeing the beast aloft in the air just inches from his friend with fists still raised. But… the deathblow never came.

A whoosh of air and a heavy, cracking thud sounded. Wingbeats fluttered, but Antonis noticed the beast was lying on its side, moaning.

He looked around in astonishment to find ten nymphs holding an uprooted tree like a battering ram. And as it turned out, that's exactly what it was! They backed up, their wingbeats fluttering in unison just above ground. Then, at a sharp whistle, they flew forward and in one smooth motion slammed the tree into the beast's side again. It groaned and flinched.

Dropping the tree atop the beast, all ten nymphs turned to Antonis and Rick, who stood looking dumbfounded.

"Well... RUN!" The nymph who looked to be in command called. That was all that Antonis and Rick needed. They bounded down the forested hillside, accompanied by their rescuers. Antonis would have choice words for his friend later, but for now, they ran like their lives depended on it. At that moment, another rattling roar rose from behind them. The beast still lived... and sounded very angry.

The air grew warmer the farther down the mountain they went. After an agonized pace and frenzied run downwards, Antonis, Rick, and their rescuers had put enough distance between themselves and the trolls that they could slow their pace. They couldn't hear the beast anymore and assumed it had returned to the trolls to accompany their descent toward Narco's fortifications.

As they marched, they neared the base of the mountain much sooner than they had realized. Where were all the cliffs?

When asked, the nymphs laughed, saying only the trolls used the caves and cliffs; the nymphs knew all the hidden trails up and around the mountains, through all the Nav'Arian forests, and beyond.

Antonis decided not to share with them just how many of those cliffs and caves he, Rick, and Aalil had gone through to find the trolls... or rather, to get captured by them.

As they walked, the nymphs informed them of the war.

"Wait? Morta?" Antonis started, paying closer attention and setting aside his concerns for Aalil for the time being. "What about Narco? I have not heard you mention him this entire time."

The nymphs stopped. The commanding officer, Talen, landed on his feet and turned to look both men in the eye. "You have not heard? My apologies, you have been with the trolls longer than we realized. Narco is dead."

Rick, who had been using this as an opportunity to drink from a proffered waterskin, choked, spraying water from his mouth. "What did you say?" he croaked.

"Narco is dead… slain by the King."

Antonis whistled through his teeth, placing his hands on his hips in a proud stance. "Well, that is an outcome I have longed to hear for some years."

"So, the war is over then? Soldiers are being dispatched to kill Morta and any remaining loyalists…. Wrapping things up nicely, I take it?" Antonis said cheerily, ripping the waterskin out of Rick's stunned fingers and drinking greedily. "Cheers," Antonis said loudly, raising it aloft.

"Tony," Rick tugged on his shirtsleeve.

Antonis scowled at his friend. *What is his problem?*

Then he looked back to the nymphs, who seemed to be avoiding eye contact and shifting uncomfortably.

"Well, what is it? The war *is* over, is it not?"

"No, Sir," the nymph replied. "In fact, the King now believes that it is only just beginning."

"That makes no sense," Antonis cut in, scowling at them.

"Shut up and let the man speak," Rick drawled, elbowing Antonis as he came to stand beside him.

"After the battle, a voice spoke aloud into the minds of all combatants. Morta announced that he is the true mastermind and has begun preparing a force larger than we have seen yet. Prince Darion believes that—"

"Wait, Darion? You have seen Darion. Tell me he is alright," Rick blurted, jumping forward and grabbing the nymph's olive-green tunic.

It was Antonis's turn to chide Rick. "Back up! Back up so he can speak, you idiot." Admittedly, Antonis felt his pulse increasing by the second. *News of Darion!*

"Yes," the nymph responded, smoothing out his tunic and shooting a look of reproach at Rick. The other nymphs had stepped up alongside their leader and were glaring at the men.

"Please, tell us what you know of Darion," Antonis asked in a calmer voice.

The nymph nodded at him, continuing, "Prince Darion and his companions returned from beyond the border at the end of the battle—they are safe," he added, staving off Rick's questions with a raised palm. "The Prince spoke of a hidden community across the border and believes it is connected to Morta. Nymph scouts have been sent out to patrol all territories. That is why we are in the mountains, a place we usually try to avoid," he added, his lip curling as his meaning became evident. *No one likes trolls... especially bloodthirsty, red-eyed, murderous bastard traitors loyal to Narco... and Morta,* Antonis thought.

But Morta? The enemy? Antonis remembered not that long ago when he'd had the sniveling, weak man in his possession. He should have beaten the shit out of him then and left him dead in the woods. He wished he would have known. His skin began to crawl as he recalled the cackling laughter of the man, who though being held captive, had seemed to think it all a game. He seemed to have actually taken pleasure from his beatings.

Antonis rolled his shoulders, looking around instinctively. "We should keep going," he murmured.

Rick was still interrogating the nymphs about Darion.

"The last communication we received, beyond our orders, was that the King and Prince would be gathering the warriors to march upon Castle Dintarran. I know not whether they have begun their march, but we are nearing our network pathways. Once we get down from these mountains, I can make contact and find out."

"Then we move," Rick snapped and started marching ahead, the nymphs fluttering to keep pace.

Antonis rolled his eyes as he drew up position in the rear to keep watch. *I did not know Rick was the commander all of a sudden,* he thought. Yet before long, his mind wandered back to Aalil. He could only pray she was alright, and that none of the bastards were hurting her… he would rip them apart if they tore one hair from her head. Picturing her, though, he smiled. She wasn't the type to take shit from anyone… she was a warrior. If she hadn't managed to escape on her own, he hoped she was giving them hell. The former seemed far-fetched, yes, but it eased his mind some as they began their final descent down the gravel-strewn trail heading back into the heart of Nav'Aria… and straight toward the battle to come!

CHAPTER 21

The Trail

Lyrianna shivered, rubbing her arms as she rode upon Trinidad's back. She was grateful that he allowed her to ride him, for even a king or queen had to be invited first. As she looked around the dark, dense woods that edged around the base of the mountains and toward the far edge of the Kingdom, and with that, the Castle, she felt unease. Were there spies watching her now? She had been bold in both her planning and her heated discussion with Vikaris—*that stubborn man!*—but now that she was alone, she did wonder if they'd made the right decision. She remembered intermittently coming awake while traversing these dark trails with Cela and the newly freed nymphs and centaurs, but that seemed ages ago. In reality, it had only been months, and now she was voluntarily headed back.

"You were correct in your summation, Lyrianna. There is no one else who can go or who knows the Castle as well as we do at this time. We will protect our loved ones by having success on this mission," Trinidad whispered. "No harm will come to us."

Lyrianna brushed her hand through Trinidad's lustrous mane. Oh, how she loved him and prayed he was correct. However, Narco had been a maniac, and now to learn that there was one perhaps worse than him made her skin crawl. Morta was wicked, she knew, but feared they did not know enough but about this new adversary. How would Darion beat him?

"Thank you, Trinidad," she murmured, still lost in her thoughts but aware he deserved a response.

He whinnied softly, his horn lighting their path.

Cela, who marched before them, weapons at the ready, had demanded Trinidad dim himself before they started. She had said, "A glowing unicorn is not exactly stealthy, Trinidad."

Trinidad had fumbled a few moments, but finally his brilliance dimmed a little. He explained that if he focused on it, he could disguise his pure aura.

"I do not need to know what you do, but make sure you keep it down back here. The enemy may have scouts, and if you start glowing, that will be an obvious target."

Lyrianna smiled at the memory and at her friend. Cela was a fiery protector. *Who else would dare boss a unicorn?* The Queen believed that her friends would protect them. She only hoped she did not become a burden. She knew how to use a blade—not expertly—but she had requested one be belted upon her waist.

Cela raised her arm, signaling for them to stop. She didn't speak but peered around.

Lyrianna didn't hear a thing but knew Cela must have.

It is the nymph Adelina returning with word, Trinidad told her telepathically.

Lyrianna perked up at the mention of the nymphs who had accompanied them and volunteered to scout ahead on the trails. *I wonder if they found anything,* she questioned, fingering her sword hilt as she waited.

She didn't have to wait long, for all of a sudden, a pink-winged, petite form appeared. She smiled and dipped her head.

"Report," Cela growled.

Lyrianna shook her head to rebuke the centaur... Cela was fiery alright, if not downright rude to those serving in her guard.

The nymph squeaked, landing softly and saluting Cela. "I bring news from my sisters who are scouting farther ahead. They have found a nymph outpost and learned that a party of nymphs has gone into the mountains to track the trolls. They believe that the trolls are leaving their mountain holdings to join the Castle forces."

Lyrianna shivered again, leaning closer toward Trinidad's neck and light. *Trolls,* she shuddered while thinking of the beasts she'd encountered at the Castle. One had continually accompanied Narco, breaking her fingers and issuing other torturous pains—though oddly, he had never seemed to revel in the pain as others she'd seen had... like the one who'd attacked Cela. She watched her friend's shoulders square at the mention of them.

"I hate trolls," Cela snarled but nodded to the nymph. "Is there anything else?"

"Well… there is one more thing," the nymph paused, peeking over Cela's large form to make eye contact with Lyrianna and Trinidad, who up until now had remained quiet.

"Well?" Cela pressed.

"My sisters heard from the guard at the outpost that the mountain nymphs are returning… and they are not alone. They are bringing with them two humans."

"Did they describe these humans?" Trinidad inquired.

The nymph's wings beat faster, lifting her in the air so she could directly respond to him.

"Yes," she whispered softly. "Antonis and Riccus are with them, mighty Trinidad… Your Majesty," she added nodding to Lyrianna.

They had freed them? Lyrianna's mind was a whirl of thoughts. *That is great news!*

"Wait… what of Aalil? Have they seen Aalil? Are Antonis and Riccus unharmed?"

The nymph seemed to hesitate, biting her pink rosebud lip nervously. "The men are unharmed, Your Majesty. No one has seen Aalil, though," she looked down as she spoke.

Lyrianna knew Aalil was well known amongst the nymphs and centaurs as a great warrior. She felt her stomach grip but couldn't worry for her now. "We must find Antonis and Riccus before the trolls do. Can you lead us to this outpost?"

The nymph dipped her head again and flitted forward.

Cela turned to them, her eyes intense. "Your Majesty, I do not know if this is a good plan. Perhaps we should move away from these trails? I fear risking your exposure to the troll forces."

Lyrianna scowled at her. They had not come this far to back down now!

Trinidad spoke up, "We know the risks we are taking, Cela. We must go. The Queen promised Prince Darion she would find Riccus... as did I. If he is with the nymphs ahead, then that is our destination."

Cela furrowed her brow, shifting on her ivory haunches as she looked around the forested pathways. "Alright but keep your light down... and no talking. Stay alert."

"As you command," Trinidad replied. His light diminished fully, and they were plunged into darkness.

"Watch your step," Cela grumbled after tripping upon a rock while turning to move forward.

Lyrianna feared she or Trinidad would twist an ankle, but she also knew that, if there were a troll force coming down the mountains, that was one group they did not want to meet. *Trolls!* She thought again. *Why did it have to be trolls?*

It could be worse, Trinidad countered. *I prefer trolls over Rav'Arians.*

Lyrianna trembled! *I forgot about them for the moment... I have been so focused on Morta and these 'Watchers'... yes, you may be right. Rav'Arians are pure evil...* and then after a pause, she swept her eyes over the dark forest, barely able to make out a thing before her and added, *You could sense them if they were near, right?*

***

The scraping talons made Dabor's skin crawl. He hated Rav'Arians almost as much as he hated Morta, his new Master. He knew that Narco was dead, and if he were truly loyal, he would have felt sadness, but in his heart, he felt only relief. He'd hated Narco, but unfortunately, he was coming to find out that his crazed former leader was a child compared to this new one.

He walked quickly, one leg dragging, only furthering his annoyance with this human. Dabor rounded the corner toward where Morta stood upon the massive ramparts. He seemed to prefer it up here, where he could look over the stone wall and out upon his gathered forces encamped around the Kingdom and beyond. Lake Threat glistened in the light, and all was quiet—save for Morta's terse words for the pale female at his side, Tav'Opal. Dabor didn't trust her… she had the same look as Morta, with coldness in her eyes. That very coldness, he noted, seemed to be present in all the eyes he met in this Castle.

"Faster," the Rav'Arian croaked behind him, bumping into Dabor as he'd unconsciously slowed his pace. He'd wanted to listen in on the conversation before Morta detected their presence.

"… the only reason I keep you around. Remember that," Morta spat at the woman, who then quivered slightly but didn't back down from the force of his stare.

Looking up then, he caught sight of Dabor and the two Rav'Arians trailing him. The once seemingly weak, aged adviser now stood straight-backed. He revealed a newly embossed metal hand, and a dark intensity emanated from him. His amber eyes practically glowed with malice. "What is it?" He snapped, spittle flying from his mouth and speckling across Tav'Opal's face. She did back up then, Dabor noted with grim satisfaction.

Dabor stepped aside, gesturing to the Rav'Arian. It cackled as it approached Morta and pulled back its hood.

Dabor loathed the sight. So unnatural. Its mottled skin, sprouting red hairs, and its giant maw, reeking of fouled flesh, made Dabor sick. He hated everything about his life. But he couldn't dwell; he forced himself to snap alert and listen.

Listening was what he was good at. He had learned a lot of information over the years. The trick was to listen, but not appear to be listening. He crossed his arms, feigning a look of resignation. *Act like a dumb troll, and they will forget you are here,* he thought.

The Rav'Arian dipped his head at Morta before rattling off the same tale he'd already told Dabor.

"Is that so?" Morta said, a bemused expression taking hold of his features. His pale skin and amber eyes looking more reptilian by the day. "And they mean to attack… without me?"

The Rav'Arian, sensing that this may displease his master, stepped back. Keeping his head low, he croaked, "Yes."

Morta inhaled deeply, turning on his heel and returning to inspect the tenements and landscape surrounding the Castle.

After a hair-splitting silence, the woman spoke softly, "The trolls overstep. They cannot fight unless you command it. They must watch and wait… as all Tarsin's peoples do."

Morta erupted with laughter, and just as quickly as it had come, he turned toward her, viciously grabbing her by the throat with his metal hand. In one smooth motion, she dangled in the air. Dabor watched in horror as the metal hand began to squeeze Tav'Opal's throat. Her hands tried to pry his grip, her stout legs kicked outward, and her amber eyes widened in panic.

Dabor dared not breathe. The Rav'Arian seemed to sense the tension, too, and froze mid-bow. The other backed up behind Dabor, as if to make its break.

"As I said earlier, I only keep you—and your kind—around for our blood connection. But I am beginning to question that, due to your many mistakes. My pet possesses what you lack—fortitude. He will terrorize Vikaris's forces, tenderizing his men, and preparing them for my destruction!"

Morta opened his hand suddenly. Tav'Opal fell heavily to the floor, curling into a fetal position and sucking in air deeply. Her wheezing continued, but Morta lost interest immediately, turning quickly to Dabor and the Rav'Arians.

"When will the battle begin?"

The Rav'Arian, head still bent, whispered, "Today, Master."

Morta sneered, "Then why are you still standing here? Gather the Rav'Arians, assemble the troops. We leave immediately."

Dabor flinched. *Today? Morta is letting the trolls set the battle?* The morning light rose to announce the start of a new day. To make ready a force of thousands to march without preparation was near impossible... Dabor swallowed, saluting Morta and taking big limping strides toward the staircase that would lead him from the outer ramparts to the castle's interior.

Just as he opened the door to the stairs, he looked aside to see Morta bending over Tav'Opal, snarling commands to prepare the unicorns and watchers. She was on all fours, trying and failing to stand as he kicked her again in the stomach. Behind him, heads of all those who had displeased first Narco, and now Morta, adorned spikes.

Dabor had no doubt that Tav'Opal's head would soon adorn the Castle wall if she—or the pale watchers—displeased him further. Dabor did not linger. To survive, he kept a low profile and did what his masters bid, even though his insides screamed for him to rebel. To fight back. To run.

But he knew it was futile. Morta had a hold on him, and if he wanted to survive, he had to obey... and listen. He wondered how it would be to see the full mass of trolls again. There were warriors here, yes, but not all. Not yet. And especially not the 'pet' Morta had referred to. Dabor felt ire boiling as he remembered that hulking beast who had come into the mountain pass all those years ago and changed everything. To be free, Dabor knew, that beast—and Morta—would have to die.

***

D'Ania cried softly as they made their way through the winding mountain tunnels and caves, coming upon a well-worn trail that Aalil could only assume had taken the main force of troops downward.

Having freed the stone from the male guard's leg had revealed much to Aalil. She had to get to the King and warn him of the trolls and of the dark forces which kept them obedient to the enemy.

D'Ania, along with three other troll females around her age, had insisted on accompanying Aalil. The rest—the older females, children, and a few too timid to even consider uprising—clustered together with the male in the cave. The old mother had promised to watch over the children who had been in D'Ania's care, vowing she would take them all to the remote caves farther up the mountains beyond the lake. There, they would be safe and wait for D'Ania… or for the males to return.

Aalil had not wanted to be rude, but this waiting made her impatient. She needed to get to the King fast so that she could return her attention to rescuing Antonis. Every moment they waited could be putting the people of Nav'Aria—her love included—in danger.

The trolls had picked up on her impatience, she knew, and said their goodbyes. The male had seemed dazed still and waved awkwardly as they left.

That had been hours ago. They had been behind the males. Aalil knew now for certain, since they'd been traveling in the opposite direction. She set a hard pace, worried that the female captives whose muscles surely waned over years in captivity, would be unable to keep up. It seemed their determination won out though, and they pushed hard. There was little chatter throughout the day, for which Aalil was glad. She was too caught up with her thoughts and survey of the land to make idle talk. D'Ania seemed to be lost in her own thoughts as well. Aalil knew it was hard for her to leave the children. She wondered then, why was D'Ania coming with her.

She peered toward the troll at her side. Face stoic, save for tear-streaked cheeks, D'Ania looked determined.

"Why are you coming with me?"

D'Ania blinked, looking down at Aalil who stood much shorter than her. "Help," she shrugged.

Grateful for the company and the help, Aalil nodded. She never would have made her way through the tunnels alone. She hated the dark and enclosed places. The confident trolls strode right through. They must be able to see in the dark better than her. It worked to her advantage, because they were able to keep a fast pace— even through those dim areas—guiding Aalil along as if she were a blind child amongst knowing adults.

Making faster pace than anticipated, Aalil breathed a sigh of relief as they made their way into the compressed forests at the base of the mountains. If she recalled correctly, these would lead her, if headed West, toward the Woods of the Willow. The King was most likely there, she reasoned, and so set off in that direction. Her companions didn't argue. They seemed nervous, the further distance they put with the mountains, however.

Aalil could understand this. They had most likely never left the mountains. Many of them hadn't left the small island they'd been imprisoned on for many years.

Again, she found herself studying D'Ania from the corner of her eye. Could she trust her? Fully? Was this all a ploy to gain access into the King's secret encampment? She questioned whether she should dart ahead and leave the trolls to their own devices.

As if hearing her thoughts, D'Ania glanced at her. "Friends?"

Aalil ceased biting her lip and smiled reassuringly. "Yes, we are friends. You have helped me a lot. But… tell me, why help? What is in it for you?"

D'Ania blinked as if struck. Confusion flashing across her face. She gestured from herself to Aalil. "We help you… and males." She pointed at Aalil's leg, indicating the place where they'd removed the stone from the male.

Aalil nodded her recollection. The trail grew dark as evening swept over the land, marking yet another day she'd spent without Antonis.

The troll inquired, "Why you help?"

Aalil looked at her, about to laugh. *Why am I helping? Obligation to the King? A love for Nav'Aria? A longing to prove myself? A desire for recognition? A need to win Antonis's respect?* These thoughts and more flashed through her mind, but she replied lamely, "I… want to."

D'Ania raised a bushy eyebrow but didn't press. "Good."

A hand grasped Aalil's elbow then, causing her to gasp. She spun alert.

One of the other trolls with her, Calwayie, bobbed her head. "Trolls," she pointed out in a whisper.

Aalil squinted to see in the dim light what she was pointing toward.

D'Ania knelt down to inspect the trail.

Aalil followed and gasped softly as she looked, cursing herself. Though she was no tracker like Riccus, she was still better than most. How had she missed these? There were footsteps—large ones—all over. They were now in pursuit of the troll army, she had no doubt.

Gulping, she tried to calm her nerves at the image of the beast's omnipotence. But what were they doing heading this direction? She felt her nerves change to exultation! If the trolls were near, so too must Antonis be!

Speaking in hushed tones, she ordered the trolls, with their keen eyesight, to keep a close watch of the area and to stay quiet. They were to pat one another for signaling rather than speaking, if at all possible. As the moon and stars shimmered above, Aalil bit the inside of her cheek to remain focused—and quiet. It was too dark to see a thing! Luckily, D'Ania now held her elbow and led her, just as she'd done in the cave tunnels. Where before Aalil had felt embarrassed—resentful at having to be led like a child— now she felt gratitude. Antonis must be near, and she was going to find him.

Signs of a sizeable force became unmistakable, and soon Aalil was struck with a grim realization. If the army was headed this way rather than joining the forces at the Castle, that could only mean one thing. They were headed straight toward the King. She prayed they would be in time to lend aid in the fight!

CHAPTER 22

The Scream

As swiftly as the warning had come, the veteran troops donned their swords, forgetting their fatigue. The unseasoned new recruits fumbled around trying to act brave, all the while appearing sickly.

Darion glanced at Edmond, who stood stolidly at his side. *Edmond the behemoth,* he thought. His loyal friend found him as soon as the horn sounded. With his shoulder-length hair now pulled back with twine like Darion's, he declared he would not leave his Prince's side... but added at Vikaris's raised eyebrow, "unless my King commands it, of course," his cheeks flaming red.

Darion, punched Edmond's shoulder with familiarly, jesting, "Of course, you're standing next to me. Didn't Barson say together we make one fighter? I'm not doing this without you." Though his nerves were on high alert, he tried to make his friend and those around him smile.

Vikaris smiled at him, though Darion noted with sadness that it did not quite reach his father's eyes. His brilliant green orbs swept the area, the tanned skin around them creasing with tension.

As soon as word had come about the trolls, additional scouts had been sent out, and guards stood watch. Garis had ordered the troops to assemble on the southern section of the camp where the horses had been hitched. It was open ground and what the commander had called ideal land for fighting. Lit torches blazed all around, and every third soldier in the formed lines had been given a torch. That, along with the unicorns in the center illuminating the area, made the force a very easy target.

After Kragar had complained about their lack of stealth, Garis explained that the need for secrecy was up. Their position had already been compromised; therefore, the additional light would serve them well. The warriors stood ready. This close of contact wouldn't allow for pikes, archers, or a decent cavalry charge, but still, they stood ready. Archers had been sent up into the trees on the edges of the camp to harry the enemy as it approached. Catching them off-guard would prove a real advantage. And soldiers in the back of the line were told to light their arrow tips wrapped in a thin oil-soaked linen, and shoot them high, again, to rattle the enemy and pierce as many in their force as possible.

Darion stood with Edmond, Triumph, Soren, Vikaris, and Trixon. Around them stood the entirety of the unicorn warriors led by the enraged and snorting Drigidor. Again, they risked themselves, and with them, all that was good in Nav'Aria. Darion hated seeing them here… and the youths—many much younger than him—

clustering around their commanding officers. He furrowed his brow as he watched one trip and nearly stab himself with his own blade, while a centaur youth dipped his entire head into a bucket of standing water before proceeding to vomit.

He wanted to ask his father if these younglings really needed to be here, but before he could open his mouth, a bloodcurdling scream exploded from just outside of range. Cries of pain and surprise rang in the new day. The sky seemed to lighten except for one area, Darion noticed, trying to ascertain what was happening. He drew heavily upon his senses. He heard the elevated heartrates of those near him and smelled the sweat on the men, the urine streaming down one youngling's legs, the newly spilled blood, and the... evil! He could taste it in the air. Not the tar of the Rav'Arians, but definitely the feel and scent of wrongness. He glanced at his father to see if he, too, sensed the darkness sweeping in.

It reminds me of the beast we faced in Rav'Ar, Triumph murmured, beginning to step unconsciously as the unicorns and guards shifted. Somewhere out there they were coming.

Darion focused on the blotch of darkness the lightening sky didn't touch.

"There!" Darion pointed, feeling as if he'd been hit in the stomach. Triumph was correct. The trolls were approaching—at a run—and in the lead was a hideous, ginormous beast with blazing red eyes and a face that Darion knew would haunt his dreams for years to come.

Vikaris was shouting off commands to the soldiers near him, just as Garis came thundering through the rows of troops, bellowing as he galloped on his powerful four legs, his russet coat gleaming in the changing light. "Archers, ready! To arms! All soldiers to arms!" He drew up just in front of Vikaris, Darion and their party. Garis brandished his sword, and then, to Darion's astonishment, readied the axe that had hung at his waist. Bare chested, save for a rope cord with a small, nearly indistinguishable stone at his throat, his muscles rippled. "Sire, hold. This battle must not get away from us. I will lead the first charge, and you, the second at my signal."

Darion wasn't surprised to hear Garis issuing orders. Vikaris and he had a working relationship, and if Vikaris disagreed, he would make it known. He was the King of course, but he respected his Commander and his battle experience. Garis's war commands deserved to be heeded.

"We await your signal, Garis."

The Commander nodded, rearing up on his back legs—much like a wild stallion—and let loose a mighty war cry. His soldiers bellowed in response.

Darion swallowed nervously. He had never been in a battle. Never seen one. Nothing like this, at least. Yes, he'd fought some Rav'Arians and the monster in Rav'Ar, but he had never seen so many adversaries. He feared for his safety and for that of his friends.

"You are braver than you give yourself credit, my Prince. Together, we will defeat them," Triumph spoke, his tone chilling. Instructor Triumph was gone, and in his place was the lethal warrior.

Garis's front legs hit the dirt, and with a ferocious cry, he signaled to the archers to let fly their arrows. Then charging directly into the beast's path, wielding both sword and axe, the massive centaur's assault transfixed soldiers from both sides.

The sight gave Darion the push he needed. This was it. Garis was risking his life for them all, and no matter what came of today—*a victory*, he prayed—he knew that he, too, would die to protect those around him. He looked over to see his father jumping into the majestic war saddle on Trixon's back.

He caught his father's eyes and remembered their quick words earlier. "Do whatever it takes to stay alive, son. If we are separated, stick with the unicorns, and if I fall—" Darion had cut him off then, grabbing him in an emotional embrace. No more parents were going to die. *Not on my watch*, he thought angrily, watching the charging monster who looked to be straight out of hell, blood streaking its face and dripping down its front. Darion knew that he was the killer and cause of that terrible scream from moments ago. The beast was their main target.

"Hurry, Darion. You should ride for this fight."

Darion didn't argue with that! He knew he wasn't supposed to ask to ride Triumph, but damn, if his friend had waited any longer to ask, Darion might have accidentally blurted it out. It would feel better to have a higher vantage, particularly with all the looming trolls and a freaking monster headed their way.

Steel met steel, and soon Darion's senses were awash with screams and clatters; smells of blood, earth, and sweat; and the distinct wrongness of the troll multitude swarming the land. Their heavy footsteps and quickened pace pounded the ground, causing dust to swirl in their wake. Horses screamed, men cried out, and trolls roared in angry anticipation as they clashed. Archers released their lit arrows, and quickly, enemies began to fall and snarl in pain—and annoyance—at such tactics.

Darion noted there seemed to be no organization to the enemy... only sheer force and numbers, just as his father and Garis had conjectured. They weren't military strategists, but simply beasts intent on an "easy kill." *We will prove that idiot notion wrong today*, Kragar had snarled. *Strategy wins out every time.*

They came in droves. Their large, bare torsos streaked with scars and jutting, bulbous veins didn't distract from their massive arms. Darion looked to his side, surprised to see Soren ordering Edmond atop him for the fight.

Edmond reached across to squeeze Darion's forearm and nodded. Darion nodded back, feeling his friend's calmness wash through him. This may be their first battle, but this was far from their first fight. They were no longer untested youths like the fools pissing themselves in the lines. Darion and Edmond knew how to fight, and they had been preparing for this moment for weeks. It also helped to have Triumph and Soren, who had fought with them and protected them across the border. This felt familiar. Together, they would face the enemy.

The three men astride their unicorns and surrounded by a circle of unicorns made for an easy target. The beast, Darion observed, narrowed in on them, and his purposeful strides brought him near. The front lines of trolls and the men and centaurs clashed, officially commencing the battle.

The unicorns held steady as commanded... though Darion eyed Drigidor. Like a crazed bull intending to charge, he was pawing the ground madly in front of the other unicorns. He had not been pleased to find that he would not be used in the frontlines. He had argued and gnashed his teeth before being smacked upside the head by Kragar for his insubordination. "You heard your King and Commander, now do as you are told," the Lieutenant had snarled.

Darion thought Kragar must be insane. *Who hits a unicorn?* And yet his reprimand had seemed to cow Drigidor... for the time being. And so, he fumed and pawed the ground, his anger and angst rubbing off on the others as they waited and watched.

Having raced ahead to lead the frontlines in the initial attack, Garis moved out from his soldiers and slammed full force into the beast, knocking it from its path.

Darion heard his father's intake of breath as he gripped the sword at his belt and watched Garis challenge the enemy. The beast roared while shielding itself from Garis's fast moving blades. Man, troll, and centaur dove away from the of the crazed centaur warrior, making space and picking off easier targets instead.

Darion, though a good distance from the front, could see the beast. It was larger than he'd imagined! It snarled, leaping and snapping its bloody jaws at Garis and catching his shoulder. Garis cried out in pain and rage, slashing his sword at the creature's neck. The arm that held the axe hung limply. The beast had snapped his collarbone and drawn blood.

Darion watched in horror as the axe fell from the Commander's hand, crimson liquid trailing down.

"NO," Drigidor roared, spinning and looking toward Vikaris. "Garis needs us!"

Vikaris, though visibly angry, hesitated. His Ruby shone brightly, casting the unicorns' white light into a pinky glow, and he drew his sword.

Another roar of anguish came from the front. Darion's eyes shot back to the front. Garis still stood fighting, sword cutting the air as it came down again and again upon the beast who parried his every blow with what looked to be a metal club.

The unicorns around the Royals danced on anxious feet, awaiting the command to run.

Still Vikaris waited, brow furrowed.

"Father," Darion urged, looking from him back to Garis, whose expert swordsmanship was beginning to wane. Men at the front seemed to sense their leader's weakening and tried to intervene, taking decisive stabs at the beast. Darion watched in horror as the beast swatted them away like flies. The men and other centaurs had the entirety of the troll force to contend with also; they couldn't turn their backs for long to come to their

Commander's aid, so intense was the fight. Screams and bellows filled the land.

"Vikaris," Trixon snapped. "What are you waiting for? He is severely injured. He cannot give the signal. We must ride."

"Garis chose the first wave. We agreed. I would lead the second wave of attack," Vikaris said, sounding uncharacteristically unsure of himself and glancing at Darion.

"That plan is moot," Trixon roared, gesturing with his horn toward the frenzied front lines.

"Well, I am trying to figure out how we are supposed to beat something like that," Vikaris snapped back, a little softer. A hybrid unlike anything he'd ever seen pricked at Vikaris's confidence. When he glanced at his son again, Darion understood. His father was distracted by his presence here. Did he truly think soldiers should die while the rest held back to protect him? As if Darion was a swaddled infant?

Anger bloomed in him. He drew his sword, arm and Ruby aglow as if they sensed his new resolve.

"If you will not go, then get off my back," Trixon growled. "King or not, friend or not, I will not stand by and watch my Commander die. The unicorns will fight!"

Darion gaped at Trixon's vehemence... and insubordination. Trixon was true to his reputation, Darion observed. He was rash... and he was right!

Darion watched his father's eyes bulge with outrage—and fear—looking again at Darion. "Father, quit worrying about me. Trixon is right. They need us!" Darion snapped.

Vikaris nodded, "then go!" he commanded and waved his hand, motioning for the rear guard to join the fray. The unicorns jolted forward, as if set free from a cage, making their way toward the front. As they neared, the beast slammed his muscled shoulder into Garis, vaulting him off the ground. The centaur's heavy landing rattled his head and left him without a sword. Trolls and men battled all around, obscuring him from their sight.

Pressing forward, Darion stretched over Triumph's neck, trying to catch sight of the centaur as they rushed to his aid. Knocking soldiers out of the way, Darion's eardrums nearly burst from the shattering screams simultaneously erupting from his father and Trixon. Making their way into view, Drigidor, along with the unicorn warriors, set to work at clearing away and fighting off trolls surrounding the beast and Garis. Darion watched in horror as the beast, eyes staring boldly at the King, clamped his massive jaws around Garis's head. Teeth tightening and wrenching around, he ripped Garis's head from his body. The beast then spat it out. Garis's dull, lifeless eyes stared up at Darion, and his head thudded in front of Triumph's skittering hooves.

The beast stood slowly back up to its full height, while the blood sprayed out from Garis's severed neck. The beast snickered and spread his arms wide for his next attacker.

Darion erupted in an ire unlike anything he had ever experienced. He held his sword and prepared to charge.

"YOU BASTARD," Drigidor screamed, suddenly rearing up on his powerful hind legs before colliding with the beast.

Trixon, shaking off an unsuspecting Vikaris, reared and bellowed a war cry of his own. Vikaris yelled for him to stop while drawing his sword and racing after his companion, Kragar fast on his heels. Bravely—and rashly—Trixon fought the beast, pummeling him with his hooves as the beast deflected Drigidor's rampage.

Darion had seen enough, and apparently so had Triumph, for a beam of bright light streamed out of his horn, temporarily blinding the beast in his rush to avenge his friend.

Near Trixon and Drigidor, Vikaris faced a troll twice his size. Triumph rushed into the fight, and Darion slashed his sword at the troll's back as Triumph cut with his horn. An angry roar erupted from the towering creature as it spun, still waving its club around in an effort to fend off the other unicorns. Triumph danced back, just inches out of the club's reach, before rushing in.

"Darion, look out," Edmond from nearby as he jumped from Soren's back and deflected a blade aimed at Darion's heart.

Triumph growled, turning from his rush at the beast to come to Edmond's aid. As it happened, there was no need, for as a vein began to pop out in Edmond's thick neck while he held off the enemy, a gurgling sound of surprise came from the troll as it collapsed heavily. Behind him, Soren stood with dark black blood staining his silver horn and velvety nose. Edmond looked surprised only for a moment before turning back to take on another troll near the King. Trixon's entanglement with the beast left Vikaris vulnerable.

"Protect the King," Triumph bellowed.

"Hold on, Triumph," Darion ordered, patting his neck and jumping off. This close fighting afforded no rider. The tight press of bodies became intense. Darion had to get to his father. He followed after Edmond, slashing at a troll that thumped past in pursuit of a younger soldier. Triumph called for him to stay back, but soon he became occupied fighting off another red-eyed beast whose club smacked his rear, provoking Triumph's angered shriek.

The beast and the Royals fought with savage ferocity, encircled now by unicorns, whose formerly pristine coats now bore streaks of blood and gore. Light shot from their horns, blinding their enemies.

Trixon and Drigidor, together with two other unicorns closed in on the beast, taking turns kicking and slashing at him. The beast may have been able to slay one combatant, but he was no match for the unicorn warriors.

Baring many slashed cuts upon its arms from the unicorns' hooves and horns, the beast roared wildly, then seemed to notice easier prey. Glancing toward the side, the beast noticed Vikaris and Edmond, and Darion close behind.

Jumping recklessly, the beast lashed out at Edmond, narrowly missing his head, which would've likely killed him given the force of the blow.

Darion shouted angrily at the troll who had Edmond and Vikaris in his sights. Slicing cleanly through the distracted creature's heart, Darion needn't waste any time watching his enemy fall. He was already dead. Effortlessly pulling his sword from the collapsing corpse, he then rushed to his friend. He found Edmond in a defensive stance, staring down the beast who radiated with mirth at the mere thought of killing.

The unicorns shrieked and growled threats while hammering the trolls that had enclosed them when the beast shifted positions. A fear-rendering scream came from that area, and Darion glanced to ensure Triumph was safe. His friend was currently fighting off two trolls, one holding together its recently slashed open stomach clumsily as it swung its club. It was finished. Triumph could hold. The scream wasn't his. Darion prayed that whoever had fallen had died quickly, for he knew without a doubt that a unicorn had just met its end.

Reaching Edmond, he sliced low at the beast's legs. His sword tip struck true, while Edmond cut at the creature's trunk, trying to fend off the blows from the ever-moving club.

Darion pulled back to prepare his next strike when Edmond stumbled—right in the club's path. Edmond's foot was caught in the entangled corpses of a troll and two humans beneath him.

The whooshing sound of the club soared through the air. Darion knew he only had moments before the club collided with his trapped friend.

"Edmond," a voice roared nearby. It sounded like Soren, though he was still too far to help.

In a moment of haste, Darion pushed Edmond down. He jumped off the troll corpse and slashed wildly as the club made impact with his stomach.

Hearing the sickening crunch of cracking rib, Darion groaned and fell to the ground. His head hit something hard as he landed beside Edmond, who was calling his name and reaching for him. A pair of hands quickly grabbed at his chest as he toppled over the piling corpses. The beast's grinning eyes peered down at him, its massive jaws widening to finish him off. Darion heard his father scream his name, and a blur of motion caught his eye before everything went black.

***

Zola paced, replaying over and over again the conversation she'd had with the leaders! Looking over the four children she had been charged to care for, she sighed in frustration. This wasn't fair. Elsra herself had named Zola a unicorn warrior, and here she was playing nursemaid. Why? Because she was female? And why were these nuisances even in a war camp? Didn't they realize she knew next to nothing about being a mother? Being a nurturer? Her abducted son was proof of that, she thought sadly. All she knew was that, when faced with a fight, she didn't back down. She would have never believed it herself had she not experienced it. She was indeed a powerful fighter, and instead of feeling fear, an emotion she sensed emanating from one too many of the soldiers, she felt nothing but a cold calmness sweeping over her.

She recalled her conversation with Soren just days earlier as she'd shared some of what had taken place during her captivity and getaway. She had commented that it seemed like fighting was the only thing she knew how to do—she certainly couldn't read, raise her son, or be an instructor like her father. She was uneducated and thus even more different than the other unicorns. Soren had just laughed. She remembered how she'd felt embarrassed at the sound of the handsome unicorn mocking her. *"You think I am dumb like a common stable horse!"* She had snapped angrily and stormed off, but he ran after her and rubbed his nose upon hers, the touch sending an electric charge through her body.

You misunderstood me, I am not laughing at the fact that you have been held in captivity. I would never jest about that, Zola. He had said, his eyes looking into hers with such earnestness that she believed him, and he continued. *I think you are one of the strongest fighters I have ever met.* At her flat stare, he pressed, *Honestly. To spend so much of your time under the drug that they used and still have such strong instincts tells so much. You are a warrior spirit... That is your gifting. Just like Trixon and Drigidor. You do not need to know all the scrolls of old, or medicine, or how to be an administrator. Your instincts are sound... and you have already beaten enemies. I think with more training, you could become one of our greatest warriors.*

She had blushed at his praise; that was, of course, before her horn was returned to her, so at the time, his words had seemed impossible. And then the impossible had happened. She had been gifted her horn. Named a warrior and member of the Unicorn Council by the dying

Regent herself, and yet, here she stood while the warriors faced the onslaught of trolls.

"You are wearied from your own fight and travels," Triumph had said in a voice brokering no argument. The other unicorns and King himself had agreed. She would be needed for the fight to come, they assured her, but she must care for herself and protect the few younglings that Vikaris deemed too young to fight, though they'd been conscripted. She glared at the diverse group. One unicorn white as snow… so different from her young colt… two blonde and ivory centaurs, and a nymph. Having seen few nymphs, she studied the olive-skinned creature with its iridescent wings. The young creatures didn't seem too pleased to be sitting out of the fight either. Clustered together at such distance from the fight, they clambered onto tree stumps, the nymph trying to remain aloft to report what she saw. Zola gritted her teeth at their excited talk. This was a game to these untested youths, but she knew this was far from a game. That was her family in the fray!

When the enemy came upon their forces, her skin crawled at their leader's menacing roar. So far off, she could not make out much beyond the stain of darkness moving over the land and headed for her fellows. She could hear the thundering footsteps and war cries of the trolls, and likewise, the pounding of hooves from the centaurs, and eventually, unicorns. The humans' boots thudding on the ground in accompanying cadence as they raced toward the enemy.

And then, she'd watched idly as Garis fell. The unicorns fought ferociously to destroy the hideous beast. She squinted her eyes to see humans near the beast, as well. The King... and the Prince! She watched as Darion fell, and the passion within her blazed. She was no mere nursemaid. She was Zola, kin of the First Horn, and member of the Unicorn Council. She was a warrior, and she was not going to miss this fight.

With curt orders that she'd punish the younglings herself if they moved from their spot, she raced to join the troops. For if Darion had fallen, she knew her father would be close at hand... and maddened with grief. She could not lose him too.

Dodging bodies of all sizes, and slamming trolls down in her wake, she felt the calm coolness of battle overtake her. She smiled, feeling the assurance that this was where she was meant to be, where she felt the most alive. Her body responded and her horn ignited with light flooding every direction. As she passed them, trolls bellowed and covered their eyes, the humans and centaurs not hesitating for a moment threw down torches and struck while their enemies stumbled blindly.

Like a flaming arrow, she streaked from the edge of camp directly into the heart of darkness. The beast was being held off for now. Trixon pummeled it valiantly, seemingly unphased by the bloody gash on his foreleg. Baring multiple wounds, Drigidor, the mighty warrior and mate of Elsra, was flagging. Her father looked near collapse, blood and dirt covering his entire side as if he'd been knocked down or dragged. He was looking from the troll toward Darion and back, and tears streaked his face. The King, Zola noted, fought bravely alongside his horned warriors, his arm aglow and his face a picture of rage. The beast, having been pushed back from Darion—who lay either dead or unconscious—looked to be enjoying itself. It was larger than she had at first assumed. Its red eyes and tireless swinging of its club kept its assailants back.

Nearing them, she gasped. *Soren!* She could see him at the edge trying to fight off a troll while nudging at two human forms. Having sufficiently battered the troll he resumed trying to pry free the pinned humans suffocating under a pile of corpses.

Freshly renewed, the troll limped forward, grasping a jagged blade in both hands and preparing to plunge it directly into....

She slammed into the monster's side, completely catching it off guard. Her horn penetrated the troll's side and tore through flesh, organs, bones, and muscle, nearly severing it in two. Tumbling back, trying and failing to catch its spilling organs, the troll screamed in agony. Shaking off the blood and grime, Zola turned toward Soren with a reassuring glance.

He stood stock straight, ears perked up, and in any other moment, she might have laughed at his complete surprise, but not right now. Not while the coolness of battle coursed through her veins. There were still more enemies, and they did not know about the newest threat.

Zola growled. This beast was no match for unicorns. It was filthy. Evil. And about to die. Power unlike anything she'd ever experienced flowed through her essence, lighting her horn like a star beam. Swiftly, her newly enhanced muscles, restored with her horn, rippled from the pleasure of use. She felt invincible... and with her blood and horn aglow, she vaulted over the corpses, the live humans, and Soren to catch the beast off guard.

As she landed just out of arm's reach of the beast, more light burst from her, causing the fighters and onlookers to fall back. Her father, Trixon, Drigidor, and the King were blasted out of harm's reach, clearing a space for her to face the beast alone.

The beast flinched, recoiling from the light, but the brilliance was unrelenting. It roared angrily, swinging the club around, unsure where its attacker stood.

It was Zola's turn to laugh. Her eerie mirth echoed off the suddenly quiet battlefield.

Fighters all around had ceased, mesmerized by her approach, as if time stood still.

She breathed deeply, with the certainty of the beast's fate. It bellowed and tottered like a pouting child. "You are weak," her lilted voice taunting him.

It snarled, spinning around and waving the club haphazardly.

She heard her name being called and knew her father was trying to reach her. She had to stop this before he did something stupid. Pawing at the ground before her, she lowered her head, slipping beneath the sweeping club, and ran her horn through its stomach. She didn't stop there to gloat, however.

It roared in pain.

Evading the club again, she darted back and unleashed two powerful front kicks to its arm. The metal club fell with a heavy clang. Her horn, still ablaze with light, kept the creature blinded.

He bellowed. Snarling, teeth bared, it snapped its jaws.

Her cold laugh bubbled up again. She moved behind the creature, lithely slashing at its legs, until she heard the snap of its hamstring muscles. The creature screamed in agony and fell to the ground, its arms flailing about wildly.

For good measure, she landed another heavy kick, putting her full force of gifted power to its head. The creature flew backwards, snorting and whimpering as it crashed to the ground.

She walked forward. Pressing her front hooves upon its chest, she pinned him and whispered lethally, "I told you, 'you are weak'… and so is your Master," and as she said it, the brilliance of her light faded, allowing the beast's red eyes a final glimpse of its killer. The eyes seemed to hold a tinge of amber for a moment. Fear and confusion flickering briefly. Before it could respond, she swiped her horn across its throat, and as the blood sprayed upwards and defiled her face, she turned to look around the gathered fighters.

The beast was dead.

As soon as its eyes closed, the trolls seemed to shout at once, and heavy footsteps sounded with their retreat. Their leader was dead. The fight was over for today.

Vikaris yelled to catch them, take any captives they could, and kill any injured trolls left on the field.

Zola stepped down from the corpse and made her way toward her father, who had been restrained by Trixon and Drigidor. All eyes wide as they stared at her as if seeing her for the first time.

"Can someone please tell me why the hell she was not on the front lines?" Kragar snapped.

Her eyes searched the area where she'd last seen Soren. Upon seeing him and the others assisting Darion and Edmond to their feet, she felt her pulse slow with relief. Though dazed, they would live. She then caught sight of the Commander. Garis was dead. She felt only gladness that she didn't remain back any longer. She vowed there that she would never sit out a fight again.

CHAPTER 23

The Sentry

The carpeted trail filled with the softest grasses, ferns, flowers, and shrubs was lighted by dancing fireflies and the luminous glow of his horn. Trinidad knew he should be humbler, but he could not stop the pitter patter of his heart whenever he thought about it. *His horn!* He had been found worthy. His ancestors and Creator—through Darion as their vessel—had transferred an awe-evoking gift upon him. He felt immeasurable gratitude... and responsibility. He would not fail this time.

He knew failure had blotted his life up until now. His haste into battle, much to his shame and heartbreak, is what had led to Rustusse's first death—the one Rinzaltan's life blood had restored—and then, there was his captivity with Lyrianna. He had allowed himself to get captured along with the Queen. She had been tortured while he stood apathetically entranced, thanks to the hallucinogenic ointment applied his horn's stump. He knew he should hate himself. Loathe his errors as

Triumph had loathed his own. And yet, Trinidad felt instead an insatiable desire for remedy. To fix things. Restore all that had been stolen from the land and make peace. He did not dwell on the past but rather looked toward the future. He remembered his father, the wise and mighty Rinzaltan, had always commented on how Trinidad was able to look ahead. See what others could not see. His father surmised that this perspective was one of his giftings, as well. *Perhaps*, Trinidad thought. Regardless, he knew now that he had been given a second chance, one he would surely not squander.

He beamed with pride aside the elegant Queen, his treasured friend and companion who strolled next to him, hand upon his mane. Lyrianna trusted him fully, and that faith, when all hope had seemed lost in captivity, had been his salvation. It had brought him back from the brink of despair. Oh, how proud he was of her... and of his son, Trixon, and of the young but already-capable Darion. Trinidad felt his heart soar thinking of all the wondrous friends he had that would—

"Are you trying to alert everyone nearby of your presence, Trinidad?" Cela tersely remarked. "Turn down your light."

Trinidad's joyous thoughts ceased as he tried to focus on dimming his horn, his cheeks flushing as if he were a chastened young colt once more. "Sorry," he murmured.

Lyrianna chuckled, patting his mane while Cela heaved an aggravated sigh with a flip of red flowing locks, turning to scan their surroundings.

Suddenly, wings flitted with the Adelina's return. "We are close. The party has returned to the outpost. They wait for us there."

Lyrianna's hand dropped. She picked up her skirt with both hands to increase her pace. Trinidad hastened to match it.

Rounding the base of a towering Cedar tree, Trinidad spied a small thatched roofed hut surrounded almost entirely by Cypress trees. If not for the small cookfire tended by a nymph out front, the outpost could have been overlooked. They had taken great care, the renegade nymphs who patrolled this close to the enemy, to protect their position. Drawing closer, the fire sizzled and cracked from the grease of cooking meats and roasting vegetables. Trinidad's stomach grumbled. Though he did not eat that fare, he realized he was indeed famished from their trek. He spied some tasty weeds and grasses he'd eat soon… just as soon as they found their friends.

A nymph stood apart from the hut to greet them. He bowed lowly at the sight of Lyrianna and Trinidad, for though they were far from the Royal War Camp, *it did not take a genius to recognize the Queen… and to pay tribute to a unicorn*, Trinidad thought. He knew that his kind—well besides the poor wretches kept by Narco and Morta— were rare in this part of Nav'Aria. He hoped his presence would uplift their wearied spirits. For weary they truly were, he noted. The nymph's pale face looked sallow and worn. Still, he was courteous and gestured for them to enter.

Lyrianna went first... after Cela had looked over the area and nodded that it was safe to enter. Trindad stifled a laugh. Many things could be said about this fiery centaur, but shirking responsibilities was not one of them. Nodding back to her as she took up guard at the entrance, along with the nymph sisters, Trinidad dipped his head low to peer inside. Unable to fit his bulk through the narrow doorway, he would have to be satisfied only peeking.

He observed that two of the farthest cots held sleeping humans. Two in fact. Nearby the room, sat silent nymphs who quietly polished weapons, unpacked bags, and neatly folded linens and garments, using utter care to not wake their companions. Or at least that was until the Queen of Nav'Aria and a unicorn strolled in.

As one, the nymphs stood saluting her and dropping whatever they were holding. One nymph dropped a water cup that clattered on the floor.

Trinidad smiled as he heard a familiar voice gripe about the noise.

"Do not rebuke them too harshly, my friend. It is because of us that they make noise."

A snort, then a gasp, came from somewhere in the back. And then a thud, and a loud grumbling "ouch" as Antonis snapped to alert, waking Riccus.

Trinidad smiled, the light growing ever brighter and illuminating more and more of the area.

"Trinidad, can you turn that down? You are blinding me," Antonis jested to his long-time friend. Striding up with a huge grin, he bowed first to Lyrianna before embracing Trinidad's neck... that which he was able to fit through the doorway, at least.

"Well, I must admit seeing you two is a welcome sight," Riccus drawled warmly walking up. The nymphs remained standing quietly. Awkwardly.

Catching on to the strange atmosphere and noticing Trinidad's predicament, Lyrianna gestured. "Let us all gather outside to speak."

Once seated around the fire, the nymphs passed out food and drink for all, even indulging Trinidad in a large pile of the delectable grasses and flowers spied earlier. The party shared in the bounty and all told their stories. The female nymphs, clearly at ease with their kind, shared news from the Woods of the Willow.

Antonis and Riccus regaled them with their mountain trials. The anguish in Antonis's eyes betrayed his stoicism as he told of Aalil's capture. This tore at Trinidad's heart. He prayed to the Creator that she was safe.

Once their news was shared, at Lyrianna's bidding, she then explained what had since transpired, and what she, Trinidad (and Cela) were up to.

Antonis gaped. "My Queen. You cannot go back there! It is evil."

Lyrianna smiled warmly at him, but her resolve did not waver. "We know the area better than any others of recent times," waving her hand toward Trinidad and Cela with a sad smile. "We must all play our part. Though I am so relieved to see you, Riccus. I promised Darion that we would search for you. And here you are. A gift from the Creator."

"Can you tell me, Your Majesty, how is my son?" Riccus spoke so quickly, that his eyes bulged when realizing his mouth's mistake. Raising his hands immediately, he began apologizing.

"Our son," Lyrianna said, softly placing her hand upon his and squeezing it. "He is well. Darion has grown since his ventures in Rav'Ar, and because of him—"

"I am whole once more," Trinidad blurted.

At Antonis and Riccus's look of confusion, Trinidad shared quickly how Darion had healed him... and then spoke of his attempt to heal Zola, of Trigger's capture, and of the Watchers' infiltration of Kaulter. The mood darkened then. They all stared into the fire's flames lost in their thoughts.

The nymphs had kept fairly quiet up until now, but as the conversation died down momentarily, their leader, Talen, spoke. "Your Majesty, you would do me the great honor if you would allow us," he gestured toward his comrades, "to accompany you to the Castle. We know the trails and hidden pathways better than anyone." He looked over to Cela, recognizing that while the Queen and Trinidad had a say, the saucy centaur would be the one to consent. She tilted her head, eyeing him in consideration.

"At least one of you should continue to patrol this area, since we know not where the trolls will appear. And..." she added, looking in Antonis and Riccus's direction, "someone should inform the King of our findings."

As soon as she spoke, Antonis and Riccus alarmed each other in their synchronous adamance.

"It is my place to protect the Queen. I too will accompany you," Antonis stated.

While Rick drawled matter-of-factly, "My place is with Darion... I will find their camp and inform them."

And just like that, it was decided. Antonis furrowed his brow at his friend. "Are you sure you will be alright? What if the trolls ambush you along the way?"

Riccus snorted and punched his friend's shoulder. "You know I am the best tracker around here and can keep myself hidden...." Before adding, "you take care of yourself too. You know Rav'Arians will be there."

Trinidad watched the pair of long-time friends while munching on his evening meal. They had a special bond, similar to his and Lyrianna's. Long-time service and captivity did that. He thought that this might be the first time they'd been separated since before Darion's birth. "You both carry great responsibility upon your shoulders." Trinidad said, nodding to them. "Thank you for all you have done for Nav'Aria, and all that you will do in the days to come."

Antonis nodded curtly. Riccus rubbed the knot in his chin, as if uncomfortable with the praise.

Lyrianna stood personally thanking each nymph and man for their assistance in this before announcing that they would leave at first light.

Riccus apologized but announced he would be leaving immediately. If Darion was this close, and a troll army was on the move, he wanted to get to the boy as soon as possible. Lyrianna kissed his cheek at that... and moments later, they watched Riccus depart with his few belongings—a fur coat, a small blade, and a tied bundle of rations. He and another nymph—Copa—headed off in the direction of the King's camp to share the news.

"Take care of yourself damnit," Trinidad heard Antonis whisper, too quiet for all other ears but his own. He walked over to the former Commander, who watched forlornly as his friend disappeared from their view.

"He is a good man," Trinidad spoke softly, turning to look at Antonis. "You are both good men, Antonis. Thank you for remaining with us. Knowing the Queen has your protection is a comfort to us as it will be to Vikaris as well."

Antonis turned away from the now empty trail and patted Trinidad's cheek. "You always were a charmer, Trinidad."

***

Following the troll prints and careful to keep quiet, Aalil and her troll companions pushed hard through their trek. The army had passed through here alright. Aalil bit the inside of her cheek again nervously as she studied the ground. They had slept very little. The trolls didn't seem to mind. They too seemed intent on finding the camp. Aalil had been impressed by their vigor. They had been half-starved and imprisoned for years yet still pressed on. Knowing the troll army was loose upon Nav'Aria was all the motivation she needed to press her sore muscles and foggy brain forward. They could not dally here, lest they be captured themselves and risk the King's army being taken by surprise by that malicious beast.

Making her way through a barrage of "what-ifs", a horn sounded, shattering through her worries and moving her to action. That horn had been close.

"Where?" She mouthed, looking up at D'Ania standing at her side.

D'Ania and the other trolls were scanning the area before another horn blast sounded again. She pointed up ahead and to the left. *South from here.* So not as close as she'd thought. *How had the trolls gotten that far? And,* she gritted her teeth, *why were they sounding a horn?* She had a feeling it could only be for one reason.

"Move," she whispered tersely.

The females began to run in the direction of the horn blasts—and an oncoming battle—Aalil had no doubt.

Dodging tree roots and scattered gravel as they crashed through the forest trails, Aalil considered the trolls' location odd. Why hadn't they headed toward the Castle? Was she too late?

The muscles in her legs burned. Her side cramped, but still she pressed on. She could eat and sleep when this was all over. There was no use thinking on what couldn't be helped. The warrior in her pushed faster and farther ahead of the lumbering females. The shouts and cries in the distance confirmed a battle was taking place, and she was in it!

Running, she nearly collided with a man who was bent down on the trail, inspecting something.

Standing suddenly and defensively turning on his heel to take on this threat, he heard the female gasp before both toppled to the ground.

A stream of curses drawled out, and Aalil knew without a doubt that it was him. "Riccus?" She blurted, trying to push herself up and off this grumbling older man.

"Damnit, Aalil." He groused, standing back up and brushing off his pant legs. His face, though bruised, split in a huge, toothy smile. "I am sure glad to see you." He paused, his brows knitting together as he caught sight of D'Ania and the others over her shoulder.

"Come on out, Copa," Riccus drawled, and at Aalil's surprise, a petite young nymph, not more than twelve or thirteen years old, flitted out from behind the undergrowth.

Words seemed to fail her, and as she gaped at him, the only thing she could utter was, "Antonis?" His absence could only mean one thing. Antonis was dead. Her breath caught, and she felt like her heart was being ripped from her body. So much for looking tough. She collapsed to the ground weeping. She felt arms grabbing at her but made no effort to comply. Antonis. He was truly gone. The trolls had already found the King's army. She had failed. She had failed bitterly.

The oppressive shroud of grief pressed in, and just before she crossed into the brink of despair, she choked, "Why did you push me?" Her tears turned from grief to anger.

Riccus bent over her, his fierce scowl glaring down. "I said, 'knock it off. He is not dead, you daft woman. If you would let me explain…"

"What? But… he… where… you…" she garbled further unintelligible phrases.

Riccus threw his hands in the air with an eye roll. "Aalil, he is fine. Antonis is with the Queen and Trinidad and headed toward the Castle. I only left them a few hours ago. We escaped a few days back." With a grin, he added, "And boy, is he going to be glad to see you. He is all eaten up over you."

Aalil's head swam with this information. D'Ania, glaring at Riccus, grabbed Aalil's armpits and heaved her to her feet.

"We go," D'Ania said sternly.

Aalil scolded herself, wiped her cheeks upon her shirtsleeves, and nodded. The sounds seemed to be fading, as if… as if the trolls were on the move again.

"Is it over?" she whispered.

Riccus's eyes looked tense as he surveyed the trail, "I think we should go find out."

And with that, two humans, a nymph, and a sorority of trolls ran down the trail toward the distant fight.

Aalil's pain and exhaustion had left her, and though she felt more confused than ever, she at least knew one thing. *Antonis is alive!*

CHAPTER 24

The Change

The walk back to the village was heart-rendering. L'Asha. Could she really be gone forever? Can life change this drastically from one moment to the next?

His love taken from him. Stolen. Torn from his grasp forever. The shroud of death seeming to come upon her in only a hair's width of a moment.

As he walked back toward his village, a brightly lit area with a beautiful pond reflected the hot summer sun, and fields of vegetables and crops grew nearby. The trees and flowers which clustered around the pond did not warm his heart as they usually did. L'Asha liked to go and feed the fat fish and birds that lived there. Always sprinkling seeds and caring for the wildlife. Her soul had been pure....

His heart throbbed painfully as he pictured her face. In anguish, he realized that without seeing it again, he may one day forget what she looked like.

His stomach gripped painfully as he neared the village. Rows of clay brick houses with thatched roofs dotted the area, and villagers *walked leisurely around, visiting and carrying baskets as they went about their daily work. Farmers toiled in the fields and small children laughed and chased each other teasingly around the pond and through the smattering of trees nearby.*

Tarsin felt anger at the children as he watched them playing— defiling!—L'Asha's favorite place with their grubby hands and loud, uncaring voices. He wanted to scream at them to stop. He wanted to lash out at them, but as he stepped forward, another stomach cramp seized his intestines.

He fell to his knees, sweat breaking out on his forehead, the pain in his stomach nearly unbearable. He leaned upon a small tree, scaring off a hen and her fledglings that had been enjoying the peaceful afternoon shade.

He reached for them, wanting to hurt something as he hurt. He caught the tail feathers of one of the tiny creatures, its squawking alerted the mother who turned back chirping and shrieking in alarm. Just as he pulled it in to squeeze the life out of its wretched, miserable little body, another cramp seized him. The tiny bird scurried away, the mother urging her young on. Away from the evil presence.

Though beginning to feel foggy, Tarsin gasped momentarily. Evil presence? Is that what I am?

He was unsure when the change had taken place, but he felt a heavy darkness settling upon him. Weighing him down. His hand, he noted, looked pale… Hot bile suddenly shot up his throat, and he leaned over to spew out the remnants of his stomach. Again, a moment of clarity came to him, and he wondered, alarmed why none of the beast's heart had been vomited out? Surely his body couldn't have digested it that quickly?

He had decided to gorge on it. It had been a moment of rash decision-making. But the symbolism of it had been too great. He wanted to rip out its heart, taking from it what it had taken from him. And yet... now... he questioned whether that had been sound. Perhaps the beast was sick? His vision blurred, and he saw with alarm that the vomit was indeed liquid... no food had come up, but what worried him was the blood. So much blood. He couldn't stop. Wave after wave of nausea hit him, and soon he was lying alone at the edge of the pond, face down in a pool of bloody bile. His vision blurring... his stomach burning... and his heart bursting with grief. "L'Asha," he whispered.

He waited. Knowing death would soon take him, gladdened by the fact that he'd soon be returned to his beloved L'Asha. In Nav'Aria, all knew that when you died, you joined the Creator. The unicorns spoke of it, and even in his tiny, rural village so far from the presence of unicorns, their teachings were known.

Soon, he would be with his beloved. And all would be well. Soon.

Morta glared at the pale woman retreating from his bed chamber. He watched the slightly hitched gait and sneered. He had decided to teach Tav'Opal a lesson. A painful lesson in obedience. Knowing he had hurt her had pleasured him greatly. She was too proud... she needed to be broken, just as Narco had. And yet, strangely, having her in his bed had made his mind wander, the likes of which had not happened in far too long. He had... been there. He could almost see Tarsin. Feel him buried deep.

The thought sickened Morta. Not because he wanted to go back to that time, but because of the evident weakness in the man. Heartbroken and hurting. Vulnerable. Rushing off to cry over his beloved, as if it even mattered. Nothing mattered except power... and that power—a tumult of writhing evil—swirled within him. For too long he had kept it hidden. He had concocted the plan long ago to lay quiet. Dormant. Watching. Let the fools of this world think they were in power, and then take it from them. It was a game to him, something he'd long grown to enjoy. Not love... for he loved nothing. But the pleasure of wielding such power. Seeing the pain and fear in one's eyes... it was everything to him.

Morta laughed as he lifted his embossed hand. Inspecting it, he noticed mirthfully, that a trickle of blood ran down his index finger. Yes, Tav'Opal had learned a lesson today.

He was not the man he had been. The beast that he had tasted had taken root within him, granting him supernatural powers and abilities. He would never go back to that weakness. He would rule here, spreading his tainted contagion upon the land until all knew his power. He had slain the beast that day, but rather than killing it, he had become it. That foreign agent planting itself in him, and thus, in Nav'Aria.

A wicked laugh erupted from him as he moved toward the Chalice. He was in his Tower apartments, preferring them over the soft Castle... though he had had Narco's gruesome desk, ever a favorite of Morta's, brought to the tower. The bones that had been used to ornament it always brought him great pleasure.

Tracing his fingers along one thin bone in particular, Morta strode to his Chalice. He had decided to hold off his attack a few days… calling instead for all the creatures of Rav'Ar to join him. Most had already come but he still had a few surprises up his sleeve. He wanted his force ready when they met the trolls and together crushed Vikaris. It was nothing personal to Morta, not like Narco's vendetta had been. Morta cared little if Vikaris lived or died, but in order to do the most destruction, he knew the king should die. At his hand. He could practically taste the tension in the air. The salty tears of the widows of his making. He reveled in it.

Gripping the Chalice rim with his steel, magically powered hand—another gift from his dark talents—he leaned over the Chalice, and the tempest of the churning dark liquid swayed, allowing him to see through the eyes of his creatures. He laughed as he watched the Rav'Arians scuttling across the border heeding his words. He watched as the unicorns of his making growled and snorted at their attendants, awaiting his word to be unleashed. And then he moved out toward the trolls. He knew they had already collided with Vikaris by now. His time with Tav'Opal had not been long, but long enough that the battle may have progressed. Searching, he finally found his target.

He entered the beast, feeling shock as a blazing silver streak slew the beast. His eyes bulged at the intensity. At the power. At the recognition! *Zola!*

The image disappeared as life left the beast. Morta roared, clutching the rim harder and searching for another unguarded mind to enter. He crept into the mind of a troll nearby, watching it writhe and cry with fear, running away from the battlefield. He saw in alarm that all the trolls were running. Fleeing like cowards.

"YOU IDIOTS," he bellowed into their minds. "Attend me immediately." Though he didn't wait for a response, he could see the trolls snapping their eyes around looking for him. Some bent down to rub the hidden stones implanted on the back of their legs. The brutes would return to him. There was no question of them ever disobeying. But his prized beast would not be with them. He had purposely designed that creature with such care, making it nearly invincible. How had she done it?

A new sensation overtook him as he considered Zola the unicorn, whose light shone pure and whose horn had miraculously regrown. He would enjoy breaking her... starting with her son. He smiled a predatorial gleam consuming his whole face. He threw open the door, barking orders to Dabor outside. As he watched the retreating troll lumber off to do his bidding, he laughed aloud.

"Tarsin, you fool. You are dead. No human emotions can penetrate me now," Morta purred to himself. His eyes fell upon two Rav'Arians who stood at the bottom of the tower, ready to lead him to the tiny colt whose mind was so ripe for the picking.

***

After having his shallow arm wound dressed, Vikaris walked the field. His mind was in turmoil. He tried to keep a brave face while nodding at soldiers and patting arms and backs whenever he could. He pretended not to notice the somber looks from his troops. So many of them avoided his eye. He walked by the tent where the injured had been gathered. They would soon be marched back to Kaulter to be treated by Lei in the Fortress.

At the edge of the field he came to the gathered corpses. One in particular stood out. A headless centaur whose russet coat gleamed in the light. His lower half appeared resting on his side. That was, until you looked at the shredded, bloodied stump of a neck where his head should have been. Someone had found his head and set it near the corpse.

Vikaris fell to his knees at Garis's side, finally succumbing to his grief and fatigue. What had he done? He continued to berate himself over and over. He could have saved Garis, and yet he had hung back. He claimed it was following orders, but everyone knew that was horseshit. Vikaris was the King. He didn't take orders, and yet he had clung to them in the battle. It was the first time in his extensive military history where he had clammed up. And it had come at great cost. "What have I done?" he whispered, reaching out and clutching fistfuls of Garis's thick coat. Tears falling freely, "I have failed you. I am so sorry," he choked out. His throat thick with emotion.

Trixon, still undergoing treatment for his injuries, had been mute, staring off into nothingness. Vikaris questioned for the first-time if they'd be able to get over this. So overcome with his emotions, he didn't hear the approaching footsteps.

"Father."

Only one word spoken, but it jolted Vikaris, evoking a strange mixture of fear, anger, resentment, and shame. He knew why he had done it. He had held back out of fear... not for himself, but for his son. He had chosen Darion over Garis. And though perhaps that is how it should be—a father has that right—a King does not.

Dewey grass squelched as Darion walked to his side and squatted down. A slight groan escaped his lips.

Vikaris turned his, tear-streaked face to see his son's torso bare, save for the wrappings around his already black and blue bruising. One shattered rib, the healers said.

Triumph had immediately insisted on trying to heal him, but Darion had brushed him away. "It's nothing. You need your energy, Triumph. You look like crap," he had heard his son telling his unicorn companion. In any other circumstance, that comradery would have made Vikaris chuckle, but not this day.

"Father, we need to speak. I don't want you blaming yourself for this. I am sorry for Garis, I really am. But the troops need you to be strong. They're scared, and having you upset isn't helping."

Vikaris felt like he'd been slapped. Standing up, he glared at his son, blurting, "I am well aware of the mood of my soldiers, Darion. I can hear their whispers. See the disappointment in their eyes."

Then Darion did something Vikaris could never have believed. He pushed him. Hard.

"Vikaris," Darion snapped, treating his father as if somehow an equal. "We don't have time for this. I know

I'm supposed to be respectful and give you your space, like Triumph says, but I can't. I'm sorry, but we don't have time for this."

Vikaris gawked and then prepared to launch into a tirade. He longed to explode all his pent-up anger and shame. First Trixon, now Darion!

"Can't you feel it?" Darion shouted, waving his arms around them. "He is calling them. All of them. I can sense it. Morta is coming. I am sorry for Garis—really. But we don't have time! We need to prepare. This fight," Darion paused, licking his cracked lips, his green eyes ablaze with passion, "is just getting started."

Vikaris wanted to bang his own head on a tree stump. Why had he ever thought he could protect this headstrong son of his? He didn't need his protection. All along Vikaris kept thinking of him as a child, and Darion was the one shouting sense into his face.

He blinked, sighing and looking back at Garis. "I have failed here, I—"

"Seriously, Dude, stop!" Darion snapped. "You don't get it, do you? Your men aren't looking at you in disappointment... they're feeling bad about themselves. They think they failed YOU. Didn't you just say you could hear their whispers? I can hear conversations all over this field. Every damn one of them feels responsible for Garis's death. And maybe that's good. Maybe we need that to remember exactly how fucked up this enemy is. I saw what that beast did to him. So, instead of crying about it," he raised his hands as if warding off an argument, "we have to act... and I have a plan," he pressed.

And, as if a light had ignited inside, Vikaris found truth in Darion's words. He looked around at the slumped shoulders and broken spirits of his men. They needed him. They needed both of them, he conceded as he listened to Darion's intent.

Saying a final prayer at Garis's side, Vikaris strode back to the Camp with his son. He squared his shoulders and joined Darion in comforting his troops.

Vikaris grabbed a soldier's arm, "Find Kragar and the unicorns. Have them meet me at the War Tent."

Burning hair and flesh permeated the air as the pyres were lit. There was no time or means to bury their dead, given the staggering loss of forty soldiers. This, unfortunately, had become a common practice in Nav'Aria. Darion felt slight dismay at the idea of these troops not having graves, but he found there was something strangely beautiful about watching the flames lick upwards into the sky, the smoke swirling and carrying the souls away. The trolls' corpses were left for the birds.

Returning to his tent, Darion walked with Triumph and Trixon. Drigidor had remained with the other unicorns at the pyres. Zola had declined Triumph's offer to walk her back, choosing to stay instead with the unicorns there... next to Soren, Darion had a feeling. Though he knew very little about romance, except his brief interlude with Nala, he could tell that Zola and Soren had a thing for each other. While he and Edmond enjoyed discussing the subject, Triumph seemed to be clueless of it. *Love is a funny thing*, Darion pictured the flirting unicorns. And then Darion's heart panged with sadness as he recalled the image of Drigidor—the fierce and powerful warrior—collapsing to the ground in tears. The widower, unable to mourn at his wife's graveside, had let his tears fall here, unabashed.

Darion snapped back to alertness at Trixon's interruption.

"I want to thank you for what you said to the King earlier. I do not know all that transpired, but I can tell his spirit was strengthened... and chastened," Trixon paused, his deep voice filling the night air as he looked sideways at Darion. "What may I ask did you do to make that stubborn man see reason?"

Darion gulped at the recollection. He had been rather heated in the moment. "Well, I yelled at him... and pushed him as hard as I could. He needed to snap out of it."

Trixon and Triumph froze mid-stride.

"Wait. You pushed the King of Nav'Aria?" Triumph blurted.

At Darion's guilty expression, the two males burst out in laughter. Full-bodied mirth erupting forth. It was much needed and uncontrolled levity.

Darion glared at them but couldn't help but laugh too. *What was I thinking?* And then a thought hit him, and he replied, "That's not illegal, is it?"

Gales of laughter boomed from them at that. Trixon was crying and snorting, breathing heavily as he managed, "It is something I have dreamed of doing on many occasions."

CHAPTER 25

The Snap

"No, really, I'm fine," Darion said, trying to fend off Soren's advances, but the unicorn wasn't having it.

Darion had spent enough time with him in Rav'Ar to know that, when he insisted on his ministrations, there was no getting around it. He and Edmond both sat on a bench in the War Tent, along with Vikaris, Kragar, and most of the unicorns. Edmond's eyes were wide with shock at having been invited to the Tent by the King himself!

Darion rolled his eyes at his friend. Vikaris knew he was loyal to Darion... and possessed knowledge that was much needed.

As Soren finished touching his horn and speaking words of healing over Darion and Edmond, both of them sat up straighter. Darion's stomach rumbled loudly, and he realized he was famished! Had the battle really been earlier that day? Though they were exhausted, Vikaris insisted they plan for tomorrow's march.

"We could follow after the Queen and Trinidad, hugging to the mountain trails and attacking from there?" Kragar was suggesting. The bags beneath his grey eyes resulted from more than just fatigue, Darion knew. The man grieved his friend greatly. They all did. Without the formidable centaur taking charge at the map table alongside the King, there was an emptiness to the room.

"That could be," Vikaris started, then narrowed his eyes at Edmond. "But I have a different idea in mind."

Darion chortled as all eyes fell upon Edmond, and his friend's face flushed like a tomato.

"Edmond, how familiar are you with the ground surrounding the Stenlen?"

"Ummm... very familiar, my King," Edmond replied weakly, reddening at Triumph's haughty snort from the back of the Tent.

This opportunity brought a smile to Darion. Vikaris had been there before, of course, and Darion had suggested that they head that direction in pursuit of the trolls. Darion also could feel the onslaught coming from the border and a strong tug in that direction. *Besides*, Darion had pointed out as they stood talking upon the battlefield earlier, *you said you wanted to check if there were survivors in the Stenlen, and here's your chance.*

Vikaris's eyes had gleamed dangerously at the idea. *Yes, and drawing them out toward the Stenlen and Plains might save Lyrianna. Then she would be safe in the Kingdom.* Darion hadn't thought of that yet recognized the value in that tactic too. His mother was brave, Darion would give her that. But no need to send her into the enemy's lair if it could be avoided.

A rustling at the tent brought a red-faced, sweaty human sentry into their presence.

"Yes, what is it?"

"My King, we have... visitors."

Around the room, blades were drawn and bodies, though injured, jolted alert. The sentry raised his hands to calm them, "No, no need for that," he stammered. "Riccus and Aalil, my King... and their prisoners—"

Riccus... Dad! Darion thought, excitedly jumping to his feet, suddenly grateful for Soren's healing as he ran from the tent. "Take me to him," he ordered the sentry, who turned on his heel obediently pointing toward a crowding of soldiers near the medical tent at the north of camp.

His father's voice called for him to slow down, but Darion did not heed it. The King could yell all he wanted, but nothing was going to keep Darion from seeing his Dad.

"Wait for me," Triumph snarled, his thudding footsteps coming nearer.

"Me too," Edmond called, catching up quickly with his long strides.

Darion heard the rest emptying out of the War Tent behind him. He ran toward the group.

"Dad!" He yelled, as the shorter wiry man with the kind eyes and knotted chin turned, his face breaking out in such joy that it nearly overwhelmed Darion.

"Darion," Rick's familiar voice drawled as he wrapped him in a tight embrace. Darion felt his eyes fill with tears when his father cupped the back of Darion's head as he'd done ever since he was a boy. Darion felt safe with Rick. He hadn't realized how much he'd missed his presence. The stalwart security that had been ever-present in his life. He smiled as Rick held firmly to his shoulders, examining the man before him.

Whistling through his teeth, Rick commented, "Well, you seem to have grown since I last saw you."

Darion smiled. His tanned skin from time in the desert, the rapidly growing symbols upon his arm, his long dark hair held back in a ponytail, and his bare, muscled torso just healing were drastic changes, for sure. He now stood inches taller than his Dad—and stronger, something that had never seemed possible as a child, but months of training with a sword will do that.

His smile found Aalil, who was surrounded by soldiers slapping her shoulder and welcoming her back with gusto. But then he frowned, breath catching. "Where's Tony?" he asked, fearing the worst.

Catching on instantly, Rick said, "Oh, he is fine. Do not worry about him. He is with the Queen," and then, as if remembering, grinned, "with your mother, Darion."

Confusion and relief flooded Darion's body.

"You have seen her then? How? Where? Is she well?" Vikaris's voice interrupted the chatter, and Rick flushed slightly under all the attention.

With a nod to the King, Rick replied, "Yes, Your Majesty... we saw her just a day ago," waving toward a petite nymph nearby.

"And Antonis, after escaping the trolls—and with the help of a nymph patrol—offered to accompany the Queen and Trinidad on their mission, Your Majesty," Aalil explained, bowing to Vikaris. "And... there is more, my King," she arched an eyebrow and glanced around. "May we speak with you in private?"

Vikaris was already waving the soldiers away. "Of course, let us go to my Tent."

Aalil didn't move, and Darion peered at her. "My King," she paused, still looking around and stepping closer to the men while the unicorns leaned in, "We need to show you something," she whispered.

She tilted her head toward a group of trolls, Darion now realized as he squinted in the darkness, they looked much less threatening than the ones he'd seen before. *Female*s, he noticed. But most intriguing were their eyes. They didn't hold the same red glow that many of the males' eyes did.

"Trolls," Vikaris said coldly, examining them.

Kragar drew his sword, stepping toward them, his lethal rage evident.

"No, wait," Aalil said, quickly putting her hands up as if to ward off the Lieutenant. "These are my friends... they are loyal to you, not to Morta, like the males."

Vikaris scowled at her, but Darion knew his Father had picked up on what he himself had observed.

"They seem... different," Vikaris said carefully. "I do not sense the darkness in them as I do with the others."

"Nor do I," Trixon rumbled.

"Who are you then?" Vikaris snapped.

"We help King," one troll female spoke, stepping forward to stand next to Aalil.

Rick stepped back to stand at her side, as if he too considered her a friend.

Darion looked at her, and though her grey-skin and jagged teeth were still glaringly frightful, there was something almost pretty about her.

He reached out with his senses, wonderingly, without thinking... and as he did, he gasped. "You aren't tainted like the others," Darion blurted.

The troll female, D'Ania, she said her name was, nodded sadly. "No stone," she whispered.

Aalil explained quickly, surprising even Rick, it seemed, who it turned out had only been back in her company for a matter of hours.

Darion listened in horror to tales of their capture and of how Aalil had been separated from Tony and his Dad. She, it seemed, had learned a great many things though. Useful things.

"If this is true," Vikaris ruminated, "then the trolls are not traitors as we assumed, but rather, prisoners possessed with Morta's dark power."

"It is true," Aalil said passionately. "If there was a male around, I would show you."

"Well it is good then that we have a pen of troll prisoners," a low voice boomed. Drigidor stepped into the torchlight, all traces of grief vanishing as his warrior persona took hold.

Had Aalil not explained it beforehand, Darion wouldn't have believed it. Who would? Supernatural stones embedded into the legs of every male troll to force them into obedience. It sounded like something from a video game he would have played in his other life.

And yet, here they stood watching as one troll after another was pinned down, and a blade driven into the leg flesh carved out each stone and flicked it off the bloody metal. The roars and cries were hair-raising, but Vikaris didn't waver. The unicorns illuminated the area, and the King instructed Kragar and the troops nearby to hold down every male troll. After each stone was pulled from skin, Aalil and D'Ania, gripping heavy hammers, crushed it. As the shards scattered, a dark black vortex swirled and dissipated into the air.

When the moon reached its zenith, Darion watched in wonder as the last stone was broken and the wicked hold that had gripped these troll's minds for years faded away.

The trolls sat huddled together. Crying, lips quivering as they looked around. Confusion and uncertainty took hold. Where were they, and how had they come to be held in their King's camp.

King. King. King, they all repeated and bowed to Vikaris, who had no need to introduce himself. His blazing Ruby and illuminated arm, which sparkled as a new image rounded out upon his shoulder shone bright.

Darion felt his own arm tingling while a spiked symbol crested around his elbow. As he watched this change in the trolls, he felt that tug again pulling them south toward the Stenlen and beyond to the border. Something was brewing.

Reaching into his pocket, Darion pulled out the yellow ribbon that he had found what seemed like a lifetime ago in Rav'Ar. As the mysteries of Narco and Morta—or rather, Tarsin—were revealed, Darion felt hope thrumming in his chest. They had beaten the beast and now discovered the key to Morta's hold upon the trolls. And with this knowledge, they could disarm half of Morta's force.

"Father," Darion whispered, stepping up to Vikaris's ear, ribbon entwined in his Marked fingers. "If we catch up to the trolls…"

"We can remove more of the stones and bolster our numbers," Vikaris finished, looking at his son with an unfamiliar expression. His father reached out, taking hold of his Darion's Marked Arm with his and igniting a shower of green light while the yellow ribbon swayed in the wind beneath their joined hands.

***

Tav'Opal felt the breath leave her as she was thrown against the wall by Morta's impressive strength. She had not had any time to recover from the previous evening. Though her old mortal bones protested the agony, she had come again, knowing to deny his bidding would mean death.

They stood in the tower, Morta stark naked and peering over the Chalice. Tav'Opal's blood smeared his lips. A moment ago, she succumbed to his ravaging teeth, and now she lay against the wall, weak and dazed. Her failure to glean useful information from the colt had displeased him. He then insisted on using the Chalice to enter the creature's mind, instead. After doing so, he dealt out her punishment; she knew not if she could walk. Blood trailed down her legs, and the wall's impact may have cracked her skull. She watched through one eye, the other so horribly swollen she could no longer open it.

And then something changed in Morta. Shifted. Snapped.

She watched, her one amber eye growing large and fearful. As he turned to her, his features seemed more reptilian than she remembered. His skin ashy.

"Where did he get that ribbon?" Morta whispered, yellow eyes narrowing.

Tav'Opal gulped. She knew not what he spoke of, but the quiet voice he used sparked terror in her. She wished he'd yelled or laughed. This cold, unfeeling, menacing voice brought gooseflesh over her entire body.

Glancing back at the Chalice, Morta screamed. Not a human scream… but something feral.

Her blood ran cold. Believing she was hallucinating, she watched as a brilliant green light flashed out of the Chalice. Morta seemed to be shaking. He darted to his desk, snatched a blade, and in one smooth stride, returned to the liquid. Holding his wrist over it, he bled himself, and Tav'Opal whimpered as she saw his unnatural blood pour out. Not red like a human's, but tar-like. Black. It dripped slowly from the wound, and the swirling liquid within seemed to respond immediately. A red cloud lifted over the Chalice. It began shaking in its hold, as if from its own volition. The entire Tower trembled.

Tav'Opal screamed at the contents' explosion. And before her eyes, the pale skin of the once-aged adviser fell away. A huge black reptile burst out, his talons pushing against the tower stone as if it were children's toys, knocking away the entire section of wall and soaring outwards. Its screeching filling the night air with terror. Its eyes ablaze and glowing red. Tav'Opal could just make out the winged form as what had been Morta now flew down to the courtyard.

She shook her head, which led to a heavy pounding in her skull. *Hallucinating*, she thought foggily. *It is a dream.* But as her vision faded, she was met with a horrible thought. All this time she had been watching, but she had never really seen. Tarsin had become the beast. And she feared he would devour them all!

CHAPTER 26

The Dam

"What does this mean?" Lyrianna wondered aloud.

Trinidad seemed to be thinking the same thing as he nibbled his lower lip.

Having traveled the last days on the trails, they had come back to pathways that would lead them back to the Castle, and with it, Lyrianna's place of torment. She had known returning would trigger certain memories and emotions, but what they found had caused a lot more questions and emotions to arise. Upon arrival at the hidden area beyond the Castle walls, Antonis had nearly choked on his water trying to get them all to look. Just over head from their position, the tower building exploded. Lyrianna shuddered thinking of what had flown out.

Its screeches had haunted her sleep, and they'd all decided to remain hidden until they knew what this new enemy was.

Antonis and the nymphs took turns scouting, reporting that the creature looked to be organizing the troops that were marching out from the Castle barracks and military encampments. Men flooded out, followed by the occasional troll and a number of Rav'Arians. A caravan of tearful, somber humans watched as their men rode away, before they were forced in the opposite direction by a few remaining Rav'Arians. Trinidad had growled seeing the midnight black unicorns—more of Morta's creations—unleashed and galloping after the troops. They, too, were leaving the Castle. All of them.

"What does this mean, Trinidad?" Lyrianna said more forcefully. "Vikaris is expecting a siege. He will be caught unaware by this force, and that... that... thing!" Her blood ran cold.

Trinidad murmured that he was trying to reach out to the other unicorns.

Initially, Cela had suggested they go after the force, but Trinidad had dispelled the idea. *Perhaps we can use their departure to our advantage*, he had said. *If only we knew where the Nav'Arian force was.*

Crinkling her brow, which grew sweaty in the midday heat, Lyrianna glanced again at the Tower. Shielding her eyes, she considered it.

From what she had heard—for she did not remember the Kingdom, having been so young at the Fall and living her entire life in the Camps and Kaulter, she knew that the Tower had not been there forever. She had mentioned it to Vikaris upon her escape, and he had grown angry. *There*, he told her, *was where Morta fashioned himself as Narco's adviser*, and they were only just now learning of all the abhorrent practices that had been performed behind those walls. Vikaris had mentioned that not even old Seegar could quite remember when or how Morta arrived at the Castle. It was as if he had always been there, or their minds had been tampered with, Vikaris had quipped. Now, considering it, Lyrianna saw more truth in it than she'd like. *Is he up there?* she wondered. *Did he make that creature?* A part of her hoped that he was lying there dead, killed by a creature of his own making.

She inhaled deeply, feeling the sun upon her cheeks and the warm breeze tickling the tiny hairs on the back of her neck. She had tied her hair back like she'd seen Darion do. *A ponytail*, he'd called it. She smiled thinking of him. His strong spirit filling her with a deep maternal pride. Resolved, she stood up and brushed the tree needles from her forest-green dress. "Well, the only option I see is to go into the Tower and see for ourselves if Morta is there."

Trinidad and Cela both shook their heads adamantly. Surprisingly—well, perhaps not too much of a surprise—Antonis jumped up right away in agreement. *He is not good at sitting still*, she thought, smiling.

"I will go," he offered.

Lyrianna nodded… "Yes, with me."

Cela and Trinidad let loose a barrage of opposition. "Absolutely not. No way. That building is unstable. What if Morta is up there waiting for you? What if this is a trap?"

Lyrianna, ignoring them, looked over to the Tower again. It looked stable enough. Only the very tallest section had crumbled. They should be able to get in safely, she thought, but looking at her four-footed friends, she understood their concern. The tall, narrow building was most likely not made to accommodate their kind.

"I will go, but you stay here, Your Majesty," Cela said, a stern expression marring her otherwise youthful and vibrant face.

Lyrianna arched an eyebrow. "You will remember to whom you are speaking," and though she said it in a voice filled with authority, Lyrianna wasn't truly upset. Cela only had her safety in mind, so Lyrianna smiled. Adding with a rueful grin, "Besides, if the tower does begin to collapse, I will need your strong arms to catch me."

Cela muttered under her breath, swiping a hand over her equally sweaty brow and looking to Trinidad to reason with her.

Trinidad stepped forward, interrupting, "Lyrianna, there is darkness up there. An evil unlike anywhere else. It lingers in the air. Do not do this," his warm and tender voice made Lyrianna's breath catch in her throat.

I will be alright, Trinidad, she spoke into his mind, as was their way. *You will be with me the entire time. We will be fast, and Antonis and the nymphs,* whom Antonis was snapping orders to, *will protect me.*

You better be right, for if anything happens to you, I will run into the building myself.

Lyrianna didn't doubt him. The Trinidad she had known in captivity had changed. He was restored, and his renewed power strengthened her.

She nodded, lifting her chin only slightly. Regally. She had set out on this mission, and there was no time to sit around any longer. The Kingdom was empty... and she needed to find out whatever she could before they returned to Vikaris. The plan had changed.

Antonis whispered to her that he would go first, and the nymphs were to surround her as they entered the dark tower. As they approached, Lyrianna observed that the wooden door stood ajar. *Someone is still up there*, she thought nervously.

Antonis looked every inch the Royal Commander: tall, intimidating, and formidable. His heavily muscled, broad frame led the way. The narrow passageway could have perhaps fit the unicorn and centaur, but Lyrianna feared they'd have no room to turn around if a threat came. She felt good then—about her decision, at least.

Climbing as surreptitiously as possible, Lyrianna's nose tickled from the dust and the dank smell... almost rotten. Like a crypt. She swallowed nervously, gripping the small blade that she carried with her. The soft flutters of nymphs' wings sounded in her ears they hovered just slightly over the steps as they ascended.

Lyrianna hadn't known what to expect but was surprised that so far all they'd found were winding stairs. No other rooms. That left the top of the tower as their destination. She felt a slight tremor of fear. *Would the building hold?*

Finally reaching the top, the stairs ended on a platform and opened into a spacious room. Two things caught her attention immediately. Beyond the horrific décor and sulfurous odor, a mishmash of vials and metal instruments littered the room.

Firstly, Lyrianna gaped at the hole in the wall which seemed much larger than it had from down below. Blue sky and fluffy white clouds filled the space as if a painting or a window, instead of a plunging drop to one's death. Secondly, she realized, they were not alone.

A strange looking pale woman, bloodied and bruised, leaned against the far wall, eyes closed. Her foreign clothing unlike anything Lyrianna had seen.

Initially Lyrianna presumed the woman dead. She quickly surveyed the area fully expecting Morta to come from any nook or corner. But no one else was in the room, save for a sickly foreign woman.

Lyrianna squinted at her. Something about her seemed to spark a recollection, though Lyrianna could not say what.

As they advanced, one of the woman's eyes, an unsettling amber color, peered at them. The other eye was badly bruised.

A nymph knelt at her side, whispering to her softly and inspecting her wounds. Blood marked the wall behind her head and trailed downwards.

"Who are you?" Lyrianna asked. "Why are you here?" Unsure if the woman could even speak.

The woman's head lolled slightly as she licked her lips, finally meeting Lyrianna's eye. "We watch," she whispered quietly. "We always watch."

Remembering Darion's tale of the strange people of Rav'Ar, cold terror gripped Lyrianna.

"Where is Morta?" Antonis cut in.

The woman's eye flicked to the hole in the wall. "We watched... wrong."

The silence that followed those words seemed deafening. Lyrianna couldn't breathe. *Is this woman crazed? Surely, she does not mean... he....*

As if in understanding, the woman sneered. "Tarsin warned our people of the winged beasts. Our elders said they turned traitor and killed the King. That they allied with the unicorns and Nav'Arian humans for evil." She paused, her chest heaving, as if even uttering a few words was a tremendous effort.

At the word *Tarsin*, Lyrianna shuddered. She knew what Darion believed, that somehow Tarsin and Morta were connected. The same man, perhaps. How that could be possible? No man could live that long. Could he?

The bloodied woman croaked, "We watched the wrong one...." And then, in a voice that made Lyrianna's blood run cold, she whispered, "Tarsin—Morta—is the beast."

Antonis whistled, studying the impressive hole in the wall.

The woman's breath rattled.

The nymphs were looking her over. It was no use, Lyrianna knew. She was too far gone... unless... Trinidad could help her, she wondered.

Ask her, what is her name, Trinidad's voice instructed.

Consenting, Lyrianna inquired as she stepped closer.

The woman's eyelid fluttered. She swallowed and blinked as if trying to recall. "Tav'Opal," she croaked.

Lyrianna stifled a gasp. *Tav'Opal! This is the woman who tried to set the Rav'Arians on my son. The leader of the Watchers.*

In a voice no longer holding its musical warmth, "Come," Lyrianna said to her companions.

Antonis turned from the hole and cocked his head. "Should we...," he gestured to the woman.

The nymphs were standing both alert and transfixed looking from Lyrianna back to Tav'Opal.

"Leave her," Lyrianna said in her most authoritative voice, no longer pitying this spawn. "Leave her...to watch," she said.

Tav'Opal's eye fluttered open, and Lyrianna saw that they understood one another.

The woman didn't protest or cry out. She only did what she was known for. She watched as Lyrianna spun on her heel, followed out by her confused, yet obedient, guards.

"Can someone please explain what is going on? Why did we just leave that old woman? And who is Tarsin?" Antonis pressed once they returned to Trinidad and Cela down below.

Lyrianna shivered despite herself, rubbing the goosebumps from her arms.

"She is the leader of the Watchers," Trinidad shared. Continuing at Antonis's confused stare, he explained, "Morta has a secret community of humans across the border, near the Rav'Arian breeding ground, that are loyal to him."

"Darion and Triumph discovered it," he added. "And barely made it out alive."

Cela flinched slightly at that. No one liked to think of the place... Lyrianna certainly didn't like to recount it, especially the thought of how close her son had come to dying there. He could have been captured. Tortured. Killed!

Antonis's gaze hardened. "I see I have missed much while in the mountains." Furrowing his brow, he looked them over. "Who is Tarsin then? The woman mentioned another man."

Trinidad lowered his head, giving it a slight shake. "Though improbable, it would appear that Morta was once known as Tarsin, a lifetime ago. The best we have sorted out is that he was attacked by an evil winged creature in Rav'Ar many cycles ago. Darion discovered a gravesite of a winged skeleton—he is insistent that it differs from the winged ones, these Reouls, whom he met. And..." Trinidad paused for emphasis, "the skeleton was found with a human skull."

Lyrianna, despite already hearing the story, listened raptly to the enigmatic tale.

"It is the belief of my brother, Triumph, and of the Prince, that Morta became callused after an attack on his beloved and has somehow managed to live longer than any other being since Creation. He has made the Watchers in Rav'Ar his pawns—how and why we do not know— but they tried to capture Darion and offer him to the Rav'Arians as a sacrifice."

"And that is why we left that woman—their leader—up there," Lyrianna piped in. Anger boiling inside her.

Antonis growled, instinctively thumbing his blade, "Maybe I should finish her then?"

Knowing that Tav'Opal was most likely already dead, Lyrianna shook her head. If Morta was indeed a winged creature, impossible as it may sound, then he was headed straight for Vikaris... who would be caught unawares.

"We need to warn my husband," Lyrianna insisted.

The nymphs had returned, this time with grave expressions. "There is something we must show you," Talen said. Lyrianna nodded, making to follow them, when Trinidad spoke.

"Wait," he said, tilting his head, his horn beginning to glow softly as he looked around. "There is one who needs us."

And completely out of character for him, Trinidad ran off without another word.

Lyrianna wanted to call after him, just as Antonis was doing.

Cela was muttering about a 'fool unicorn', when Lyrianna finally heard it. A soft whimpering.

Lifting her dark skirts, she dashed after her companion through the courtyard until nearing the back of the Castle, where she and Trinidad had made their daring escape only months before. The chattel cages were still nearby, though empty. All sense of rationality left her as she listened to the crying. Another prisoner of Morta's. Though seemingly abandoned of soldiers and guards—a victim remained.

A fury bloomed in Lyrianna's chest as she listened, knowing whom she would find. The diamond upon her forehead glowed softly as she made it to the entrance following swiftly on Trindad's heels. Cela's protests and heavy footsteps not far behind her.

Caring not a whit for stealth, Lyrianna followed Trinidad through the winding passageway and stairs, down to the lowest level of the Castle, the abominable place where Trinidad had been imprisoned. There, below the stone Castle, was a holding cell—a room—and Trinidad informed her that this was where Zola had been held during her years of torment. It smelled dank... like spoiled food and excrement. The foul odors affronted Lyrianna, but she did not slow her pace. As they came to the room, Trinidad pressed his horn into the lock.

Just then, a shadow caught Lyrianna's peripheral gaze. "Trinidad, watch out," she cautioned. Her Mark aglow, brightening the area, as Trinidad jumped back just in time to avoid the crush of a heavy swinging club.

A troll stepped out of dim hiding and into the light. It swung its club again, and once more, Trinidad dodged it.

Lyrianna tried to make out its face, but the shadows— save for her and Trinidad's glaring light—obscured it.... until it stepped ever closer.

She gasped! "YOU," she cried, baring her teeth in a snarl. This was the troll that had hurt her all those times. She knew it. She recognized his youthful face. This one was different than the others, and she'd stored his image deep in memory. He had the same apathetic look to him.

Not crazed or maddened like some she had seen, but...
distant. Unfeeling.

Cela's footsteps clattered after Lyrianna's. The troll
stood, arm suspended in the air, staring as if seeing a
ghost. His mouth worked soundlessly as his eyes bore into
Lyrianna's.

Trinidad and Cela moved forward. Lyrianna felt
claustrophobic within the tight confines. This passageway
wasn't intended for a troll, a centaur, and a unicorn. She
began to step back, intending to allow her friends room to
slay the enemy.

"Queen... help!"

Lyrianna wanted to laugh. Did this miscreant expect
her to help him? He, the bringer of so much pain during
her months of captivity? She pictured Tav'Opal's bloodied
face, dying alone in the ruined tower at this very moment.
She gave no mercy to monsters.

"Sorry... Hate Master most," the troll spoke quickly.
"Stone fault."

Trinidad and Cela had been edging in closer, waiting
for the unspoken attack signal once Lyrianna was out of
the way.

"Wait," Lyrianna called, hesitating. Watching the troll
lick his lips nervously, she noted, unlike many of the
others she'd seen, his eyes didn't have the reddish glow.
He could have already attacked them, yet he held off.
Waiting. Pleading, she realized, noting the tears forming in
his huge coal-like eyes.

"Why should I believe you, Dabor?"

He gasped, stepping forward timidly at the mention of his name… something brightening in his face.

Impossible, she thought. *A troll cannot possibly feel hope. They are monsters. Tricksters. Traitors!*

Glaring, she pressed him. "If you hate your master so much, why do you follow his orders?" Holding up her bent fingers, she reminded him of his torturous attentions.

He closed his eyes, shaking his head as if he didn't want to see the proof of his barbarity.

Why? Narco would have gloated over it. Lyrianna felt confused.

Dabor babbled something.

Cela glared at her. "Lyrianna, get back so we can finish him." There was no mercy in her voice, for Cela loathed trolls ever since her mistreatment.

"Stone, stone, stone, stone, stone," the troll babbled, tears falling freely before he collapsed to his knees. He placed his throat before Trinidad's horn, as if wanting to make his killing easy.

Trinidad stepped back, startled. "Stone?" He asked, "what stone?"

Dabor wept bitterly now, snuffles and snorts erupting. He leaned back to his bent leg.

Cela stepped forward, her blade at its throat. "One wrong move, and I will gut you," she snarled.

Dabor nodded, tears falling freely. Slowly, in the awkward, cramped space, he was able to pull up his pant leg, revealing a large, dark stone embedded into his upper calf.

Trinidad clearly becoming more interested then, ushered Cela out of the way despite her protests. The unicorn's inquisitive attention illuminated the area on the beast's leg.

Lyrianna's eyes widened at the sight of the stone. Watching the troll—the terrifying brute who was responsible for many of her nightmares—crying like a babe perplexed her.

"Where did this come from?" Trinidad asked in a soft voice, peering at it.

"Master's beast... must obey," Dabor whined. "Hate it... Hate hurting." Dabor's head dropped heavily as the sobs wracked his body. The anguish in his voice breaking down the walls of Lyrianna's heart.

Cela sucked in her breath as realization hit them. The trolls were not traitors—at least not this one. Dabor was a prisoner.

"Can we get it out?" Lyrianna asked.

"I will try," an authoritative voice spoke from behind.

Antonis! How long had he been standing there? Lyrianna wondered.

Cela backed up, allowing the former Commander to step forward. He bounced a blade in palm, the metal gleaming in the unicorn's light.

Crouching over the troll, Trinidad and Cela still on alert if this ended up a trick, Antonis took his blade and made quick work of digging the stone out. Dabor did not cry out but trembled with emotion, pain, or a mixture of both.

At one knife flick, the stone popped out of its holding place within Dabor's flesh, clattering to the ground. A faint trickle of blood ran down it, and as Antonis jumped out of the way. Dabor's whole body seemed to convulse for a breath before lying still. He lay sprawled out on his stomach, chest heaving.

Lyrianna stepped closer as Antonis and Trinidad inspected the stone. Cela grabbed Lyrianna's arm, pulling her back as Dabor began to get up, despite their protests to lie still.

His eyes, Lyrianna noted, looked even clearer and kinder than before, and his face took on an entirely different cast as he broke out into a beatific, toothy smile. "Free," he whispered.

Gooseflesh formed along Lyrianna's body. She understood how that release feels. Though still unsure how she felt about the troll that had caused her so much pain, she could not deny that he seemed different.

"Must destroy," he said suddenly, approaching the stone and before anyone could stop him, Dabor stomped down with his heavy boot. The stone crunched and a dark swirling force rushed from the shards beneath his foot and blew down the corridor.

"Well, I was not expecting that," Antonis announced with another whistle.

Before anyone could speak, a pitiful wail sounded on the other side of the door. *The prisoner*, Lyrianna thought with shame. All this time they had been distracted by Dabor, forgetting to free whomever was inside.

Cela and Antonis led Dabor away from the door as Trinidad pressed his horn into the lock and kicked open.

Inside, Lyrianna exhaled with relief. Though terrified, the prisoner did not seem to be injured, so far as she could tell.

"It is alright, little one," she cooed, walking in, palms slightly outstretched. "It is alright now. You are safe."

A tiny sniffle was the only response she got.

She smiled and kneeled down to its level.

"Trigger, right? That is your name?" She asked warmly, watching the tiny colt whose life up until now had been nothing but hardship. "Your Mother is worried sick about you, little one. We will take you to her, OK?"

Trigger's eyes widened at the mention of his mother. After another sniffle, he crept tentatively closer to Lyrianna, who now knelt in the soiled hay strewn about the austere cell.

She did not reach out for him, allowing him instead to come to her, but once he did, she cooed softly in his ears, wrapping her arms around the trembling infant and casting his fears away. "You are safe, Trigger. No one will hurt you," she whispered, smiling as she felt Trinidad's warm presence at her side.

"Yes, child. You are safe," he said softly, leaning down to nuzzle Trigger's cheek. The tiny unicorn's horn catching lightly in Lyrianna's curls as Trigger looked up wide-eyed at the shining and strong unicorn before his eyes.

Lyrianna was struck by the beauty of the two of them. Both so different in coloring and yet so pure and pristine.

Their horns shining, one like diamond and the other like obsidian. *This*, she thought, *is the proof that Morta has failed. What he tried to make for evil has been beaten by love.* For she had no doubt, that just as Zola cared for her son, so too did his grandfather, Triumph, and his great-uncle, Trinidad.

She wiped a tear that had fallen. *There is still good in Nav'Aria*, she thought. There is still beauty and though Narco and Morta had tormented so many, they would not—could not—win. Lyrianna felt more determination than ever looking at the tiny colt that had been born into captivity, imprisoned, and left to die. *That man*, she thought, will *pay for his crimes*.

"It is time to go," Lyrianna said, rising. "We need to get to Vikaris."

***

Soft moss tickled Shannic's fingertips as he felt around the dam. The wall that had been hastily built to keep the merfolk trapped for cycles was of constant consternation to him. He swam the length of the wall, as he did every few days. Feeling every nook, crevice, and stone. He combed the lake bottom beneath it trying to find any clue as to how to unleash the water and bring down the dam. Yet, he thought morosely, if there had been a key, a way out, or a rescue attempt, it would have come long past. In the murky water he swam slowly. His tears mixing into the liquid.

Jasra.

He could picture her clear, bright topaz eyes. Her radiant auburn hair and pale skin. The freckles dotting her sun-kissed face, for she loved to hold her face up to the sun. She always said she could still dream of freedom when she felt the warmth of the sun's rays. Her teal and violet scales a beautiful, iridescent sheen within the muddy lake water. He longed to run his hands through her hair. Kiss her lips....

The tears overcame him then at the memory. They had come for her—for them—days ago. Morta, who seemed to be in charge now, though how or why Shannic did not know, ordered the guards to seize one of the merfolk to show his displeasure. The trolls had leaned off the ferry and caught Jasra just as she floated on her back, eyes closed enjoying the sunshine.

Shannic had heard the screams, and joining the other merfolk, broke the surface just as he saw to his great horror Jasra being strung up by her tail on a large post that had long been used for their executions. The stout, heavy wood bore numerous holes from the stakes that were driven through the tails of the tortured merfolk.

Jasra was screaming and clawing with everything in her as the beasts held her down, driving the stake through her tail. The post was just far enough that the merfolk could not reach out for her. The trolls seemed to enjoy it, laughing, all save for one who hung back.

Shannic thought of his beloved. That had been days ago, and yet, things since then had been oddly quiet. Usually when one of the merfolk was tortured, they were to be made an example. Narco would come and give a great oration over their supposed heinous crimes against him and threaten to string up their dwindling numbers.

But no visit ever came. A great frenzy had taken place on the surface, that much was known, for the merfolk scouts—those in rotation—had commented on the constant ferrying of troops across the water. It seemed that the entire Castle—entire village—had been emptied out. Shannic could not see why Narco would do that. Unless it was Morta's doing? He had heard less of Narco of late, and much more of Morta on the soldier's lips as they moved back and forth over the water. Shannic's prison.

No one seemed to be coming to check on them. All any scout nearest Jasra's position could do was splash water upon her throughout their shift. So far, they had been able to continually keep her damp, though many of them were tiring, and some wondered aloud if what they were doing was only drawing out Jasra's misery. Shannic had only just left his post there, being told by his friend, Cal, to go for a swim. To rest.

But how could he rest? Jasra was dying up there. He had been restrained on multiple occasions from crawling out to get her. Too dangerous, they said. She was a good dozen feet from the water, and even if he reached her, he could not stand. He would have to wriggle on his belly like a fish, and then what? He had no way of pulling the stake free.

Almost without realizing it, he had been ignoring something. So lost in thought, he had not realized until now that it wasn't the crying or his heart breaking but instead voices calling for him…. He shook his head, looking toward the dam wall.

"Hello," a voice carried through the water. Merfolk, having a distinct inflection in their lilting voices, were very recognizable.

He spun in a circle. He was alone. All the other merfolk had left him to his swim. Many knowing his pain, having suffered the loss of their own mate.

"Hello," the voice called louder, and this time, punctuated it with a pounding.

The fish in the area scuttled away. It was as if someone were on the other side of the dam. That could not be! This had to be a trick. A nasty trick by the evil villain himself. Shannic would not give in to the game.

Shannic turned, keeping low near the lakebed, beginning to swim away, but he froze.

"Hello! I am Marman. We come from Kaulter." The voice sounded more urgent this time.

Shannic called out a long clear note, signaling to the other merfolk to join him. Other calls echoed his own— from both sides of the dam!

The merfolk appeared, eyes widening as they themselves heard the unique lilting voices and calls from the other side.

"They have come for us at last," Olgan whispered, glancing around excitedly. The mermaid swam to the wall, pressing her palms upon it and her ear up against it. Her nearly white hair undulating with the water.

"We come from Kaulter. We will help you," the voice crooned from the other side.

Shannic's eyes widened, unsure of how they possibly could help.

"How many of you?" He called out.

"All of us," the voices thundered in unison, and as soon as they spoke, they began to push against the dam.

Shannic could hear them collide with the wall and then swim backwards, preparing to slam into it again. The merfolk possessed a strength beyond many of the land walkers. Narco had learned to send the trolls, since the merfolk could often overpower the humans escaping their grasp.

It seemed incredibly unlikely that they would do any damage, and Shannic feared for their capture. "No, stop," he and his fellow imprisoned merfolk on this side of the lake cried, knowing that this much noise would surely bring the attention of the guards.

The slamming thuds of powerful forms in unison bludgeoning the dam filled their ears, and all Shannic and his friends could do was wait. And pray.

***

"I will go first," Antonis ordered, glaring at Cela.

Trinidad was growing tired of the constant competition between the two of them. But he held his tongue, as it seemed did Lyrianna. A loud pounding sound continued somewhere not far from the village, which they now strode through. Trinidad was distracted by it. Uneasy. He had warned the Queen, but after searching much of the Castle and finding it nearly empty, save for a few cooks and kitchen aides, he could safely say the area was deserted. Same with the village. Where had they gone?

Trinidad felt his ire escalating as he thought of the children under Morta's "care," fearing they faired no better than Trigger had.

Then he looked back at the presence tottering along in silence. He felt only love for the tiny frame... and a fierce paternal affection. It was his brother's grandson, after all. They were family. *And family means everything*, Trinidad thought, holding strongly to this belief.

Cela shot out an angry retort, Trinidad blinked back to the conversation at hand. "Oh, you two stop that bickering. You are squabbling like children. Antonis, please search ahead. Cela, watch the rear... Trigger is too exposed." And though he didn't say it, Cela's eyes shot to Dabor, who ambled behind them all.

It was rare for Trinidad to give an order, and the two stopped. Cela's pointed finger, directed at Antonis's chest, froze in midair with disbelief.

Lyrianna cleared her throat slightly, bringing both back to attention.

Trinidad stifled a laugh as Antonis, looking somewhat flustered, and Cela, red-cheeked from the rebuke, both fell to doing his bidding.

That pounding! Trinidad thought, forgetting almost instantly their petty squabbles. *Where is it coming from?*

"Do you hear that?" he asked softly.

Lyrianna tilted her head, then shook it. "No, nothing. What do you hear?"

All knew that unicorns typically had heightened senses far superior to their human counterparts, save for the Marked Royals. He continued walking, unsure of how to describe it. They passed the thatched roof homes. The desolate village caused his spine to tingle. It was silent. Not even a dog barked or bird chirped. It was as if even the animals knew to take cover, for the beast—Morta—was now unleashed upon the land, and no one was safe.

Animals, he paused his thinking. His eyes shot to the water. "There," he said. "Something is happening at the lake!"

Antonis trotted down ahead of them, all eyes catching sight of another victim. Their nymph friends gathered there inspecting it.

"Oh no," Lyrianna gasped, lifting her skirts once again and running toward the dock. There, a heavy wooden beam was driven into the ground, and on it was a mermaid. A stake driven through her tail. The nymphs were trying, but failing, to pull it out.

Antonis made it to her, and as Trinidad arrived, he could see that Antonis, kneeling down at the poor wretch's face, was speaking to her. "She lives," he said quickly. "Barely. She needs to get back in the water immediately."

Trinidad peered at the stake, pressing his horn upon it but unsure if he could draw it out. As he inspected it, a big grey hand appeared in front of his nose. He balked, looking up quickly, surprised to find Dabor there. With one smooth grasp, the troll pulled the stake out, his grey bulbous skin tight over well-worked biceps.

Antonis, having picked up on Dabor's nature, caught the mermaid's head and upper body as her lower half became free and fell to the ground.

Trinidad and the rest stepped back while Antonis and Dabor spoke to the mermaid. Her head lolled from side to side, and she was murmuring something. Her skin baked red from the sun and her scales flaking off in patches.

While Antonis and Dabor were busy carrying her to the water's edge, Trinidad looked askance toward the dam. He still heard pounding. Rounding the dock, he walked to the water's edge. Dipping his horn into the water, a streak of light shone out as if a beacon led directly to the dam... and an entire gathering of merfolk. Trinidad watched tails and heads surfacing as a number of merfolk came forward. One head came nearest, and as the green-eyed merman looked them over, his eyes caught sight of Antonis lowering a mermaid's form into the shallow lake.

"Jasra!" The merman cried, arriving at her side in one giant splash.

Trinidad came closer, seeing with relief that her eyes fluttered open as Dabor lowered her into the water. The merman gently grabbed a hold of her upper body from Antonis and drew her into the depths. The heads disappeared for a moment, and Trinidad wondered if they'd spooked them, until the green-eyed merman appeared again.

"Thank you," he sobbed, coming closer, his eyes ringed with relief. "But... why?" He spluttered, eyeing Dabor, in particular, who stood near Trinidad. "Who are you?"

Lyrianna, who had remained nearly hidden behind Trinidad and Cela's imposing forms, appeared trailed by Trigger, whose ears perked up in alertness.

"I know you." The merman said, astonishment filling his voice.

Trinidad at first thought the merman was referring to the Queen but followed his gaze to the tiny form of Trigger. Looking between them, Trinidad asked, "Do you know... Trigger?"

The merman was nodding, looking perplexed. "Yes. But where is his mother?"

And then Trinidad understood. He remembered lamely, wanting to knock his head against a wall for his sheer slowness, that merfolk had aided Zola and Trigger's escape. He understood. "Zola is not here. You must be the one who helped her." It was more of a statement than a question.

The merman nodded, introducing himself as Shannic and flooding the party with questions.

Trinidad looked at the infant and breathed heavily. "Morta captured Trigger from Kaulter and searched his mind for memories. He," Trinidad gestured toward the water, "is how Morta found out about your involvement. I assume that is why she was tortured?"

A bitter glare swept over the otherwise handsome merman's face. His eyes darkening and looking at Trigger, and then finally, softening as Trinidad spoke. "It was not intentional, I can assure you. He is but a child. For I have searched his young mind, as well. Trigger has been no better treated than you—perhaps even worse."

Shannic nodded when another loud pang sounded nearby.

"What is that sound?"

"The merfolk of Kaulter," Shannic explained. "They appeared only today. They are trying to bring down the dam."

"From Kaulter?" Lyrianna questioned, and for the first time, Shannic studied her. His eyes widened with sudden recognition.

"Your Majesty?" he questioned softly, as if in disbelief. "How are you—" He looked around himself with sudden confusion. "But you were captured, we heard of it many moons ago. How is it possible? Forgive me," bowing his head quickly.

Lyrianna knelt down and extended her hand.

Shannic swam up reaching for it and pressed his lips to her hand with another bow of his head.

"I fear we have much to discuss, but first, I would like to visit with the merfolk of Kaulter. We left there recently, and it troubles me to think of them leaving there. Why now? After all this time," she replied smoothly, motioning for them—save for Shannic—to follow her back down the dock and around toward the dam.

As they neared, Shannic called for the merfolk on the other side to stop. Explaining that the Queen and Horned Ones were present. He called for them to explain why they had come.

"We learned of you from Zola," a voice called out, Shannic speaking louder so that those not submerged in water could hear the response.

But as Trinidad dipped his head to listen to the rest of the explanation, a severe shock rang through every nerve ending in his body, for with his heightened hearing, he could discern the voice under the water.

"… and we came because Kaulter is no longer safe. The Regent Elsra has been killed, and the Portals were closed just days ago."

Trinidad fell to his knees, his emotions in turmoil. "Mother!" He cried out. *This cannot be.*

But as his glassy eyes met those of his companions and then landed on Dabor, reminding him of the stone, he knew that it was. Morta's tricks, his vast evil taint, were only just beginning.

CHAPTER 27

The Arrival

Trinidad gasped. *Mother, gone? How could she have died without me knowing*, he wondered. He had always thought if a relation passed, he would have sensed it. But no. She had died—without him. He needed the full story. And in order to do that, he needed to speak with all of the merfolk. He needed to bring down this dam!

"Stand back," he roared to those around him.

At this, Antonis ushered Lyrianna and Trigger back while Dabor and Cela stood at a distance.

Trinidad stepped into the water at the edge where the manmade dam of piled stones stood barricading the Kaulter merfolk from their kin. His heart in turmoil, he felt a renewal of passion seize him, as if a power unlike any he'd ever known was fueling him forward. *Mother*, he thought. Her spirit was strengthening, or perhaps it was just her memory. Though he would never know, he chose to think of his lost parents and their support of his next efforts.

Striding knee-deep in the cool water, he bent his head down so that his horn pierced through the murky liquid. He closed his eyes and drew upon the fount of power growing in his heart. He pictured Rinzaltan's death. Narco's treachery. Lyrianna's face when captured. Cela when she was ravaged before they could save her. Darion's brilliant green eyes. Tav'Opal's bloodied form. Dabor's stone. He saw everything. And, as if releasing a great exhale, he focused on the immense light that he felt in his heart, a gift from the unicorns of old, and he expanded it. In a flash, the entire lake radiated with a magnificent light, revealing the merfolk on both sides of the walled dam.

Trinidad stepped further into the water, and as he did, a trembling began at the lakebed. The merfolk didn't hesitate for an instant. The Kaulter merfolk, now able to see everything—every nook and cranny of the barrier—renewed their impact. Seizing on the weak points, they swam and collided with the wall in unison. As they did, the lakebed trembled with greater intensity, as if nature rebelled against this violation of ill will. The quake's magnitude nearly knocked Trinidad from his powerful stance. He knew not what he was doing, only that his innate giftings demanded justice. Demanded to be released upon this evil. And so, he held his position and kept the lake alit.

Another crashing from the merfolk and then a crack. Angry waves threatened to drown Trinidad. The trapped merfolk, all but Shannic, retreated. Trinidad could see his brilliant scales tracing the wall…. Though laboring against the turbulent waves, Shannic scoured every crevice, even though he ran the risk of being crushed if the wall came down.

He surfaced near Trinidad a moment later, revealing huge bright eyes! "That is it, Trinidad! All this time I knew there had to be a key, but I searched for a literal one. I think, instead, you are the key. A unicorn. Here, press your horn onto the wall itself," Shannic directed him.

Trinidad walked carefully at the water's edge, keeping his horn submerged, and as the merfolk opposite pulled back for another collision, Trinidad focused on Elsra's image and pressed his horn to the dam.

Shannic quickly ushered him away when a massive force met with the wall and a thundering erupted from both sides of the churning water as stones and debris fell away. The connection of the unicorns and merfolk had long been a part of Nav'Arian history, and so it was, that their union in this common need was honored by the spirits of old. A flash of iridescent light, like that of a mermaid or merman's scales, flared across the water.

Trinidad looked up, raising his head to watch as a multitude, more numbers than he'd even known resided in Kaulter, rushed to be reunited with their counterparts. The water clarity was brilliant, as if the connection between Trinidad's horn and the merfolk had cleansed it of its murkiness. Furthermore, the land here had been healed. The fractured relations had been brought back together.

This is the beginning of the new Nav'Aria, Trinidad thought. Now, they must go face Morta to end this darkness.

***

"I mean, it's possible, right?" Darion pressed Edmond.

While in pursuit of the trolls, Darion had found Edmond to walk beside. Triumph, Soren and Zola trailed behind, leaving Vikaris to his military commanders. Vikaris walked beside Trixon, Myrne, Kragar, and Drigidor. They were doing what they always did: discussing plans and strategies. His father had dark circles under his eyes, and his brow seemed permanently furrowed these days.

"I guess," Edmond said apprehensively, drawing back Darion's attention.

Both longed to talk of Nala and Ati. To see them and know that they were alright. Darion had made up his mind, and though he knew he should be focused on the fight to come, he couldn't keep his thoughts from returning to Nala. Her foreign, slurred speech, interesting style, strong-will, and stunning beauty.

"I say, as soon as this is all over, we go find them. If Morta is defeated, then we can tell Zalto that everything is safe. The girls can live here—with us…. I mean, if that's what we want," Darion finished lamely. He thought he heard a snort from one of the unicorns. Triumph, most likely.

"Yeah, but…" Edmond cut off, glancing in Vikaris's direction. "Do you really think he will let you leave? Again? After all of this?"

Darion scowled, though secretly he wondered the same thing. "He's not the boss of me," and at Edmond's caustic stare, Darion admitted, "Well, I guess he is as

King, but still. I think we can find a way. We won't need a border anymore if Morta—and the Rav'Arians—are wiped out. So, that's what we need to do."

Edmond nodded along, his cheeks flushing as his thoughts, most likely, drifted to Ati. Darion didn't blame him. Just thinking of Nala made his own skin grow hot. He missed her. The smell of her hair…. her endearing left cheek dimple… the form of her body as….

A loud snort and a grunt came from behind this time.

"Damnit, Triumph," Darion snapped embarrassed. "Mind your own business."

This time Zola joined in the laughter, and soon all three unicorns were chuckling and snorting like fools.

Darion grabbed Edmond's arm, and drew him up ahead, away from the chortling unicorns who were making quite a scene.

"Just like old times," Edmond laughed, winking at Darion, and though feigning annoyance, Darion couldn't help but grin too.

The days had come quickly since leaving Kaulter and fending off the troll force. With the knowledge of the stones, the loyal Nav'Arians pushed ahead after the troll force. Drigidor had wanted to set off after them immediately, but Vikaris had insisted on seeing the funeral pyres lit and sending scouts back to Kaulter to warn them of the many injured that would need immediate attention.

After that, Vikaris had commanded they head towards the Stenlen and beyond, for Darion had shared with his father that he felt a growing pulsing energy near the border. Vikaris admitted he could feel something as well but couldn't articulate what exactly it was.

If this weren't worrisome enough, Vikaris also had the nymph scouts' news to deal with. The portals to Kaulter would not open. They had been closed… and since no unicorns were in control in Kaulter, and none on this side—nor the King—had activated this command, Vikaris feared the worse. Once again, Morta had tampered with the portals. The significance of this was dire. There would be no retreat. No escape. The injured had to be left in the woods under the care of a few of the nymphs until the portals re-opened. That was all that could be done.

Watching the tall grasses and rolling hills of Nav'Aria, remembering crossing similar ground on his secret quest to Rav'Ar, Darion considered this. Now, he had an entire army at his back… though what they would find… was anyone's guess.

Still alongside Edmond and the unicorns, he walked distractedly, pondering this.

"You seem to be in deep thought, My Prince," a rich voice mused nearby.

Darion blinked, glancing over, surprised to find a centaur near him.

The centaur towered over many of the others. Darion had seen him before but had never been introduced. The centaur had the deepest ebony skin Darion had ever seen. It ran almost seamlessly from his fleshed upper body into a deep, glossy coat on his four legs. The small ornaments in his long swinging braids tinkled lightly in the warm breeze. A pink puckered scar ran along a portion of the centaur's side, marring the otherwise pristine coat, and one of his arms ended in a stump just below the elbow.

The centaur caught Darion glancing at it and chuckled, a warm booming sound. "Yes, my Prince. I have not always been fortunate in battle. This," he paused, lifting his arm into the air, "this came years ago, from a Rav'Arian blade. It sliced my hand clean off," and then his stare grew deadly, "but he did not live to see the result," he replied, snickering darkly.

Darion gulped.

He certainly looked the part of a warrior. Though one-armed, two sword hilts arose from the strappings on his back, and his biceps far surpassed Antonis's... which was saying something.

"I am Drogs," the centaur replied, smiling. A bright white smile illuminating his dark, handsome face.

Darion smiled back and suddenly wondered if this centaur was related to the younglings he had seen on his first day in Nav'Aria. He felt guilty for not getting to know more of his 'subjects.' Looking at the kindly, yet lethal, centaur warrior, he vowed that once this battling was finished, he would meet every single Nav'Arian.

"Nice to meet you," Darion replied after a moment, finally remembering his manners. "I am Darion."

The centaur dipped his head in respect. "Please, my Prince, I have heard whispers of your travels to Rav'Ar, and I was wondering something."

Darion nodded for him to go on.

"The Rav'Arians have always come from there... so I am wondering, do you think we are walking into a trap heading toward the border? If Morta comes from the Castle and his reinforcements come straight from the border instead of having joined the enemy force, are we going to be caught in a pincer?"

Darion frowned, *Is he a mind-reader?* This was something he and his father had only just recently discussed. And yet, they decided there was no other option. Even if the trolls were luring them into a trap—if there was even a slight chance they could free more of the trolls and bolster their side with them, they had to take it.

"Drogs, I wish I knew. All I know is that we need to catch up to those trolls if we're going to have any chance."

The centaur studied him. "Yes, I see. That is what Myrne has repeated to us as well." He seemed to hesitate before stopping completely and turning toward the King, "Then I believe I have somewhere to be, my Prince," and with that he bowed and turned back, pushing gently through the oncoming troops toward the King.

Darion turned to watch him. "What was that about?" He asked aloud, not expecting any answer.

Soren approached. "He means to do something foolish," Soren replied. "Brave, but foolish."

Soon enough, Darion understood what Soren meant. It seemed Drogs felt that they should not waste such time marching. He pleaded to the King for the centaur contingent to be sent ahead to find and attack the trolls, for if they came upon the trolls too late and were surrounded by Morta's forces from multiple sides, they ran a very big risk of being defeated. Soren explained later that Drogs and Garis had been very close friends and sparring partners who were raised together as boys. He needed to avenge his friend.

At dawn the next day, the centaurs—all save for Myrne—who remained at the King's side, gathered. With war horns blaring, the formidable warriors—male and females alike—set off, thundering across the Nav'Arian land in a heightened pursuit of the trolls.

Pushing hard that day, Darion could hear the distant war cries and bellows of battle. As they crested a hillside spilling out into a lush green pasture of rich farmland and luscious, vibrant greenery, Darion and those near the front of the line witnessed the centaurs clashing with the trolls. It seemed that they had been able to capture more, and a handful of bodies lay strewn about. No centaur corpses were among them.

He heard his father's call for them to join and surround the trolls, and Darion set off at a run, Triumph keeping pace. Soon, the reinforcements made quick work of the final combatants, and they surrounded an angry, roaring group of a dozen or more trolls.

Drogs trotted up, winking at Darion before bowing to Vikaris. "My King, at least half of the force continued running and did not stop to help these," he waved back at the surrounded group.

Vikaris replied, "You have done well, Drogs. We have strengthened our numbers without losing any," placing emphasis on the last word.

Drogs caught his meaning and responded quickly, "Yes, my King. We were fortunate today. No losses."

Vikaris's shoulders visibly lowered as he breathed out. "Good. That is very good to hear."

The force made camp there, so Aalil, D'Ania, and Rick, along with the other "freed" trolls, could get right to removing the stones. The trolls' bellows and agonized cries could be heard for much of the afternoon as one after the other was pinned down and his leg cut into. And though it made Darion a little queasy at the thought, he knew that it had to be done. The trolls that had been through it days ago still seemed a little dazed albeit completely loyal, as did D'Ania and the female trolls. Vikaris ordered them kept under strict watch despite telling Darion how they reminded him of the trolls he recalled from his youth. They were amiable and mild mannered.

Making a quick camp and sleeping in the open air reminded Darion of their trek through Rav'Ar. Each step they took closer to the border comforted him, for he was drawing closer to Nala. He pictured her face each night before dozing off into the dreamless sleep that only comes from the heavy fatigue of battle and marching. Though, this night, his sleep was interrupted only briefly. His dream revealed his mother, no longer tortured in a cell but standing upon the ruins of a building looking out toward a horizon. She seemed... pensive.

Darion woke, mulling it over and hoping she was safe.

Sitting up, Darion's nose tickled from the pollen and aromatic grasses, and his stomach heaved with hunger pains. He could smell breakfast roasting—mainly small animal and venison—that troops had hunted. Beyond that, they had eaten some fruit picked from a wild orchard that had appeared almost like a mirage. Cherry and apple trees dotted the edge of camp, and the soldiers made quick work of removing nearly every piece of edible fruit.

Not nearly enough to fill their bellies, but that was the way, Triumph had grumbled. *Life as a soldier is full of discomforts. It is best to get used to it.*

Darion, as did the other humans, he noted, slept with their boots on, and so he stood stomping the sleep and fatigue from his limbs before turning to find food and catch up with his friends who appeared already awake. He and Triumph needed to continue their conversation on the prophecy. As they drew nearer to battle, he still had no idea how he was to defeat Morta.

Just as he moved toward Triumph, though, an ear-splitting screech filled the morning air, and as if appearing out of nowhere, a large, winged beast swept into view. Darion felt fear grip him as he stared at it. It looked different than any of the Reouls he had met. It had large, menacing horns on its face and spikes down its back. Huge black wings and scales gleamed in the morning light. But worst of all were its eyes. For even at this distance, Darion's senses could make them out. They burned red, and as if sensing him, locked with Darion's. It dove straight down toward the troops surrounding Darion and opened its giant maw. Jagged rows of teeth gleamed white, and then orange, as a burst of fire poured from it igniting the camp. Centaurs, humans, nymphs, and unicorns alike screamed and bellowed, diving out of the flame's path.

Darion stood frozen and staring, as if suspended, as the creature made a beeline directly for him.

***

"Thank you again for everything," Shannic spoke, squeezing Lyrianna's hand and smiling at her and Trinidad. "You have restored our hope. You have given me..." at this point, Jasra, the beautiful mermaid, swam up. Shannic stopped, smiling, and wrapped his arm around her, pulling her in closely, "You have given me everything."

"You will always be safe under my husband's rule," Lyrianna said graciously, smiling at the pair of them.

After talking late into the night, the merfolk had helped lead the ferry carrying Lyrianna and her party across the lake. She could sense Darion. He needed her. And so, they hastily crossed and bid farewell. The reunited merfolk vowed to swim back, for there was a sea between the Isle of Kaulter and the mainland of Nav'Aria. Though all other creatures relied on portals to travel, the merfolk could swim there. They vowed to return and spread the news of Morta—and the empty Castle—and all that they had learned and seen here.

Although Antonis had briefly entertained the idea of the merfolk ferrying Lyrianna and Trigger all the way back to Kaulter, the Queen shut that train of thought down almost instantly. She would not go back while others fought for her. If the battle plans had shifted, then she would adapt. There was no retreat if the portals were truly closed. She would not cower while those she loved most risked all.

"I can sense them," she murmured to Trinidad, rubbing her Mark.

He nodded as if he too could sense the battle brewing. And then, without another word, they waved their final farewell to the merfolk who swam in the clear, iridescent waters ripe with magic, and turned to head toward the tug Lyrianna felt. Darion. He was her beacon... and she was coming for him!

***

Rick nearly choked while swallowing a chunk of rabbit meat when a beast unlike any he had ever seen soared over the camp and began spraying fire.

Darion, he breathed, panic gripping him. He spit out the wad of meat in mid-jump and yelled for Aalil. "Come on," rounding up the trolls and the fierce warrior who had captured his friend's heart and whom he had begrudgingly come to care for over the past days.

Aalil, true as her nature, was already dressed, blade in hand and following him out into the fray, no questions asked.

War horns sounded. To his horror, from the far position at the rear of the camp, Rick watched an outpour of enemy soldiers stream across the landscape, headed from all directions and bound for their camp. Above, the screeching beast spewed fire and chaos wherever it passed.

Rick had to get to Darion. He was up there somewhere. Rick had tried to give him his space, letting him proceed with Triumph and the King. Besides, Rick liked to keep his hands busy and had seen that he could be of use to everyone by helping Aalil with the trolls. But as he ran, racing through the dazed and terror-stricken soldiers, he regretted his decision. *What was I thinking?* They were marching to war. He shouldn't have left Darion out of his sight for a moment. If something happened to Darion, he…. "Do not even think it," he growled to himself. He darted through the maze of cookfires and rows of tents, then passed many soldiers who were still donning their sword belts.

Fools, he spat, glaring at many of them. *How could they have let this happen? Where were the scouts?* These and many other questions racked his brain as he ran. A sulfurous odor and smoke began to fill the morning air, and Rick froze. Flames burst in front of him, and had Aalil not rolled to the ground behind him, she most likely would have knocked him into the now blazing inferno before their eyes. This route was currently cut off from the rest of the force. Rick's eyes teared from the smoke and emotion of that moment.

"Damnit," he moaned, trying to mentally block out the screaming men who were caught in the blaze. Bodies staggered in agonized motion as they collided with one another and were soon reduced to soot when another wave of heat erupted nearby. Bleary-eyed and straining to see through the haze, Rick pushed back the way they'd come. Running for Darion, he looked around to discover he was utterly alone. No sign of Aalil or the trolls in sight. He breathed shallowly, coughing intermittently from the overwhelming smoke and odor of burning flesh. Soldiers ran and ducked in disarray. Soon, Rick found himself alone in the open field. The air seemed clearer here for the moment, and that's when he saw it. Or rather, when he was seen. The beast sighted on him and swooped over the burning battle. Clangs of steel rang out amidst the screaming as the trolls, Rav'Arians, and traitor humans battled the Nav'Arian force.

Rick watched the tumult that came as the beast made its second sweep over the camp, further narrowing in on him alone. Exposed. He watched as its mouth opened, its chambers filling with flame at the back of its throat before spewing fire straight at Rick.

CHAPTER 28⟡

The Father

Vikaris blinked blurrily, recovering from a troll hit. He gritted his teeth and spat, tasting blood from a loosened tooth. He searched around him. He and his commanders had been in discussion, planning their march for the day, when they'd been set upon unawares by something out of a nightmare. Why had the scouts not blown their horns? Signaled an attack? And what was this fire-breathing monster? Surely not one of the winged ones, for Darion had said they were friendly. Had they lied to him? Betrayed Vikaris?

There was no order to the fighting whatsoever. His military strategies were all null and void as he looked around at the jumble. No ranks. No pikes. No archers. Just chaos. Half the camp was engulfed in flame. The open field, where the centaurs had clashed with the trolls just yesterday, had become a blackened, scorched land in a matter of breaths. The beast had to be killed, or their destruction would come all too soon.

Stumbling to his feet, he looked to see Trixon engaged with two trolls—evil, red-eyed ones—still under Morta's control. He ran to assist his companion, slashing his sword expertly across the nearest troll. It clutched its side and roared, growing more enraged. As Vikaris helped Trixon finish them off, the unicorn's horn already dripping in gore and blood, he called, "We have to find Darion."

Trixon agreed, commanding, "Get on my back."

Vikaris hopped on, signaling to Kragar, Drogs, Drigidor and some of the other soldiers nearest him to join them. Together, they could stave off more attacks if they fought back to back.

A shallow wound on Kragar's sword arm dripped blood, but he didn't hesitate to bellow orders. Any soldiers nearby were to assemble. Join them as they pressed across the battlefield.

"Archers, ready!" Kragar cried. Many of them had hung back, clustered on the edge of camp awaiting orders, though no formation was in place, nor could they send out volleys for fear of hitting their fellow soldiers. Kragar pointed up at the beast, directing them. "Kill that monster! Bring it down!"

Archers spread out, running to take down the enemy in the air—something Vikaris never thought he'd witness in his lifetime.

Vikaris had long since known it was never ideal to let an opponent choose the place of the battle... or the tactics. They had been caught unaware, and a fire-breathing beast was circling overhead, but Vikaris would be damned if he died without trying to regain some control of this fight. Together, his numbers grew as they pressed forward like a battering ram into the oncoming enemy. More and more Nav'Arians—humans, unicorns, centaurs, and nymphs—joined them, rather than continuing to fight isolated and alone interspersed throughout the battle. It seemed one area in particular was overrun with Rav'Arians, and the beast was circling nearby.

As Vikaris neared, he saw why. There, amid a sea of talons and claws, stood Darion, back against Edmond, and together with Triumph, Zola, and Soren. The unicorns' white coats—though splattered with some blood and muck—struck a vivid contrast to the dark Rav'Arians' scales and cloaks. Grey skinned trolls lumbered around, swinging their clubs toward the unicorns who were just barely fending off the force. They'd never survive. It was five against one hundred by the looks of it. Even as the bodies piled up around Darion and his friends, the Rav'Arian fodder never faltered. They kept coming, opponent after opponent.

Vikaris pointed at them bellowing for his troops to push. They had to get to Darion's aid. He slashed the trolls and treacherous humans, easily identified by their insignia and uniforms, still the winged crescent and colors of Narco.

Stabbing and cutting, Vikaris and Trixon tore through the enemies, reinforcing their numbers and coming to engage with those surrounding his son.

The beast—momentarily distracted deep within the camp—sprayed its fire. Vikaris could hear the screams of those caught aflame and shuddered involuntarily. Death by fire was an abhorrent way to go.

"Trixon," he growled, "my son will not die on this battlefield."

"No, he will not," Trixon rumbled, his resolve equally apparent.

They pressed on. Vikaris's sword arm bare, the Markings illuminated as they so often did, as if the act of battle triggered them. His Ruby shone so resplendently that a light pink tinge painted Trixon's neck.

None could miss the King as he rode through battle, something that Garis and Kragar had often complained about. At this moment, Vikaris was glad for it. Such recognition would likely draw attention from Darion. His son's arm, blessedly hidden under long-sleeves, did not give his identity away, at least not yet, he hoped.

"Sire, watch out," a voice cried from beside him as a force slammed into Trixon, knocking him askance.

A troll, the largest that Vikaris had seen, now battled Myrne, the centaur matriarch. Her fierce brown eyes narrowed on her opponent, her soft grey braids clinking together. Vikaris watched her expertly run a spear through the troll's abdomen. It roared angrily. As she jerked on the spear, trying to dislodge it, the beast swung its club in an uppercut motion to Myrne's chin. She cried out and somersaulted to a clearing, landing heavily on her side. The awkward lay of her neck told the story: the force of such a collision had snapped it.

Trixon yelled. Turning around, he slashed his horn across the beast's back. It bellowed. With a severed spinal cord, it began dropping heavily in writhing agony. Before it could touch down, Vikaris stabbed his sword through the back of its neck, and clear through the front of its throat. He dislodged it quickly and then turned back toward Darion's position.

He would mourn for Myrne, one of his oldest friends, later. He swallowed heavily. Darion needed him now.

The beast circled overheard. It was coming for them. Chaos abounded. Vikaris saw clustered Rav'Arians encircling his companions. He watched in horror as Drigidor reared at a Rav'Arian, hammering its head and bloodied corpse into the ground.

"Drigidor, behind you!" Unable to penetrate the tangled corpses and living, Vikaris could only shout.

A skulking Rav'Arian lurched from the margin and stabbed Drigidor's shoulder, the unicorn shrieking at the impact and limping as he shook off the opponent and stabbed him in return. His eyes blazed as they caught Vikaris's with a nod. He would live for now.... Vikaris could taste bile but pressed on. His son was what mattered most.

By this time, the King had reached the outside of the enemy cluster encircling his son. He could see Darion, now astride Triumph, and Edmond atop Soren, both battling with equal ferocity. But none compared to the pure savagery with which Zola fought. She was unlike anything Vikaris had ever seen. Such a sight made a Nav'Arian onlooker glad to know she fought on their side, for she was the most formidable fighter ever witnessed, Vikaris had no doubt. Wave after wave of Rav'Arians came at her, recognizing her as the largest threat presently. She slew every one of them. She reared, kicked, bit, and stabbed. Her shining light blinding the enemies around her, adding to her advantage. One unfortunate Rav'Arian got close enough to graze its talons across her throat—until it heard the scream. It escaped her lips and grew in piercing intensity... until it equaled her horn's blinding wrath. Her opponents covered their eyes and ears and fell at her feet. She made quick work of them, creating a much-needed opening. Vikaris tried calling out, but it was no use. Over the thrum of battle, Darion could not hear him. Vikaris watched helplessly as his son rode upon Triumph through the opening Zola had created. Edmond and Soren followed while Zola brought up the rear, though no living enemies remained nearby to challenge her.

Slamming his fist into the side of a human opponent, he roared orders, "Kragar, where are your archers?" Vikaris watched as the beast swept over the portion of camp in which Darion was heading.

"Rally the troops," the King bellowed.

Trixon was already turning around and pointing them back in that same direction.

"To the interior of camp," Vikaris cried. "Nav'Arians assemble together."

***

Rick braced for the fire to engulf him, closing his eyes with one final prayer.

The heat from the blast swept around him. He could smell the sulfur, feel the inferno's heat in the air, hear the humming of fire spraying out. He cracked an eye open. Nothing had hit him. And then he nearly screamed.

Darion was there.

"No, son," he moaned watching in horror as his son, the boy he had raised and loved since infancy, stood face to face with a monster.

Darion shouted at the creature, his Marked Arm raised in defiance, the stubborn set of his shoulders and head, hair billowing around him, unlike anything Rick had ever seen. This... this man, held his arm out... and was holding back the flames.

Rick couldn't explain it or believe it. Darion stood, his arm aglow with a green, brilliant luminescence as his Ruby, tight at his throat, shone red upon the scorched earth. The beast in the air roared angrily, jerking its head and spraying fire to the sides, but none of it touched the ground. For it was as if Darion's hand was a buffer. *A shield!*

"You will stop," Darion bellowed, his voice magnifying with an intensity Rick could hardly believe.

The creature, tilting its head, simply stopped. While its wings flapped just enough to keep it aloft, its fire ceased.

Rick exhaled the breath he didn't know he had been holding. He felt arms on him and recognized Edmond, who pulled him up and out of the line of fire.

Soren, Zola, and Triumph stood nearby... though Triumph was pleading with his companions to let him go.

Rick heard Soren press, "NO, Triumph. You heard Darion. You have to trust him."

Just then Rick's eyes shot back to his son, who still stood alone challenging the beast that would make most grown men fall to their knees, Rick included.

"Don't distract him," Edmond threatened in his ear.

Rick's eyes widened at Edmond. He wanted to push him away and run to his son, but he saw the loyalty and admiration shining in his eyes and then turned to see it for himself.

Darion tore off the remnants of his shirt, which had suffered multiple slashes. Rick thanked the Creator that none of those cuts had sliced deeper. Darion, aglow with a sheen of sweat and the light from his Marked symbols and Ruby, made an epic image.

Darion repeated, "You can't win. Nothing can destroy what we have in Nav'Aria... even after all these years you've tried to spread your evil, you have never won. Never claimed it. You have failed, Morta."

With Darion's commanding shouts, Rick saw the Nav'Arian soldiers approaching from all sides look up in confusion.

"Morta?" Rick mumbled, looking at Edmond, whose eyes were still riveted to Darion.

A loud booming chuckle filled the air! "Ah, so you do know me," the beast replied, voice equally loud. "I had wondered if you would be able to sort it out."

"Oh, I did... Tarsin," Darion purred, his voice chilling.

The beast who had seemed to be enjoying the exchange snapped back to Darion's gaze, releasing a guttural cry that made every hair on Rick's body stand.

"Do not use that name!" The beast roared and renewed its fiery blast.

Darion's still-lifted arm held off the flames. How, Rick could not be sure. Some sort of Marked magic he assumed, but Darion did step back as if the force was beginning to wear on him.

"Darion," he breathed, stepping forward, longing to do something to help his son and all the while realizing the impossibility. Where Darion might be able to withstand the fire, Rick had seen plenty of other humans that couldn't stop the incendiary force. The heat burned the tiny hairs on Rick's arms and body. How could Darion stand it? Sweat poured down his son's tan face and slicked his bare arms.

And then Darion, still staving off the flames, reached into his pocket with his other hand and drew out a long yellow ribbon. At the sight of it, the beast shrieked, and instead of diving forward to attack Darion, as Rick had expected, the beast huffed, spun in the air, and bolted in the direction from whence it came.

As soon as it left, Darion collapsed, and Rick and Edmond rushed to his side. As they stood, Rick looked to find Vikaris and a squadron rushing their way. Vikaris's eyes looked as large and concerned as Rick knew his own did.

That had been too close. And Rick would be a fool to think that was the last of the beast. He knew it would be back.

CHAPTER 29:

The Destiny

Morta seemed to have called off the attack for the time being. The trolls and Rav'Arians as one ran when the beast—Morta—fled the area. Darion knew this wasn't the end of things, though.

As his Dad and friend helped him stand, he felt groggy. *How did I do that?* The force of the blast—the evil that had radiated from the creature—was enough to make him convulse even now. Surely he couldn't combat that thing? He could barely keep it from lighting the whole camp on fire. And the prophecy said HE was supposed to defeat it. Save them all. He shook his head, trying to clear his thoughts. Edmond assisted this effort by draining a water skin on his friend's head.

"What was that for?" Darion grumbled.

Shrugging sheepishly as Darion glared at him, Edmond replied, "You looked hot. I cannot believe you are not on fire!"

Rick pushed the boy back to get a good look at Darion.

Darion ran his hands over his face, brushing his now damp hair. "I'm alright, Dad."

Words seemed to fail Rick. His mouth was pursed, as if trying to keep the tears back, as he grabbed Darion in a tight hug.

While Rick embraced him, he felt another hand clamp down on his shoulder. Pulling away from Rick, he was almost knocked over with Vikaris's fierce, paternal embrace.

Muttering much the same thing, Darion tried to reassure them both that he was alright and that Morta would certainly be back.

"I know," Vikaris said lowly. "I have sent men to retrieve the bodies, clear the field for the moment, and get something in their bellies." As he spoke, he surveyed the scorched earth all around and asked, "Any idea how we can keep him from roasting us all for supper?"

Darion could see through his forced levity. Taking a good look around, Darion tied up his hair, asking, "Well, how many of your archers are nymphs?"

Vikaris crinkled his brow thinking on it.

"Not nearly enough," a low voice boomed. Drigidor limped up to them, his shoulder injury now sewn up.

The unicorns had lost a few of their number already, and Trixon had commanded—being of the Unicorn Council himself—that none were to use their healing abilities unless it was dire. They needed all their energy stores for the fight ahead.

"Could they," Darion hesitated, looking at some of the nymphs nearby. "Could they carry spears or something?"

Vikaris was already nodding his head in understanding. "Kragar, organize your archers. Get the nymphs too. They can carry spears or rocks for all I care, so long as they bring that beast down. At least if he directs his flame toward them, they should be able to fly away. As it stands, our human soldiers do not have a chance of escaping the blaze, all except..." Vikaris trailed off, looking at Darion.

He knew he left off the "you." Darion didn't know how he had achieved it, but only hoped he could do it again. Otherwise, he'd be burned and left as a pile of ash. He had definitely pissed off Morta. *He'll be back.*

Triumph growled in agreement.

Vikaris was still barking orders. By now, the men, unicorns, centaurs, nymphs, and few loyal trolls—accompanied by Aalil, who looked a little worse for wear, soot and leaves in her hair, as if she'd taken quite a tumble—had all gathered and were forming lines. Together, they would press ahead for the next attack. The trolls, Darion was surprised to see, were placed in the center around the unicorns and Darion himself.

Darion didn't have too much time to reflect on it though. After stuffing down a mouthful of roasted meat, what kind he didn't care, and washing it down with a swish of water, a horn sounded in the distance. *Back already,* he exhaled. He hadn't wanted to say it out loud, but he feared for them all. *How could they defeat those numbers with a freaking possessed dragon leading the army?*

Morta circled in the air angrily. He could feel the evil power rippling through his body. But at the sight of that blasted ribbon, the tiny sliver—the remnant of Tarsin that lingered in him—he moaned. He felt... weak when he thought of that man from so long ago. He was more than Tarsin. More than anything that lived. And he would wreak destruction unlike anything any ever witnessed before upon this land. The darkness within him craved it. Yearned for it. He had to end it. Today. This was to be the new beginning. Nav'Aria would breathe its last breath this day.

Winging down toward his forces, he shouted his orders. His pets quivered with energy as he swept over them. Kept away from the first attack... they longed for this. He laughed, a billow of smoke escaping his jaws. "Kill them all," he bellowed, his voice amplified.

As one, the Rav'Arians—and their forces of trolls, humans, and midnight black unicorns—tore off, Morta sweeping into the air above them.

"Too bad you did not get to see any of this, Narco," he chortled, soaring away.

Again, the fighters came suddenly, but this time they were met with ready opponents. Both sides faced one another as the daylight began to fade away into evening. Their fighting and preparing had taken all day, and Darion knew they had a long night ahead.

Diverse ranks prepared to fight at all costs. Though Darion noticed some of the trolls on the other side looking uneasy as they caught sight of the Nav'Arians' trolls.

He sat on Triumph, sword in hand, surrounded by all those he'd come to love and respect in this land. He rubbed his palm absently on Triumph's neck. The unicorn whinnied softly, shaking his mane.

"Darion," Triumph began. "I—"

"I know, Triumph. I love you too. You are a true friend."

He thought he heard a sniffle from his companion, but it was soon drowned out by the roar of the beast. Morta had returned.

"Shit," Darion murmured. Though still a distance off, it seemed—once again—headed straight for him.

This time, however, the archers were ready. As the front lines held firm, they eyed the oncoming soldiers—who, as was their nature, were in disarray. Though powerful, neither Narco nor Morta, it seemed, possessed the finesse of battle strategy. The hybrid unicorns, with their dark, glossy coats and maddened eyes, led the enemy forces.

The unicorns around Darion shifted as they saw them. They had not been used in the previous attack, but Drigidor had cautioned they would come. The unicorns and horse regiment stood ready.

As the enemy force approached, nearly colliding with the Nav'Arian front line, the archers released their first volley, taking out man, troll, and unicorn alike. None were spared from the herb-tipped arrowheads. D'Ania, the troll, had had the idea to rub a certain herb known to have sleep-inducing effects all over the metal-tipped arrows. She had tasked her female troll companions with picking it ever since learning there was to be a battle. Sacks draped across her body stored large quantities of it. She had worked tirelessly, with Aalil's help, to first grind the herbs and then dip all the arrows.

Darion watched as they struck the soldiers, and just as D'Ania had described, the potent, fast-acting agent quickly dulled its victims' senses, slowing their movements. It wasn't exactly a fair fight that way, but Vikaris had scoffed, saying it had long since stopped being a fair fight when men were killed in their beds and children and women were taken as slaves. This was war... and war was ugly.

The archers directed their next volley at the oncoming force. Their third intended for the winged beast quickly coming into their target zone.

Darion in the center, protected by trolls and unicorns for now, watched the front lines engage the enemy. The sluggish trolls and unicorns were a welcome sight. The herb was working!

The arrows bounced off Morta, however. Darion watched in pure horror as he opened his mouth and swept over their lines and toward the archers, spewing his red-hot fire. The nymphs jumped into action, quickly pulling archers out of the way as best they could. Still, the inevitable screams pierced their ears.

Morta swooped over the battlefield ceasing his attack. For the moment, he seemed keen on watching. More arrows clattered against him and toward the enemies, but their accuracy and numbers were few. The archers had done their part. Now it was up to the main body of soldiers to carry the fight. Cavalry and foot soldiers pressed in all around.

Bodies pressed in as the fighting grew thicker. Trolls near Darion fell as the enemies swept in. The enemy unicorns making quick work of those who tried to stand against them.

Darion swung his sword, cutting the head off a Rav'Arian that squelched as its blood spurted. The smell was toxic, but he ignored it. He saw his father astride Trixon, likewise stabbing and hacking away amid the pressing enemy.

And then he saw a blur of white. Drigidor and four unicorn warriors found an opening to weave through until they met with the enemy unicorns. Shimmering white and black horns clanged against one another. Screams and shrieks filled the air.

Darion watched in desperation while Drigidor jumped back, kicking a troll behind him, only to be slashed by a menacing, equally large unicorn. It withdrew its horn reveling in the blood trailing from Drigidor's side. His pristine coat now soaked in red. Drigidor fell heavily, hidden by the battle waging all around.

Triumph screamed in anger as he watched his stepfather fall. There was nothing he nor Darion could do, though, as they were caught in their own fight against a cluster of Rav'Arians. Their poison-tipped blades and talons keeping Darion and Triumph on the defense. One wrong move, and they'd meet their end.

Suddenly, an opening in the enemy ranks parted, leading directly up to Darion and Vikaris, who fought and bellowed his war cry all the while.

A hideous beast—scaled, clawed, and massive—thundered through the ranks, uprooting soldiers as it came at them.

"The beast from Rav'Ar," Triumph cried, at the exact moment Darion locked eyes on it.

Another one? It looked identical to the one they had slain—perhaps a hair smaller, but just as lethal.

It roared, its long maw revealing rows of jagged bloody teeth snapping at any in its way—friend or foe. Darion gritted his teeth, poised to fight it, when a blur of white and a behemoth of a man hastened by. Soren and Edmond rushed to face the beast before it could reach Darion.

"Damnit," Darion muttered, fearing for his friend. And as if on command, the Rav'Arians they'd been battling only moments ago pressed back in, renewing their fight with gusto. Soren and Edmond were now closed off from the Nav'Arians and faced a threat far greater than any they had seen today, save for the bastard in the sky. Darion shot a quick glance up to see that Morta was indeed still hovering above, watching.

Cries, screams, screeches, bellows, and roars sounded all around. Along with the sensations, they overwhelmed Darion's heightened senses. The mix of blood, Rav'Arian filth, and smoke permeated the air.

Darion could hardly see but could hear his friend's cry as he battled the beast. His brave, stupid, behemoth of a friend, Edmond. Darion couldn't reach him! He feared for him and Soren.

Angrily, he lashed out with his sword—and his senses. His arm blazed green again, and a bright light flashed out from him, knocking the surrounding enemies off their feet. This gave him a clear but momentary look as the beast whipped its tail, swiping Edmond's legs out from under him. It prepared to bite at Soren. And then… slam!

A dazzling light streaked through the forces. It slammed into the beast, sending it flying on its back and then skittered to a halt.

Darion and Triumph had cleared enough of the opponents to see it. Zola pawed the ground. Her light— given by the spirits of old, Triumph had explained—made her the most powerful unicorn of their time. And very clearly, Darion could see she had things under control.

Running forward, she hammered her hoof down on the beast's head before turning to check on Soren and Edmond.

Darion started to call out to them when a screech came from overhead, the only warning Darion received before raising his arm above his head, shielding all within his vicinity from the flames. They licked out at the edges, men and beast crying aloud.

Darion glared up at Morta.

You can do it, Darion, Triumph was murmuring. *Push him. Fight him off.*

Darion ground his teeth together. This felt harder than before, and a trickle of fear wove into the back of his mind. As he acknowledged it, more screams came, as his shield began to wane.

You are stronger than him, Darion. PUSH! Fight him!

Darion tried with all his might, but he felt his energy failing. A motion at his side tore his attention. A troll pulled Vikaris from atop Trixon. *Father!*

The flames overhead stopped, and Darion looked from Morta back to his father. If he ran to his father, all his friends would surely be aflame the moment he lowered his arm, but if he didn't... he looked back to see Trixon rearing up in pain as a Rav'Arian stabbed his hindleg. Blood smears trailed along his coat, revealing a number of wounds. Darion could no longer see his father.

A sound brought his attention back. *Laughter.*

Darion screamed in outrage.

Morta was laughing at his predicament. And then he opened his mouth again to renew his flames. But they never came.

For just at that moment a sepia blur slammed into Morta aloft in the air.

Darion blinked away the sweat that was beading on his forehead and blurring his vision. For a moment, there it looked like ....

Darion's jaw surely would have hit the ground had he not been clenching his teeth so tightly.

Savage roars rang out from overhead. Shapes appeared from all around in the sky and battled the dark winged creature who had hurt so many over the years.

"They came," Triumph whispered.

Darion felt hope for the first time all day… and true elation. *They came!*

For it was Zalto clawing and blowing fire directly into Morta's face.

Another green creature—whom Darion recognized as Gamlin—flew around them, spewing flame when possible. And more and more winged shadows arrived. The twilight colors dancing off their shimmering scales of violets, greens, ambers, cerulean, crimson, and more. *The Reouls had come!*

Darion whooped in the air at the sight of them, causing the entire Nav'Arian force to raise cheers. For though many had no idea that winged creatures such as these existed until today, they knew anyone attacking Morta was a friend of theirs.

Darion jumped from Triumph and to where he'd last seen his father and Trixon, confident that Morta was now otherwise engaged. Kragar was limping. Blood ran freely down his left cheek from a gaping wound, but he supported Vikaris, who looked—all things considered—to be in good health.

But Trixon, he was on the ground. Rick knelt over him, examining his wounds and speaking in his soothing voice. Darion remembered it from years of watching his father tend horses. Trixon was in bad shape… that much was clear. Triumph rushed past him, followed by Soren. Both placing their horns upon Trixon's wounds. His body convulsed lightly. Vikaris wept openly, but still shouted orders to soldiers nearby. They were to gather up. Clear the dead. He then motioned for Darion to join him.

Darion felt his eyes brimming with tears. He wanted to comfort his father, but something held him back. Looking up, he noticed for the first time as the sky battle waged, and teeth, fire, and talons locked onto one another, that a small figure was perched onto the back of Zalto.

"No, no, no, no, no…." Darion was murmuring, holding his hands to the sides of his face.

Edmond gasped as he saw what had captured Darion's attention.

Nala clung for dear life to the spikes on Zalto's back. She was riding him into battle against Morta!

In a collision of fear and love and elation and rage, Darion watched as the woman he loved—whom he'd longed for these last weeks, was about to be burned alive for all to see.

***

"They are engaged already," Trinidad shared, the tremor of fear evident only to Lyrianna, for she knew him so well.

She wanted to scream, to urge him to run faster. Amazingly, he had allowed her to ride the entire distance from the Kingdom to the melee taking place near the border. They had run for hours upon hours, and as they crested the hill above the battle, they froze. Antonis sat astride Cela, though he'd grumbled about "what people would think" if they saw him riding a centaur. Dabor carried Trigger, who slept fitfully but safely. And the nymphs fluttered around them.

What they found was far beyond anything they'd expected. As the vibrant sunset colors swirled in the sky, and a thin, pale crescent moon rose, the sight that stole all of their breath, was that of scaled beasts, boasting many shades, fighting in the air against Morta while the soldiers waged war below.

"The winged ones," Lyrianna whispered, almost reverently.

"Holy shit," Antonis and Cela said in unison.

Glancing at them with a grin and feeling hope for the first time all day, Lyrianna called for them to move. She could feel Darion's strong pulse from somewhere in the battle. How she could sense him, only the Creator knew, but her love for her son—and her husband—was strong. And it was a gift. She wouldn't waste time questioning gifts, but rather, she'd use them. "We have to find Darion."

And so, they descended the hillside and ran to join the madness.

***

Zola had been momentarily shocked by the aerial battle, but perhaps not so much as her counterparts. There was much of the world that she did not know or had not seen. Really, since everything surprised her each day, nothing surprised her. She had fought off many foes today and felt her muscles tiring.

And then... a tickle in her mind. A tiny sliver of recognition. She lifted her head, ears perked, and suddenly alert. Spinning around, she searched through the smoke and shadows. *There!* She felt it. Without a word to Soren at her side, she took off toward the middle of camp just behind their lines.

As she ran, she heard him. His tiny, innocent, precious voice, *Mother?*

Trigger! She screamed in her mind and aloud. *He is here! In a battle. NO!* Her heart leapt in her chest as fear gripped her. Was he to be used as bait? Were they hurting him? She would rip every limb from his captor's body.

And then she saw him. A troll held him. "You," she shouted angrily. As she ran, preparing to slay the wretched beast, she heard her name. The evening shadows were creeping in and had obscured the others around Trigger, until a blaring light gleamed around her.

Rearing with surprise, she gasped, "Trinidad? But how?"

"We had to come to help, and to bring you your son," a musical voice replied from beside Trinidad.

"Your Majesty," Zola said quickly, bowing to her. And then looking dubiously at the troll, who stepped forward and set Trigger on the ground.

The tiny colt trembled as she ran her velvety muzzle over his face, breathing in his familiar, soft scent.

"Mother?" His precious voice stirred her heart.

"Oh, Trigger. I am here. You are safe," she whispered.

"I hate to break up this lovely moment, but we have company," Antonis murmured lowly, scooping up a discarded sword near a corpse nearby. Cela reached for another that Antonis lifted from a corpse, seemingly forgetting the blades at her waist.

Lyrianna drew a small blade and widened her gaze.

Zola spun, "Get back, Trigger," she ordered, before seeing the oncoming threat.

As she turned and locked eyes on the remaining black unicorns, her breath left her.

"He is one of ours," one of the unicorns in the front growled, nodding at Trigger.

Zola urged him back by the Queen and turned again to stare down the unicorns. They were far enough away that she could run at them, hopefully drawing them away from Trigger. But she hesitated. Many of them were her own children as well... they just didn't know it yet in their brainwashed state. She knew they fought ferociously and that Elsra had commanded for them to be killed, for unicorns that could be used as weapons were too dangerous. And yet....

They stood watching her, as if awaiting her answer. Or toying with her.

Antonis stepped up, clearing his throat softly. Cela and Dabor rose with him, protecting Lyrianna, who knelt with her arms draped around Trigger's neck.

Zola glanced to ensure he was safe before speaking.

"You cannot have him. He is mine." She said it simply, for she was a simple-minded unicorn. He was hers. And that was the end of it.

They didn't seem to agree.

With the evening shadows creeping in, obscuring further their jet-black coats, the unicorns crept forward. Only the sparkle of their horns and white of their teeth gave their presence away. In this darkness, they had the advantage. As one they began to move, and in their half-moon formation, pressed in.

Antonis bellowed, and to his credit, didn't back down at a herd of angry unicorns headed his way.

Dabor, the troll whose presence Zola was still confused about, stepped up beside her, bouncing a club off his palm lightly as Cela pawed her front hooves in angry anticipation.

Trinidad stood back as if trying to decide whom to protect. Zola or Lyrianna and Trigger.

They were a body's length in distance now. So close. Zola could make out their every feature, despite the darkness... and... she could smell them.

Though ranging from adolescents to full adults, she could smell her children. They smelled like Trigger.

"ENOUGH," she roared, the air around her crackling with energy as a bursting light flooded the ground near them, and a stream of light beamed from her horn.

The oncoming unicorns reared and shied away from her.

"Who are you?" one moaned, eyes firmly shut, pawing irritably at the ground.

Fire and screams filled the night sky as the winged ones battled, but Zola had eyes only for these. She thought of Elsra. Her words to her in her final moments. *My warrior.*

"I am your mother. Your master has kept you from me, but I found out, and kept one of you. Him," she said, turning back, the light from her horn illuminating the radiant Queen, with her flowing golden locks and pale arms draped against her son's glossy, midnight black, perfect coat. "I claimed him," she said calmly, turning back to them.

Seeing that some had begun to creep toward her again while her head was turned, she growled, "As I claim all of you," her voice grew in its power and authority. "I, Zola, family to the First Horn and member of the Unicorn Council, named to it by Regent Elsra herself, claim you. He cannot have you, for I have already claimed you as my own. You were born of my body," she knew most of them had been, at least, and cared not to know the distinction, for in that moment she knew. She was a warrior. And there was no greater warrior than a mother. "I failed you, and for that I am sorry. But I have found you, and no harm will come to you ever again. But you must leave all that you think is right behind you. I will teach you the truth."

A few of the unicorns stood up straight, ears perked, and heads cocked to the side questioning her veracity. The largest of those gathered stepped forward and sneered. "We follow no one but Morta. Now give us the youngling or die."

"I tell you this now, stop. I have given you a chance, but I will not hesitate to protect what is mine. Trigger is claimed and safe. As you can be too... but fight me, and you will die by the tip of my horn."

The unicorn charged.

Zola instinctively bent her neck and touched her horn to the ground in front of her. Immediately, the ground began to shake, and as soon as she lifted the tip away, a giant tree appeared from nowhere. Crystals shimmered in the pale moonlight and brilliance of her horn.

The enemy unicorns—her children—reared around the Tree. One—the large, angry unicorn—leapt forward, either unaware or uncaring of the Tree's presence, aiming directly for her.

His horn slashed clean through one of the thin lower branches, the crystals clinking as they bounced and scattered on the ground.

Trinidad gasped in horror at the sight, but Zola was too transfixed on the unicorn.

While his horn collided with the Tree, a scream tore from his lips. A swirl of dark matter flooded out of his body, and in a blink, he faded away. Gone. Vanished. Dead. The only trace of him was his horn, which looked like the crystals below, glossy black while the others were a silvery white.

The other unicorns backed up, as did Zola's party. As quickly as it had appeared, the magical Tree vanished. Where the small crystals had fallen, tiny saplings made entirely of crystal rose from the ground. One sapling stood out amongst the rest. Instead of crystal, it looked like a glistening obsidian tree. This marked the spot where the Shovlan Tree had been. The other unicorns fidgeted in place; their gaze rooted where their companion had been only moments ago.

Trinidad stepped forward then, his shimmering gleam equally dazzling. "The Shovlan Tree houses the spirits of all departed unicorns. All pure unicorns. They will drive out any who are filled with evil, as he was. Our ancestors have bestowed a great gift to Zola—your mother—and together she can teach you what it means to be a Nav'Arian unicorn. The Creator made you for so much more than this," Trinidad said, scowling at the ongoing battle behind them. "Admit it. You can feel the truth in her words. I can sense it in you. Your spirits changed the moment she uttered those words. As if a part of you that has lain dormant for so long has come alive. You are free, young ones. Do not squander it. This is a chance for a new start. Join us or—" Trinidad nodded toward the obsidian sapling: a permanent grave marker.

One unicorn piped up in his reedy voice, "What do you want us to do?"

Zola smiled, her warmth spreading out upon them all. She walked, again, purely following her instinct, and placed her horn upon each unicorn's forehead, just underneath his or her own horn. A few shied away until they saw their peers do it. A silver diamond shape crested each forehead below their horns. "Now," she said, smiling and rubbing her cheek upon each one in greeting. "You are claimed as mine. You are claimed… for good. Morta can never touch you again. You are free… and together we will learn what that means."

She looked them over. The red in their eyes had faded, and now she saw with relief that many of their eyes took on various shades of chocolate, lavender, azure, and more. Morta's evil possession of them was gone the moment the Tree appeared and she touched her horn to her kin.

"Will you fight with us?"

CHAPTER 30

The End

Darion watched in horror, as did most of the fighters, for it seemed all eyes—from both armies—were riveted on the fight above. Morta blew his fire, igniting the darkened sky in orange and reds, causing Zalto's shimmering sepia scales to glow. While the other Reouls fought, it was Zalto that led the attack... along with Nala.

Darion could hardly breathe! "We have to do something!" he shouted to Triumph and Edmond, who knew why he was so worried.

Vikaris knelt at Trixon's side. His bleeding had lessened, but he was out of the fight. The King was shouting orders and mobilizing his troops during the aerial distraction before they went on the offense. Rows reformed around them, barricading the enemies and pushing them back. The trolls—even Rav'Arians—seemed confused and stumbled around.

So, they didn't know about the Reouls, then, Darion thought sardonically. He knew some Rav'Arians did indeed, but many seemed just as surprised as the Nav'Arian soldiers.

He was so grateful for their presence in this fight.... But still! What could he do?

A screech tore through the night air as Zalto's front talons scraped along Morta's face, jagged rivets appearing in his scales. The archers may have been no match for him but fighting an equal enemy... he was struggling. Angrily, he blew a quick shot of fire and then zipped off out of the fight. The Reouls hovered a moment, opting not to pursue him. Instead, they circled the battlefield and opened fire upon the clusters of Rav'Arians that they could identify.

Vikaris took this as his signal and called for the soldiers to attack. The bumbling trolls, Rav'Arians, and humans who looked forlornly at the sky as their leader deserted them quickly found themselves surrounded. Darion and Triumph held back. Darion's arm glowed, and he was waving it like a crazed loon in hope of drawing Nala's attention.

A heavy whooshing sound echoed in his ears as Zalto sighted him. Swiftly, Zalto and Gamlin made their descent. Soldiers moved away so as not to be crushed by their immense bulk.

Without preamble, Darion ran to them. Nala, more beautiful than ever, hastily climbed down and in a moment, she was there in his arms. He inhaled her deeply, the exotic smell of her hair mingling with smoke.

He leaned back, cupping her face with his hands, "What were you thinking? You could have been killed!"

"Now, I did not know you wished to take on my father's role," she chided, arching an eyebrow, in her slurring speech. Her big eyes filled with tears as she ran her hands over his face and shoulders. "I have missed you," she said.

Before she could say anything else, he crushed his lips to hers, kissing her fully and passionately right there in the middle of the battlefield.

A deep rumbling sounded next to him.

Darion broke off, laughing, that is until he saw the intensity of Zalto's gaze, then he pushed Nala a few steps away to create some distance.

On his way to greet Nala and the Reouls, Triumph snorted.

"You came!" Darion blurted.

"Yes, that seems rather obvious," Zalto mused his tone as friendly as he could muster.

"Thank you for coming," a new voice sounded. Darion turned to look at Vikaris, straight-shouldered, Marked Arm bared and glowing, and despite the chaos of battle, clearly the man in charge.

Still, Darion's eyes widened slightly as he saw Zalto's giant head dip in greeting to the King.

"We fly for Nav'Aria," Zalto rumbled, and then in a softer, almost sad tone, he added, "I apologize for not coming sooner."

With Zalto pre-occupied, Darion didn't waste a moment in reaching back for Nala. He never wanted to let her go again. But he frowned, asking, "Well, what made you come? When I was with you, you—no offense—made it pretty clear that we were on our own. What changed?"

Zalto exhaled, emitting a puff of smoke from his nostrils as he surveyed the battlefield. His Reouls—coupled with the Nav'Arian force—were laying waste to the enemy.

"Tiakai died," Nala said simply. Her deep, rich, slurring voice so wonderful in Darion's ears.

He looked at her, "And that…"

"That revealed to us, that we had been kept from you—through her and through Rinzaltan—for many years. When she passed, it was as if a partition was drawn, leaving us to see the error in our ways. I learned some when you came, but it wasn't until she died that the truth was revealed. Though, I assure you, I speak not against Rinzaltan," Zalto paused, for Triumph had released a low rumble of his own.

"Explain it then," Triumph spoke in a voice too cool for comfort.

"Oh boy," Darion muttered in Nala's ear. The last thing they needed was a unicorn-dragon fight to break out. He shot a glance to the sky. Morta was still gone for now….

Zalto took up the tale. "I am one of the eldest Reouls as you know, and when Tiakai died, I was named the elder. As soon as her last breath left her body in the caves, a revelation eclipsed in my mind. As if it had been kept hidden from me until that particular moment. Magic," he said, looking them over, almost reverently. "I was with her when she died, looking at the prophecy which adorns the wall. And as soon as she passed, the images transformed. All of a sudden, the border disappeared! The gleaming figure—who we assume is you, Darion—grew in size with arms reached out to both sides as if to unite them... to bring them back together. There was no divide any longer. And as I looked at it, I heard a voice. An ancient voice." At this he paused, as he looked from Triumph to Darion and to Vikaris.

"Rinzaltan told me that long ago the border had been created to keep the evil forces that lingered there back from Nav'Aria."

"Yes, obviously," Triumph huffed.

Darion rolled his eyes.

"But..." Zalto continued, "he also explained that he had had a dream from the Creator explaining that an evil presence had already come to the Realm and would cross the border into Nav'Aria. And that one day, it would try to come for the Reouls. Rinzaltan then shared that he had created a memory barrier, a strengthened border that would prohibit the Reouls from crossing back into Nav'Aria. The symbol that he had etched on Tiakai worked as a shield, and though she could remember it, it obscured her memories and visions of the future. He thought," at this Zalto hesitated, clearly upset by it all, "that by keeping us across the border and the memory of our united lives together early on in Creation hidden, he could save us. That the evil agent that was growing in a different region of Rav'Ar and entering Nav'Aria would also forget about we Reouls. If none knew of our existence, and no Reouls crossed the border to remind everyone, then we would be safe. Until…"

Darion felt his arm tingling as this story was divulged, and goosebumps broke out along his body.

"Until you, Darion. You are the key to bridging Nav'Aria and ending the evil taint that has ravaged the lands for far too long."

Triumph snorted. "This is a rather convenient tale, I think. All of a sudden you appear with the excuse that you have never been able to fight us because of an old magical barrier my father placed on your kind cycles ago. How very hard that must have been," Triumph's voice dripped with contempt.

Darion gaped at him. But… his friend had a point. Maybe Zalto was just weaving the tale to look good in front of Vikaris.

"What he says is true," a warm soft voice interrupted, causing all to spin in amazement.

"Trinidad!" Vikaris blurted, turning and running toward them.

Lyrianna stood radiant and dazzling in the evening twilight, her beauty illuminated by Zola and Trinidad on either side.

Darion smiled watching his parents embrace, and then his father's face looked panicked as he scanned the battle. Though it seemed more of a slaughter, the Nav'Arians clearly had the upper hand now that the Reouls had joined.

"But how? Why? What are you doing here?" Questions tumbled from Vikaris's mouth.

"We have come to fight," Antonis said proudly, stepping up from the shadows.

Darion rejoiced at the sight of his long-time friend, Tony.

Vikaris grabbed his friend in a fierce embrace, confusion and joy and fear fighting for a hold on his expression.

"Now, now, one thing at a time. We can all explain and reconnect later," Lyrianna responded, regal as ever, stepping forward to embrace Darion. She kissed his cheeks, rubbing one with her thumb before letting him go. She smiled warmly at Nala but turned toward Zalto and gestured for Trinidad to explain.

"If you recall I was at the battle that your elder spoke of. I remember it well. That was the battle in which Rustusse was slain, and my father gave his life for my King." Trinidad's horn shone brightly as he spoke, his warm voice comforting them all. "Before the battle though, my father told me he had been visited in a dream by the Creator, much as you say, and he told me he would create a shield that would hopefully protect Nav'Aria from an even greater evil that was brewing... he would solidify the future by his mark. I admit, I did not know exactly what he meant, I was a foolish, young unicorn. More focused on the battle ahead than my father's dream... that was the last conversation we ever had," Trinidad said sadly.

"When Darion told us of his encounters with the Reouls and the adamant refusal by your elder who bore my father's mark, memories began to come back, and I have long since suspected that my father was responsible for your isolation. I know what you say is true, and that now is the time of the prophecy. With your elder gone, I can now remember the earlier battle, and the presence of your winged fighters before the memory was taken from me. Darion, you have opened this future up to us with your return and your discovery of the Reouls. Now, together, we shall end this evil."

As if his words were heard from above, Morta's red eyes and dark form appeared again overhead.

Darion swallowed at the sight of him. "You have to stay down here." He commanded Nala. "Please. Do not expose yourself again."

Lyrianna was reaching her hand out to Nala, who looked as if she wanted to argue. She ran to Zalto and wrapped her arms around his neck. Darion heard her whisper, "Be careful."

Vikaris began shouting orders.

Darion turned to see Gamlin quietly watching everything going on. He trotted up to him and patted his friend's scaled shoulder. "It is good to see you, Gamlin. Thank you for coming."

"It is good to fight," Gamlin replied, sounding older than when Darion had last seen him. He remembered helping Gamlin not so long ago.

"Don't do anything stupid up there," Darion cautioned.

Gamlin laughed, jagged teeth bared as he launched into the air, the wind gust buffeting off the surrounding soldiers.

The other Reouls who had been fighting all around the battlefield took to the sky moments later to take on the beast again. Soon fire and smoke filled the night once again.

Morta must have rounded up one final group of soldiers that had been hanging back. Fresh Rav'Arians poured into the decimated enemy ranks. They were naked—no robes or hoods like the other fighters. These ones were small, reptilian, and bird-like.

A wave of foul odor wafted from them.

"Fresh from the tar pits," Edmond growled at his side.

Darion agreed. These were the youngest of the beasts... Morta was growing desperate. But still they fought... with feral savagery. No skill with blades or spears. They clawed, kicked, bit, and tore their way into the Nav'Arian force. Their viciousness kept all eyes focused.

Darion could only pray that the battle overhead went well, for quickly he found himself standing with his friends and family, facing all that was wrong with their land. He stood shoulder to shoulder with unicorn, man, woman, centaur, nymph, and troll. He looked around to see Triumph, Edmond, Soren, Vikaris, Rick, and Tony who held hands with Aalil. Darion was glad to see they'd been reunited. Near them stood D'Ania and her fellow troll soldiers. Nymphs, Drogs and a cluster of centaurs, and even Drigidor and Trixon were standing alert, though weak. Surrounded by the black unicorns whom she seemed to have taken charge of, Zola gleamed brilliantly on his other side. Lyrianna, Nala, Trinidad, and Trigger stood just behind Darion. With her was a large troll, whom they called Dabor. Together at last. All of those that Darion loved most in the world. And he knew in that moment—that live or die—at least they would be together.

He locked eyes with his father's. Vikaris stood proud, Marked Arm with symbols spreading from fingertips to shoulder aglow. The Ruby at his throat cast a red tinge upon their area, much like Darion's own. They weren't hiding. The enemy could spot them easily in the crowd.

Let them come, Darion thought, determinedly.

His father raised his sword, yelling one last time, "FOR NAV'ARIA," as the enemies, their ranks newly strengthened, rushed at them. Echoing cries of "Nav'Aria" and "for the last time" and for "Rustusse" and for "Rinzaltan" filled the air, as Reoul's bellowed and roared overhead.

"No matter what, Triumph," Darion said softly. "Thank you."

Triumph turned his gaze to him and dipped his head. "Thank you, my Prince… and my friend."

Steel rang out, and the cries of bloodied, fatigued soldiers once more thrown into physical contest erupted.

Darion fought, sword swinging, yelling in the face of the mottled skinned wretches that came in angry waves, tearing and ripping as they went.

All were engaged in the fight. The brutality of it so intense that it brokered no distraction. Darion couldn't look to either side to check on his family or friends, for one wrong look would give an opening to the enemy. He thought he heard his father's yell and a shrill scream from behind. He prayed it wasn't Nala or his mother. Dabor pounded past him, having somehow become an ally, and slammed his club, knocking five or more bodies away. This opening allowed Darion to duck back momentarily. Trinidad reared and kicked at the two Rav'Arians that had snuck behind. Lyrianna and Nala stood together, blades extended, as tiny black legs poked out behind theirs.

Just as Darion was headed to stop them, a shining white light razed the two Rav'Arians as if they weighed nothing. Zola streamed in and dealt with the two swiftly, ensuring the safety of her son.

But her absence on the front line had cost that section. A unicorn shriek filled the air, and Darion watched in horror as Rav'Arians jumped upon it and began ripping it apart with their talons and maws. On his other side, Trixon was surrounded, and Drigidor was doing his best to fend off the attackers who must have seen his weakened state. Darion watched Rick slam into one of the beasts coming to their aid, Vikaris not far behind. He could hardly move as he watched both his fathers fighting off greater numbers than he thought. The Rav'Arians seemed to be pack hunters, sectioning off the front lines, coming in waves, and attacking the vulnerable points— and fighters. Their line was in disarray. He heard Rick's shout and saw him waving at Antonis, who now fought back-to-back with Aalil. An enemy troll was closing in on them. Another scream came from behind. Everyone he loved was in peril. He looked to see Edmond clutching his bloodied arm. Soren limping with a nasty gash on his back leg. And Triumph!

"Triumph, NO!" Darion screamed, rushing ahead, for in that moment, a Rav'Arian further down the line threw a jagged tipped spear intended for Triumph's heart, which was on full display as he stood on backlegs pummeling a troll, exposing his chest. Darion knew he couldn't make it there fast enough. The spear was closing in. Inches from his friend's heart.

Doing the only thing he could think of, he seized upon his senses and willed it all to stop. Raising his Marked Arm, he yelled, "STOP!"

And stop it did. It felt as if a blast had flashed from his arm—from his spirit—and come to the aid of his friend. The spear fell mid-air, and many of the enemies were thrown back from the force of his command.

Stepping forward, he exhaled deeply. Darion looked overhead just in time to see Morta close his jaws around Zalto's neck, jerking him around. Darion watched his friend—the Reoul who had answered his call and come to help—drop from the sky with a heavy, sickening thud.

Nala screamed from behind him.

Morta swept closer, hovering over Darion. The bloody markings on his torn face and jagged teeth made him even more terrible to look upon. Pure, festering, unadulterated evil. There was nothing left of Tarsin—or even of Morta—in this being. This was something new altogether.

Darion saw that this being didn't want to rule, nor did it even care about a fight; it wanted to destroy all life and bring only pain and death. He remembered the darkness that clutched Gamlin's mind and Zola's spirit. He thought of Narco and his wicked torture of Lyrianna and Trinidad. He remembered Zalto's tale of his brother Salimna's death at this creature's whim. He remembered the Watchers. Triumph's family. His father's never-ending quest to restore the Realm. And he saw… himself. He looked in the air and realized that he could sense Gamlin. A closer connection than almost anyone on the field, as he could sense Triumph.

"The winged crescent," he breathed. As realization struck him, he stared into the malevolent eyes overhead. *It is not a symbol. It is not good or bad. It is not prophecy. It is me. I am the Winged Crescent… the connection between the two.*

"MORTA," Darion bellowed, completely calm and at peace as his senses took hold. He could smell, taste, hear, and feel everything. The entire pulse of the battle was at his command. He would end it… right now.

"MORTA," Darion screamed when the beast didn't respond. "YOU AND I WILL END THIS!"

Darion blocked out the other voices, focusing solely on his Marked Arm. On what pains had been taken to bring him up safely in this broken world and get him to this place. He thought of his mother's love… both of his mothers. Lyrianna, who selflessly gave him away for safe-keeping, and Carol, who selflessly loved him even though he wasn't her own… and died to protect his family. She died for Nav'Aria. He thought of his two fathers, who even now stood back to back in this fight, both united in protecting him. And protecting Nav'Aria. It was love that had brought him here and it was love that he felt for Nav'Aria… for those on either side of the border… that led him to this moment.

A brilliant green light spewed from his fingertips as he drew in all of his heightened energy and senses. All his memories and emotions, he funneled them toward Morta. The other Reouls had landed around the battlefield, sectioning off the Rav'Arian monsters and blasting them in flames while Darion kept Morta occupied.

And then suddenly, a shield, translucent and shimmering, expanded over the entire Nav'Arian force, covering them in a strange barrier of safety, something that Darion didn't know he was capable of. As he looked, he saw that it wasn't he alone who held this strange dome-shaped shield of protection. As Morta released a fiery inferno sure to devour them all, every unicorn stepped forward following Triumph's lead and touched the ground with their horns. In that act, they not only strengthened the land by calling upon the Creator himself, but they bowed to the true Marked Heir and Chosen One…gifting him their strength. Darion had their horns.

Darion could feel their power surging through his veins as flow after flow of light spewed from his arm. He focused on the dark energy overhead.

Morta continued to rain down fire, but none of it touched them, thanks to the dome. Yet Darion could touch Morta, for as he focused in, he sensed the evil above. The writhing, wriggling mass of vitriol. The incendiary wrath with which this foul being wished to vanquish the earth. It screamed as he narrowed on it. Focusing further, he pushed, just as he had when he had entered Gamlin and Zola's minds. He could see a tiny speck of light completely surrounded by darkness at the bottom. A miniscule pinprick of light amidst a vacuum of wriggling worms. He focused on that light, calling to it.

As he did, he thought he heard a moan. A scream. A cry in terror and anger and rage and primal evil.

This enraged Darion. He reached his mind out to Gamlin and immediately he felt a flicker of recognition.

Gamlin recognized his mind, "I will help you," he seemed to say.

Darion smiled then.

Morta stopped spewing fire, and a flicker of fear crossed his face.

Darion felt it in his insides. He sensed an explosion of light in his heart as the Shovlan Tree, the house of the Cavern of Creation, the magical tree only visible to unicorns and the Marked Royals, appeared directly beneath the dome. Growing and rising and shimmering, its crystals gleaming silver and shining like diamonds, further brightening the battlefield until it looked more like day than night. The unicorns whinnied and neighed at the sight, as many of the Nav'Arians and enemies backed away. For this time, the Tree was visible to everyone.

As it appeared, a partition, as if to another world, opened in the sky. While the land above glowed, at its cavernous base, the Tree was surrounded by wriggling dark worms. The evil that was spreading through the beast's presence. The meaning was clear. This beast meant to destroy all living creatures. To destroy the very essence of creation. But the beast was proven wrong. It had misjudged the fortitude of a united force shaped in love and honor. As the image in the sky popped into view, so too did familiar shapes. Elsra, Rinzaltan, Trinity, Xenia, and many other unicorns appeared, their horns shining just as bright, lending their strength, their spirits—through the Tree—into the fight which Darion now led. And swooping over them all, a winged creature greater in size than Morta arrived. Tiakai... she looked whole and well, as she would have in her vigorous youth.

Darion focused on them, thanking them for the lending of their strength. He reached out with his mind to Gamlin and Triumph and all the rest. Morta screamed and writhed in the air, as if the light and powers surging around him were burning him. He could not move.

Darion's arm, focused overhead, was soon joined by another, his father's, which clasped his hand, followed by a smaller petite arm that reached in and grabbed them both, his mother's. His father's arm glowed brilliantly, as did his mother's forehead. At their touch, an explosion of swirling silver and green light laced together and shot directly into Morta. At that moment, the Reouls overhead, led by Gamlin, opened fire. It engulfed Morta, still immobile and writhing from the blinding light below.

The beast convulsed in the air, screeching, "DIE! ALL MUST DIE!"

In unison, the translucent images of Rinzaltan and Tikai both turned on the beast, and in one last shot of silvery light and burning red flame, the beast burst, dissolving into a cloud of smoky ash which began to fade and finally disappear.

At its bursting, Darion thought he heard a sigh, and then a name. *L'Asha.*

A tumult of cheering filled the air as the Tree slowly vanished, and with it, the fading, smiling figures of the deceased back to await their loved ones in the spirit world. For now, they left this world—without the stain of evil— to the living.

Rinzaltan and Elsra lingered nodding at him before fading away. Darion watched them go, falling to his knees as the shield and light went out. Enough of the camp was still aflame to help everyone get their bearings, but it seemed the supernatural had come to an end.

Darion embraced his parents and his friends. He clung to Nala and petted Triumph's head. The celebrations would come, but the fight wasn't finished yet.

He turned to look over the enemies who had been frozen, kept out of his dome during his duel with Morta. He watched as the enemy trolls collapsed. The red blinking out of their eyes as their evil maker was slain. His hold on them vanishing just as he had. Seeing this, the traitor humans raised their arms above their heads in surrender. They didn't appear angry or evil—just tired.

Darion cheered along with his fellows. Now, it was only a matter of killing a few more Rav'Arians!

The Reouls and the victorious Nav'Arians set to quick work. The few that escaped, Vikaris vowed would be hunted and uprooted. Every single crevice of the land would be scoured until they were wiped out.

Darion allowed himself to be pulled to a campfire that was being lit, as were many others around the camp. Nala tended to his wounds, and his mother fussed over him. He smiled like an idiot at them both. His father, King Vikaris, had clapped him on the back before marching off with Kragar to check on Trixon and the other injured. Gamlin swept over with news that Zalto was injured but would live. Miraculously the beast's teeth had missed all arteries and left only puncture wounds. He was sore from his fall, and he wouldn't be able to fly for some time, but he would live. Before succumbing to sleep, he demanded that all around him let him slumber until next year.

Nala had laughed deeply at this and promised Gamlin she would check on him soon, thanking him for his care.

Rick came and sat with Darion for a moment, congratulating him, but soon was off to help remove stones from the enemy trolls. Though inactivated, "It seems best to get rid of those things," Rick had drawled, smacking Antonis on the back and breaking up his rather exploratory kiss of Aalil on the edge of their circle.

Tony had laughed, and Aalil had glared, but both joined him to tend to the trolls.

Zola and Trigger stood amid other unicorns deep in conversation with Drogs and some of the centaurs that were awed by Zola's military abilities.

Triumph lay down beside him, as did Soren and Edmond, who both awaited medical attention. Songs and cheers broke out all around. They had done it. They had really freaking done it.

No, you did it, Darion. We owe you our thanks, Triumph rumbled to him, nuzzling his shoulder.

Darion looked at his friend, smiling, "We did it, Triumph. All of us."

And though Triumph looked like he wanted to argue, something caught Darion's eyes.

Green scales gleamed from the firelight overhead as Gamlin landed beside their circle.

Two riders jumped off, Ati and a small boy. The boy took off calling for Nala. She jumped up in a satisfied smile, scooping him in her arms and kissing his exposed tummy as his tiny shirt rode up. The squeals of joy and laughter gladdened every heart. After all, this was what they had been fighting for. To hear a child's laugh after a horrible battle made tears fill Darion's eyes—not to mention seeing the maternal love on Nala's face.

"Well," Triumph snarked, "it looks like you are to be a father."

Darion colored, croaking, "what is that supposed to mean?"

He knew with certainty that he was still very much a virgin, and then Triumph gestured back at Nala and the boy.

Darion smiled catching on. Nala was kissing Valon's sweaty face. Darion was sure he heard him say "Mama Nala."

"I guess you're right," Darion grinned, for there was no way he was living his life without Nala ever again. And besides, he liked adoption. He would happily love and raise that cute kid if that was what Nala wanted.

She smiled as if reading his mind with those big owl-like eyes enveloping her face.

He gulped.

Triumph snorted.

Nala led Valon by the hand to sit with them and meet Darion, and then they got a good look at Edmond.

One of the tallest and strongest warriors in Nav'Aria, tripped over his words, red-cheeked and awkward, as Ati stood smiling up at him in greeting.

"Kiss her, damnit," a soldier called, making Edmond's face even brighter.

"Allow me," Ati purred, standing on tiptoes and pulling Edmond's red face down to hers, kissing his lips soundly.

Whoops and cheers came from all around, and Ati ran her hands down his arms and back, until Edmond groaned and grabbed at his wound. And just like that, she went from kissing to clucking at him for not telling her he was hurt. Soon, Ati had him sitting back by the fire. She removed his shirt and tended to the wound with an efficiency that showed her great skill in healing. She grinned the entire time, though, and gave a little wink over at Darion and Nala.

Triumph and Soren chuckled, and soon their entire camp and clusters of soldiers were smiling, singing, and cheering.

Not long after, the morning light began to stream in, awaking those who'd dozed off with the warm greeting of a new day. A new world. For this was the first of many days to come in a world that held no more evil.

Narco was dead. Morta was dead. And with it, the land seemed to stir. Perhaps it was mere fantasy, but Darion felt sure that the vibrancy of the colors was even greater this morning. The air smelled sweet, as the warm breeze blew away the stench of rotten filth, death, and decay, restoring the air with a floral scent. Small birds began to sing and chirp, geese flew overhead, small rabbits and foxes left their dens and hopped and ran this way or that. The sunrise bloomed, the sky big, bright, and clear.

All around there was life and beauty.

"So, this is Nav'Aria?" Nala asked warmly, stifling a yawn behind one petite hand sitting up near him, Valon still snugly asleep in her lap.

Darion smiled at her, knowing that no matter how beautiful his home was, it would never compare to her beauty.

"This is Nav'Aria, Nala. Welcome home."

EPILOGUE✦

A Time of Peace

The war was over, and now a new age was upon them. The blood that had rained down upon Nav'Aria for the past generation was no more. *They were in a time of peace,* Darion's father called it. A time without Narco, Morta, or any of his abominations. After the battle, dispatches had been sent out and every Rav'Arian left living was hunted down. Drogs, the centaur, joined by Edmond and Soren, had led a group of Reouls to the Watcher village. The Kingdom families found there—having been forcibly removed from the city to be watched over—were safely returned to their homes... and for some, their waiting husbands who had sworn loyalty to Vikaris. No Watchers were found, but to be sure, the Reouls burned the entire area to the ground. The other Reouls scoured the land of Rav'Ar, scorching any Rav'Arian's they found, and Zalto himself, once healed from the battle, joined the party at the Watcher encampment and took part in destroying the Rav'Arian breeding grounds. No eggs remained in those tar pits. The abominations were no more. That party had only just returned last week.

Dabor, the troll, had volunteered to lead a search party into the mountains to recover the females and search out any other threats. Accompanying him would be many of the nymphs, Talen, Copa, Ida, Lula, and Adelina included. D'Ania had volunteered to go with him, and though Darion wasn't sure—it's hard to tell with trolls—it had looked like Dabor blushed! He wouldn't be surprised to hear those two were a couple.

It had taken months, but they had finally done it. The wrongs had been righted, and new settlements were set up for the citizens of Nav'Aria... including in the Stenlen, which had contained a handful of survivors after Narco's nightmarish trip through there. Municipalities were put into place for the various clans to begin rebuilding. Dabor was named leader of the trolls, Drogs of the centaurs, an older nymph Darion had not met before, Tolten, was named as their leader, and Shannic the leader of the merfolk. Zalto was recognized as the Reoul Elder. Together with the Royals, they would help their kind find places in the new Nav'Aria. To begin to work toward the good. To, once again, contribute toward society through farming, building, teaching, healing, and so much more. It was a rebirth of civilization, and everyone had their part to play.

Darion had spent weeks traveling around with Triumph, Nala, and Gamlin, visiting with leaders all over the Realm before returning to Kaulter to check on things. The portals, now magically and inexplicably frozen open.

His father and mother had elected to stay at the Castle, the seat of power for their land, to rebuild all that had been broken and overlooked for so long. Along his journey, Darion had brought his sketch book, and upon his return had shown his mother. She had at once ordered an easel, pencils, charcoal, and whatever else he might need, be brought to his apartments. His large sketches, now framed, filled the Castle. The art was no longer limited to portraits of the Marked Royals, or of the Fall (seemingly commissioned by Narco). Most had been removed, and instead images of every group were now represented in Castle Dintarran.

Yet on this particular evening, the first of many he hoped, all were gathered to honor their King, and his family… and to recognize this time of peace. The search parties had returned. Government and order had been set up, and now, it was time to usher in a new age.

Darion looked around the Great Hall of Castle Dintarran with amazement. The room was lit with dazzling wall sconces and gilded candelabras. The warm evening air blew through the open windows, causing the flames to dance as if catching on to the levity of the room. A crescent moon hung visible beyond the furthest window.

Exotic, flavorful aromas filled the air as herbs burned upon the braziers. The room was full to bursting with decadent guests of all kinds: man, unicorn, troll, nymph, centaur, and the scaled, familiar head of one heroic beast. Gamlin. Nala leaned upon his shoulder, as they peered into the room from the doorway. Gamlin had feared he'd take up too much room and did not want to limit the number of guests, though Darion had offered him a seat of honor. He smiled at Gamlin—his striking, bright eyes taking in the grandeur and ceremony—thinking of the joyous news he had brought back from the Reoul camp near the Shazla Desert. A hatchling had been born. *A new age indeed*, Triumph had happily remarked.

In the middle of all the evening's festivity, just beyond the great gilded and gleaming chandelier sat the beaming King of Nav'Aria upon his rightful Throne, polished to shine. Vikaris dressed in a silken sleeveless gold tunic with his Marked Arm visible for all to see with his Ruby ablaze at his throat. And upon his head sat the crown of old. The crown of his forefathers. His Grandmother, His Father, and now his.

Darion watched his mother's beatific face radiate with joy and splendor, her silvery diamond crest upon her brow only enhancing her outer beauty. Her plum dress was long and full; beading and intricate silver design work ran down the bodice. She sat in her throne to the King's right, her throne smaller and yet, she could have been sitting on a hay bale and still been the loveliest vision in the room. All eyes were drawn between her and her husband. His parents.

Darion smiled watching them. He sat on his father's left in his own throne. And though he knew it was his rightful place by birth, and now, through the fulfillment of prophecy, he had slain Morta after all, thanks to their union, Lyrianna and the unicorns. Yet, Darion could hardly breathe for the magnitude of this moment. He thought back to his life in his tiny attic bedroom in Gresham, Oregon. He had been an awkward, confused teen there. And here he sat dressed in silks, a smaller crown upon his head, next to his powerful and incredible Royal parents. He sat equally powerful, if not quite incredible yet—in his mind, upon his own throne, as Prince Darion, the true Marked Heir of Nav'Aria.

"I would most certainly describe you as 'incredible'," Triumph murmured appraisingly in his ear.

Darion smiled, but he didn't turn around. This, Triumph had shared before the evening began, was how it had always been. How it should have been for the past cycles, and now would be again. The Marked King and Marked Heir with their bonded unicorn companions standing just behind them and able to whisper in their left ear if appropriate... as acting advisers and partners to the Royals.

Darion thought of the hubbub from earlier as Lyrianna walked to her throne, accompanied by her own bonded unicorn companion, of course. Never before had a non-Marked Royal bonded a unicorn, and never before had a Mark been given like that which graced his mother's face.

He had smiled thinking of her love and strength and sacrifice. Perhaps it had never been seen before because there had never been a mother—two mothers actually—so bonded and united in one purpose, to selflessly and sacrificially love a shared child for the good of Nav'Aria. The spirits had rewarded Lyrianna with the Mark, and in doing so, honored what Carol had sacrificed. Darion rested his hand upon his heart for a moment thinking of the tattoed flower there in memory of Carol.

As Trinidad, horn sparkling in the candlelight, walked beside Lyrianna, all had gazed adoringly at the most striking, magical pair in the land. A wreath of greenery adorned Trinidad's neck, as well as Triumph's and Trixon's.

Cela had followed their procession and stood beaming up at them from her position below the dais before her eyes returned to scanning the gathered Nav'Arians. She was lovelier than ever, the candlelight dancing upon her ivory coat and red locks, but Darion knew not to be fooled. If anyone was out of line this night, the grinning centaur would be on them in a flash. She had been named leader of the House Guard only earlier this day. She would guard the Royals within the Castle vigilantly. Darion shuddered a little at the thought. He thought he heard a soft snort behind him.

As he sat upon the dais in his throne with his parents and unicorn friends, Darion caught the misty eye of Rick, who stood just below, knuckling his brow with a quick bow at his son.

Darion would always be his son. His heart felt peace and joy unlike anything he had ever experienced. Next to Rick stood Antonis, hands intertwined with Aalil's. Darion grinned as Tony winked at him. He smiled when his eyes met Edmond's, whose hand was interlaced with Ati's. Aside her were Soren, Zola, and Trigger. And then he caught his breath as he looked toward the back of the room. *Nala.*

Darion didn't know what the future held, but he had a feeling that the exotic, foreign beauty in the back of the room would one day fill a seat upon this dais. He looked forward to that day. She smiled her brilliant, dimpled smile and Darion tried and failed to keep his face calm as he grinned like a fool at the girl he loved.

Seegar stood at the center of the room, inviting all gathered guests to bow for their Marked Royals, his gaze lingering on his three, fidgeting wards Ansel, the King's Nephew, Anton, Edmond's younger orphaned brother, and Valon, Nala's cousin and adopted child. They would live together in the palace and get the best education Nav'Aria had to offer—that is, if they survived this party without making a fool of Seegar, Darion thought.

Seegar paused, eyeing the boys for a beat longer to ensure proper decorum before repeating to the now standing guests. "For King Vikaris. For Queen Lyrianna. And for Prince Darion."

As one, the entire crowd bowed, many wiping happy tears from their eyes.

Darion felt tears of his own form in his eyes as his father reached out to grasp both his hand and one of Lyrianna's with his other. United.

Standing themselves, Vikaris lifted both his hands, and those of Lyrianna's and Darion's, and shouted with command and extreme pleasure. "For Nav'Aria!"

The crowd of Nav'Arians, unicorn, human, nymph, centaur, troll, Reoul, and even merfolk—their lilting voices carrying in from outside—joined in the booming, long overdue cheer that erupted.

***

"Zola! You must come look at this," Soren called, for as he had entered the hall in Kaulter before Zola, his new bride, and adopted son Trigger, something caught his eye. He glanced at the frieze and was jolted with surprise at the sight of newly carved images appearing from some deep magic before them. Where the frieze had once left off with Rustusse, and then the image of Darion's prophecy as the Chosen One, a new image appeared. King Vikaris, clear as day, upon his throne, accompanied by Lyrianna and Darion.

"What is it?" Zola's rich voice called, her hooves clattering as she hustled to her husband's side.

"It is a promise," Soren said, smiling at Zola, the newly appointed Unicorn Regent—and the female he had asked to be his forever. "The Creator has blessed us. We will now have the peace that we have so long desired in our land. Nav'Aria is safe now. We will have peace and a new age."

"A new life." Zola laughed warmly, "I know I have much to learn, Soren. But one thing I know for certain is that you, my First—and Forever—Mate, will help me to raise our son together… happily… in peace."

Soren's eyes blurred, and just as Trigger tottered up, Soren leaned in to nuzzle first Zola and then Trigger. "Yes," he whispered, tears falling freely from both adults. "A family… forever."

***

Rick walked down the hall, whistling softly to himself. He looked forward to the first day of peace… without festivities. He was ready for routine. To get back to work. Vikaris had appointed him as head of the Royal stables and cavalry, while Antonis was given back his position of Commander after Garis's tragic death. While Kragar opted to retire with his family in Kaulter, Drigidor was named Lieutenant and accepted the position, not wanting to return to Kaulter. *Too many memories*, he said. Rick understood that well. He also had a feeling the fierce warrior wanted to remain close to his stepsons. Though he'd never admit it out loud, Rick was sure.

Rick looked forward to working with horses again. To being near Darion and watching him continue to grow and mature as Prince. Mostly, Rick looked forward to finding a new normal in his home. Though his Springflower was gone, and his heart wrenched each and every morning at the realization that Carol wasn't sharing his bed, he had purpose again. Darion—and the Kingdom—that was his purpose.

Rounding the hall in the palace, Rick came to a room to greet his friend and get an early start on numbers. He wanted to know exactly how many horses he'd be responsible for and the outcome of the many of the warhorses now that they were in a time of peace. He had grooms and horses waiting on him, so he had risen early.

As he knocked, he was surprised that there wasn't an answer. The occupant always answered.

He knocked again. Silence. A tremor of fear gripped Rick's gut, after everything they had been through… could an enemy still be lurking in the palace?

Without delay, Rick tried the handle, noticing the latch wasn't bolted. He swung the door open ready to face an adversary and...

What he found was certainly not an adversary, but rather a pair of sweaty faces and interlocked bodies twisted in bed.

"Rick, get out of here!" Tony boomed, as Aalil laughed and tugged at the blankets to cover herself.

"Ah, shit. Not again," Rick growled, turning quickly, cheeks aflame, and then added, "Start locking your damn door!"

Acknowledgments:

This series wouldn't have been possible without a terrific team of people supporting me every step of the way.

To my family (parents, husband, daughter, brothers, extended family, and late grandparents): Thank you from the bottom of my heart for your support and love. I appreciate you dearly for putting up with my continual spew of Nav'Aria updates/drafts/pleas for social media likes and your readership.

And, Mom, I couldn't have done ANY of my Author Events without your help! You've always been my biggest supporter. THANK YOU. I love you so much.

This ever-prevalent "family love" theme in this series wasn't a hard one for me to write. I've been blessed because of you all. Because at the end of the day, it's not blood or even a shared last name that makes a family... but love.

I hope you, my Jarica, above all, know this to be true. You are my everything, and you make me proud to be your mom every single day. We've been blessed by adoption, and through our experiences, I was able to give added dimension to the characters I had dreamed up before you made me a mom. I will love you forever, child of my heart.

And Keil, without having you by my side, I don't know if I ever would have had the guts to go for it. Thank you for believing in me and supporting me every step of the way. I mean, you even formatted the book series!!! You are the world's BEST husband and a true partner. What we have is beautiful... and that lent so much to developing a companionable, intimate love like what Riccus and Carol shared. You are my person, Keil Backer. I love you with my whole heart.

To my friends, Twitter Writing Group, and awesome Instagram Community: Jessica, Kimmie, and Shanna, Jen, Cassie, Marc, Joe, and K.T., what did I do to deserve your support?! You've been invaluable throughout this journey and really made me feel incredibly special. Thank you for continually sharing Nav'Aria with others and always making me laugh with your candid reactions to the books.

And to my school & church friends, and former colleagues/students, THANK YOU again for supporting me and my crazy idea about EPIC unicorn warriors.

To Heather Peers: When I came to you a couple of years ago, I was completely terrified. Unsure of how my writing would be received. But you believed in me... and because of that, we've now successfully launched three books. WE FREAKING DID IT! Your word magic is what took Nav'Aria from ramblings to perfected prose. This will forever be one of the best seasons of my life.

What we've created here is something truly special. Thank you for agreeing to be a part of it. *"For Nav'Aria!"*

AUTHOR'S NOTE✦

How do you say goodbye to a story that's been in your heart for nearly a decade?

I started writing *Nav'Aria* on a whim, as a substitute teacher in 2011, and continued with it on and off while teaching high school history. Upon adopting my daughter in 2017, I "retired" from teaching to be a mom… and to pursue my dream of becoming an author. And yet, I had no idea what it would become. I took a chance with book one (*Nav'Aria: The Marked Heir*), thinking that perhaps I'd sell ten copies (all to my mom most likely), and maybe someday I'd finish the series. But in just two years, I've written the rest of the series and released a completed *Nav'Aria* trilogy. That's because of YOU, my amazing readers. Hearing from YOU, meeting and engaging with YOU at events, and connecting online—it's all so energizing! I LOVE the bond readers have developed with Darion and the EPIC unicorns of Nav'Aria. Is it any wonder I'm struggling to say goodbye?

This has been such a rewarding, life-changing journey. Thank you for being a part of it. I hope you enjoyed the ending… and while it's goodbye, for now, I won't say it's goodbye forever. Darion and his companions have a very special place in my heart; perhaps their journey will continue one day, and if not, we can rest easy knowing that Nav'Aria will live on!

If you enjoyed this book series, I'd love to hear from you (connect with me online- K.J. Backer on Facebook, Instagram, Twitter, Linked In, Goodreads, and my newsletter at **kjbacker.com**). And PLEASE share an honest review on Amazon, Goodreads, and anywhere else you can! THANK YOU SO MUCH, READERS!

***

I wrote and released book three, *Nav'Aria: The Winged Crescent* during the COVID-19 pandemic of 2020. This has been a heck of a year, and I've found solace in *Nav'Aria*. If I may, please allow me to share a few things *Nav'Aria* has taught me… and that hold special significance in a season like this.

-Courage comes in all forms. It's in the big, heroic moments… and the everyday moments. Courage can be seen on the battlefield, like with valiant King Vikaris and Trixon, or when protecting others, like we see with Antonis and Zola. But courage can also be achieved in our relationships, routines, and decisions. At home. In our workplace. In our hearts… like Carol, Riccus, Rinzaltan, Lyrianna, and Trinidad. Choosing to help others. Love others. Care for others. Protect others.

25187857R10267

And... to help, love, care for, and protect ourselves as well. Be brave.

-As Darion was instructed so often, *Guard your minds.* Pay attention to where your thoughts drift, what is causing you anxiety, and what self-talk you're allowing. YOU matter. And you are loved. So, take care of yourself... and shine!

-It is okay to feel. It is okay to hurt. To be sad. To be scared. To be vulnerable. But... don't let that be the end of your story. There is more living to be done. The fight is not over yet. Breathe. Feel. Let go and forgive if possible. AND LIVE. Dream big, bold, audacious dreams... and make the most of the time you have here. We saw many moments of pain in Nav'Aria. Trixon, Triumph, and Darion all felt like failures at times... but their continued pursuit of life impacted not just their own, but many others. Darion and Triumph are experts at self-loathing, but over time they grew to see that those thoughts didn't help anything. By letting go, they embraced their futures, saved many, and learned to live fully. I want that for myself. And I want that for you too.

"BE EPIC."
K.J. Backer